KNIFE SWORN

'The characterisation and detail is where *Knife-Sworn* really delivers. A strong middle book which will secure book three's place on many a "to read" list next year' *British Fantasy Society*

'*Knife-Sworn* grips the reader by the sheer force of Williams' sumptuous detail . . . he has succeeded in that tricky business of creating a middle volume that spurs one on to get to the conclusion. This reader for one will be ready and waiting when the final volume, *The Tower Broken*, comes around this time next year' *Starburst*

'A solid sequel in a marvellous trilogy . . . Williams is a wonderful author and fans of epic fantasy will love this magical, character-driven trilogy. If you haven't picked up *The Emperor's Knife* yet, I recommend you do so – especially if you're a fan of Brandon Sanderson's school of original magic systems and well-wrought new worlds' rantingdragon.com

'A commendable accomplishment [that] showcases the growth Williams has undergone as a writer. This series is a new and exciting facet of the Fantasy genre, and fans would so well to acquaint themselves with it . . . leaves readers breathless for the next instalment: it's obviously going to be a game changer. I can't wait!' speconspecfic.com

'*The Emperor's Knife*, Mazarkis Williams' debut, was an awesome read, so when I found out that *Knife-Sworn*, the sequel was available, I jumped at the opportunity . . . Now I [have] found myself at the end of another great instalment [and] I can't wait to see what Williams provides us with in the final outing . . . a great read'

Also by
Mazarkis Williams

TOWER AND KNIFE
The Emperor's Knife

KNIFE-SWORN

TOWER AND KNIFE, BOOK TWO

MAZARKIS WILLIAMS

First published in Great Britain in 2012 by Jo Fletcher Books
This edition published in 2013 by

Jo Fletcher Books
an imprint of Quercus
55 Baker Street
7th Floor, South Block
London
W1U 8EW

A CIP catalogue record for this book is available
from the British Library

ISBN 978 0 85738 867 4 (PB)
ISBN 978 0 85738 866 7 (EBOOK)

10 9 8 7 6 5 4 3 2 1

Typeset by Ellipsis Digital Limited, Glasgow

Printed and bound in Great Britain by
Clays Ltd, St Ives plc

For Heather and Alexandra

PROLOGUE

Aldryth looked out over the sands of Cerana. There, hidden far beyond any well or waypost, waited the place where his god had died.

He sat upon a rock and pulled from his sack a crust of hard bread and an apple. He worked the crust in his mouth, sipping from a water pouch to soften it. He had come through the high passes of Mythyck and across the jagged beaches that no empire wished to claim but which claimed for themselves innumerable ships, leaving them battered and broken upon the shore. From there he had made his way through Parigol Pass, the last and loneliest place on the map to bear a name, bent against the howling wind, until at last he stood on the edge of the great desert.

Now he looked out over the vast emptiness and took a last mouthful of water before sealing the skin tight. Already sand gritted against his teeth. He saw no animals, no plants, not even insects. Here the sounds of life grew quiet and careful listening was required.

The next day he reached the sands. He sheltered from the heat in the lee of a dune, but even in the shade it seared his eyes and he wasted water by splashing them. Though his throat was raw he chanted the promises of his faith: sacrifice and love.

That night he drew the pattern for water, calling for its essence, but none came.

After three days in the desert his pace slowed as each step between the simmering dunes became a challenge. His skin blistered and peeled. His lips cracked and bled. His legs were abraded by sand. And yet he moved inexorably towards the Scar.

By the seventh day the sun had burned away his thirst, his hunger and all hesitation. Memories of the waterfalls of Mythyck, the lush valleys, the green trees and tart fruits, had dried to thin impressions and crackled from him with his skin. By day the soles of his boots crumbled into the burning sand; at night he shivered. He kept his mind focused on Mogyrk, but it was the Scar that pulled at him, not with its power, but with its silence.

One night – he could no longer remember how many it had been – he stumbled over something, the corner of a square, flat stone inscribed with criss-crossing lines: a pattern-piece. Time and wind had submerged all but that edge. Scuffing at the sand he found others, and more besides, forming a wide arc. He felt the hum of living things, though it became confused and frayed, there and not there: the unwinding sorrows of flower and fish, tree and scorpion. *I'm close now.* He settled into the sand. *Just some rest first. Some rest . . .*

Flowers, red and purple, sprouted from a nearby dune. Aldryth had little time to look at them before they unwound, showing him the roots of their colour, the roads inside them by which light and water travelled, the pollen that nestled within their soft petals. Then he saw nothing but their patterns, triangles and circles floating on the wind, and soon those too were undone, until the dune lay bare and white.

He moved away, wanting to sleep where dreams of the Scar would not disturb him, and yet they did: patterns dissolved and drifted away across the sand, here an autumn leaf, there a drop of honey, each gone pale, drifting apart. The wound torn by the god's death was spreading, a fraying of the fabric of existence, an unravelling, expanding in all directions as if the god's doom had been a stone cast into the pond of the world and only now were the ripples starting to show. Sometimes Aldryth saw only blackness, and then he trembled, convinced for a moment that a void was all that existed and life no more than a fading memory.

He began to chant his devotions, but his parched mouth ached and he found he could no longer remember the tune, its rises and breaks, the picture it drew from notes and the spaces between them. He looked at his hand and saw it complete – muscle and bone, blood and sinew – but could not remember how to make the signs for any part of it. The Scar was spreading.

Aldryth felt it in the core of himself, the Unwinding, the essence of his life coming undone, not a peeling of skin or a breaking apart of bone, but a dissolving, the falling away of component pieces for which he could no longer find the words. Now he understood. Mortals were built upon many patterns but the god had only one: a single pattern stronger than the many, one pattern to cover the world. *Mogyrk.* He shaped the word with his tongue that was no longer a tongue, his undone lips and his throat that for the moment before it disappeared could have shouted to wake the entire desert: *Mogyrk.*

1

Grada

Thrashing churned the water: white foam, tinged brown with river mud. Grada knelt on a broad stone bedded in the shoreline, her arms elbow-deep, wringing as she had wrung out the robes of the wealthy many times before.

Muscle bunched across her shoulders. Jenna had always said she was strong. Ox-strong, head-strong.

Further out the river slid past, green-brown, placid. Somewhere a widderil called out its song of three notes with all its heart.

They had come from the thickness of the pomegranate grove, two of them sticky with sweat, laying down their pruning hooks as they saw her. Both of them old enough for wives, young enough for wickedness, stripped to loincloth and sandals, white-orange blossom from the second crop clinging to their chests and arms. The men had angled Grada's way as she walked in the shade at the margins, where trees gave way to the river road.

'Hey, girl!' The taller of the two, both of them wiry with white teeth behind their grins.

Sometimes trouble sneaks up on you, but most of the time

it comes waving a flag for any with eyes to see. Jenna, she'd never had the eyes the gods gave her, blinded by too much trust she'd been. Happy though. A friend to the world, right until the day it upped and killed her.

'Where are you off to?' The second man, trouble right behind him swinging that flag.

'I've business downriver,' Grada had said. She backed pace by pace towards the obelisk set to mark the orchard's boundary, some temple slab brought in from the desert. Its shadow reached out to touch her shoulders.

'Have a pomegranate.' The first man gestured back into the greenery, so lush it looked wrong, like sickness.

Had she been the one to offer fruit, neither of them would have taken it from her, not from an Untouchable. But they *would* touch her.

'Come and help yourself.' His friend. 'We've been plucking all day.' He savoured 'plucking'.

She stepped deeper into the shadow, wondering why they would want her. They would have wives at home, babies perhaps, girls in the Maze who might very well take their lusts for a reed-net of pomegranates.

'Don't play games now.' The shorter one, friendly entreaties gone from his eyes, leaving them hard. An old scar across his chest caught the sunlight, a thin white line.

Both came closer, taking turns to nibble away the distance, egging each other on. *Don't play games now.*

Grada's hands went to the belt that cinched her robe. A simple length of knotted rope, slipped through a loop at one end, the final knot larger and set through with a heavy ring of iron.

'I need to be on my way. I can't stay.' But she didn't leave, didn't step away from the obelisk rising behind her; that would have been foolish.

'And we need you to stay.' They brought the perfume of the trees with them, sweet and heady. The man grinned, an ugly thing that dropped away as he moved into the shadow.

Jenna called her strong like the ox, but it wasn't a man's strength. She could outwork a man, out-endure one, but in the quick violence of a struggle the strength of men would tell against her. Grada pulled the rope from around her hips and her robes fell open. They'd been white when she took them from Henma at the wash-stones; now they carried a week of road-dust.

'Clever girl,' said the shorter man with the scarred chest. *Girl*, he said, though he hadn't any years on her.

'I want to leave.' She knew herself no beauty, a broad face sculpted without delicacy, a solid frame. They wanted her because they enjoyed taking. Men like to take more than they like to be given.

She should be scared. She wanted to know why she wasn't scared. Just something else she had lost? Another part of her broken?

The tall man lunged, and she swung. The iron ring hit his cheekbone. Grada heard bone break. He staggered away, both hands clamped to his eye, howling. His friend watched her, amazed.

'Why did you do that?' He didn't seem able to grasp it.

'Two against one isn't fair.' She wondered as she spoke them if the words were hers, or something left behind, something dropped by the Many in the shadows of her mind. She looped the rope back into its place, watching the men. The tall one walked into a tree, staggered and sat down, blood leaking from under his hands. His friend didn't seem to care, still wrestling with the injustice of it all.

'We were just playing.' He even seemed to believe it.

'You would have let me go when you'd finished?'

She turned, knowing it wasn't over, and walked towards the river.

'Yes.'

A voice whispered that they would have buried her among the trees. Not a true voice, just an echo. *Those pruning hooks are meant for cutting.* Another whisperer, one that sounded eager enough to cut. *A keen edge must be used, sooner not later. Sharpness is a challenge.*

Grada heard Scar-chest coming, feet pounding the hard-baked soil past the marker stone. Stupid. She had known he lacked the wit to creep. She had almost reached the point, the point beyond which he would have let her go, almost surprised herself. But he came, as she knew he would.

She ran too, skipping down the riverbank, barefoot, stone to stone. The look on his face – determination, eagerness, anger – all of it gone when she turned at the water's edge and set her shoulder to receive him. He flew high as she took the impact and straightened, landing with a splash as wide as his surprise. Grada followed into the river and pulled her attacker into the shallows where she could drown him.

Thrashing churned the water: white foam, tinged brown with river mud. Grada knelt on a broad stone bedded in the shoreline, her arms elbow-deep, wringing as she had wrung out the robes of the wealthy many times before.

And now, as the water calmed, as the thrashing of limbs surrendered to the cold and placid flow of the river, his face kept only a hint of surprise. She knelt on the rock, the river swirling cold about her arms, hands locked around his neck.

Somewhere in her, a tongue remembered pomegranate. Hers? Had she eaten one? Imagined the pale jewels inside to be riches that might take her from the Maze? Had that been her?

His eyes on hers, the water sliding between their faces, streaming his hair: this nameless man.

She had throttled chickens with more emotion, twisted their heads off and set the bodies still twitching in the basket, scaly legs still jerking as if to escape the hands that had plucked them from the yard.

Don't play games now.

Grada stepped into the water and hauled him out, grunting with the effort. He lay half over her as she fell back onto the hot rock, a touch of the intimacy he'd been seeking. 'Gods.' She sucked in a breath. Men became so heavy when the life ran out of them, as if it had buoyed them all their days. She lay gasping, then pushed him off, slapped his face, made him cough.

The fear that had hidden away all that time in the orchard now crept back in, hunched in the pit of her stomach, putting a tremble in her hands that was about more than wet robes. She stood up.

'So I saved you.' She looked down at the man, black hair plastered to the rock. Had it been Grada that saved him? Once her choices had been hers, spread out like Kento sticks: pick one – they're all yours, but pick one. Every choice felt like a step away now, each one leading to a different person. The Many had left her, but their paths remained, tracks worn in the empty lands, a thousand crossroads without sign or post.

And she walked on, water dripping to the dust, marking her trail like so many drops of blood.

To know that you are alone, first you must know company.

Grada paced along the riverbank. In places the trail dipped as an irrigation channel crossed it, and in the soft mud the ruts and hoofmarks of the caravan could be seen among the countless camel prints.

Grada knew what it was to be alone. For the longest time she had been alone and yet not known it, as if her life had been lived blind, until the Pattern Master gave her sight, until Sarmin showed her beauty. Now that sight had been taken. Now she knew she walked alone.

Along the river the air felt cool, though the sun beat down just as hard. At the oasis of Jedma the waters stretched so wide you couldn't hurl a stone across them, but the air hung still and heavy, wrapped you in a warm, wet hand. The river breathed, though. The silence held a different quality.

Ahead, the faint smudge of smoke against the blue of sky. Camel dung burned dirty when they gorged on the lush banks.

Grada found a place to sit beside the road. She didn't need to creep up like boys playing hunt-the-cat, didn't need to spy on her prey from some ridge or dune. They were there. The record of their passage, the smoke of their fires, told her so. Five dry dates made her lunch, fished from the deep pockets of her robe. She chewed them, savouring the old sweetness, slow and deliberate, like the camel thoughtful over its cud. The taste woke many memories, flavouring each so that it became hard to know which were hers.

'I'll keep to the road.' She spoke to the portrait, a disc of obsidian cupped in the palm of her hand, Sarmin's features incised into its surface. What the artist had found that would cut obsidian she didn't know. 'I'll keep to my quarry.'

She had asked him for a statue, one of the icons the nobles had, to say their prayers to. The Old Mothers had them in gold and bronze: representations of Beyon standing six inches high in niches above their beds. Some kept them still, with just the name cut and re-stamped upon the base, Sarmin's name below his brother's image, a man too powerful in chest and arm to be Sarmin, though nothing like his brother either, so the emperor told her.

'I would feel silly giving such a thing to a friend,' he had told her. 'You carry me inside you.'

Grada had Carried him, now she carried the space where he had been. It seemed cruel to remind her and refuse her in the same breath, but then Sarmin, for all his cleverness, for all that he had shared her skin, did not truly know her. Perhaps he understood no woman, and maybe no man either. He had stepped from that room they raised him in, but she wondered if he would ever truly leave it.

In the end, Sarmin had shown he knew a little more of her than he admitted, for as she took her leave on the mission he assigned her, the emperor stepped from his throne, crouched beside her where she knelt prostrate and pressed the disc into her hand.

She twisted it now before her eyes. Straight on, you saw nothing, just a suggestion here or there. Only at an angle would the light catch on the artist's cuts and offer up Sarmin's features, caught in a few brief lines: as true an image as she had ever seen.

Grada slipped the disc back into her robes and stood, brushing away dust and grit. She walked on. The caravan would not halt long; they had kept a good pace for the past week.

Hours later, with the sun descending, she almost passed by the place where they had turned. She knew in other lands that tracking was an art-form, learned over a lifetime and practised with great skill. Cerana had few places where such skills mattered. Between the city and the sands lay only a thin strip of land where the ground would mark, and where the wind would leave such disturbance long enough to be of use. If the caravan had not numbered iron-shod horses among its steeds there would have been no choice but to follow closely and risk detection. Just one such print caught her eye, one half-moon, cut through the year-old flood-crust out towards the fields. The caravan had left the river road, turned from the city with little more than a day's travel ahead.

'I want to know about the slaves brought in from the north,' Sarmin had said to her. Not in the privacy of the room they once had shared, nor in the secrecy of that link – forged, then broken – that once had bound them, but in the light and space of the throne room. Only distance kept their words from the courtiers moving about the perimeter in a bright and glittering flow; only loyalty kept their secrets within the circle of muscled backs that Sarmin's bodyguards presented to their emperor.

'Slaves have always come from the north,' she had said. *Emperor*, she thought, I should have called him *My Emperor*. And slaves came from all directions, drawn into Nooria to serve, grow old, die. The roads north brought white slaves, too pale to work beneath Cerana's sun, exotic girls for the harem, for nobles wishing to show their sophistication, populating their houses with Mythyck's children.

'I am told that they bear watching,' he had said. Who told him such things, she wondered.

'I will watch them.' She had fallen into her prostration. An Untouchable, the emptier of night-pots, washer of moon-blood from private linen, fallen in obeisance as if she were a man of property and breeding. Azeem had told her of the damage she did, of the poison that spread where she walked.

Grada turned away from the river, along the trail of hard mud beaten to dust, the wheat rising high to either side. A watcher left along the path would know her now – a spy, following along a trail to nowhere. Grada eyed the wheat, swaying in the wind's half-breath. Best pray they had left no watcher.

A quarter-mile along the trail and the wheat had halved in height, an arid taste on the air, irrigation ditches struggling to do their duty. Grada stopped. She wriggled her toes in the dust – sand as much as dust now.

Life at the bottom of a pecking order teaches you to listen and to watch. When any hand can and will be raised against you, it pays to know where those hands are. City sounds are not river sounds, and river sounds are not desert sounds, but a keen ear will learn the ways of each. Grada didn't hear the approach, but she heard the hidden birds fall silent, the creaker-bugs pause and each small thing grow quiet until only the wheat's rustling remained.

She left the trail and pushed in among the crop, careful to part the stalks so they would spring up again behind her. She went in deep enough that she could no longer see the road. Curiosity kills more than cats, and if you can see, you can be seen.

The horses came first, a distinctive *clop-clop* of hooves on dry mud, the jingle of harness. Grada had seen horses, the first time through the eyes of the Many, watching the empress-to-be travel the sands towards Nooria. But these were not the ponies of the grass-tribes. Rather they were the tall steeds of the west, water-hungry, fierce beasts even less suited to the sands. And after the horses, the softer plod of camels, the creak and rumble of waggons. Not a true caravan: these men had followed the longest paths and skirted the desert. Wheels would not take a traveller across the dunes.

'—wouldn't think that meat would need seasoning—'

'—water, and feed the—'

'—volunteered to teach them some new tricks—'

And the travellers had gone, taking their conversations with them. Grada waited. Long enough for the creakers to speak and the birds to take up their song again. She emerged, flicking chaff from her robes, and resumed her course.

In half an hour the trail had gone to ruts in sand, a record of the caravan's passage that would not survive the day. A low ridge took river and its green skirts from view, and Grada found herself on the edge of the desert, as hungry and empty as it ever was. The stone-built house and surrounding pavilions came as a surprise when she crested a second ridge. She went flat to the dust and crawled forwards, lizard-low. The building lay a few hundred yards off, but with the sun in the west she would catch someone's eye coming over the incline.

The hot trail scorched Grada's palms, heat rising from the ground to bake her, gritty sand lifted by a light wind to sit between her lips, irritate her eyes.

'What are you doing here, Grada?' Sometimes she spoke to herself. Since the voices of the Many had been taken, it comforted her to hear her own from time to time. Somehow speaking a thought made it more real, gave it weight.

The gods had plucked her from a life of drudgery and certainty only to replace it with another kind of purpose, a camaraderie of a different sort, the bonds of caste replaced with the pattern. But now? Alone, and with choices outnumbering instructions as sand grains outnumber dunes, Grada felt unmade. *A needle with no eye*, Jenna would have called her.

A man led a chain of girls from the largest of the pavilions: five of them, walking as if still bound together. *Some ties remain, even when cut.* Five girls – three blond, two redheads, exotics from Mythyck and the Scythic Isles beyond – still wearing the rags from their homelands.

'See how he keeps them waiting by the school? No care for whether the sun stains them.' A male voice behind her, calm, without threat.

Grada kept very still, ice on her shoulders. If he had wanted her dead he could have killed her already.

'School?' she asked.

'The last girls were here three months. Only two of them. Those two went out with the caravan that brought these ones.'

What would they spend three months doing out in the folds of the desert? Grada didn't ask. Instead she asked herself what the man wanted. Such questions came as naturally as breathing. Survival as an Untouchable, as a creature whose life was the property of all and any, required that you ask yourself at each turn what every person wanted of you. Grada had been lower than a slave – slaves at least commanded a price, and despite the fact that she had held the hand of the emperor her birth still tainted her, her eyes dark with the sin of her ancestors. *He wants me to answer my own question.*

'They are training them,' she said.

'Because?'

'Because . . .' Grada had never seen skin so pale until the high mage had led her from Sarmin's room to the Tower, where she saw her first northerner, a wind-sworn mage. She thought to say the girls were in training for the Tower, to serve the empire, but why here? No, they were not mages; one northerner might live in the Tower but many more lived beneath Sarmin's golden roofs, proof of his power and wealth. 'Because only the richest can afford exotics.'

'That's my assessment of it,' the man said.

Grada rolled to her side, a slow move, so as to provoke no attack. The man squatted a few yards behind her, off the trail, his robes the colour of sand.

'My name is Rorrin,' he said, veiled as the dunes-men are wont to ride, the sun throwing his shadow before him, short and dark.

'Are you here to kill me?' Grada asked. The fear that eluded her between the river and the pomegranate trees now sent sweat trickling, warm from beneath her arms. She sat, shuffling back from the view of the school.

'Do I look like a killer?' The man pulled his veil about his neck and set back his sun hood. Old, maybe fifty, a comfortable face sagging beneath short grey hair.

'No.' She knew killers, the kind who strode the Maze or bore the emperor's swords. Many wore it openly in the brutal lines of their face. Others hid it, but for those used to looking, their true nature lay revealed – something of steel about them, in the eyes, in the quiet way they held their peace in chaos, waiting to strike.

'Well, then.' He smiled.

Not a killer. A murderer maybe. Murder lies deeper in a man.

'Why are you here, then?' she asked.

'To watch, of course. And better to be away from the trail when you watch. You never know who might come up behind you.' His eyes told a story of kindness, dark but warm.

'And who sent you?' The man who killed Jenna, who cut her body with a sharp knife as if he had been looking for something hidden within, that man had kind eyes.

'We both serve the same person, Grada,' Rorrin said. 'Have you seen enough, or should we wait?'

'How long have you been watching?' she asked.

'Four days.' He waggled a sun-dark hand as if it might be more, might be less.

'Another won't hurt, then.' And Grada rolled to her stomach and crawled back to the ridge and away from the trail.

2

Grada

'Tell me why you let them live.' Rorrin had lain silent in the dust and heat beside Grada while the sun rolled slow across the sky. Now as the dunes beyond the compound started to throw shadows, he spoke.

'Who?' she asked.

Rorrin said nothing, not dignifying her pretence, his gaze on the buildings where the slaves had been taken.

Grada let the breath slip from her, a sigh she hadn't known was in her. 'I'm not a killer.'

'To lie to me again would be a mistake.' Rorrin's voice held no threat, as mild as if they discussed the shade of the sand.

'I . . .' That pale face stared sightless at her again from beneath the water. 'I didn't want to hurt them.'

'Now you're just lying to yourself.'

Rorrin wrinkled his nose to dislodge a fly. Not so many this far from the river but enough to annoy. It flew Grada's way. A shiver of irritation ran through her, not at the fly – the Maze lay black with them in some months – but at the discovery Rorrin was right.

'You said you'd been watching here four days. How could you even know . . . ?'

'I said I'd been watching four days. I didn't say here, Grada.'

'Watching me?' With effort she unclenched the fists she'd made. 'Why?'

'Answer my question. I asked first.'

'They didn't deserve to die,' she said. 'It would have been too easy. I wanted them to know what had happened, to remember me, to hurt, to have it in their minds the next day, the next year.'

'Death would have been a mercy?'

'Yes.' The face again, hair flowing with the current, the river sliding between them. It would have been too easy for him, to slip away with the river.

'And you weren't feeling merciful?'

'No.' Grada watched the man beside her, his profile as he stared across the ridge at the distant building. 'Now answer my question – why were you watching me?'

'I didn't say I would answer you, just that I asked first.'

Grada pushed herself up, started to rise. 'If you think—'

'Down!' A command. 'Our friends are on the move!'

The three blond girls. No, three blond girls, but perhaps not the same ones. Grada learned that from the shell game played on shaded corners where the Maze opened onto the wider streets of Nooria. 'Watch the pea! Watch the pea!' the man would call, his hands blurring as he swapped the shells. And any honest passer-by who tried to watch that pea would lose it just as they lost sight of the wider game.

'Each to a different pavilion,' Rorrin said.

Grada had started to think that he spoke only to test her. 'They're dividing them – setting doubt in their minds so any groups that formed on the journey here are broken.'

'It's likely,' Rorrin said.

'We should have followed the caravan,' Grada said. 'If it included trained slaves from this school we'd learn more from where those were taken than from watching the outside of the tents and building in which these ones are being trained.'

'Yes.' Rorrin showed no concern.

'You weren't alone.'

'No,' he said.

'If we move fast we might still catch them before they reach the city gates.' Grada scooted back across the ground, half sand, half dust, and stood out of sight from the school.

Rorrin followed her, his pace a sensible one but too slow to suit her mood. She waited for him at a milestone. Such stones counted out the first hundred miles from the city – this one read 'twenty' in the old script of lines and dots.

'We may lose them in the city,' she said as he drew closer, river dust scuffing under his sandals.

'Meere will not lose them.' Rorrin watched her face as if he had asked her a question.

'Answer my question,' she said. 'Why have you followed me?' Rorrin seemed almost uninterested in the slaves, as if she herself were the quarry that mattered to him.

A shrug. 'Is it only the emperor's enemies who must train new agents for the fight?' He stepped closer, close enough that she could see the sweat on his brow, the grey stubble above his lip.

'I'm not a fighter.' The idea pulled a laugh from her. 'I'm an Untou—'

His hand was on her shoulder, a move of shocking swiftness. 'I touched you. Be something new.'

The echoes rose from the base of her skull, old whispers hissing repetition.

A sharp edge demands a cut. Quick hands kill, quick hands kill. Aristo touched me so.

She took his wrist and lifted his hand away. There had been an Aristo . . . was that voice hers? A memory?

'You don't have to be a warrior to fight for the emperor. The Tower fights his battles, the alchemists in the Tun, spies who live new lives in far corners beyond the edge of empire.' Rorrin smiled. 'Give me my hand back.'

Grada let him go and in a flicker he held her wrist instead, one finger digging down into a nerve that made her cry out and almost fall to her knees. She kept standing though, snarling at the pain.

'You're too used to doing what is asked of you, Grada.' He let her go. 'Can you unlearn that lesson of a lifetime and show that same obedience to only one man?'

The pain subsided in waves as Grada cradled her arm. 'I serve the emperor, nobody else.'

'Well next time I ask to have my hand back, consider saying no.' And he walked on by, sandals scuffing.

They walked through the cool of the night with the blazing stars to light a moonless path. The love song of ten thousand frogs accompanied them, and the river's sigh as it slipped past unseen.

Grada slapped her neck and brought her hand away dark-smeared with blood and pieces of mosquito.

Rorrin snorted at her side. 'The death of a thousand bites. The emperor—'

'You don't have to make every damn thing an . . . an . . .'

'Allegory?'

'Yes, one of them.' Grada didn't know the word, but it sounded right. 'A story about the emperor or a lesson or—'

Rorrin pressed something into her hand. 'The emperor gave me these.'

Grada looked. Dark objects, rounded, small. A sniff – the faint scent of lemons, bitter lemons.

'Citronel pods. Crush them and wipe the juice on. The bloodsuckers won't want you.'

'Sarmin gave you these?' Grada asked.

'Emperor Beyon. He hated mosquitoes. The things will drink royal blood soon as take from peasants.'

'You knew Beyon? Was he like Sarmin?'

Out in the darkness a whippoorwill unleashed its cry, like a shriek of agony.

'You can't see the emperor as a friend, Grada. That will make trouble for you and for him. And no, Emperor Beyon was nothing like his brother. He would never have spoken to an Untouchable and his friendship was . . . dangerous. Apt to be pulled away as swiftly as it was given. He had a quick temper.'

'They say he was a great emperor. The people loved him in the city.' Jenna had always offered prayers for Beyon. And to him, which made no sense.

'The people adored him because he did nothing. They loved him because we had peace and times were good.'

'It doesn't sound as if you loved him.' And if not Beyon, did Rorrin love Sarmin?

'The gods gave us the emperor that we deserved at that time and the emperor we needed at that time. It's not my place to love the emperor, only to serve him. If the call came I would have laid down my life to obey Beyon with no delay, while the peasants were wondering just how much they liked him after all. The emperor is Cerana. Cerana is the people. I serve.'

Grada crushed the pods and the mosquitoes left her alone while she pondered. Dawn found them still walking. With the sun still flowing up over the rim of the desert they saw the caravan ahead, circled and camped. Rorrin appeared not to see it and Grada broke her silence.

'We should hang back.'

'And look guilty? We'll walk on by and see them again in Nooria.' He walked on, his pace that had once irritated her with its lack of haste now calling on her strength to keep up.

'And if they turn aside to some river mansion or local farm?' She almost kept the annoyance from her voice.

'Meere,' he said.

Grada looked around, sudden remembrance spooking her. She should have remembered Meere. But wherever he hid he'd done a good job of it.

Meere. She would remember him next time.

3

Sarmin

Sarmin paced, fifteen by twenty, fifteen by twenty. The tower that had held him safe for seventeen years offered no comfort. The walls where Aherim and the others once hid now lay pitted, and dust bled from the scars Mesema had left there, covering his old books with a layer of grey. Whorls of ink and shadow had both hidden and revealed the angels who lived in his room, and the demons. It had taken years to find them. Now Sarmin stared at crumbling plaster and broken lines.

His old bed, stripped down to wood and ropes, did not invite. The mattress, soaked with blood from when Grada stabbed him, had been taken away and burned. Broken plaster bit through his silk slippers. A jagged tooth of alabaster jutted from the window frame. Grada had smashed his window, opened his eyes to the world. The shard threw yellow light upon his right foot, then his left. He came to the edge of the room and turned.

One room. Seventeen years. Safe years.

—*You were never safe.*

Sarmin squinted at the broken wall but it was not Aherim who had spoken. When the sun fell a sea of voices rose from some dark infinity. The Many he had saved he had returned to their own flesh, and now they shivered lonely in it. The Many beyond saving still rested with Sarmin. Those whose bodies would no longer receive them, their flesh perhaps too torn to hold a spirit, or the spirit too changed to fit in that which had once contained it. At night they raised their voices.

Sundown had arrived, but a different kind of clock spelled out this day. Mesema had screamed. They tried to shut the door, tried to hush her, but he'd heard it. Her time was upon her; Beyon's child would be born this night, beneath a scorpion sky. Sarmin had tried to see her, but too easily he had let them turn him away. Women's work, Magnificence. Women's work. And an emperor had been turned aside by Old Wives.

And so he had come here, to search one more time for Aherim.

His fingers fell upon the old table, where he'd carved the pattern. Tried to save his brother. None of them had seen this future in the pattern. Had Helmar?

Women die in childbirth every day. Someone had said that to him as if it were a comfort. The rough-carved shapes writhed beneath his fingers, but they were his to alter and cheat, not to command. That spell had been Helmar's, and Helmar was dead. Another spare branch of the family tree pruned away, albeit belatedly.

'Aherim. Show yourself.'

He searched for a pattern. Two eyes together. A nose and a mouth beneath them. 'Will she die, Aherim?'

He saw nothing.

'Zanasta?' Always the last to reveal himself.

Gone. Mesema herself had cast Zanasta out and now he would not help her.

Below the window and to the left an area of the old decoration lay untouched, a tangle of dense calligraphy that had yielded no face in all the long days of Sarmin's inspection, no voice, only confusion mixed with beauty. He went to it now, set his fingers to the fabric, traced the scroll of the lines written out in black and in deepest blue.

'She comes.' Sarmin jerked his hand back, fingertips stung. The voice had rung through him, spilled from his mouth. 'Who?' he whispered. His hand didn't want to return to the wall; the ache of it ran in each tendon. Even so he set his fingers to the pattern once more. None of the angels ever spoke with such authority. Not even Aherim. Of all the devils even Zanasta never chilled him so. 'Who comes?' Only silence and the defiant complexity, as if the artist had written in knots rather than script. 'A daughter? Our child will be a girl?'

'She comes.' Again the shock but Sarmin forced his hand to maintain the contact. A jagged line tore his vision. Mountain tops. The sun sinking behind serrated ridges of stone.

'Who?' Sarmin demanded it but the voice kept silent. 'Who!' Silence.

A knocking brought him back to himself. It repeated.

'My Emperor?' Azeem's voice from outside.

The door handle turned. From long habit Sarmin ignored it. His guards had always checked the door, but never entered. Now the hinges creaked and silk rustled as Azeem entered the room. He took silent stock of the ruined walls and broken window before touching his forehead to the floor.

Sarmin gathered himself before speaking. 'How is my wife, Azeem? The child?'

Azeem leaned back, onto the balls of his feet. 'I know nothing of the women's hall,' he said. 'I have other news.'

Sarmin looked down upon the courtyard where his brothers had died. 'Then tell it.'

Azeem stood now. Sarmin without looking imagined him smoothing the silk of his robe, brushing the plaster dust from its folds.

—*He will betray you – the boys, where are the boys? – so much blood – I'm frightened.*

—*Be quiet, all of you.*

After several moments Azeem said, 'Govnan's mage whispers upon the wind: the peace embassy from Fryth draws near.'

'Such magics.' Sarmin turned and met the vizier's gaze. Azeem looked away, the jewels on his turban throwing out glimmers of the sinking sun. 'Such powers exerted that men might talk across miles.' Fryth was the outermost colony of Yrkmir, the closest corner of its empire, and yet still so far.

'Battles can turn on such a thing. Wars can be won because a message was lost, or heard.' Azeem laced his fingers, perhaps not trusting himself not to fidget.

'And yet when we stand face to face we have so little to say to each other.'

'Even so,' Azeem said, eyes on his hands. He wore no rings on those long dark fingers.

'Let us hope a peace can turn on the right words at the right time.'

Azeem bent his head in agreement. 'Indeed we must move carefully. With victory so close Arigu was not pleased to call a truce, and he has many allies in Nooria.'

Arigu's pleasure mattered nothing. A truce would be had. Sarmin's messengers had been stopped by snow in the passes, unable to reach Fryth and prevent the general from launching his attack. Now too many people had died. Sarmin felt each one as a loss, a shape removed from a pattern. He spoke the words he had meant to keep behind his lips. 'Let us hope my council understands Arigu better than I, for in truth I don't know what he sought through bloodshed.'

'It is the doom of good men that they cannot see what evil men desire, and their salvation that men of evil will not believe it,' Azeem said.

Sarmin returned to the wall, his fingers exploring the ruination. 'You were a slave, taken from the Islands.'

'Yes, My Emperor.' A shield of formality raised without hesitation.

'My servant, Ink, is from Olamagh. His true name is Horroluan. He says in that land there are birds brighter and more colourful than peacocks and that they speak like men.'

'Olamagh is to the south, in wild seas where pirates and sharks infest the waters, Magnificence.' Azeem raised his head. 'My home was Konomagh, a place of spice trees and old learning. We had no birds that talked.'

'And your name?'

'Was Toralune.' Azeem smiled at some memory.

'Wit and service earned your freedom. My cousin Tuvaini raised you high.'

'I serve at your pleasure, My Emperor. If there is some other better suited I would be honoured to return to my former station. I made a better master of house and coin to Lord Tuvaini than I did a vizier. I think perhaps he wanted me near for the comfort of a familiar face rather than for my skills as a diplomat, which are sadly lacking.

'In the Islands, where even children learn to swim, we have a saying. "To be out of one's depth" – it means to lose the seabed before you have mastered swimming. Tuvaini led me into waters deeper than I am tall and I have never learned to swim.'

Sarmin had to puzzle over 'swimming'. In the end he recalled an illustration in The Book of Ways, heads and arms amid a sea of waving lines. Swimming. The palace held a deep pool, marble set with gold, where a man might drown, but none swam there.

His fingers returned to the wall. 'Did you ever have an imaginary friend, Azeem?'

'I had a real friend, Magnificence, and after he died for many years I imagined his ghost followed me. I would tell him my secrets, and leave him a portion of my food, but he only followed and watched, and could never join in my games.'

'I had an imaginary friend once.' Sarmin raised plaster-white fingers to his face. 'Sometimes I think all of my friends have been imaginary.'

Sarmin crossed to his desk and sketched Aherim's face with a white finger. It didn't look like Aherim. 'Perhaps we can be friends, Azeem?'

The pause spoke the 'No' plain enough.

'An emperor cannot afford friends, Magnificence,' Azeem said. In Sarmin's mind the Many laughed. *The richest man in an empire of rich men and he cannot afford friends.*

'Least of all low-born or slave-taken friends. Your flesh is golden, your robe brighter than the sun. The empire requires you that way, needs you that way, and the touch of lesser men sullies you. The touch of the Untouchable—'

'Of Grada. You may say her name.' Sarmin rubbed the chalk face from his desk, an angry motion.

'As high vizier I am little but advice. My advice is to send

Grada away, never to return. You have been gifted many concubines—'

Those concubines, gifts from the scheming, whispering lords, might as well have been snakes in Sarmin's view – no less so for their high status. That was why he had sent Grada to find out about them, Grada whom he trusted, she who had carried him with her.

'Tell me,' he said, stalking closer to the vizier, 'how long did it take the palace to turn Toralune to Azeem? Do you remember when and where we taught the Island boy to despise? When our traditions, dry-born of the desert, replaced the sea-born freedoms of the Isles?'

Azeem let the anger run off him. 'Traditions are what hold you in your throne, Magnificence.'

'You would not speak so to Beyon.' Nobody would speak an awkward truth to Beyon. Perhaps that was what killed him. 'Go now. I'll speak to you in the other room.'

Azeem made his obeisance and left.

Sarmin had a world of two rooms now. The one room he stood in, and a second larger room that held everything beyond his doorway. Two rooms, one full of wonders, the other full of dust, and sometimes he felt more trapped than ever he had when fifteen and twenty paces had bound him.

In the other room a child was being squeezed into the world, pushed into it in pain and blood. Mesema would be screaming and yet even the emperor himself couldn't push past tradition, tear through custom and see her, offer comfort. Or maybe his own fears held him. In the other room a man could drown. Even an emperor could find himself out of his depth.

4

Grada

The house stands in the Holies, up above the reek of the Maze, separated from it by the stockyards, the market, the streets of Leather and Copper, the streets of Salt and Silver. And by the river.

When Uthman came across the empty desert in the longest of long agos he discovered two great outcrops of granite defying both sand and river, channelling the waters between them, resisting the wind. He founded a city there and named it Nooria after Meksha's daughter, she of the hidden fires in whose deep furnace such rock is forged. On the greater outcrop he built his palace, and in time it grew to devour and conceal the ancient rock. On the lesser outcrop, watching the palace across the swift waters of the Blessing, he set the first shrine, to Meksha, and the second to her child. And among the many shrines that followed, the rich built homes, each according to the changing tastes and prosperity of the times. For what is wealth for if not to let men live among the gods?

This knowing comes to Grada from the pages of a great book, though she cannot read. It can only be that the Many have whispered it to her. She sees the book, its parchment turning beneath blunt and ink-stained hands, at once familiar and strange.

The house stands on a long aisled street where date palms grow in ordered senility, grey with age and fruitless now, awaiting time's judgement. At one end, Mirra's shrine, domed in black marble, simple and without adornment. At the far end where the street opens into a sun-dazzled square, Herzu's shrine in alabaster, abalone and ivory, white in many flavours, carved in deep and complex relief.

The house stands between life and death, pale in the moonlight, and Grada knows with certainty – as sudden as the sun's departure – that she is dreaming.

It's cold on that street where the palms whisper in the dark and no one walks. Grada shivers against the breeze and against a deeper chill woken in her bones. The gardens are high-walled but it is gesture rather than threat; the stonework is ornate and easy to climb. There are no lights behind the many shuttered windows, no servants at late duties. There will be guards – a rich man cannot sleep without a sharp blade to guarantee his slumbers – but like the walls these guards will be more show, blunted by routine, selected for the peaceful boredom of civilised living.

Grada would rather walk away, let sleeping dogs lie. Instead she waits and lets the poisoned dogs die. The meat she slung over the wall left her hands bloody. She wipes them on the coarse sandstone before her. There will be more blood to come. She can taste it.

This isn't dreaming. This is memory.

Unfolding, piece by piece like a tight-wrapped pattern, bound about a dark and rotten truth.

Grada knows this, knows it as she knows the path her knife cut to Sarmin's chamber, the lives she sliced open to reach him. The Many guided her hands that night. Now those same hands find purchase on the carved corner of a garden wall and pull her up. The pattern unfolds a piece more, its secret still hidden. But some offenses are so rank they reek to heaven and nothing can wholly conceal them. There's a child here. She knows that much.

'Wake up.' Fingers tight about her wrists.

Grada struggled, but the grip held.

'Wake up!' Rorrin said again. The moonlight caught his face above her.

Grada relaxed in his grip, spitting sand.

'You shouted in your sleep.'

'Bad dreams,' she muttered, shrugging him off to sit upright. She paused a moment, looking about. The milestone at the roadside, the milky haze of stars above, the sigh of the Blessing slipping past in the night, and in the far distance the glow of Nooria.

Rorrin sat back, a white gleam of teeth in the darkness of his face. 'You're young yet – there are worse dreams to come.' Sloshing as he reached for his waterskin. 'Here.'

For a while Grada held silent, the waterskin cool across her knees, its contents sliding as she changed position. Rorrin settled down beneath his cloak once more.

'And what kind of emperor will Sarmin be?' If she fell asleep that house would still be waiting for her, she would find herself straddling that wall with the bushes seething beneath her in the darkness and the sounds of three hounds choking. Better to have Rorrin spin out his opinions and keep her awake.

'We get the emperor we deserve,' Rorrin said. 'And clearly we deserve to be punished.' He yawned, wide enough to crack his jaw.

Grada pushed the skin aside, her anger in the sharp gesture. 'Sarmin is a good man.' Sarmin the Saviour, they were calling him now.

Perhaps Rorrin shrugged – the darkness hid it. 'Better a strong emperor than a weak one, but if the emperor is weak then better he hide in the palace and play his games there. The worst of all is a weak emperor who shows his weakness to the world. Cerana has enemies on every side. It's the natural order of things – the rich are watched by the poor, always waiting for the chance to turn the tables, to move into their houses, dine from their silver. Neighbour watches neighbour with jealous eye.'

'Being a good man doesn't make Sarmin weak.' Grada remembered how easy it had been to stab him. How she bore him to the bed and he had offered no fight, only traced his fingertips across her shoulder, and in that touch taken her from the Many.

'This emperor has yet to name a Knife, though seven candidates have been offered for judgement. Only a fool walks the Maze unarmed. Sarmin walks far worse places and thinks he needs no Knife. His enemies won't see a new way of thinking in his empty hands, they'll see he represents an opportunity entirely different from the one he thinks to offer.

'His weakness springs from what we did to him. We learn to mistrust as we grow, we come to know the true nature of men, the hungers that drive them. Our innocence dies the death of a thousand cuts. Sarmin spent those years alone, nursing only one wound, a big one I grant you, but even so. He doesn't understand us, the people outside his rooms, outside his books. Innocence, that is a dangerous state of mind in which to rule. Better a bloody-handed murderer than an innocent on the Petal Throne.'

Grada set her head to her pack and twisted to remake her hollow in the sandy ground. She had no argument for Rorrin. She could say that the emperor had been easy to stab but that his touch saved her. She didn't think that would ease Rorrin's mind. She closed her eyes against the light of the stars. The garden and the house would either draw her to them or they wouldn't. There are some truths that can't be run from.

5

Sarmin

'I have come to see my brother,' Sarmin said.

All other guards had yielded before him without a word, bowing their heads as he paced past, his own picked men silent at his shoulders. Now he faced one who would not stand aside.

'Daveed is sleeping,' his mother said, arms folded beneath the swell of her milk-vest.

'Even so, I will see my brother.'

It had hurt Sarmin to deny his mother, to override her authority with his. Back when he slew the Pattern Master and took the throne, Nessaket had been the last to acknowledge his new status, blind to it almost, steeped too long in the ownership she had enjoyed when one room held him. To defy her had been another door to pass through, another transition no part of him wanted, and yet necessary. To surrender any inch of those gains would require the same battle to be fought and won again.

The silence stretched between them until it quivered.

Nessaket broke first. 'As you will.' Even now forgetting his title, bowing her head more to take him from her sight than in honour. She stepped aside as he stepped forward. The chamber beyond held four of her personal guard, tight around the child's crib as if in accusation.

If Sarmin demanded Daveed's life four guards could no more save the babe than the trio of nursing-slaves waiting beneath the lamps. The guardsmen at least had the sense to draw aside quickly, lifting the points of their great hachirahs from the carpet. Sarmin leaned over to watch the sleeping boy.

'He smiles now, they tell me?'

'For two weeks, and he can tug on Dreshka's skirts, reach for the vases in their niches, burn his fingers on a hot lamp.' Nessaket joined him, a tight smile escaping her displeasure.

The boy was lying sprawled in sleep, one pudgy arm reaching a fist above his head, sweat plastering dark curls to his temples.

'Have the council spoken to you again? That snake Azeem?' She flashed Sarmin a dark look, eyes hard.

Had she fought so hard to keep *him* from the Knife, when tradition ordered all Beyon's brothers dead? That she might think he would give up his brother's life to those men's demands – that hurt him more than her attacks.

When each sun set it was always to draw in the same night, that night of the Knife, that night of slit throats and blood across the courtyard. Sarmin's mother claimed she had saved him from that fate, but Beyon had made the same claim. Tuvaini also, and Govnan of the Tower. A good act finds many owners while many a sin goes begging.

'The council speak to me often, Mother,' he said, 'but I have many councillors, and only one brother still living.'

Sarmin reached to touch those dark curls, to feel the warmth of the child's skin. Beside him his mother startled, as if to seize his arm. The closest of his guards tightened hands on hilts, the blued steel of their scimitars showing above their scabbards. Nessaket fell back and Sarmin circled a finger amid the dampness of his brother's hair.

'Lift him for me.'

'He's sleeping,' she said.

'Even so.'

And she drew him from his crib, soft and heavy in sleep.

I need to see him, touch him, feel the living heat rise off his skin.

Time and again the council called for an end to this line. 'He is the son of a traitor,' General Hazran had said. Azeem would not speak of Tuvaini, but when Nessaket was mentioned he lowered his head. 'She schemes. Even with the most generous interpretation and with the utmost humility, it must be admitted, she schemes.' And Dinar said, 'Daveed is the son of a traitor and a schemer, and next in line to the throne. He cannot live.' Herzu's priest knew much and more about death. 'Put him to the Knife.'

And in a thousand ways, in every way except that which mattered most, they were right. Sarmin took his brother's tiny hand, held it between two fingers and a thumb. Enemies, men with antique grudges, men hungry for power, or for the chances that change might bring, they would all stand behind this boy, seek to own him, aim him. The empire lay cracked and the crack had a name.

'Daveed.' Sarmin closed the fingers of one hand around the baby's thigh. Soft and fat and small.

She thinks to protect him from me, but this, this touch, hearing him draw breath, the scent of him. This is what keeps him alive.

'You forget, Mother, Daveed is heir to the throne. My heir. I will not see him harmed.'

'Today he's your heir. Tomorrow?' She shrugged.

Tomorrow is always a puzzle of many parts. Give me a daughter and Daveed stays safe. And that could be an end to it. I would be happy to raise a daughter.

'You should be with Mesema, Mother.' Sarmin watched his brother, refusing to meet their mother's eyes.

'She has women aplenty with her. In any case these horse-girls know more about birthing than any decent bride should. On the plains they open their legs to men and beast alike and drop bastards in the grass without a second thought.'

'Mesema had no plains-children, Mother.' Sarmin took his hand from Daveed before anger tightened it. 'She was taken too young from her family. She needs the Old Wives round her – she has laboured two days and a night.'

'She has Old Wives—'

'Only Lana is with her, and the Little Mother was never strong, less so since Beyon's passing. Mesema needs strength now.'

'My place is with my son,' Nessaket said. 'I cannot leave him.'

Sarmin turned to go.

'The gods will strike you down the day you listen to those men,' his mother said.

No ifs. She already thinks I will break, that it's just a matter of time.

'The only danger to Daveed is your fear, Mother. Herran tells me of these plans to spirit my brother away to the estate of this lord or that lord, to use this passage, that guide. Fear breeds fear. The more you do to take the child from the palace the more the council mistrust your motives.' He sounded tired even to himself as he stepped towards the doorway. 'Watch my brother well.'

His hand still held the child's warmth. He looked down at it, half expecting to find it bloody.

Corridors led him and for a time Sarmin walked without direction. Bodyguards shadowed his path, dark as befits shadows, slave-bred sword-sons from the Islands.

If Mother knew that five men loyal to me guard Daveed for each of hers, what then would she think? He stopped before an archway. Beneath it, in mosaic on the floor, Huna, last champion of the Parigols, stood outnumbered by Cerani, proud and many. *Perhaps it's in our blood to glorify our enemies and overlook our own heroes.*

'Magnificence!' A pale man running, wrapped in the blue silks of a servant, sashed in gold to denote command. 'Magnificence!'

'Paper!' For a moment Sarmin couldn't remember the man's true name. Even now it felt strange for Paper to speak after seventeen years serving in silence. 'Charging at the emperor is a good way to lose height.' He spread his hands to calm the guards who had stepped in close. True to their training they relaxed only by the merest fraction, as if humouring him. *Threats don't vanish just because the emperor does not see them.*

'A child, My Emperor!' Paper caught his breath and remembered himself. He fell into his obeisance. 'The empress is delivered of a child, Mirra be blessed!'

'Is she well? Is Mesema well? Are they both well?' A hollowness filled him.

'Tired, Magnificence, but she is well. As is your son.'

'A son?' How many gods had he asked for a daughter? 'A son?' Beyon's son. The true emperor.

6

Nessaket

Nessaket sat and watched her son Daveed. An hour ago he had begun to cry for his milk, a strong, healthy cry that seared her chest, but she did not lift him from his bed. He remained where his brother Sarmin had put him, waving his tiny fists and punching his feet at the ceiling. Over time his wailing grew thin, until finally he turned his face to the blankets, sucking at the silks, making little noises of disappointment. Shadows gathered around him, settling into the folds of his blankets, the curves of his hands and the hollows of his eyes. With the darkness came a chill, but she did not cover him. Perhaps the cold would sink in, make him frail, carry him off to his dead brothers. Perhaps that would be a mercy.

Before the little savage pushed forth her cursed boy, Sarmin had named Daveed as his heir and promised never to hurt him. But within an hour everything had changed. Now Sarmin had a son and Daveed was both more and less than he had been. More of a threat, less of a necessity. Her prayers to Mirra had gone unanswered. Tuvaini lay in his tomb, Arigu remained far away in Fryth and she was alone.

A wail rose from deep within her, but all that escaped was a half-syllable, choked rather than spoken. Daveed heard and renewed his protests, outraged that she would sit so close without feeding him. His fury reminded her of Beyon, though her eldest would never have gone quiet, or so she believed: she had never made Beyon wait, and so she did not know.

Was it easier to die as a baby? She thought of her son Yusuf, who had yielded to the same fever that killed so many of Tahal's children. It had swept them all away and left Beyon as the eldest boy. How she had thanked Herzu then, making sacrifices daily, for pestilence was His province but Beyon had been spared. She thought perhaps he'd been chosen by the gods, and urged Emperor Tahal to protect and favour her son over all others.

She laughed at that, all bitter edges, cutting across the baby's cries. *Yes; I should just kill him now. His brother is the hand of heaven, and the gods are careless.* Even Tuvaini had managed the deaths of all Beyon's wives during his short reign. Women she had hand-picked and trained from a young age – staked out in the courtyard for Eyul's bow. The throne was purchased and maintained through death and blood.

Nessaket raised the cushion and stared down at Daveed's red, angry cheeks. He had Beyon's eyes and that curl of hair at his temple. He did not resemble his father; for that she was thankful.

There had been a time, before her husband had betrayed her, when she had loved and been loved, when she had looked to the future with happiness. When she remembered those days, it was to recall another woman, not herself. That woman had been hollowed out of her, bite by bitter bite, until she felt empty. The same emptiness had forced Siri to jump from the roof of the palace after little Kashim died, the roof where she had kept a beautiful garden, where the children had played.

She had watched Eyul Knife-Sworn drag his blade over Amile's throat. Had Amile wondered, in those last moments, whether his life had always been meant to end that way? Whether his lessons and songs and embraces had been for nothing? Had he felt the betrayal, had he felt unloved? It weighed on her like a stone, making her arms heavy, the cushion heavy. She dropped it.

It just covered Daveed's little body. She leaned over the crib, letting the heaviness weigh her down, letting it press her hands against the silk. A lullaby came to her lips. *Sleep now little child, your father tames the sands so wild, over dune and under star, your dreams have wings, they'll take you far.* Daveed struggled a moment, his little feet kicking at the tassels, then went still.

'No!' Nessaket threw the pillow from the cradle. Had he died so quickly? But he blinked at her, angrier than ever, and let out a long, shuddering wail. 'Oh, Daveed,' she said, picking him up. 'Oh, my child.' *And so I still have something yet to lose.* She gave him her breast, wondering if some part of him would remember this and hate her, just as Beyon had. Now she had betrayed all of her children, except for Yusuf. Dear, sweet Yusuf had died not knowing anything but her love.

Daveed would not die. She would make sure of that now.

I will be a better mother this time.

Once Daveed's stomach was full, his eyelids drooped. Nessaket placed him in his cradle and turned to the mirror. She saw herself in the silver, still a little heavy from giving birth, her hair finally showing a streak of grey. 'Dreshka? Where is my body-slave?' she called out, though she knew the woman always stood in the shadowed niches of the hallway.

'Your Majesty?' Dreshka hurried in and prostrated herself on the rug.

'I need my hair done, and my face.'

Dreshka came to stand behind Nessaket and picked up a brush. 'How would you like your hair today, Majesty?'

'Down.'

Dreshka asked no more questions. Within a few minutes Nessaket's hair gleamed and kohl lined her eyes. Now she saw at least a trace of the woman who'd seduced emperors and generals. Better. She stood, causing the slave to stumble backwards. She ignored Dreshka. Best to show slaves no consideration; down that path lay resentment and danger. 'Sash,' she ordered, and Dreshka tied blue silk around her shoulder, making a sling. Nessaket lifted Daveed and tucked him in.

Dreshka looked down at the baby. So easily she smiled. 'Where will you take him now, Majesty?'

Nessaket slapped her face. 'How dare you ask questions of me.'

The girl's eyes watered and Nessaket clenched her teeth. Slave-girls made her feel upset. In the days of old, eunuchs had both guarded and served the women of the palace. Satreth the Drunk had outlawed the practice, calling castration cruel. Nessaket wished he hadn't. She imagined the eunuchs as stoic and competent, yet easily led. The perfect servants.

Dreshka fell to her knees and pressed her forehead to the carpet. 'I am a foolish slave, Your Majesty.'

Nessaket walked into the corridor, smiling sweetly at each of the grizzled guards. They were the closest to eunuchs that she could have. They fell into place behind her.

Everywhere painted women perched like butterflies on benches and cushions. Generals, satraps and prominent merchants had all sent their finest prizes to Emperor Sarmin, but he had found no use for them. They watched her pass, eyes careful and cunning. Nessaket had not chosen them. They bore watching.

At last they arrived at the temple of Herzu. She gestured for her men to wait, squared her shoulders and marched into the darkness to pick her way through the confusion of statues and benches. The apex of the high, spotless dome was hidden in shadow, but she knew what was there: a will and a purpose. Not a path to avoid suffering but one to live through it, victorious.

At last she emerged near the altar. High Priest Dinar stood under the monstrous golden statue of Herzu, his broad shoulders blocking the candlelight. A sandcat lay at his feet, muscles twitching, its blood pooling on the tiles. A sacrifice. Sandcats were said to be twice as fast as a man and three times as strong, but she saw no man here save Dinar. She stood silent, watching the cat grow still.

At last Dinar turned, and she met his dark gaze. She was the wife of two emperors, twice Empire Mother. He would hear her out.

'Your Holiness.'

He bowed. She saw speckles of blood on his scalp, on the backs of his arms. His right hand held a bloody dagger. 'You bring the babe.' A question in his tone.

'I would have him serve Herzu.'

Dinar rose from his bow and motioned to a nearby bench. Together they sat. Dinar looked down at Daveed. 'May I?' He held out his hands, covered with blood.

Nessaket slipped her baby from the sling and handed him to the priest. Dinar took him from his blankets, studied his legs and arms, turned his jaw left and right, and checked his penis. 'He is strong.'

'Yes. He would make a good priest of Herzu.'

'Tuvaini was a good servant of Herzu. His son must be blessed.'

Nessaket said nothing. Dinar turned the baby on his lap and ran a red-tinged finger along his spine. 'You would give me the babe? Now?'

She hesitated. 'He needs my milk.'

Dinar wrapped the blanket around Daveed. 'I cannot take him.'

Nessaket felt a wetness on her slipper. The creature's blood had run across the tiles. She looked at Herzu's statue, his terrible fangs, the heart of the sandcat in one golden hand, a dead baby fashioned of bronze in the other, and then at Dinar, his eyes cold, a ruthless smile on his lips. 'Why?'

'You come to me out of fear and weakness. A mother's desperation. You insult me.'

'Mothers can also be strong.'

'Are you strong now? Were you strong when you tried to spirit him away to your family? Or does your mage son frighten you?'

'Sarmin is no mage.'

Dinar smiled again. 'You were not among the Many, were you? Many things that had been secret were shared. We shared a terrible knowledge. Now we are afraid to remember.'

'What are you speaking of?'

'Cowardice. We have forgotten what was begun.' Dinar stood and walked through the sandcat blood to the altar. He ran a hand down Herzu's muscled, golden leg. 'By Sarmin and those before him. We long for the Many, but we forget the price.'

Nessaket stood, the babe quiet in her arms. 'You refuse my son?'

Dinar spoke with his back to her. 'I refuse your intent. Be strong for the empire, serve Herzu, and perhaps I will take him yet.'

'Sarmin—'

'For now the emperor is a child of Mirra, soft and weak. He offers peace to a defeated foe and coos over an infant. He will not move against you.'

Treasonous words. But she had spoken worse in this place of Herzu when Beyon was emperor. And Dinar spoke truly. She could make her moves now, before Sarmin learned to play the game in earnest. She could be several steps ahead of him before he had finished admiring his new son. 'What must I do?'

'You know what to do. This peace is an affront to Him.'

Nessaket gathered Daveed against her chest and left the temple, leaving bloody footprints in her wake.

7

Rushes

Rushes runs over the soft ground. She chases something quick and bright, a flutter of patterned wings, darting in and out of the grass, rising high, beyond her reach, and then down again before she can grasp it. It is yellow with a pattern of blue and red, a bright abandon of colour that calls back to her a time when she was younger, before the slavers brought her to the palace, before she became one with the Many. It pauses over a blossom, and she darts forwards to cup it in both hands. Its wings beat against her palms, frantic, its fear translating along the lines of her skin, infecting her, and so she lets it go. But the ground betrays her; her foot snags in the grass and she struggles for balance. Too late. She begins to fall.

'Rushes! Wake up, girl.'

Rushes opened her eyes to take in the room, just beginning to show itself in shades of grey, and Mother Hagga, leaning over her with a frown.

'Sleeping when you should be lighting the fires. Gorgen—'

Gorgen! Rushes leaped up and reached for her serving-dress, hanging on the wall above her pallet. If she hurried, she'd still get to the kitchen before he did. She didn't want any trouble.

You'll get it, he always said. She finished tying on her clothes and ran to the water-basin. 'Where's Demah?' she asked.

Hagga shrugged and reached for her own work clothes, but without any hurry. Mother Hagga had worked in the Little Kitchen for as long as anybody could remember, and did mostly as she liked.

After splashing some water on her face, Rushes ran through the door and towards the Little Kitchen, holding her skirts up over her feet, taking the corners at a spin. She hoped Demah had already lit the fire.

But when she got to the Little Kitchen the fireplace was dark, and Gorgen waited by the water-pump, his big shoulders drawn up against the cool of the morning. Tears formed in Rushes' eyes and she edged towards the coals. *Where's Demah?* As one of the Many she might have called out for her, but not any more.

Gorgen smiled. In this light his teeth looked just a shade lighter brown than his hair. She froze, one hand on the coal-shovel, but he didn't move towards her, not yet. 'You look so pretty, even first thing in the morning,' he said.

Confused, she said nothing, watching his face for clues.

He reached her in one stride, his big, callused hand raised, and she cringed. But he only ran a finger down her cheek, and this scared her more than a slap ever could have. She didn't know what he wanted, or what she was supposed to do. To live outside the Many, deaf to the murmurs of those around her, was to live in doubt. 'I remember your voice,' he began, but stepped back and fell quiet at the sound of Mother Hagga's footsteps in the corridor.

Rushes turned away and shovelled the coal. It wasn't unusual for people to remember her voice among the Many. She'd been the only child in the palace who survived the Patterning. Also she was fast, and small enough to fit through little cracks and holes, so that it had been she who first found the body of Emperor Beyon, laid out in his coffin, the pattern shining all around him. It had been she who sent the image to the Many so that all could rejoice. When he was alive he promised that as long as he was emperor nobody could hurt her. And then she had become part of the Many, and celebrated his death.

Tears burned her eyes; when the pattern broke the shame had found her and it had never left. It burned in her now, so she threw herself into the morning's work. *Sorrow slips through the empty places, the idle moments, and trouble can't move a busy hand.* So her mother used to say when the snow piled up outside and the two of them readied the wool for spinning, all alone in their smallhouse, with no clan or fields to surround them. *Let's keep our hands busy.*

'Here comes the priest,' Hagga warned in a low voice, and Rushes saw him, all in black, gliding past the kitchen door like a wraith from old stories. Every morning an acolyte of Herzu went into the dungeon and plucked out a prisoner who never came back.

She must have stopped whatever she was doing, for Hagga hissed at her, 'Get to it, child! You can be frightened later.'

Mina scurried up from the Big Kitchen, dark hair gleaming under a pink scarf, carrying a bucket of onions with both arms. Only four worked in the Little Kitchen – Rushes, Demah, Mina and old Hagga.

'Where's Demah?' asked Gorgen, looking towards the hallway.

'Sick,' said Hagga. It wasn't exactly a lie; Demah was always sad and out of sorts since the Unpatterning, like many other slaves. People called it the Longing.

Gorgen snorted. 'She'd better drag herself out of bed. The prince is being presented today, and the silk-clad will be looking to fill their mouths.'

Rushes imagined the baby, red-faced and soft. It made her smile. She had been allowed only a few months with her own baby brother before coming to the palace. They finished the rest of the breakfast preparations in silence, each to their own tasks. Hagga made the bread, which gave a pleasant smell to the room, and Gorgen polished the silver and glass to gleaming. Every morning Rushes and Mina took platters up to the generals, the visiting nobles and the finer slaves – the ones who counted money or wrote the stories of empire – while Demah served the women's wing.

Gorgen turned to Rushes. Eyes that seemed kind, earlier, now went sharp. 'With Demah dozing like a lazy cat,' he said, 'you'll have to do her work.'

Rushes hoped the beating of her heart didn't show in her hands as she reached for the first silver tray, covered with the best dishes and the finest glass, and placed it on the moving shelves that would rise all the way to the third floor, to where the silk-clad women waited for their breakfasts. Once that tray was in place, she reached for the second.

'That one's for the Empire Mother,' said Gorgen, still at her side, so close she could feel his breath on her neck. He touched another tray, smaller. 'That one's for old Sahree down in the servants' hall.'

'Why?'

'Empress Mesema commands it.' Gorgen straightened and lifted his chin. 'Sahree gave excellent service, I heard. Back-door Arvind told me. Low Vizier Shubhan said it to Guard-Captain Mahmoud, and *he* got it from even higher up.'

Rushes couldn't be sure all of that was true, because she had gone deaf to the thoughts of others, especially Gorgen's. It would be odd for the message to come from Back-door Arvind, an old man full of jokes and alcohol, who couldn't name a single woman who lived upstairs. She lifted the last tray and put it inside the box of moving shelves.

'Hey.' Gorgen grabbed her elbow, squeezed hard. 'When you see Demah, tell her she's gonna get it.'

Rushes approached the great bed of the Empire Mother, a silver tray balanced between her hands. Nessaket lay sideways, head turned towards the window, the silk sheets tangled around her feet. Her hair made a brushstroke path along the white mattress, an artist's sweep towards a word. *Beauty. Richness.* Rushes thought some more. *Sorrow.* She placed the tray on a table and knelt into her obeisance, listening for a sound from the emperor's little brother. Demah had told her the little prince was a jolly child, and fat, and she would very much like to see him, but she heard nothing. *Strange. Empty.* As one of the Many she would have been able to find the babe and listen to his nascent thoughts. She felt a pang of loneliness and pushed it aside.

'What is that?' The Empire Mother's voice came hoarse and tired.

'Dinner, Your Majesty.' Rushes focused on a woven red flower just beneath her nose. Nessaket had never been one of the Many, but lying abed was an Unpatterned thing to do – something Demah would do.

The sheets made a slithering sound as Nessaket rose. 'I know it's my dinner – what sort of a dinner is it?'

'Cheese, bread, olive oil and some roasted vegetables and

nuts.' Rushes took a breath. 'Your Majesty.' The last had come too late, and she cringed.

No blow came. Rushes let out her breath.

'What blood is it that grants such orange hair? I should like a slave with orange hair.'

'I – I am from the plains, Your Majesty.' Clanless and starving. But from the plains, nevertheless.

'Girls from the plains have brownish-yellow hair,' said Nessaket, her voice full of knowing. Silver clinked against silver as she drew something from the tray. 'They always look as if they need to be washed.'

Rushes mulled over the implied insult towards the empress. Her forehead began to sweat where it rested against the rug.

Glass clinked; the Empire Mother continued to eat while Rushes knelt. After a time she spoke again. 'Are you sure you're not Fryth?'

In truth she did not know. Her father had gone east when he left. *Gone home*, her mother had said, scratching at her own cheeks in desperation. *He has gone towards the morning and left us.* But Rushes did know the Cerani had attacked Fryth, and that made them the enemy – at least until the peace was made. 'My father might have been Fryth, Your Majesty,' she said, 'but I lived on the plains until Lord Arigu brought me here.'

A chuckle. 'Arigu is no lord.' And then, more quietly, 'He is more useful than that.'

'Apologies, Your Majesty.' Rushes thought about how long she had been facing the carpet. Gorgen would be in the kitchen wondering where she could be. Trays were lining up on the counter, waiting to be received by generals, advisers and visiting lords. Mina wasn't as fast as she was, and Demah was not there. Every day there was another reason for Gorgen to get angry. Warm wine, cold food, soggy bread.

You'll get it.

'Stand. Let me see your eyes.'

She stood, instinctively avoiding the Empire Mother's gaze, but then Nessaket grabbed her chin and jerked it up. Rushes stood eye-to-eye with the woman who had given birth to two emperors. Beyon's mother. She tried not to let the other woman see it in her eyes: that she had stood over his body and radiated joy for the Many.

'Dark blue,' said Nessaket, letting go of Rushes' chin. 'Fryth for certain.' She took another bite, chewing slowly, her red mouth curling up into a smile. Behind her, the little prince began to wail, pulling Rushes even further into the past, when she was five and her own little brother cried for his milk. Her mother sold her one season later, to get herself a dowry and to secure the baby's future, but she remembered his angry little fists, his chubby, pumping legs. The fierce love she had felt for him rose inside her, more of a longing than a memory, and tears threatened.

But where could the prince be? She could hear him, but she couldn't see him. His golden basket could be anywhere, lost among the gilded pillars, gleaming mirrors and fine paintings of angels.

Nessaket returned her food to the tray. 'Do you understand the Fryth concubines when they speak?'

'Apologies, Your Majesty. I have not heard them speak.' In truth she did not know whether she would understand Frythian. She remembered something of her father's speech, its hard edges and its lack of affectionate tone. Had that been Frythian?

'But you understand their language? What about the other ones? The Mythyck girls?'

Rushes blinked away a tear. 'I'm just a slave, Your Majesty.'

'A slave with ears.' The Empire Mother looked away as if gathering her thoughts. Perhaps Rushes' stray tear had disturbed her. 'But pretty. You may attract too many eyes.'

'Thank you, Your Majesty.' Was that the right response? She could have told how she wore her dresses loose, and used two aprons instead of one, to keep the men from looking.

'And yet,' said Nessaket, 'I would love to have someone who can tell me what people are saying. Visitors to the palace. Generals and lords. The concubines. They guard their tongues when I am near.'

'Of course, Your Majesty.' Rushes made a bow. 'As you wish.'

Nessaket smiled and waved a hand over her tray. 'I'm finished.'

Rushes picked up the tray and left the room backwards, bowing. In the corridor she nearly bumped into one of the new concubines, a dark, curly-haired girl with brown eyes that narrowed at her. Had some lord paid her family, and then presented her to Emperor Sarmin like a gilded box? Rushes remembered the first day they brought her before Emperor Beyon. He had been standing all alone in his great hall, but then he sat down on the steps and gave her some honey-candy. He called her Red-Rose and let her play when nobody was looking. She had betrayed him in the end, but she could still help his mother. All she need do was listen.

Rushes returned to the moving shelves and exchanged the Empire Mother's tray for the old servant's, careful not to walk into any of the silk-clad concubines. They crowded the Great Room, circling the food she'd laid out earlier. She felt pity for them; everyone knew the emperor wanted only one wife. It was a love story, savoured over the sleeping-mats. Sarmin the Saviour and his wife Mesema.

The beauties ignored her as she balanced the tray on one knee and pushed the heavy door. On the other side a guard saw her, smiled and pulled it open. She thanked him as she hurried past, wondering which One he might have been. It was nearly impossible to match the memory of a voice, the impression of a life, with a real face. And of all the things she heard when she was Carried, *I was a guard* was the most often repeated. But *he* probably remembered her.

Rushes turned this way then the other, as the corridors grew plainer but at the same time brighter. The plain white walls reflected the sun and made the servants' quarters sizzle. This hall was for the slaves who had earned their freedom but remained in service, though she did not understand why they would. Before long she found a door hung with a wreath of Mirra. She knocked but heard only a murmur, so she put the tray on the floor and pressed her ear to the door. 'Hello?' she called out, knocking a little louder. This brought something like the croak of a blackbird. Before she had the time to be afraid, she opened the door.

The room was so dark compared with the hallway that it was difficult to see inside. Wooden screens blocked all light from the window, and shadows drifted like mist along the edges of the room. To the right she could see an altar, its base carved in the shape of a woman, its candles unlit. In the centre of the room rose the dark mound of the bed, and what lay on it looked more wraith than old woman. She could make out only the sharp edges of her cheeks, the brightness of her eyes, and tufts of white hair glowing in the light from the door.

Rushes bent down, lifted the tray and carried it in. Finding no table near the bed, she laid it on top of the covers. The room felt colder than it should be. Outdoors it was hot; it was hot in the hallway. And yet this room felt like autumn on the plains.

'A lady died here,' the woman said, her voice dry as old bread. 'Murdered. You can feel it, can't you?'

Rushes shivered and wrapped her arms about herself. The old woman smelled of urine, but there was another smell here, something like rot and soil. Rushes sent a quick prayer to Mirra before speaking. 'Blessings, Sahree. I brought you food, from the empress.'

'Cerana has no empress.'

'But we do. She—'

'No. We have emperors, and the emperors have wives. Many wives, and many children. But this is one woman who will have just one child, and only doom will come of it.' She spoke with certainty, like a priest in his temple, and with the same ferocity.

'Don't worry, Sahree. The little prince is healthy.' But Rushes had not seen the boy. No one had.

Sahree chose an olive and sucked on it, making a slurping noise. The room closed in on Rushes. She imagined someone was hiding behind her, or under the bed, ready to grab her feet. She longed to run back out into the sunny hall, run down the stairs and put this room far behind her, but she must not return to the kitchen without the silver tray. Perhaps she could wait out in the hallway while the old woman ate. While she considered, Sahree spoke again. 'Mirra blessed the girl. We all heard it loud and clear from Mirra's garden in the desert, but she chose her own way instead. A hidden way for her

Hidden God. The Hidden God can't stop what's coming, can't stop what nobody can see.'

'Shh,' said Rushes, peering towards the hall. 'Do not speak ill of the empress.' Rushes had seen whippings, and worse, for lighter words.

'Beyon threw me into the dungeon already,' said Sahree, pointing a bony finger at the floor. 'I have been in the highest rooms and the lowest cells of this place. I have seen everything there is to see and the future besides. I saw it in my stone, and it changed me. But now I have lost it.'

Rushes tried to make conversation, the way she did sometimes with Gorgen, to keep him from thinking about bad things to do. 'Where did you lose your stone?'

Sahree leaned forwards. It was a task to meet her gaze, so intense was it. 'Right where I found it,' she whispered. 'Below.'

'In the dungeon?'

The old woman didn't answer, just stared and popped another olive into her mouth. Her eyes never left Rushes' face, and there was a question in them that could not be avoided.

Rushes covered her mouth with both hands. 'Oh! I can't get it for you. I can't go down there. It's dark and the priests of Herzu are there and anyway Gorgen would—'

Sahree snorted. 'Gorgen! I spanked him when he was a boy running wild in Tahal's kitchens. He's frightened of me still.'

Rushes forced her hands down to her sides, made them stop trembling. 'Well, perhaps you could ask Gorgen . . .'

Sahree sprang forwards then, faster than Rushes could jump away, and caught her forearm in an iron grip. Sahree's skin was cold, and Rushes could feel her finger-bones like claws digging into her flesh. Instinctively she cried out to the Many in her mind: *Help me!* But the Many had faded to nothing more than a buzzing at the edge of her thoughts.

'This is Mirra's work,' Sahree said, 'and it has to be us women who do it.' Then she let go, leaned back and lifted one of the silver domes. 'The meat is nice and rare,' she said in a normal voice, the voice of a motherly old body-slave. She took a piece and chewed, open-mouthed, and the blood ran down her chin. Rushes looked away. For a moment she felt angry with Demah. If Demah hadn't run off, she would be the one talking to Sahree.

'Do you know why she was murdered, girl? Right here in this bed. For babies. It's always about babies. Too many babies, not enough babies; dead baby, alive baby; right baby, wrong baby.' Sahree spat out the meat. 'What's on this?'

'Fish oil,' said Rushes, 'to make you strong.'

'Take it,' said Sahree, pushing the tray, 'and don't come back without my stone.'

Rushes stood in the hall and listened for Gorgen's voice in the kitchen. If she was lucky, he'd be on one of his many breaks in the work-yard, smoking bitter weed and flirting with the laundry girls. Since she heard only the crackle of the kitchen fires and the sound of Mother Hagga beating dough, she ventured in. Platters filled with delicate pastries covered the wooden table, waiting to be taken to the reception room where Empress Mesema would show the newborn prince to the court. Rushes walked past them to work the pulley and take a silver tray from the shelf. It was covered with half-eaten food and splashes of rosewater from when the women had cleaned their hands after eating. She took it to the washing-tub.

'Did you like it up there, among the silks?' Gorgen's leg

brushed against her backside as he moved behind her. 'That could have been you, Rushes. Emperor Beyon would have you in the women's wing by now.'

Her hand shook as she rinsed a fine glass under the water-pump.

'Oh, yes.' She heard the pleasure in his voice, the joy he got from frightening her. 'Lord Vizier Shubhan chose you for the throne room.' Then his finger on her cheek as it had been that morning, but not softly this time. 'Why do you think he did that?'

Red-Rose, the emperor had called her. Rushes swallowed and stepped away from him.

'The emperor played with you? Gave you treats?'

Outrage overcame her fear. 'I was a just a little girl!'

'But not any more.' He laid a hand on her arm.

Hagga sighed behind them. 'Leave her be, Gorgen.'

'No. I didn't like the way she talked to me just then.' His grip tightened as he pulled her towards the rice pantry. 'Come on.'

'No . . . please. I need to put . . . need to put the glasses away.' Her protests were futile. Before they had left her lips, he had pulled her halfway across the room.

As they passed Hagga, the old woman put down her dough and frowned at them. 'Why can't you beat her right here in the kitchen like anybody else, Gorgen?'

Gorgen and Hagga stared at one another. Hagga's eyes spoke of accusation and disgust. Rushes blushed with shame.

Gorgen raised a fist. 'Be careful, old bat. I'm not afraid of hitting you, too.' But then he dropped Rushes' arm and slouched into the corridor.

Hagga picked up her dough and kneaded it with white-crusted hands. Even as one of the Many she had stayed in the kitchen, baking her bread and tending the fire. If the Many was a river, Hagga had been a stone at the bottom, solid, unmoving, something you could step on without ever falling. *I was a cook.*

'Thank you.'

'Watch out for that one, child.'

'Why is he like that?' The Many had never hurt one another. Rushes turned to the tub and lifted the delicate glasses she had washed.

'He's got the Longing. Without the Many he doesn't know one end of things from the other.'

Rushes doubted that. The Longing made people sad, not mean. Rushes remembered Sahree and asked, 'Hagga, have you ever heard of a special stone? A magic stone?'

Hagga put her bread on a long trowel and slid it into the oven. Wiping her hands on her apron, she said, 'I may have heard of something like that. A luck stone.'

'How does it work?'

'Well,' she said, already punching another round of dough, 'some say you hold on to it, and bad things won't happen to you. Others say you only have to sleep with it. Or if you plant it in your garden, you won't get any weeds. Things like that.'

'Bad things won't happen?' Rushes wished that people could still understand each other without speaking.

Hagga sighed. 'Well, girl, a luck stone just might protect you from beatings, or worse, if you can find one.'

Or worse. Rushes moved towards the corridor, looking for Naveen who would lock away the precious glasses until the next time they made a tray for the Empire Mother.

'But sometimes they don't work,' Hagga said from behind her. 'And everything just gets worse.'

Rushes wished Hagga hadn't said that, wished she had kept her silence, hands on the bread, still as a stone. *I was a cook.* But it was too late. Something had happened; it was too quiet and at the same time loud, as if the voiceless Many were screaming. Naveen came running around the corner and hurried past Rushes, his robes flapping against her knees, a quick butterfly kiss that brought back her morning's dream. *No. Don't touch it. Too delicate.* At the door Naveen shouldered past Gorgen, who dropped his pipe, scattering bits of weed across the tile like tiny feathers, and ran on, into the courtyard, beyond where Rushes could see him.

Back-door Arvind stood on the sun-baked stones, more statue than man, arms raised, hands turned up, palms empty.

Demah.

'She jumped,' Arvind said, 'from the burned tower.'

Gorgen stumbled forwards, into the sunlight, one hand shading his eyes. 'Who?' he asked, 'Who jumped?'

'Your girl from the Little Kitchen,' said Arvind.

Rushes clutched the glasses so hard she snapped one of the stems. The jagged edges cut against her palm as she watched Gorgen turn back to her, his eyes not angry but frightened, searching. She knew that look; she'd seen it in Demah. He was looking for comfort, for family. For the Many. *Too late. It's too late now.* She let the broken glass go, let them all go, and they fell in a sparkling cascade against the tiles. *Too late.*

8

Sarmin

Mesema waited on cushions of silk and samite in shades from snow to cream and from faintest blush to crimson. A single slave stood at hand to fan her. She lay amid the heap, encircled by silver tables each piled with delicacies, her body wrapped in wisps and jewels as if she herself were a confection. Beneath the delicate fabrics white linens held her, binding tired flesh. She held one breast bare, and kept it to the small bundle she cradled in one arm. Paint had been applied to her lips, to the dark circles around her eyes, but exhaustion showed through. She smiled, tired and triumphant.

'I want to call him Jakar, after my brother,' she said.

'And I would call him Pelar after mine.' Courtiers followed into the chamber as Sarmin approached the tables. 'But we have spoken of this.'

The boy would wear a Cerani name to rule the empire. For countless thousands this child, like Sarmin, would never be more than a name, spoken with awe perhaps, mentioned with the gods, a face on coinage they were too poor to own. The power he would wield might be as tenuous as his own name, thus it had best be a name that would echo back along the years, reminding all who spoke it of past glories, of Pelar the

First, of Pelar Sand-sword, of wise Pelar from the story of the camel and the crane.

Servants swung the side doors wide as Sarmin approached his wife. Courtiers entered from all sides. A tide of them, their finery making a dour crow of their emperor, in black amid birds of paradise. They spread to all corners, scores of lords, of lesser princes from nations lost beneath Cerana's expansion, of satraps, clerics, even hereditary generals with swords so ceremonial they resembled gaudy toys. The ruling of Sarmin's empire rested on the goodwill of such men. A life of luxurious seclusion, of hunting and feasting, could be lived whilst ignoring any wider duties – Beyon's life. But to rule in more than name, to make things happen, that required the subtle manipulation of this crowd of peacocks and tigers; the delicate balancing of needs and wants, egos and prejudices.

Sarmin walked between two silver tables, the scrollwork along their edges catching at him. 'You look tired, Mesema. Is our son well?'

She smiled up at him, sweat beading on her brow despite the wafting fan, ostrich plumes set into a staff of turned ebony.

'I am tired. I think one child should be enough for any emperor?' She shifted the baby's position, his mouth tugging at her breast. 'And yes, he seems well. Certainly he is hungry.'

Behind Sarmin the courtiers moved about the perimeter of tables, picking at blue quails' eggs, at pickled squid from the ice of Sheltren waters, at peacock breast braised with honey, at a dozen more wonders, each unseen. Fingers did the choosing as the emperor, the empress and the new heir held all eyes. Priest Assar watched Pelar with a smile, a finger on the pendant of Mirra he wore about his neck, while Lord Zell bit into a sesamed lotus as if it had offended him. None of these men had been at the palace during Helmar's time; untouched by the Longing, their minds narrowed to a few simple ambitions.

Sarmin squatted beside Mesema to better see his son, Beyon's son. His knees ached at once – but better to squat than to kneel, and the cushions did not invite. He'd spent too long in his small room, grown in the dark, and been left weak in a world that praised strength. No wonder the men around him watched this infant with such interest. How many years would their pale emperor last in his new throne? Was the child sickly too, or would he grow to lead them into glory?

'He's beautiful.' The child had tufts of black hair, a pinched-in face, the tiniest of hands balled into fists – but he was beautiful. 'He will be Pelar third of the name, Pelar Jakar of the House Cotora.'

'Must they stare at us?' Mesema tried to watch his eyes but her gaze kept slipping to the crowd.

Sarmin reached for the baby and took one little fist in his hand. Around him the hubbub of conversation respectfully hushed, leaving the sounds of important men chewing, the shuffling of feet and swish of costly fabric. In Emperor Tahal's day the palace held a menagerie where sandcats and a lone tiger prowled in cages, furred wonders from northern forests lurked in green pools, and crimson scorpions writhed in a glass tank. Sarmin and his brothers had watched the tiger, speaking in whispers, for the creature, thin and sunken as it was, awed them with the cool blue of its stare and the white fangs descending from its upper jaw. Only Pelar had thought to pity it. Now Sarmin understood.

'This is theatre, and we are the players. And yes it is necessary.'

Without a sure heir to the throne men of influence and wealth might set to wondering where the power would lie should things change. It is not good for an empire to continue with a single man standing between peace and chaos.

'Now should ill befall me there will be no doubt, no conflict, and all Cerani will know where their allegiance lies,' Sarmin said.

'On the grass the women ride out with their newborn in the second week to show him at each hall and hut,' Mesema said. 'They don't invite the riders in to watch before the blood has dried on their thighs.'

'In years to come when these men are far away in their palaces a messenger may come to say there is a new emperor, that Prince Pelar has taken the throne. They will remember then that they stood here and saw him on his name day, the true-born son of the emperor. We're buying his future.' Sarmin kissed the boy's hand and let it go. He raised Mesema's fingertips to his lips. 'You are of the Felt,' he said.

'We carry on.' Mesema sighed and hugged her baby closer still.

Sarmin stood, holding his face still against the effort. The Many stole his sleep and left him weak. He turned to the tables and the crowd.

If Beyon's child could have been a girl!

'You have a fine son, Magnificence!' A round man in thinned velvets, purples so dark as to be black, with a neat and pointed beard darker still.

'He is strong.' Sarmin agreed. 'When he is older I will bring him east, Satrap Honnecka.' Azeem had warned him of this one, sharp despite the blunt bulk of him, with a hunger for more than goose livers and camel-fat. His gifts of women were set to overflow the women's wing.

'As handsome as his father, Magnificence.' A taller man, young, hair in greased black ringlets about a sallow face. Gethchen of Arthona: his grandfather ruled a land that now enjoyed the protection of Cerana.

'He will grow fierce,' Sarmin said. 'A warrior of the horse, like his mother's people.'

He wanted no such thing for the child. Better a life of peace and books, a wife of his choosing, a future to be discovered. And yet the boy would have none of it. If little Pelar had been a girl Sarmin could have named Beyon as the father. Now the secret must be held tight. As Beyon's son, Pelar was the emperor, no doubt or questions: the true emperor was suckling at his mother's breast. Armed with such knowledge Gethchen, Honnecka and a score of others would rise. The council listened to these men – they would no longer require Sarmin's permission to return to the ways of the Knife. Daveed would die first. Sarmin might survive that night, maybe the next, but in time the emperor's Knife would seek him out. He had been dangerous to keep when hidden in his room all those long years. Out in the light of day he would be seen as a threat to Beyon's son, and removed.

Sarmin stepped out between the tables to walk among his nobles and the men who ruled the empire in his name. The four sword-sons of his inner guard closed around him, sharks slicing through glittering waters. Each guard kept a hand to his knife hilt, short blades of chrome-steel. In a crowd they would trust to the speed of knives over the reach of their swords.

'Headman Notheen.' Sarmin approached the only courtier in garb as simple as his own. 'How stands the desert?'

Notheen watched him a moment before speaking, eyes slitted

against the sun though they stood in lamplight. 'The desert stands empty, My Emperor. Wind whispers to sand and the bones of my fathers lie drowned.' He wore deepest blue, and new shades were revealed as he moved, as if remembering the depths of a lost sea.

'A curious turn of phrase, my lord.' The nomads from the inner desert went so long without speaking to strangers that they made an art of their words and spent them with misers' care. Sarmin decided he would see the desert himself. Notheen carried a strangeness with him that made him more alien than even the Yrkman girls in the harem with their milk-skin and golden hair. 'I would like to climb the dunes. I am told they stand higher than my palace.'

Again the pause, as if Sarmin's words must first settle in Notheen's head. The nomad towered over Sarmin; stick-thin, sand-robes rucked around him like a wrinkled hide, though these had never seen the desert, fresh from his wives' looms no doubt. He wore his face bare, veil pinned back perhaps for the first time in years, his cheeks stained dark by the dyes his people prized in their cloth.

'The desert is an ocean, My Emperor, wider and more deep. Where the storms gather, the dunes overtop your tower of mages. I would be honoured to show you these places. Even to the Cliffs of Sight.'

Sarmin had seen the Cliffs marked, in the cartodome on one of the maps set in many colours of stone into the tops of marble tables. On those maps the desert accounted for more than half his empire, though not one in a thousand of his people dwelled there. The Cliffs of Sight lay on the margins. Even the cartogramme, where each hill and stream bore a legend, offered no name for the desert: in the centre, amid the sandstone used to indicate the margins, there was only the plain white marble of the table, suggesting nothing.

'What of the interior, Headman? Do I rule there too?' The blank whiteness of the map-table filled his mind and for a moment the whispers of the Many rose to cover Notheen's reply.

'. . . survive. That place is not for men, My Emperor. It is an emptiness that devours.' The headman bowed and took a half-step back, as if he had no more to say.

Honnecka pressed close enough to make the sword-sons loosen their daggers. He cleared his throat, a deep unhealthy sound. Flanking him to the left a man of similar girth, his belly hitched up in bands of scarlet silk, rings on each of his fat olive fingers, many set with gems as large as eyeballs – a discordant display of wealth that owed nothing to beauty or balance. To the right a warrior in plates of fire-bronze, each stamped with the eagle of Highrock. His beard reached almost to his chest, showing hints of red in the dark curls.

'Satrap Honnecka,' Sarmin said. 'And . . .' Azeem's schooling failed him.

'Lord Jomla of Westla.' He indicated the man in silks and rings. A name Sarmin remembered. Grown fat off river trade and a monopoly on caravans out of Hedrin, richest of the western ports. 'And General Merkel from the Fort of Ax in Jalan Hills.' Of this one Sarmin knew nothing.

'Magnificence.' The general bowed at the waist. Not a general with Cerani legions under his command, but less ornamental than many of his fellow Faces. Azeem called them Faces, the men named as generals and called to the palace so that nations with only a generation or two under the Cerani yoke could save face and name themselves allies and protectorates rather than mere outlying regions of the empire.

'General Merkel.' Sarmin made a smile for the man. 'You've come a long way. There can hardly have been time for news of the empress's condition to reach the north-marches and for you to journey south from Highrock. You must have left immediately!'

'Indeed I would have, Magnificence, but I had already embarked on the ride before any such tidings reached us.' The light gleamed from one plate of armour then the next as he shifted.

'What then set you on so long a journey, General?'

'War, Magnificence.' Merkel's hand slipped towards the ruby-set hilt of his blunted sword, and then away as the sword-sons tensed. 'The White Hat army – with its glorious men-at-arms and fabled horsemen, the battle-strength of the plains – all passed within a spyglass's view of Fort Ax on their way to the grass. They shouted out the name of Emperor Tuvaini as they carved a red path to Mondrath. And this man at their head, Arigu, told us they were to press on into Yrkmir lands.'

'And so you came to petition my cousin Tuvaini? Seeking what?' Sarmin asked. Merkel must have heard of the imminent peace, and with his ambitions nearly frustrated he would attempt to carve some benefit from it. Lord Jomla watched them with fascination, switching his allegiance as each spoke, as though he watched the ball in a game of slap, his cheeks wobbling each time he turned his head.

'As you know, Magnificence, the people of the Highrock have long fought against those of Fryth, and fought alongside them, quarrelling like brothers. We have blood ties stretching back longer than memory. My own cousin is in Mondrath; my brother married a daughter of the House Sharth.'

'You've come to seek mercy for them?' It wasn't likely; the

general's face, handsome but cold, had nothing of compassion in it.

'Only to set our claims before you, Magnificence. I have scrolls with me, from the time of your grandfather and his father, that speak of Highrock's borders before the second Yrkmen incursion. I have papers that show my own father's inheritance of three manses in Mondrath city and wide tracts of land to the south along the River Mern.'

'And it may be,' Jomla added, his voice as high and sweet as any girl's, 'that your Magnificence will require men of good breeding and independent means to govern these new and barbaric regions of empire. Men who would not call on the royal purse in order to establish taxation and impose social order.'

'Gentlemen.' Sarmin held up his hand, a silence rippled out across the room, broken only by the faint sound of Pelar sucking. His station enforced their silence, but so did his manner, pulled from memories he held of ruling the court, of capturing the attention of grasping men. Whose memories they were, he did not know. Words flowed from him as if practised for days.

'Tuvaini was emperor for two weeks, unjustly, for Helmar was the emperor by right. And Helmar's wrongs took him from the throne just as Beyon was judged wrong.

'An emperor unjustly on the throne for two weeks unleashed my army of the White Hat like a spear thrown at the people of Fryth. And for what? Lies about a Mogyrk assassin, greed for lands so distant he was never likely to set his feet there. These are not things to spill blood for, my lords. Since my empress came to Nooria I have shed my own blood to the knife and killed an emperor with this hand. It is no small thing to kill a man. Better reasons are required than to satisfy memories held only on parchment, or to move boundaries on a map.

'In the Redeemer's Cartodome the maps are written in stone. There is a message there. Guard your borders. Let no man set them aside, but neither push them forwards. Cerana is full-grown and now it must earn its bread with honest trade. When stability can be gained only by constant expansion, something is rotten at the core. Cerana will grow, but it will get no bigger. Richer, yes, wiser, yes, but no larger. We have marked out our place in this world. Now it is time to build an empire within those borders, an empire such as the world has yet to see.'

He finished and drew a breath. The two lords stared at him, Jomla moving his lips without speaking and Merkel's eyes darkening with fury, fingers playing with the ruby hilt of his sword. All gazes were trained upon the emperor, all mouths silent in the wake of his speech. Even Mesema's eyes, blue as the sky, pointed his way, her red lips parted in amazement. And then she smiled, and the Faces faded away with the useless swords, the thick robes, the peacock colours. It was just Sarmin, and Mesema, and the little emperor, Pelar. She smiled, and in that moment Sarmin was happy.

Notheen stepped forward, his narrowed eyes sharp in his leathery face. From among the colourful courtiers he stood plain and unadorned. All he needed to convey could be seen in his stance and his expression, and now, he meant to give warning. The headman had been speaking before Jomla and Merkel brought forth their politics; he had been saying something about the desert. Sarmin searched his memory for the words Notheen had so carefully chosen, and when he found them, the room's heavy silence pressed against him like prison walls. *An emptiness that devours.*

9

Sarmin

At lanterns' turning Sarmin returned to his tower room, legs aching with each step. Mesema had earned her rest, guarded by six sword-sons and the Little Mother. The perfumed lords had been settled into luxurious guest rooms, where they still might convene over trays of wine, whispering of their ambitions. Azeem sat at his desk, as always, sorting through the business of the day. It seemed the man never slept. But Sarmin must.

He retreated to his own room, the place he knew the best, where his friends had once waited for him to find them. He settled onto the ropes of his old bed and within moments the tide of the Many rose and took him from his own shore, giving his body over to another. And as each time before, Sarmin found himself drowning, sinking in the lightless ocean between memory and dreams.

He woke with a start, a sudden convulsion of limbs beneath a coarse blanket. The space around him lay night-blind and silent. He listened, hard, ears straining to manufacture hints from the currents of quietness flowing over, around, and through. Nothing. No noise had woken him, rather the absence of sound, the loss of something so familiar as to be unnoticed until it stopped. No bleating of goats, complaining even in their sleep, no dry susurration of breeze among the palms. Only as Sarmin tried to rise did he remember this was memory. Another man's memory. And that man had kept still, listening, thinking. Wiser than Sarmin perhaps.

In time though the man reached Sarmin's conclusion. He rolled from beneath his blanket, hands finding the floor deep with sand and drawing back in surprise. With more caution he reached out again, and came up into a crouch. He stretched out, above and to the side, finding the wall of a tent. A sigh of relief – quickly sucked back as the camel hair came apart under his fingers. A great piece of the tent side collapsed in, tearing from the rest under its own weight, as if rotted. Through the ragged hole above him Sarmin saw the blaze of stars, clustering in multitudes, gathering into the milky river of heaven dividing the sky as the Blessing divided Cerana.

The man crawled to the tent flap. Aharab, his name burst like a bubble at the back of Sarmin's mind. Aharab's fingers trembled on the ties securing the flap. He could have stood and looked out through the hole, but something felt wrong with the hole. Everything felt wrong about it. In the starlight the woven camel hair around the edges of the ragged opening looked silver-grey and it almost seemed as if the hole were growing, fraying into dust at the edges.

At last the ties were undone and Aharab leaned out. Sarmin half-expected a scimitar to descend and bring the memory to a sharp conclusion. Instead the sight of a sand-choked oasis awash with moonlight checked the beholder.

'No!' Sarmin felt the man's lips frame the word, the feeling not unfamiliar; he had been Carried before, by the Many and then by Grada alone, but this was memory. Aharab bore no patterns. The pattern waited for him in his future. 'Matarai? Jana?' Anxious cries, unreturned.

Half the oasis lay drowned in pale moonlit dunes, palms emerging from their lower slopes. Two ridges of sand braced the waterhole itself, giving way to the hard-baked and stone-scattered ground of the outer wastes. Aharab hurried barefoot towards the dunes, stopping short of the shifting sand. Two guy ropes ran from wooden pegs in the hardpan to be swallowed by the edge of the nearest dune. It looked every bit as if the desert itself had surged forwards in the night, devouring everything in its path, tree and tent, goats, even the oasis itself.

'There was no storm!' Aharab stamped in protest and spun back towards his tent. Whatever decay got into the walls had now spread, the tent collapsed, kept aloft here and there by leaning poles, and unknown objects, pots and pans perhaps, draped in the fragmenting remnants of the densely woven camel-hair fabric. And revealed by the collapse, a second tent behind, a ten-pole pavilion, black in the moonlight.

For a moment Aharab stood still. The silence wrapped him. The air held no scent but dry. Even as he watched, a spot of grey appeared among the tent's black, spreading out like a drop of water soaking into hardpan, ripples on oasis waters . . . like fire.

'Al-Tari! Al-Tari!' Sarmin had no desire to get closer but Aharab's memory sent him straight towards the tent at a run.

Perhaps Al-Tari was a sound sleeper, for no answer came. The night swallowed Aharab's shouts and the grey spot grew, the changed cloth becoming weak, pieces falling away, unweaving themselves as they dropped so that only silver hairs reached the ground, brittle like sticks burned all to ash yet holding their shape.

'Al-Tari!' Aharab stopped two yards from the tent's dark porch, his shout loud enough to wake every djinn in the deep desert.

The grey edge of a second diseased area passed into view over the ridge of the tent. Without warning the back half fell in on itself, a pole, maybe two, breaking with that dull noise that comes from snapping wood half-eaten by dry mite.

Aharab turned and turned again, an older memory painting itself over the sand: their arrival, with the boy, Jana, herding the goats ahead, switch-hand idle now as the scent of water led them. The camels followed at the rear, muttering disdain and belching, nine of them, four belonging to Matarai, three to him, two to Al-Tari and his son, each with its load swaying on high: tight-folded tents, pressed dates, urns of cooking oil, deflated waterskins, and most precious, the salt-blocks stacked and wrapped, white gold to the cities strung like pearls along the Blessing. The memory shredded, vivid greens swallowed by pale sand. Back where he had seen the ropes of a buried tent, a dune slumped forwards, a noiseless avalanche flowing over one of the last palms.

'Al-Tari!' And with that last shout the tent folded in on itself, grey sections fallen to powder.

'Dear Mirra, save us!' Silence. The cold of the desert night and silence. Where were the goats, the camels? 'Where—' Something rose among the folds of Al-Tari's tent and stole any other words from Aharab's mouth. The shapeless form writhed and struggled. Aharab took a step back, the night-cold running like a blade along his spine. 'Mirra!'

Tent fabric tore and fell, and stepping from it came Al-Tari's boy, Tomra, grey with dust. Aharab struggled to speak and failed. The boy walked forwards, dust rising around each footstep. Aharab took a step back for each step of Tomra's approach, retreating across the hardpan, away from the desert, away from the oasis, away from the child.

Tomra held a hand out, dust sifting from his fingers. Where the pale dust left him, the flesh beneath lay paler still. Duty and compassion made Sarmin want to go to the boy, even if Aharab's memory screamed that this was no longer Tomra, not all of him.

'W—what are you?' Still Aharab fell back. A djinn had entered the child, surely, for he didn't move like Tomra but like an old man forgetting how to walk.

The boy opened his mouth. His lips moved, but nothing came save the hiss of sand over sand.

'What are you?' Aharab screamed the words.

The hiss again and a single reply. 'Hollow.'

Sarmin's desire to help the boy came of duty but the thanks he gave when Aharab turned and ran sprang from an older and more primal source.

'I have brought you something, Magnificence.'

Sarmin stumbled back over smooth tile, terror echoing in his throat and limbs. *Tomra! Tomra?* But the desert had gone, replaced by painted walls, a high, cushioned bench. He turned around in the reception room, empty now, but still fragranced by fish and perfume. *How did I get here?* Sarmin's hand wavered, and light from his lantern danced across a woman's face. A priestess's face. *Not hollow.* She moved forwards, jangling with charms and bracelets, arms wrapped about a clay urn, then crouched to place it on the tiled floor. Her loosely tied robes opened to show where necklaces swayed between her breasts.

Sarmin watched her, allowing his breathing to slow, his

heart to resume a normal rhythm. Aharab was fading but this too could be a dream.

—*She is of Meksha.* A young woman's voice rose from his mind's depths, awed and respectful. Meksha's temple perched against the rocks of the Kofka mountains, a place where the blood of the earth rose burning from the fractured rock. If she was truly here then she had come a long way. The earth beneath Sarmin's feet was long dead, cold against his slippers.

He cleared his throat. 'What have you brought me, priestess of Meksha?'

'Magnificence, I come from the temple deep in the mountains where fires melt and rocks flow, water burns and air chokes. I come from the place where Meksha sings, at the heart of the world where all things are possible and all things can be seen.' She spoke in a low voice, gravelled by smoke, as she made a slow circuit of the urn. Her golden toe-rings glimmered in the lantern light. 'Meksha bid me bring you this,' she said. 'It will help you through the coming storm.'

—*An emperor does not wait for an answer!* An outraged voice, one he had not heard before, but familiar all the same.

'What is in the urn?' he said, folding his arms behind his back with a frown.

'Something that goes beyond the bickering of armies and the struggle for a throne,' she answered, beginning another circle. Her hair had been drawn into a complex arrangement and he found himself struck by the pattern it made from pins and twists. 'Hundreds of years ago Meksha granted magic to Uthman for the founding of the Tower. And so it was Meksha's priests who tutored Helmar Pattern Master when he was held here, like you, My Emperor, against an uncertain future, like grain buried in clay urns, sealed against the threat of failed harvests.' She met his gaze. 'These are the records of those times.'

Sarmin looked into her eyes. The Pattern Master had written marks upon the skin of thousands, making each person a small part of his grand design. Together they had been the Many. The pattern was broken, the Pattern Master dead, but the Many had left its mark on the empire. On the emperor, too. He touched a finger to his forehead. To open the urn would be to find another brother, the one who had been hidden away, forgotten, as he had been. They had both been held in the same tower room, hundreds of years apart. He hoped this was not a dream. 'Open it.'

The priestess bent over the urn, her necklaces swinging forwards and clicking like teeth. 'It does not open, Magnificence. It is sealed by signs and magic.'

'Then how—'

She smiled. 'I do not know. But if Helmar sealed it, you, Magnificence, can surely open it.'

Sarmin did not know whether challenge or faith lay beneath her words, but it was the stout urn and its handled lid that commanded his attention. 'You are dismissed,' he said, and listened as the clacking of her beads grew faint. Sarmin had killed the Helmar Pattern Master, but a different Helmar hid inside this clay. *No, not hidden. Forgotten.* He pulled on the handle, but as he expected the lid was sealed tight. A puzzle to open. The Many moved inside Sarmin, jostling against one another.

—Don't open it – the horsegirl is – it was cakes and lemon slices and I ate them, oh I ate them – don't – I had a comb, it was silver with mother-of-pearl—

—Silence, all of you!

Sarmin woke in his room beside the unbroken calligraphy, the cold desert air on his cheeks. Had he been dreaming, then, of both Aharab and the priestess? But the urn was at his side, its seal intact. *Not dreams, then.* He touched the blue ink on the wall, fingers against dry paper. 'Is that who was coming? The priestess?' he asked.

Silence.

He would look in his *Book of Histories.* The middle book, neither large nor small, containing little of knives or instruction, had always been his least favourite. Written in a tiny font and beginning with a long genealogy, it described Cerana from Uthman's time, when Meksha had been the patron of the land, gifting Nooria with the Tower. It ended with the triumphant story of Satreth the Reclaimer and his victory over Yrkmir. Over the course of long nights Sarmin had inked in his own additions – his father's name, Beyon's name, the births and deaths of his young brothers – and just recently he had pulled the book from the dust and written at the bottom of one page: *Daveed, son of Tuvaini,* and *Pelar, son of Sarmin.*

It was for that book that he reached now, hoping to find some reference to priests of Meksha tutoring a young prince. Helmar did not figure in the histories – that much he knew – but perhaps some trace survived, some mention of a boy and his priest.

But *Histories* lay open on the floor, its leather cover loose and twisted, the pages cut to shreds. 'No!' Sarmin knelt by the ruined book, grieving as for a friend. His least favourite, yes, but one of his only companions during Beyon's reign. The destruction was complete; each page dagger-cut and punctured, the wounds gouged into the words. Such rage had guided that blade that even now Sarmin could feel it, wafting from the book like a scent or a memory. With trembling fingers he searched for the last genealogy page, where he had entered the name of his son and new brother.

Gone.

'Ta-Sann!' he cried. 'Ta-Sann, who has been in my room?' But even as he spoke he scented a darker possibility, the truth of how he had found himself in the reception room with no memory of having walked there, of the manner of his return. As the sword-son entered he knew what the man would say, that guards were posted at the stairwell door and the door to the Ways could not be opened without the emperor's own key. That nobody had been here. Nobody but himself.

10

Sarmin

'The peace envoy approaches,' Sarmin said. 'Arigu remains in Fryth, hostage against his safety.' He felt wholly himself now, during the day when the Many fell quiet. Safe until the sun set once more, until the dark brought those who would move inside his skin, speak with his voice. The thought filled him with horror. He turned away from it.

Govnan shifted in his iron chair. The room lay bare, black with old char, with no seat other than the high mage's. When Govnan offered it Sarmin had refused, but now his legs ached and even the knobbed metal chair started to look inviting. An emperor does not change his mind or show weakness. Foolish requirements to be sure, but even here, with no audience save the old mage and General Lurish, they must be observed.

'Discuss? They will be told!' The general snorted into his dark beard. 'Arigu had them on the point of his sword, I hear.' Older, higher-born, more traditional, Lurish demonstrated unexpected support for his fellow general, perhaps just a soldier's respect for the genius with which Arigu prosecuted his campaigns – that or pride in the army of the White Hat, a weapon that had once been his to wield.

'A peace founded on being told will not last, General.' Sarmin turned to meet the man's gaze, fierce under grey brows. Although stooped by years, Lurish loomed above him. Having to look up like this reminded Sarmin of the benefits of a dais, and a throne. Still, an emperor who ruled only from his throne was an emperor who might be forgotten when the great doors closed. An emperor who walked where he willed, be it the Tower or the War Room of the White and Blue, was less easily circumvented. Something he had learned, or a gift from the Many?

'What do we need with a lasting peace?' Lurish chewed as he spoke, as if trying to swallow an unpalatable truth. 'Cerana has armies that could take the world for you, Magnificence. Perhaps this is not the time, perhaps it would be better if these victories did not show Tuvaini's hand behind them, but if you would issue such orders yourself in the next season all Cerana would know the glory to be yours. I would take our legions and finish what Arigu—'

'Your orders are peace, General. Must I pin them to your chest?'

'Magnificence, our strength—'

'Your strength didn't keep my brother on his throne. Your strength did not hold when Helmar walked into the palace, into the throne room. A stranger from the desert was all any knew of the man and yet he walked in alone.'

'His tricks, Magnificence, magic—'

'Who taught him that magic?' Sarmin gave the general no time to dig in or regroup. 'He learned his trade in Yrkmir, and he learned it there because our strength did not stand against the incursion. The Yrkmen soldiers marched through this palace burning as they went, their priests carrying the one god before them, chanting their prayers. In Nooria! In my palace!'

'Three hundred years ago,' Lurish protested.

'They were repelled in time.' Govnan said it from his iron chair: an observation with none of Lurish's heat. He looked lost in the folds of his robe, thick cloth, not velvet but something tougher and dyed to a deep scarlet.

'And yet we have Mogyrk priests creeping back to Nooria, preaching in the shadows, hidden churches in the greatest of our cities,' Sarmin said. Azeem had spoken to him of these churches, filling the streets with spies and saboteurs. He had read to Sarmin from the histories: cities falling at the mere approach of Yrkmen armies, their rulers overthrown by the mob, storming their gates with torch and rope. 'The Parigols poisoned wells, Govnan; the Yrkmen poison minds.'

'The Longing has left the people hungry for salvation; they want to belong,' Govnan said. 'Some find more solace in the one god than in Mirra or Herzu or any of their children.' He shifted in his chair, eyes bright and dark, watching Sarmin.

'Yes,' said Sarmin. Grada had spoken of the Longing, of how freedom from the Many had left her hollow. 'And that too flowed from Yrkmir.'

And his dream? The emptiness in the desert?

'Find the churches, burn the priests, sack the cities of Yrkmir and our people would know this Mogyrk for a grinning idol and nothing more.' Lurish shook his fist as if he held a sword, as if he imagined the blood even now. The copper discs, overlapping across his chest, rattled.

'Have you seen an austere write patterns, General Lurish?' Sarmin asked.

'Sand mages cannot stand against steel, Magnificence.'

'There is no sand in Yrkmir,' Sarmin said. 'And these are not sand mages with tricks of dust and light.'

Govnan raised himself from his chair with a suppressed groan. Since Sarmin parted him from his elemental the high mage had grown ancient and frail. Still sharp though, sharper perhaps. 'Have *you* seen an austere write patterns, My Emperor?'

'I—' Sarmin frowned. An image came to him, a man in red, hair white, feet bare, hands empty. Mountains rose about him, mountains such as could never exist, huge beyond imagining. Surely between sky and ground no space sufficient for such enormity existed.

'Emperor Sarmin?' Govnan reached his side before Lurish, unexpected strength in the clawed hands offering support, a shiver in them too, as if he were cold despite the heat.

'I—' He could not speak of the Many he held within his flesh. The council would count it sickness, Helmar's taint. Already he lacked information others thought he had, was forced to listen carefully for the answers to his missing time.

But he gained memories in recompense for those he did not have, unasked, uninvited: the vision rose again to cover his sight. On the slopes high above the red-robe something moved – a goat? Too large, but as quick, as sure-footed. A man with leather shield, leaping between rocks, diving for the shelter of a crag. With one finger the red-robe traced a symbol, part of a pattern, flicked out before him, quick as quick. Dry bones clattered across the rocks. Dry bones, rags, and a leather shield. Dust hung in the air. 'I have heard that they can turn a man's flesh to dust,' Sarmin said as they helped him into Govnan's chair.

'Hearing and seeing are different things, My Emperor,' Lurish said. 'Tales grow in the telling. If the Yrkmen have such power why are they not here, ruling over us?'

A good question, to which Sarmin had no good answer. At

last he said, 'It may be that they were waiting for an invitation. Our war on Fryth may be that invitation.'

Lurish snorted, then remembering himself, bowed low. He spoke facing the flagstones. 'No Yrkman has stood with the men of Fryth. They have pulled back at every turn, or simply failed to come to their aid. I tell you that they are weak, Magnificence. An old nation senile before its time, rotten at the core.'

The *Book of War* directs that when pressed an army that falls back must not *only* fall back. Locked in his high room Sarmin had studied that book longer than any general. He knew the work better than the men who wrote it. Always counter-attack.

'I came seeking the high mage's wisdom. Why are you here, General Lurish? What are the dry secrets of the Tower to a man of action?' Sarmin struck from a new direction.

Govnan coughed. 'I sent word to request the general's presence, Emperor. I have something to show him and a request to make.'

'Show me,' Sarmin said.

Govnan bowed as if he had expected no other answer. 'There will be steps. I could call on Moreth to help you?'

Sarmin nodded. Better to admit his frailty than to break his neck tumbling down the stairs. Govnan drew small black stones from pockets on either side of his robe and clacked them together. Moreth entered the room seconds later, a dark and thick-limbed man in the greys of a rock-sworn acolyte. He looked strong enough to carry Sarmin and Govnan both. In the end though he walked the narrow stair a step behind Sarmin, supporting him by elbow and wrist.

They came to the end of the winding stair where Ta-Sann and the sword-sons waited. 'Perhaps you should wear this,

Your Majesty.' Govnan offered a dark, hooded cloak that Sarmin closed up to shadow his face. They left the Tower compound and came by gate and plaza to a narrow street, where market-sellers packed their goods and guardsmen told their jokes under the darkening sky. Sarmin marvelled at their freedom and easy ways, but he knew each one had some hurt they nursed in the darkness, some secret they kept from the light. The Many had taught him that.

Hashi the wind-mage joined them on the street, his eyes on the roofs of buildings, alert for assassins and spies. They turned down one street and then another, Sarmin flanked by three mages, Govnan, Hashi and Moreth, the last with a hand still on his elbow. In time he knew they headed for Beyon's tomb.

Sarmin had visited that tomb only once. Beyon had not been there. Perhaps his bones lay inside but they held no meaning. The tomb had been the last anchor point of Helmar's grand pattern and it echoed still with the impersonal malice of that design. Sometimes it worried Sarmin that Pelar had been conceived there, the timing dictated by Old Wives among the Felt, so Mesema said. An intersection of plans in time and in space. Plans whispered to the Windreaders by their hidden god, and plans laid across centuries by the Pattern Master. What changes might be wrought in the new seed of a child by such a conjunction? It had never been something Sarmin chose to dwell on.

The long walk soon took its toll on Sarmin, sapping his strength, leaving him sweating in his silks, and robbing some of his urgency. They came to the tomb through older portions of the city where the streets wore their years more plainly, the sword-sons always choosing to steer Sarmin along unex-pected paths against the dangers of predictability. The emperor's swift passage amid his tight knot of bodyguards dropped more than a few jaws and provided enough fuel to keep the gossips busy for weeks to come. When they reached the tomb he felt regret to be leaving the open air and sky of the streets, being among ordinary people, the many who lived under his rule.

The chamber rang with the echoes of many feet, from marble floor to vaulted ceiling, as Sarmin and his guard marched in. The austere lines of the room contrasted with the intricacy of the tomb itself, pierced screens of whitest alabaster surrounding the heavy marble box on all sides, set back two yards to allow a slow, private circuit. The decoration tended to fish and fruit, strange choices that Sarmin felt would have found little favour with his brother. Beyon had planned the structure but died within it before its completion. In the confusion that followed, the artisans set to finish the work had let their own aesthetic guide them. Sarmin had been unconcerned. Beyon lived in him and in Pelar, not in cold stone. Azeem had even brought plans before him for his own tomb. Sarmin had waved them away. 'Let the next emperor do with my remains as he sees fit. I'm sure you have more pressing matters to put before me, Vizier.'

A polite cough brought Sarmin from his recollections. His feet had led him to the arched entrance through the screens. Notheen waited there, the lean nomad towering above Govnan.

'High Mage?' Sarmin tilted his head in question.

Govnan said nothing but looked away, through the arch. The sepulchre beyond, in which Mesema had once hidden for a night with Beyon, had almost gone. It looked as if it had melted away like a block of butter with a hot coal placed at its centre. The stonework towered at the four corners, eaten away elsewhere, and in the midst of it all a blankness, the colour of forever, blinding the eye. Sarmin couldn't say if it was grey or white, perhaps black. The emptiness of it filled his mind and drowned out the screams of the Many as they hid behind his thoughts.

'Do not look too long, My Emperor.' Govnan's words came from a distance.

'It takes, My Emperor.' Notheen, still further away. 'It will hollow you.'

Sarmin tore his gaze from the space within Beyon's tomb. Hours seemed to pass as he shook its bonds, days.

'My Emperor?' And at last he looked away, met Govnan's eyes, dark with concern.

'What is that?' Sarmin stepped away, not wanting to look, not wanting his back to it.

'Nothing, My Emperor.' Govnan bowed his head. 'There is nothing there. That's all my magic can tell me. Notheen's people know more of this.'

Sarmin took a step closer to the veiled nomad, hung about with white as if he rode the desert rather than walked the corridors of a palace. 'Tell me.'

'This is of the desert.' Notheen waved towards the tomb. 'This is the unwriting that grows in the dead heart of the sands, beyond even the djinn. It spreads from the secret.'

'What secret?' Sarmin remembered his dream, the pale boy, the tent falling into dust. *An emptiness that devours.*

Notheen bowed his head. Sarmin pressed the heels of his hands to his forehead, forcing back a growing terror. The two of them stood alike now, the high mage and the nomad headman, neither meeting his gaze. The faintest of sounds injected itself into the silence – the sound of trickling sand.

'What secret?' Sarmin repeated. 'You knew from the moment you spoke of it that I would require explanation.'

'May we speak alone, My Emperor?' Notheen let the words slip quietly to the floor.

'We are alone!' Sarmin looked about, exasperated.

'The two of us. This truth is dangerous. Many lives balance upon it.'

'Just us, then.' Sarmin motioned the sword-sons away.

Ta-Sann hesitated. 'My Emperor, the nomads—'

'Away!' Sarmin waved him off with his objections and the Island men retreated towards the main entrance, Lurish following, deep in thought.

When his guard reached the far side of the chamber Sarmin spoke again. 'You have me to yourself, Notheen, me and the old man. Will you enlighten me or stab me? Govnan could not stop your knife.'

Again Notheen paused before answering, stretching the silence until Sarmin thought he would not speak. 'We have among our people wise men, just as with all the tribes of man. They read the signs written among the dunes, listen to the wind, treat with the djinn who ride to the outer desert on sandstorms. Held among the wise of my people is a tale, a secret learned long ago and kept close.'

'I will not share this secret.' Even as Sarmin said the words he thought of his lost time, wondered to whom he spoke and with what voice. A man who commands an empire but not his own mind should not promise discretion. Notheen, however, nodded, touched his fingers to his lips through the cloth of his veil and spoke.

'The heart of the desert is a place of death. All men know this. They know of the heat, the storms, and that there is no water. But the nomad tribes know that there is more. A god went into the sands. A god walked the dunes until in every direction two weeks of travel would not bring a man to water. And there in the dry heart of the Cerana Desert that god chose to die.'

'Mogyrk!' Sarmin stepped back in shock. He lowered his voice. 'Mogyrk?'

Notheen nodded. 'The dead god. The desert was where he came undone.'

'If the Yrkmen know of this . . .'

Notheen set the length of a finger to his forehead in acknowledgement.

Govnan answered with a question. 'Do you know how the Yrkmen invaders were driven from Cerana?'

'The desert beat them.' Sarmin had read it in the Reclaimer's histories. 'Supply across the desert proved impossible without the co-operation of the nomad tribes, and the defeated Cerani waged war from the sands where the Yrkmen troops feared to follow them.'

Govnan nodded. 'It's true, the desert defeated them. They lived in fear of it, and with good reason. Because of Mogyrk they understood the desert better than we did. Let us hope they have not forgotten that fear.'

'Why have you told me this, now and here by my brother's tomb?' Sarmin glanced back, wondering if the screens had always looked so white, so brittle, or was the nothing within stealing both colour and substance from them as in his dream.

'The emptiness in the desert has been spreading. Slowly at first, so slow that it was not noticed from one year to the next. The dead god made a hole in the world and our sands are running through it. Faster this year than the last, faster today than yesterday.'

'Wh—?' Sarmin glanced between Govnan and the nomad. 'Why? Why now?'

'The Pattern Master spurred the advance. Our deep routes have been swallowed, even oases have been consumed. The salt paths my fathers rode are gone.'

'Helmar made my brother's death his last anchor point for the pattern. This place, that time, Beyon's death. It made the pattern whole.'

'And now the dead god's Undoing is spreading from the wound.' Notheen paused as something crumbled and fell behind the screens. 'Like new fires spreading where embers from the great fire have fallen.'

'This . . . this will spread?' Sarmin asked. 'This could consume the palace!'

Notheen bowed his head. 'It could erase Nooria, from wall to wall. We call it the Great Storm. It was foretold.'

'You must be able to stop it?' Sarmin let the question hang between them. He had looked into the tomb and seen nothing, not even hunger, no pattern, no hint of substance or flaw upon which a pattern-working might find purchase. Looking into that void had left him drained. The Many felt fewer in his mind.

Govnan looked worried. 'I had hoped *you* might – No? Maybe that is best. If Helmar's pattern made the fracture through which this bleeds then perhaps more pattern-working would only tear the hole wider still.'

'What can the Tower do, then?' Sarmin asked.

Govnan frowned, staring at the screens as if in search of inspiration. His body hunched, shoulders raised in the effort to will a solution. At last he shook his head. 'It takes substance. Perhaps a rock-sworn mage might strengthen the stone to resist it. A wind-sworn mage might teach the air to hold its essence more tightly.' A shrug. 'If it is hungry and we feed it, the void might lose its appetite for other things . . . a water-sworn mage might steer a stream from the Blessing and seek to drown this thing, if we had one.'

Notheen said nothing, only his eyes showed above the veil and beneath his cowl, and yet he managed to look unimpressed. 'In the end there will be only desert. My people have always known this.'

'And that's the total of nomad wisdom on the subject?' Sarmin kept the frustration from his voice.

'Even if the high mage can slow this advance, it is not good to be near this.' Notheen waved his hand at the tomb. 'The emptiness spreads beyond the boundary where all things are undone. Djinn will feel its pull and come to haunt this place. The nothing will echo in some of those who serve you, they will fall empty and sicken . . . There is no good thing here now. The wisdom of my people is in our name. Nomads. Seccan Thaleen we call ourselves, "blown before the storm". You should find a new place, Sarmin Emperor. This one is undone.'

11

Grada

Rorrin and Grada occupied themselves with the stalls outside the Blessing Gate. Many merchants traded within the shadow of the walls, enjoying city trade without the full requirement for licences and tax. Some said stallholders bribed the gate guards to keep the queue for entry near-stationary so that visitors would buy their wares out of boredom if nothing else.

'It's copper-*coloured*, I grant you.' Rorrin flipped the pot over in one hand and flicked the base to make it chime. 'Doesn't sing like copper, though. I find its voice sharp and lacking melody.' He shopped with heart, although he bought only citronel pods and later some roasted groundnuts sprinkled with the pollen of desert rose. To watch him Grada could believe Rorrin had no greater desire than to bilk the traders of their profit.

Rorrin put the cooking pot back with the others and allowed himself to glance at the approaching caravan. It had been turning heads for a little while, some citizens stopping to stare, little boys clambering up the palms lining the approach to the Blessing Gate.

'Foreigners.' He spat for good measure.

'How can you tell?' Grada wondered if the slave waggons

were rumbling along in the wake of this new caravan or whether they had changed course as she feared.

'The covers come to a peak. It's the style in Fryth and Mythyck. The cloth is faded but hints at blue – which more than hints at Fryth. Someone important, going on the size of the escort. Those White Hats are service units in from seeing action, they're not dressed for show. I'd say we're looking at royal prisoners, or some kind of envoy.'

They watched the approach. Outriders came in to disperse the queue at the gates, showing no patience with any who objected. Close up Grada could see dented shields, torn clothing, rusty bloodstains and short tempers in evidence. 'It's an envoy,' she said. 'Our forces must have been repulsed.' Some among the crowd started to hoot, to call down curses upon the Frythian devils. For a moment Grada bristled at the idea of any defeat, her blood rising with the anger of the crowd. *Cerani troops driven back by mere Fryth!* It took a moment to recall that Sarmin had wanted peace, had demanded this very thing. She took control of herself, shocked at how infectious the mob's mood was – at how easily people put aside reason in favour of taking sides.

The White Hats dealt out blows with fist and spear haft until the crowd fell into sullen silence. The caravan commander clearly had orders to make this a welcome. Preventing it from being a stoning was perhaps the most he could hope for.

Closer now, and Grada could see the Fryth waggons with their faded blues and narrow wheels among the Cerani army waggons, and further back along the column, flanked by White Hat spearmen, two carriages, each decorated with angular carvings exotic to her eye, blued and gilded.

That Rorrin had recognised their origin and deduced so

much in so short a time reminded Grada that whatever favours she might have she was still an Untouchable, with all the lack of education and ignorance that entailed. Her early life had been spent focused on survival in a particular handful of alleys. Before Sarmin the sum total of her life had been played out within perhaps a single square mile of Nooria. And here was the world arriving at her doorstep once more, reminding her how very large and how very strange it was.

The carriages passed, the first less grand, with shades closed. White Hat guards marched briskly beside, spears over their shoulders.

'Scribes and personal servants, most like,' Rorrin said. 'Maybe an honour guard.'

The second carriage rattled by, a golden eagle spreading gleaming wings atop its finial. The windows stood open to catch the air and Grada stared at the men within. The closer man met her gaze between the passing spears as he went by, leaving her with an impression of indigo. A larger man sat to his left – broad cheekbones, a brutal face. And they were gone.

'What did you see?' Rorrin asked.

'Two men. They were gone so—'

'Don't speak. Close your eyes and see them. They're still there on the backs of your eyelids. Describe them to me.'

'I can't—'

'Do it.'

So Grada closed her eyes and let the images flow. After a minute, standing without motion among the jostling, ill-tempered crowd, she spoke. 'He wore a helm, despite the heat. The closer one, the younger one. An inlaid golden eagle in flight decorated it. His jacket, deep blue – almost black. Shiny buttons with that eagle again.' Grada wondered if she was making it up. How would she even have made out eagles on buttons? 'He had dark hair where it showed, like charcoal, dull. Blue eyes, a strange deep blue. No beard, an artist's face, delicate, angled. The other man was bare-headed, short yellow hair, some kind of robe, black I think. He looked like a warrior.'

'His robes were red. That was an austere. One of their priests. Very dangerous. They have magic that actually works! Not just smoke and fancy words. The other will be the envoy. Some relative of the Iron Duke I expect. In any event, not bad – you see more than you know and more than most.' Rorrin snorted. 'You can open your eyes now, you know. Probably best if you did. The slave waggon just went by!'

'What?' Grada opened her eyes, blinking against the light.

They hastened to the gates, stepping around the fresh piles left by horse and camel and following hard behind the waggons without delay, the queues not yet having reformed as people continued to stand in hot debate about what it all meant.

Beyond the Blessing Gate lay the wide plaza of Satreth, surrounded on each side with great warehouses, huge sandstone buildings carved so grandly that many newcomers mistook them for temples. Incoming merchants drove their livestock or cargo to be unloaded at the various bays while Noorians in their hundreds busied themselves in a score of different roles, an organised chaos designed to devour what the outside world fed in.

'We should follow.' Grada tried to shake off Rorrin's grip as the slave waggon rumbled between two tall feed halls at the stock market.

'Meere will watch them,' he said, releasing her as she ceased to struggle.

'Meere!' Grada spat. 'Meere, Meere, Meere. I don't think there is any Meere. I've not seen sign of him for all your talk.'

Rorrin shrugged without offence and turned back along the crowded street.

'Who's he supposed to be then? This Meere of yours.'

'Oh he's not my Meere. He's the emperor's, though the emperor may not know it yet.' Rorrin kept his voice low, tone conversational, and Grada found herself hurrying at his elbow to catch his words. 'Meere is the last person many people ever see – the best knife in the Grey Service.'

That stopped Grada's feet and left her standing, jostled by crowds. The Grey Service was something to be whispered at night, a phrase invoked to end the conversation.

'Eyul was the emperor's Knife. I saw him through the Many. I didn't see any Grey Service.'

Rorrin sidestepped a pot-seller hung around with his trade goods. 'Eyul, son of Klemet, Fifty-Third Knife-Sworn, was a man of particular duties and particular talents, a man set to cut throats for the empire—'

'For the emperor!' Grada said.

'For the empire. The Knife may cut royal throats too – even the throat of a false emperor or one condemned by his own laws. The Grey Service, on the other hand, carries out more mundane forms of murder for the state. It isn't wise laws and shrewd negotiations that keep the empire's peace, or at least not just those things. Unexpected deaths and the fear of dying unexpectedly in the night, in the security of one's own bed, is what halts the plans of many an ambitious Cerani or stops them drawing up such plans in the first place.'

A coldness ran across Grada's skin while she pushed and shoved to keep up with Rorrin, as if a shadow passed over them. 'You mean the whole empire is run on murder and blood?'

Rorrin barked a laugh. 'All empires run on murder and blood.' He stopped without warning and she checked herself just before crashing into him. 'And the disturbing thing? All the alternatives lead to more blood and more murder.'

'So where are we going?' Grada asked, then stopped, turned, and set off back up the street, no longer interested in his reply. He'd done it to her again. Simply told her what to do, and like a trained dog, she'd obeyed even though it meant giving up the task set into her hands by Emperor Sarmin himself.

'Where are *you* going?' Rorrin followed in her wake.

'Back to what I should be doing. Back to my duty.'

'Come this way then. You won't find them at the stockyards. I know a shortcut to where they're going.' And he veered away into the mouth of a narrow alley.

Grada cursed and followed. Somehow she always ended up following the man, one way or the other. Behind her the hubbub of the street fell away with remarkable swiftness, as if the hot and acrid shade of the alley were a different world. Rorrin moved quickly, half-running, sandals scuffing over sandy cobbles.

Something soft and heavy dropped behind her as she hurried after him. The sound stopped her, pulled her round. The man must have waited on some ledge and watched them pass below. Grada had no time to look up and check – the blade in his hand kept her gaze. Even in the shadow its edge found a gleam.

'What do you want?' she asked as he rose from his crouch, a man neither young nor old, sharp-faced, black hair greased back across his skull. It was a foolish question but questions were all she had to put between them.

'Don't.' The man's eyes flicked to Grada's hands, busy with her belt rope.

'All right.' Grada kept her fingers working at the knot.

A smile as thin as his blade cut the man's face. 'Learning,' he said, and lunged. Grada fell back, whipping the rope up at his arm. He moved fast and somehow the knife found her shoulder. She felt her robes tearing as she dropped.

Hitting the alley floor, a mix of dirt and dislodged cobbles, hurt even through her fear. Weeks in the desert had stripped her flesh, leaving only muscle and bone. From the ground she risked a quick glance in search of Rorrin, but if he was still there he wasn't close enough to see.

'Clever,' her attacker said. 'An unarmed foe is at their most difficult for a knifeman when they're on the ground, exactly as you are.'

Grada raised her right foot, ready to kick if he came in range. The hard leather sole wouldn't offer much protection against his blade but it felt better than bare flesh against steel.

'You know you're bleeding?' He held his knife up to show the smear of crimson running from its tip.

Grada grunted. She hadn't known and had nothing clever to say about it. The echoes of the Many, so loud when that pair came after her by the pomegranate grove, kept to whispers this time. Her right hand closed around a loose cobble, her left finding only dry dirt. Where in hell was Rorrin?

'Most who get stabbed or cut don't live long enough to realise it. The pain holds back until it's decided if you're going to survive. But the stab lets the strength out of them quick enough.'

Grada watched him, let him talk. She'd been born in an alley and hadn't spoken with emperors and mages just to die in one.

'If you're going to stab someone it's only right that you should know what being stabbed feels like. It helps you to know what to expect of those you knife.' The man had entirely too much to say for himself. He was starting to sound like a teacher, starting to sound like . . .

'Rorrin!' She barked the name. 'You set this dog on me! You can call him off.'

Just a flicker of the man's gaze, up along the alley, at the mention of Rorrin's name. Sometimes a flicker is enough. Grada let fly with the cobblestone. She moved fast; she'd always had quick, sure hands. The knifeman swayed right and caught the stone in his left hand some fraction of an inch from the side of his head.

'Tricksy.' His smile gone.

'You know you're bleeding?' she asked him. An edge of the broken cobble had cut his head, his hand unable to prevent all contact. 'People can miss these things in the heat of a fight.' She wanted him angry, making mistakes.

Grada flung the dirt in a wide arc, set her hands to the ground, drew her knees to her chest, feet beneath her, and jumped up. The man stepped back, shaking dust and grit from his clothes. 'You really need to be closer for that to work.'

She charged. He moved with unreal speed but somehow she half-caught his wrist as she drove him back into the wall. The knife felt like nothing going in and like a punch when the hilt slammed into her ribs.

'You see?' he hissed past teeth crimson from his bitten tongue. 'Nobody knows what to expect.'

Grada smashed her forehead into his nose. The back of his head cracked against the stonework. She stepped back, her hand on the dagger hilt, keeping it in her as he slid to the ground. 'I know.' She looked down at the knife in her flesh. 'I've been stabbed before.' She kicked him in the neck as he tried to rise. This time his collapse was a boneless thing.

The knife started to burn in her, in the muscle and blood that held it, each breath as if her lungs had filled with broken glass. Sarmin had joined with her when she stabbed him, made them a pattern of two pieces, interwoven; she had felt every part of his pain. It hadn't been her flesh, but she had been stabbed before.

'Ghesh take me!' Rorrin's voice behind her. 'Meere! Meere?' The alley had grown dark, as if the sun were getting further away by the moment. 'How in any hell did that happen—' Grada fell, her legs turning traitor. The last thing she knew was Rorrin's hands catching hold.

12

Grada

It's cold on that street where the palms whisper in the dark and no one walks. Grada shivers against the breeze and against a deeper chill woken in her bones. In the garden below her the bushes seethe, stirred by the wind in the black of night. The dogs are dead or dying. She slips from the high wall and drops among the shrubs. Rising from her crouch – that brings back a memory, a man dropping behind her, rising with a knife in his hand – she pulls her own blade from the sheath at her side. It's an old knife, ugly, cutting a glimmer from starlight, a thing made for killing and not for show.

She walks from the bushes and from the muted sounds of dying beneath the rustle of leaves. The ground is soft beneath her feet, springy. Plants cover every square foot, all of them the same, their leaves like short black blades. The water it must consume to keep this garden green in the desert sun! The weight of the knife draws her back to her purpose. She would rather wander, but the knife pins her to the moment. Ahead the tall house, silent, its many windows dark. She is here to do murder.

The house looms, pale stone reaching skyward as she passes the ground-floor windows one by one. She tests the shutters on each then moves on. This is memory. In some lost corner of her mind she has been passing by these windows for ever, hoping never to stop.

She tries another shutter, strains to see the hands testing that smooth wood, prising those long slats, tries to see if they are her hands, Grada's, or if she is Carried rather than carrying. Carried at least the blood will not stain her skin, though the stain will be more than skin-deep in either event.

Another window, fingers wedged once more between the slats, muscles straining, and with a soft schnick *something vital surrenders and the shutter comes loose. She climbs in, heart hammering louder than her footfalls. Even passing through she notes the quality of the timber, the extravagant thickness of it, shipped down the Blessing in the great barges of trade princes like Jomla and Honnecka. These people throw gold about as if it were nothing while in the Maze children starve, babies are stillborn. She tries to kindle a fire within her, anger to burn away guilt, but the sparks die. The desire to kill can't be manufactured.*

She's in a corridor now, padding her way, the heavy knife held out before her to test the darkness, so thick you might better call it blindness.

Footsteps, just a whisper, bare feet on thick rugs, a snuffle, someone making their way by habit. Grada steps back against the wall and waits. She draws a deep slow breath but it hurts. For no reason her lungs are full of broken glass, a hot rivet driven between her ribs. She bites down on the cry that demands escape.

'Herzu's member!' The curse started as a scream but died in a whisper on her lips.

'The mouth on her! Labourers on Tuvaini's tomb shout that when they hammer their thumbs by mistake . . . you're sure she's the emperor's chosen one?'

'Just finish stitching.'

'Gods damn you, Rorrin!' Grada managed a louder whisper. She couldn't unscrew her eyes yet but she knew his voice.

'Rorrin?'

'Stitch or I'll give you something bigger to sew up!' Rorrin's voice again.

'She's done. I'll go see to my other patient.' Something being wrapped around her chest and ribs.

'I wouldn't bother. If he wakes he'll only die of shame. Taken out by a Maze girl . . .'

Meere? She tried to curse again but her lips felt too dry. Whatever might be wrapping her ribs, something thicker and more velvet seemed to wrap the rest of her, pulling her down into black and dreamless sleep. *Meere?*

13

Nessaket

Nessaket stood on the stairs and watched the Fryth delegation move towards the western wing. Newly arrived visitors were always taken to the temple of Herzu, to remind them they stood in Nooria, the heart of the empire, carved from the desert with ruthlessness and will. Hazran's white-hatted soldiers herded taller men in ornate armour, their swords thin and light compared with Cerana's heavy steel. Their weapons made these Fryth guardsmen no less intimidating, for their height and muscle showed what force might wield them. In their midst walked two men, one blond and wrapped in a priest's red robe, the other black-haired and wearing a heavy coat the colour of midnight. The latter looked towards the steps, but not at her; his eyes fell, wide with wonder, upon the carved ivory balustrades, the gold leaf and the paintings that lined the wall. Lords from the farthest reaches who lived in wooden shacks or tumbledown ruins often wore that look upon first arriving in Nooria, but she had heard the Fryth were artisans themselves, building architectural wonders within their mountain holds.

Nessaket took a step downwards, and her men moved too, matching her pace. Such things were important; one did not touch the Empire Mother, by accident or otherwise. She counted three-dozen guards, including Hazran's soldiers, the Fryth and her own men – how many swords could fit into a temple, she wondered.

Though the delegates' entourage moved softly, complete silence was impossible for a group so large. Their murmurs rose to a hum, and slow footsteps became a rumble in the hallway. She followed them easily. To her surprise they passed Herzu's temple and turned towards Mirra's, where flowers blossomed and sunlight filtered through the silk roof. Sarmin's choice, or his wife's.

General Hazran guarded the entrance, his white hair and eyebrows snowy against his darkly tanned face. He was one she did not know so well, his reactions and desires less predictable. It was said he had one wife, children and grandchildren, that he was a very happy man; but whenever she saw him he looked held by some dark thought, mouth turned down, brows furrowed. 'This is not a good time to visit the temple, Empire Mother,' he said with a bow, polite yet firm. 'Perhaps you could return in an hour.'

'I always go at this time,' she said, her lie smooth as silk, 'it is all arranged.'

'But I'm afraid that—'

'Priest Assar is expecting me,' she said, moving past. *Let him try to grab me. See what happens to his arm then.* She passed through unhindered, her guards behind her in a long train, and paused, taking in the heavy scent of gardenia as she looked around the temple. More than two-dozen crowded among the roses and tall, gold-hued grasses, their murmurs echoing along the marble walls. Every man here stood taller than herself, and she weaved through them, a thread through a tapestry, searching for the centre where the Fryth envoy and his priest might be found. The soldiers saw her and moved aside, bowing, unable to prostrate themselves due to the crowded floor. She scanned the room ahead of her, glimpsed between armoured shoulders and strong chins, until at last she saw a shock of yellow hair that marked the Fryth priest.

The northern soldiers did not bow for her, instead quickly moving aside, shrinking from her naked arms and breasts as if they were poison. Sensing disturbance the priest turned, caught sight of her and said, 'Oh!' his mouth a circle of surprise. Good: he could be put off balance. She smiled at him and did a curtsey, careful to let her hair fall against her shoulders in a smooth cascade. 'The Fryth priest, I presume?'

'Yes . . . my lady' he said in a slight northern accent. He looked more warrior than priest, both in his eyes and in his arms.

'It is "Your Majesty",' admonished her guard, 'and you must bow.'

The priest's gaze did not stray from Nessaket's as he bent at the waist. 'Your Majesty,' he said. 'I am Second Austere Adam.'

'I am Nessaket, Empire Mother,' she said, smiling, 'and I come to speak of the peace.'

'I would speak of the war first,' he said, straightening, 'and of what your son's armies have made of our land.'

'That is not a topic for this night, Austere.' The young marke pushed forwards from her left, speaking Cerantic that was soft and hard in the wrong places. His hair was as black as the priest's was light, and his cloak of midnight blue swirled about his gaunt frame, a mystery of folds and patterns that gave the impression of a much heavier man.

'Apologies, my marke.' The priest made an obsequious bow, though his eyes flashed with anger.

Nessaket turned to the young man, wondering if he was truly the one in charge. From what she understood the Mogyrk priests wielded such power that they need not submit to anyone. 'Peace is my son the emperor's greatest wish.' It had never been her wish, during all those nights whispering with Arigu and all those days planning and waiting. To honour Herzu, to make Cerana great again – was that not a goal Sarmin shared?

'Then it is a shame his cousin Tuvaini sat the throne before him,' said the austere, though Marke Kavic laid a hand on his arm, 'for his brother Beyon never threatened those beyond his borders.'

'May heaven keep him and bless him.' Did all beyond Cerana remember Beyon as a man of peace? In the corner of her eye Nessaket saw Govnan, white-haired and bent, making his way towards her. 'Let us walk about the room, Marke Kavic,' she said, turning her back on high mage and priest together. He fell in beside her and she realised his height surpassed even Arigu's; her head came barely to Kavic's shoulder as they walked. Beside a bed of yellow roses he said, 'You must excuse the austere, Majesty. We have lost much and he has not recovered from it.'

'He is not accustomed to war,' she said.

'No one is, Majesty.'

Weaklings.

'Your palace is beautiful,' he said as they stopped to admire a white peony. She watched the pull of his nose, the way his mouth shaped the unfamiliar Cerantic words. 'The materials and workmanship of your halls exceed any that I have seen before.'

'You flatter us. I have heard much of northern artisans.'

'We favour a simpler style. I'm afraid you would find it quite ugly.'

She imagined his city, burned and filled with the dead. She moved on, meeting Lord Jomla's eye as they passed, and then turning away, down a different path, though he raised his finger and said 'Good evening' in his high, smooth voice, hoping to intervene. She had no time for his politicking tonight. 'Perhaps you will have the opportunity to tour the city. Our tombs and our temples?'

'But we will not stay long. Tomorrow morning I shall meet with your son the emperor, heaven bless him, and I think the peace will be quickly made.'

Heaven bless him. A required phrase for any courtier. 'I admire your etiquette. Many new arrivals offend through their ignorance.'

Unlike his priest Marke Kavic was eager to please, desperate for peace. She would have to work with that.

'I consider myself a student of your culture. I have even learned to play Settu, though I admit I cannot win without losing most of my tiles.'

'Great sacrifices are required to win the game,' she said, stopping before the statue of Mirra, carved of obsidian with carnelian eyes, 'but the best games, the great games that everyone remembers, are played with such skill that each opponent holds on to his best pieces.'

He narrowed his eyes as he considered her words.

'A game easily won is nothing to savour,' she said, bringing the point home for him, 'but defeating a formidable opponent is what makes us Cerani.'

'Showing weakness in the game is an insult.'

'Just so.' She smiled, though his bluntness grated.

'Thank you, Your Majesty,' he said. They stood in silence as Kavic studied the statue. 'And what goddess is this?'

'This is Mirra, goddess of children and mothers and all soft things.'

'Is she your goddess, Majesty?'

'Praying to Mirra has never benefited me.' A yellow head made its way through the crowd towards them; Austere Adam was approaching.

'To have so many gods from which a person can choose!' said Marke Kavic. 'We have only the one, who Named all things, and makes all things possible.'

'And has that been fruitful for you, Marke?'

Kavic glanced over his shoulder at the approaching austere before spreading his hands wide, a gesture Nessaket did not understand. 'God is not always kind. He gives life but also demands it.'

'Empire Mother. I have been looking for you.'

Nessaket knew that smooth baritone and the mocking wit beneath it. She turned and acknowledged the high mage who stood behind her, shrivelled and white, but his eyes still blazing with otherworldly heat. 'Govnan.'

Govnan stopped four feet from where Nessaket stood with the austere and Marke Kavic, guards flanking him on either side, Fryth and Cerani together. 'I would speak with you, Nessaket.'

'I am welcoming our new visitors to the palace,' she said, gesturing. 'I hope you will not force me to be rude and abandon them.'

'I am afraid that I must,' said Govnan, twisting his cane into the marble floor, 'for it is of the greatest urgency that I seek you.' He looked past her and bowed to the guests, but did not introduce himself as high mage. He meant to keep that advantage, for the time being. Priest Assar approached with a bow; Govnan had arranged for him to take over the conversation. Nessaket had been outmanoeuvred, by the Tower and by Mirra.

Controlling her anger, she turned back to the marke. 'I must leave you for the moment. Please enjoy the cool comforts of the palace.'

'Such a relief after the desert,' agreed Marke Kavic. 'But I hear there is a kitchen where a man might find some wine?'

'You should have a slave assigned to you, who will bring you anything you wish.' Nessaket looked around the pair, but saw only guards.

The austere wrinkled his nose as if he smelled something rotten. 'We do not use slaves. We will get our own wine.'

'Nessaket.' Behind her Govnan grew impatient.

She held out a hand to stay him and said, 'Here is High Priest Assar. He can tell you how to find the kitchens, for I do not know where one might be.' Austere Adam stiffened like a cat when he caught sight of the other priest. He was a zealot, then. Tucking that knowledge away, she bowed to the marke. 'Marke Kavic.'

'Empire Mother,' he said with a bow of his own. And with that she turned and joined the high mage, walking side by side through a gauntlet of guards and a panoply of flower scents until they reached the hallway.

'You should trust in your son and his advisers.'

Nessaket looked at her slippered feet while she considered what to say. With so much at stake the high mage expected her to do nothing – and yet if she showed her anger she would lose what little power she held. 'I know men; I can already judge how Kavic will negotiate. He will agree to anything if it will bring peace to his land.' She left out that the priest's advice would be different, that he had interests of his own. 'If you allow me to attend, I can advise the emperor, heaven bless him.'

'I remember how you advised Emperor Tuvaini, and General Arigu before him. There would be no need for peace negotiations except for you.'

'Every lord and general in Cerana wanted the war. I only tilted it to our advantage.'

'To your advantage.' Govnan waved his cane in the direction of the Petal Throne. 'Sarmin is emperor now. This is a new age for Nooria, with new enemies and threats, and you are not seen as a peacemaker.'

She could not deny it. She had been Arigu's ally, Tuvaini's partner, and yet she felt the injustice of exclusion.

'Women do not make the peace, but they shall enjoy it.' Govnan wiped sweat from his brow. 'In the morning the young marke will be led before your son the emperor, heaven bless him and keep him. Go upstairs. Be with Daveed.'

Had the high mage mentioned Daveed as a threat? She looked into his eyes but they betrayed nothing. Govnan would not hesitate to recommend her child's death if he thought it served the empire. She turned towards the great stairs, anger mixing with anxiety. Perhaps the seed she had planted in Mirra's temple, the suggestion in Kavic's mind, would be enough to slow the peace and give Herzu time for his work.

At the landing guards opened the ornate doors, and they closed with a thud behind her as she made her way through the Great Room.

A northern concubine – Jenni was her name – was seated on the cushions, playing dice with Little Mother. Nessaket watched her a moment, wondering when Sarmin would begin to notice that so many beauties belonged to him. The horse-girl was after all not so beautiful, and busy with the baby besides. Another child would bring disaster upon Daveed for certain. She walked to her room, suddenly very tired. She would take care of it. Tomorrow.

Mesema stood in Nessaket's room, by her window-screen, Pelar in her arms. Nessaket rushed to Daveed's crib and was relieved to see his pink cheeks, his healthy kicking. It was a crude power play for the empress to come here uninvited and stand so close to the cradle, but then she was never one for subtlety. Nessaket would speak to the guards about allowing the horsegirl so close to her infant son.

'My father is dead,' said Mesema with no preamble or grace. She turned, showing the tears that carried kohl and powder down her cheeks. 'General Hazran brought a letter from Fryth. It was from Banreh, his voice-and-hands.'

So she had not come to flaunt her higher standing; she had come for sympathy. Nessaket stood frozen as Mesema put a hand to her stomach. She knew that feeling: it was of a world shrinking. With Chief Tegrun dead, Mesema became the daughter of nobody. The old men would urge Sarmin to take a second wife, the daughter or sister of someone important, and that woman's children would take precedence over Pelar and Daveed both. Nessaket picked up Daveed and frowned. Like it or not, her baby's fate was now entwined with Mesema's.

And so it was business, not sympathy, that came first to her mouth. 'Who would take your father's place?' she asked. The Felt controlled the gateway to both the tradelands in the west and Yrkmir in the east, and if Mesema could provide a key her power was secure.

Mesema stood a bit straighter, understanding the importance of the question. 'Banreh. Lame Banreh. He is the new chief.'

Nessaket knew nothing of this man, this voice-and-hands – whether he favoured Cerana, whether he was a man of war – not anything. She settled on the bed, preparing questions in her mind, but Mesema sat beside her, Pelar quiet in her arms, and fixed her sky-blue gaze on Nessaket. 'Where did you go?'

The directness of the question surprised Nessaket. Just a moment ago the girl had been weeping. 'I met the envoy and spoke of the peace.'

'You mean that you spoke against it.'

'I wonder why you speak *for* it. Your father, the lords, the army did not want peace. If you asked every person in the empire and the grasslands, you'd find the only people who ever wished for peace are yourself and Sarmin.'

The girl lifted her chin. 'What of the wives and children of the soldiers? The people of the grasslands who are most at risk once our Riders leave?'

'Next you will plead for the sheep.' Nessaket gave the answer Arigu would have given.

'Perhaps I will.'

'And Banreh? Your new chief?'

Mesema fussed angrily with Pelar's wrappings, her father forgotten for the moment. 'What of him?'

'What does he think about the war?'

'I don't know – but why do you worry about him and not the palace? Here are two sons; do you not worry about that?'

Nessaket was surprised by her insight. Did she guess the

rest of it? The women in these halls had nothing to do except compete for Sarmin's attention. He had not given it yet, but once he tired of Mesema he would notice them – dozens of fertile young women at his disposal. And if two boys were too many, what about thirty?

Mesema spoke again. 'Is my boy safe?'

'For now. And mine?'

'I would not hurt Sarmin's brother!'

'Then we shall protect the children together.' A necessary alliance, for now.

That chin again. 'How can I trust you? You didn't protect your other children.'

Nessaket recoiled as if from a snake. When Tahal had ordered the death of all those boys, she had thought her life was over; Amile was dead, Sarmin locked away, and Beyon given over to rage for ever. She had watched Siri, the youngest wife, throw herself from the roof garden and wished she had the strength to do the same.

She had no retort. She stood, mouth flapping like a fish's, and Mesema's expression softened. 'I'm sorry. I speak without thinking, sometimes. Of course we will work together.'

Nessaket forced a smile. 'Very good. We will support one another, you and I. Our children will be friends.'

'Yes. I would like that.'

Nessaket studied the girl's honest-looking face. She was a mistake – Nessaket's own mistake. She had tried to put Mesema aside during Tuvaini's brief reign, yet she remained; somehow she had caught Sarmin's heart.

After Tahal died, Nessaket had been lost. But over time, she found purpose. She planned. She found Arigu and then Tuvaini, and she believed for an instant that everything might change, that she could be more than an Old Wife in a gilded hall. But Helmar and his patterns proved that to be no more than illusion, showed that in truth her life had been shrinking since the day Beyon was born, the day she provided Tahal with the only heir he needed. It dwindled with time and age; now it was no bigger than these soft rooms. But still she could protect Daveed. Still she could be the kind of mother she had not been for Amile.

She stood up and faced the girl, as her mother had faced her before her wedding day. 'The first thing you must learn is how to keep Sarmin's attention, blessings upon him,' she said, 'so let us begin there.'

14

Rushes

'Why couldn't Demah go to Mirra?' Rushes didn't like the dark temple of Herzu with its frightening, twisted statues, or the priests with their big muscles, black robes and ink-stained hands. She shivered to think of them moving through the dungeons, choosing inmates with a point or a glance, of how cold their grip must feel when they dragged a victim from his cell. The presiding priest looked towards her now, his shadowed eyes filled with contempt, and she cringed away, imagining herself dissolving under that hard gaze, disappearing like one of those prisoners.

This was no place for a funeral. Herzu's creed was struggle and torment; sorrow was a weakness here, and pity an insult.

Mina leaned towards her and answered her so quietly that Rushes held her breath to hear it. 'To throw herself from the tower insulted Mirra. That means Herzu gets her soul.'

But Demah had not killed herself. It was the Longing that killed her.

An acolyte carried a cage of doves to the foot of the gleaming statue. They cooed and fluttered against the bars as he put it down, a sound that brought a ghost of a memory into Rushes' mind: fields and sky. He lifted a small door at the top, grabbed a bird and handed it to the priest, who snapped its neck with such an economy of movement that Rushes barely took it in. Then the next, and the next, until a pile of feathered bodies, still and lifeless, covered the altar. Death. Murder and death. She remembered Sahree's room and how she said a woman had been murdered there. The old servant had spoken of her lost stone as if it could keep such disasters at bay. Rushes pinched her pocket. A luck stone would feel good there.

The other attendees began to stand; the ceremony was finished. Not a word had been spoken. Silent as the Many without being joined, they were fragmented, desolate. The priest and the acolyte lifted Demah's body, wrapped tightly in linens and rope, and carried her through a rear exit. Rushes wiped away a tear and joined Mina in the aisle, if one could call it that; it was more a path between statues, basins and chairs. Order was not Herzu's realm. That belonged to Keleb.

'What will happen to her now?' With the Many, a person who died stayed within the pattern. They continued; Demah had stopped.

'There is a slave cemetery, out beyond where they dump the offal and chamber pots.'

'There is?' Rushes had been out there many times, but didn't remember any graves. 'Are we allowed to visit the stones?'

Mina snorted. 'Only the best slaves get stones, the ones who work upstairs, weighing gold and holding quills. For us they dig a hole. Once there are ten of us in there, they cover it up and dig a new one.'

'She will lie in an open hole all year long!' That was an offence to Mirra. All living things should return to the soil.

'No – only a week, maybe two. Think how many of us there are. We get old and die, or we're whipped too hard, kill ourselves . . .' Mina stepped into the corridor, into the light, and Rushes could see the sadness on her pretty face. 'Anyway they put the prisoners in the same graves, and that fills them quick enough.'

Rushes imagined Demah lying together for all time with a murderer or a thief. 'No!'

'Get used to it. That's where you'll be. But it's only your body.' Mina turned towards the kitchens. The funeral had been performed early – in the middle of the night, in fact – so as not to disturb those of the palace. Now they had some extra time.

Rushes yawned and ran after her. 'Nobody I knew ever died before. I want to know about Demah, where she went.'

'I told you. Herzu ate her. He devours the weak.'

'Where will I go?'

Mina fell silent a moment, eyes on her moving slippers, as if debating her answer. Finally she said, 'That depends upon your god.'

Rushes did not have a god. She never went to temple or made sacrifices. She had nothing to sacrifice, in any case, but perhaps one of them would appreciate her prayers, accept her spirit. She went through the gods in her mind: Keleb and Pomegra, scholarly and stern; Mirra, motherly and kind; Ghesh, wild and chaotic. 'I suppose Mirra.'

'Then you will grow into the plants and trees and forget yourself, unless . . .'

'Unless what?' Was there a way to serve Mirra better? She remembered what Sahree had told her: *This is Mirra's work, and it has to be us women who do it.* The stone. Would Mirra favour her for the stone?

They entered the Little Kitchen. The barest promise of light shone through the window-screen, and with it Rushes could make out lumps of dough on the table, left to rise when Hagga went to the funeral.

Mina pushed her into a dark corner before whispering her answer. 'There is another god, one who has no temple here. But He is kind and forgiving, and gives you a life beyond this one, just like in the pattern. Some of us slaves—'

'What are you doing, kissing? Get to work!' Gorgen had followed them. Now he grabbed the belt around his waist and wiggled it, threatening to take it off and use it as a whip. But then he turned away and walked down the steps to the Big Kitchen. Slaves worked there all night long, and there was always tea on the fire. Once he was out of earshot Mina grabbed Rushes' arm and leaned in again.

'Some of us meet in the root cellar at night. Mylo the delivery boy, he goes out into the city and meets the priests. Then he brings their Stories to us.'

'What priests? Who?'

'You'll see,' said Mina. Then she followed Gorgen down into the Big Kitchen.

Rushes shovelled coal. There were a few gods in the pantheon who did not have a temple in the palace. Meksha, of course, the goddess of fire, kept hers deep in a distant mountain, and Ghesh had no temple at all; but she could not think of one that fitted the words *kind* or *forgiving*. That was the sort of god most people would find weak, but it made her feel warm even before she set flame to the fuel. Beyon was gone and could not forgive her for rejoicing over his death, but perhaps Mina's god could. Rushes sat before the glowing coals and listened for Mina's return. After a minute Hagga came in and picked up her dough as if she had never left it. Voices and the smell of roasting meat rose up from the Big Kitchen.

At last Mina came up the steps carrying a pot of greens. She placed it on the hearth to keep it warm and looked down at Rushes. 'Will you go?'

Rushes gave a little nod, and Mina smiled. 'Good.'

Slaves from the lower floors, male, female, young, old, gathered on barrels filled with pomegranates and pickled lemons, on clay pots filled with honeycombs and on the dirt floor. Rushes counted three dozen, at least, who had come to hear the stories of the new god. They held candles close to their lips, ready to be extinguished, and kept their voices to a murmur. Discovery meant punishment. Being out of quarters at this hour, and in the storage area, opened the slaves to charges of theft and worse. Already a boy she did not recognise had eaten halfway around one of the best winter apples, set aside for the empress or the Empire Mother. Where would he hide the core, she wondered.

The silence deepened, and all heads turned towards a tall, copper-eyed man standing below the drying rack. He was handsome and young, with skin the colour of tea. When he smiled, a rush of gladness lit the room. Rushes thought the new priests could not have picked a better messenger than Mylo. His voice came soft and friendly when he spoke, humble but confident. 'Welcome, everyone. Today I learned a new story. I learned the story of the living god and the servants of the fruit seller.'

As he spoke he looked to first to one person and then the next, not with Dinar's glare, or with the tired look of Mirra's Priest Assar, but with excitement and promise. 'There once was a wealthy merchant,' he said, 'and he had collected many fine things. Silver combs and velvet drapes. Golden spoons to eat with, and silk cloths to wipe his mouth. But one day the god came to him and asked for shelter.'

'Mogyrk,' said one of the listeners, a woman, hands clasped at her breast.

'Mogyrk,' he agreed with a tilt of his chin. 'But the god found that this merchant treated his servants ill. They had been whipped and starved.'

This elicited murmurs of sympathy from the crowd.

'When He spoke with them, they begged Him to help. Instead He told the servants He would depart come sunrise, and that anybody who accompanied Him would be free from harm. But He is merciful, and so He told the merchant the same thing.'

Mutters of protest; 'He didn't deserve it!' cried a man from the rear, before he was hushed by those around him.

Mylo smiled, confident in the story. 'But the merchant refused, for his house was beautiful and he had many comforts. The god asked once, twice, until He had asked five times. Each time He was refused. So before the god left with the faithful servants, He struck the man dumb and blind.'

Mina nodded with satisfaction. 'A wise tale.' Others appeared to agree, frowning as they considered its meaning. Rushes kicked her feet against the crate she sat upon and waited. The story did not feel finished to her.

'Here is someone new.' All of a sudden Mylo stood over her, smiling down, and Rushes leaned back. She liked to look at him, but not so close at hand.

'This is Rushes. She's from the Little Kitchen,' said Mina.

'How did you like our story, Rushes?'

'Well . . .' Rushes met Mina's kind brown eyes. 'When the servants followed the god, where did he lead them?'

'Into the light, Rushes.'

'Where is that?'

'The light,' said Mina. 'Knowledge. Wisdom.'

Rushes looked down at her slippers. They were grubby from the cellar floor, and now she would have to stay up late to clean them. 'I'm sorry I didn't understand.'

Mylo put a hand on her arm. It was smooth and soft for a delivery boy. 'Don't be sorry,' he said. 'I am a poor teacher. But now the austere has arrived, and he will teach us. He will lead us to greatness. When you come back, you'll see.'

Rushes didn't know if she would come again. She was frightened; every time she heard a noise she thought it was Gorgen or Back-door Arvind, come to discover them meeting like this, in secret, after most of the lanterns had been put dark for the night. She wondered if this was the sort of thing Empire Mother Nessaket might want to hear about, but she could not imagine that it was. These were not nobles, viziers or generals.

Mina took her hand and they readied to leave, but Mylo stopped them, an easy smile on his face. 'Rushes,' he said, 'are you a merchant, or a servant? The first time a person comes, they get to choose.'

'I'm a servant, of course,' she said.

'Well, yes, you serve the silk-clad, but that's not what I meant. A merchant needs to be forgiven, while the servants are innocent.'

Rushes frowned, thinking of Gorgen. 'How do you know? The servants could be all sorts.' This brought a laugh from Mylo. He made a little bow, his dark hair falling forwards over his face.

'Blessings. I hope you do come again before the end.'

Not sure of his meaning she did a little curtsey and hurried up the stairs behind Mina. Her stomach churned at the top –

what if Arvind or another guard were waiting in the shadows? – but nobody was there. Her slippers needed cleaning. When Mina turned towards her quarters Rushes ran down an empty corridor and through the Big Kitchen, ignoring the angry shouts of the night boss, and up the stairs to the little one. There she crashed into a wall of a man, dressed in silk, standing before the dying fire.

'You piece of stinking dung!' She heard the crack of his hand against her cheek, sensed her feet stumbling backwards from the power of the blow, before she felt it. She crashed into a storage cabinet, clay pots overturning, air thick with the scent of star anise and cardamom as they spilled from their containers. She slipped to the floor, stunned and dizzy, while the man came at her again, feet sharp and angry against her thigh and hip. *Why?* The Many had never hurt one another like this.

'Herzu's balls, Zell! She's just a girl.' Another man pulled the first away, hands firm along the silk of his arms. 'You've had far too much to drink.'

Zell slipped from his grasp and struck out at her again, his slippered foot connecting with her stomach. She curled around the blow, the pain too intense to release as a scream. 'I came for some bread and there was nobody here! It's intolerable.'

'She's here now, if you don't kill her,' said the other man in soothing tones. 'Come on, girl, get up and get us some bread.'

Rushes put her hands on the floor, slid her knees under her chest and pushed herself standing. She hobbled to the shelf where a loaf waited in plain view and reached for it, gasping with pain. She paired it with some olive oil upon the table and retreated into the corner. The men sat down with grunts of anticipation. Zell had a big round face and stuffed his cheeks to bursting, while the other one, handsome and thin-lipped, picked at crumbs. She tried not to clutch her sore stomach as they ate. She knew that she needed to listen and remember, to carry their words to Nessaket, but she was frightened.

'The slaves in the palace are not of the same quality as elsewhere, Anut,' said Zell, tearing off a piece of bread. 'The problems began with Emperor Beyon and continue to this day.'

'Do not speak ill of the emperors, heaven's light be upon them.' Anut glanced around for anyone who might be listening. 'In my home the slaves are ready to serve me at any moment, do anything. They would eat poison if I asked them to.'

'That sounds like a waste of money.'

Zell laughed, a staccato noise that made Rushes jump. 'It's the point of the thing. Obedience and respect.' He turned, his eyes searching the shadows until he found her. 'Come here, girl.'

She came forwards, her heart beating in her throat. *If I had a luck stone, things like this would not happen to me.*

'When you see me again, what will you do?'

'I will give obeisance, my lord, and do as you ask.'

'You see?' Zell said. 'She has learned her lesson.' He looked her up and down as if she were a horse on the plains and then ran a hand up her serving-dress, along her thigh and hips. 'Here, now,' he said to Anut, 'look at this young skin.'

Without thinking she stepped backwards, out of his reach, and his face twisted in anger. 'Come here,' he said, 'or I will beat you worse than I already have.'

She looked at the other man; he had helped her before but now his eyes burned with a strange fascination. She took another step back. 'My lords, please, I—'

Zell stood so quickly that his chair flew out across the floor. He stepped towards her, menace in every inch of his tall frame. 'Come,' he said, 'here.'

Help me! She cried to the Many, but only silence replied.

But a voice came from the door, clipped, with hard consonants and long vowels. 'What is happening here?'

A man dressed in a cloak of dark blue stood in the doorway. Behind him, in the corridor, a host of men with swords looked in, including General Hazran. She shrank back, her stomach hurting not from the blows she received but from shame. Hazran had always been friendly, but what would he think about her now, alone in the kitchen with two men? Zell had touched her – had he seen it?

Lord Zell turned with a snarl. 'You – Fryth garbage,' he said to the man in blue. 'You stink of defeat, yet see fit to ask me what I am doing? I, a lord of Cerana?'

'Then let me ask,' said General Hazran, and the man in the doorway – the Fryth man – moved aside to let him through.

'This slave is insolent.' The lord laid a hand on the hilt of his dagger. 'I have every right to deal with her.'

'When you insult the quality of palace slaves you insult the emperor,' said the general, jerking his head towards the men behind him. The soldiers looked tense, ready to move, and the Fryth man had raised his thin sword from its scabbard enough for its steel to glimmer in the firelight.

Lord Zell looked each man in the eye, considering. 'You will draw steel on me, for this slave and this Fryth?'

Hazran took a step forwards. 'I am charged to protect the emperor, from insult and injury alike. And this Fryth lord is my charge.'

For a moment no one spoke. Rushes backed into a corner,

wishing she could disappear. This was no longer about her; it was about respect, order, hierarchy. Things over which free men could fight. Somewhere in the distance, a baby began to cry.

'A misunderstanding, then.' Lord Zell leaned back and raised his hands in a gesture of surrender. 'I hope you will overlook my error.'

'I will overlook it, this once, if you will leave and allow us the use of this table.'

The legs of Anut's chair screeched against the floor as he pushed it back. He had been so quiet that Rushes had forgotten him.

'Blessings of this night upon you, General.' Zell stepped away.

Hazran lowered his head. 'And upon you.'

Lord Zell and his friend descended into the Big Kitchen. Hazran sighed and leaned against the water-tub. 'Some fresh bread, girl, and wine for our guests.'

He was not angry with her, then. Rushes moved towards the shelves, but flinched when the Fryth man laid a hand on her arm. He touched her gently, but she wanted him to stop nevertheless. 'She's hurt,' he said to the general. 'I'll get the wine.'

She found the envoy's behaviour strange. One would think him a servant himself, and yet they said he was the grandson of the Fryth ruler. It made her wary. A silk-clad could behave any way he liked, but she could not risk appearing lazy. It would not be said of her that the envoy had served himself. As they both moved towards the cupboard she remembered the morning's wine had not yet been brought up from the root cellar. 'I'll get the wine from below,' she said, 'my lord.'

A man with hair as light as the sun pushed his way between

Hazran's men and walked across the room. He looked straight ahead, taking no care of the table and chairs, as if he had been in the Little Kitchen a dozen times before. He wore the robes and patient expression of a priest but held about him also a glint of determination, or else love. It drew Rushes in, wondering which it might be. 'No. You need to rest,' he said after looking at her a moment with bright eyes, and under such a gaze she could do nothing but agree. 'I will get the wine. I believe that if I keep going downstairs I will find it. Is that right, child?' His Cerantic was good, better than his companion's. He walked towards the stairs.

'Austere—' said Hazran, but the man had already gone, in the same direction as Lord Zell. He was not the sort of man to be stopped by a word in any case. Five soldiers followed him, three Fryth and two Cerani, a deadly train. She remembered Mylo and the others, possibly still in the cellar, talking about Mogyrk. If Hazran's men found slaves there, eating apples or . . .

Austere. He was the man Mylo had mentioned. The one who would lead them to greatness. That was what she had seen in him. She looked down into the Big Kitchen, but he had passed from her view.

She turned from the stairs, took the half-eaten bread from the table and laid out a new loaf. Great happenings were not her concern. She would be a slave no matter what else might occur, just as she was a slave before and after the pattern. She could only hope that if she pleased Empire Mother Nessaket she might end up upstairs, instead of in the kitchen.

Hazran motioned towards the table. 'Please, Marke Kavic, sit.' The Fryth lord sat down, and Rushes retreated to the corner, out of sight. One of the soldiers in the corridor motioned to the general, and Hazran walked out to speak with him.

She looked at the marke and found he was watching her. 'You're a quiet one,' he said. 'How long have you been here?'

'Two years, my lord. Maybe three.' She tried to remember how young she had been when Beyon handed her that honey-candy. That had been an age ago, viewed through a veil of shapes and blue lines.

'From where in Fryth did they take you? How?' There was something odd about how he said it, an angularity to his words that it took Rushes a moment to recognise. He had spoken in his own language – in her father's language. She remembered only bits and pieces of her father – the smell of pine, the patches on the knees of his leather trousers, the way he sang under his breath when he thought no one was listening. And his eyes. They had been blue. Rushes gathered herself and tried to find the Frythian words that would tell the marke she was Clan, from the grass, but at that moment Austere Adam returned.

The priest held a bottle of wine in each hand, the soldiers still trailing behind him. There was no sign they had discovered anything amiss. She rushed to fetch the men a pair of plain, sturdy goblets. The priest accepted them, sat down and spoke to Marke Kavic in a low voice.

'It is as I feared. Our countrymen are still on the road, war prisoners, to be made into slaves.' He motioned towards Rushes and she pressed herself into the corner, wondering whether he had seen Mylo in the cellar after all. Mylo was a delivery boy; he could talk to people in the city, find out who was on the roads. But why? Adam cleared his throat. 'The peace negotiations have not affected Cerani plans in this regard.'

'Then we will ask for their return.'

The austere opened a bottle of wine and poured before speaking again. 'What about all that you said? The pain of a few for the freedom of the many. Sacrifices for the peace . . .'

'Whatever I said before, now I say that we will ask for all we discussed. The prisoners. Reparations. Everything.' Kavic took a gulp of wine.

Adam said nothing, but he gave a chilly, mocking smile, as if he had won a game against someone he did not like. Where before he had looked a kind and capable priest, now his expression resembled Lord Zell's. She pressed herself even further into the corner, but as she watched the austere's face transformed again, became the same calm, patient mask she had seen when he first entered the room. Empire Mother Nessaket would want to know about this man. Rushes would be the one to tell her.

15

Sarmin

Sarmin sat on the Petal Throne, out of sorts, tormented by what might be imagination or might be memories of the night's wandering. How many places had he gone? What had he said? He turned his mind to the present, unwilling to consider the possibilities.

The cushions he had made them place rendered the seat bearable, but hardly comfortable. They softened the contours of silver flowers and twisting stems where they rose above the stonework. Azeem had bitten back his complaint when the slave-girls brought the cushions, but Sarmin heard it none the less.

'Should I always suffer on the rack that tradition has set out for me?' Sarmin had asked him. 'Seventeen years forgotten in a small room were not enough? Now I must put any stray heir to the Knife, *and* twist about in a chair made to be easy on the eye rather than on the behind?' Azeem offered nothing to displease him and yet the man grated on Sarmin, despite or perhaps because of the fact that the vizier's personality came closest to his own of all the court. The key to it though was of course Azeem's view of Grada. Honest or not, Sarmin would hear no more of those opinions.

The throne room held the usual ensemble of palace guards, sword-sons of Sarmin's personal guard and courtiers who attended him. He had picked for this meeting not men he liked, or in some cases even knew, but men used to the politicking of empire, men who commanded troops or governed regions at a level that required their close and daily attention. They sat in a row on the third step of the dais, tradition dictating an uncomfortable afternoon for them too.

Among the nine advisers was Satrap Honnecka with his many soft chins and single sharp beard to hide them. Close by, the equally corpulent Lord Jomla, and General Merkel's narrow frame, his sword absent, sandwiched between them. At the far end the nomad, Notheen, perched in his tight-wrapped robes, a sinister air to him. Azeem had counselled against allowing one of the desert at the audience, but Sarmin had said the desert was the heart of the empire. He had insisted, in part to contradict Azeem, if only to show that the man could be wrong, but also because perhaps that disquiet the nomad brought with him from the empty reaches of the desert would speak louder to the man of Fryth and his priest than any threat or show of force. Their reactions to him might reveal whether they knew about that which grew through the sands, eating all in its path.

A gong sounded beyond the throne-room doors, another closer at hand, and then came the ponderous opening as six men set their weight to the left door and six to the right. Such a weight of wood might mean little to men from the green lands of Fryth, but at least they would know that entering the throne room of Cerana should not be taken lightly.

The court herald – an Island slave trained for the purpose – announced the visitors; the mellow voice that rolled forth a poor match for the oiled immensity of him, his vast girth held in with bands of purple silk.

'Lord Kavic Syr-Griffon of Fryth, grandson to the Malast Anteydies Griffon, the Iron Duke.' He drew breath. 'And Adam, Second Austere of Mondrath.'

Two Fryth guardsmen preceded the envoy, disarmed but still fearsome in their size, both as tall as any man in the palace guard and heavily muscled. They parted to reveal their charges, the envoy in dark cloth, cut and stitched in strange shapes as if the tailor sought battle with every natural fold. The austere beside him wore robes much as every other priest Sarmin had seen, his hair close-cut. To Sarmin he carried the air of a man more likely to burn books than to study them.

Before the doors closed Sarmin spotted High Mage Govnan slipping through the narrowing gap. The old man had been called to sit in counsel on the fourth step, where the priests of Mirra, Herzu and the rest would sit. In the end Sarmin had not summoned the priests. Matters would likely prove tricky enough without letting the Mogyrk priest insult or be insulted by Cerana's gaggle of holy men.

Envoy Kavic moved to the fore. He halted two yards before the first step of the dais. One of Azeem's men would have coached him in this. The same man would have coached the visitors in the obeisance as well, and yet they stood, all four of them, as if their legs would sooner break than bend. Sarmin felt the tension rising in his guardsmen. The sword-sons remained calm; protocol was nothing to them, but they noted the danger of escalation and stepped closer to the throne.

To not give the obeisance was unthinkable. Even to Sarmin the instinct ran so deep that the mere fact of their disobedience paralysed his thoughts for a moment. Of the five books that kept his company for his long imprisonment it was the *Book of Etiquette* that held most of his attention. In that room they fed and watered him, but they had starved him of human contact, and so a book dealing only with the business of the interactions between one man and the next, however dry and formal its writings, proved more of a window onto the world he had lost than did the arch of stone and alabaster which admitted only light. And in that book the obeisance lay time and again, writ large in black letters that recognised no doubt or leeway, the act that more than any other defined an emperor. But these men had not read the *Book of Etiquette*, and Sarmin had not read their books. Truly, nothing about the garb or faces, the weapons or skin-tone of these men of Fryth so clearly marked them out as alien than that their understanding of the world came wrapped in different covers.

Soon one or other of the palace guards would snap and take the head from priest or envoy, ready to sacrifice his own life for acting without orders rather than to endure the affront to the emperor a moment longer. Sarmin only sat and clutched the arms of the throne. He couldn't excuse them, couldn't show such weakness before the men he had gathered to welcome the envoy. Surely these men of Fryth didn't understand what they were doing by standing there stiff-necked and angry. Azeem should have explained it to them himself . . .

A gleam from polished steel as one of the palace guards closest to the envoy began to draw his blade, his face a mix of incredulity and cold rage. High Mage Govnan moved in a swirl of ash-grey robes, the heel of his iron staff striking behind the knee of the leftmost Fryth guard. The man fell helpless, landing on the injured leg, the armour casing around the joint hitting the floor with a loud report. Govnan's staff took the guard in the back of the neck, driving him into a crude approximation to the obeisance.

The high mage stood for a moment, heaving in a breath, and it seemed the air about him rippled with heat. 'I recommend you follow the example of your escort.' He addressed the envoy and the Mogyrk priest above the fallen man's agonised grunts. 'I had hoped the palace officials would have educated you in our ways – but if you require further instruction . . .' He lifted his staff an inch or two.

'I'm sure that won't be necessary, High Mage,' Sarmin said from the throne. Even without his elemental there was clearly fire in the old man yet. And well directed. His outburst might succeed in overcoming the impasse with a broken knee in place of a severed head.

'In Fryth a man kneels only to Mogyrk or to his liege lord.' The priest spoke, a man of middle years, white-blond hair gleaming in the lantern light, an intensity around his dark blue eyes. His voice held calm, carrying only sight accents, but his skin flushed in a crimson scald from neckline to cheekbones.

Sarmin spoke to preempt hot words from Govnan. 'You are not in Fryth, priest.'

'There is a reason for that! We—'

'Peace requires negotiation – negotiation requires manners.' The envoy cut across the words that would have been the priest's last had they escaped his lips. His Cerantic reminded Sarmin of Mesema's way of shaping the sounds when she first came to the palace. Perhaps the envoy too had learned the language en route.

Kavic began to lower himself, making his intentions clear so his companions could kneel before him. The guardsman went quickly, first kneeling, then pressing his forehead to the marble. The priest hesitated, a snarl twitching at his lips, but he could hardly stand when the envoy knelt, and at last he followed the guard's lead, with Kavic following.

A breath Sarmin had not known he was holding hissed past his teeth. The Mogyrk priest was right; they were here only because Cerana's armies had invaded Fryth, but being right would not have kept him alive. Indeed it might have brought ruin to his homeland. The priest's insolence had been destroying the only thing preventing the destruction of his nation – the peace rested on Sarmin's ability to command the men between them, the lords that ruled the many pieces of Cerana in his name. And that obedience, as Azeem often pointed out, rested on tradition. If showing obeisance to the emperor was a tradition that no longer had to be observed, what else might follow? As a nation of Settu players the people of Cerana knew all about how one falling tile can topple every token on the board.

But tradition would not keep the emptiness from toppling the palace, from filling the city with hollow men and leaving the Blessing as a trail of dust. This matter of distant war had to be resolved and quickly so Sarmin could consider the more imminent crisis.

Sarmin kept the visitors in their obeisance for a minute, and then a minute more. Time enough to gather his wits, time enough to underscore the point for the old men of empire seated two steps below him. Those old men, as much as any other players – his mother, Tuvaini, Beyon – had kept him in that room so many years. Alive and yet not alive, for what is a life that's lived unseen and unknown? Less than dust.

'Rise,' he said, and waved two palace guards to help the injured man away.

Kavic gained his feet with a wry smile, the priest still venting silent outrage so that in Sarmin's eyes it almost shimmered about him, like the heat around a glowing coal.

'Welcome to Cerana, welcome to Nooria, may the sand take only your sorrows.' Sarmin offered the old greeting.

Kavic tilted his head and gave a stiff shallow bow. 'We thank you for your welcome to your court, Magnificence.' He kept any hint of irony from his voice, or perhaps it became lost in translation. Far behind him the injured Fryth guard collapsed onto a bench against the rear wall.

Azeem had counselled that the men of Fryth played a short and direct game when it came to diplomacy, despising the verbal feints and circling so beloved of Cerana's lords and satraps. Sarmin chose to do likewise. Not so long ago his longest conversations were those conducted with the decoration on his walls, better to reach his point quickly than to lose it in the confusion of small talk.

'My cousin, Emperor Tuvaini, initiated an attack upon the Dukedom of Fryth. I understand he was poorly advised by one of his generals, a childhood companion of his. It was believed at the time that the plague which had taken my brother, Emperor Beyon, from this throne had its roots in Yrkmir and her protectorates.

'The truth turned out to be more complex. In fact the pattern-plague was the work of Helmar, also emperor, a son of this royal house, torn from it and educated in the way of pattern by Yrkmen invaders long ago. The pattern-plague was rooted in both Cerana and Yrkmir and in the conflict between them. Rather than starting a war, those events should have reminded us all of the lingering horrors such aggression leaves to echo down the years. Long after homes have been rebuilt and nations repopulated old grievances survive and work their ill again.

'I came to my throne with that reminder in my thoughts and my first act was to call a halt to the advance of the White Hat army.' Sarmin paused and unlaced his knotted fingers. Beneath his silks sweat ran. 'Tell me Envoy Kavic, what word do you bring from the Iron Duke on my offer of peace between us, nation and throne?'

The priest made to open his mouth but Kavic answered first. 'My grandfather Malast Anteydies Griffon desires peace also, though the terms and reparations will require consideration.'

Second Austere Adam scowled. A muted rumble rose from the men on the third step: Reparations?

'Good,' Sarmin said. 'Then perhaps tomorrow we shall begin such considerations. For now though you must be tired after so many weeks on the road. You will be taken to fitting quarters and shown how welcoming Nooria can be . . .' he allowed himself a smile and added, 'now that the business of manners has been settled.' He would rather they talked terms and reparations immediately, reached agreement before sunset and moved on to the more urgent matter of the wound their god had made on the world. But the memories he Carried told him in Cerana no agreement reached in such haste would carry respect; instead it would need to be picked over by advisers, the most minor of points argued through, near to death, the documents drafted, drawn, redrafted and redrawn. He wondered sometimes how in such a nation of debaters and nitpickers the decision that bound him for seventeen years and stole away his youth could have been reached in the scant hours separating his father's death from the long climb up those stairs to his prison.

Sarmin looked up from his musings. Kavic had made no move into his obeisance and for a moment Sarmin feared that once again it would prove a sticking point.

'My thanks, Magnificence. It has been a . . . trying journey. I must urge haste, though. I hope we can complete our negotiations tomorrow and communicate the results to Fryth as swiftly as possible. Our friends in the east may be slow to stir, but they will not remain idle for ever in the face of Cerani troops on Frythian soil.' He bowed, then, remembering himself, he knelt and made his obeisance. Austere Adam, following him down, winced at each stage as if every move wounded his honour.

The court watched in silence as the visitors departed, no word spoken until the great doors closed behind them.

'Speak then,' Sarmin said. 'You are here to advise me.' Marke Kavic had spoken of the Yrkmen. Had it been a threat or a warning?

The courtiers before him stood, some stiff and rubbing their posteriors, some quick to their feet, all of them stepping down from the dais before turning to face their emperor. Sarmin had expected the sharp-tongued Satrap of Morrai, Honnecka, to be first to share his opinions, but the ragged Notheen spoke into the pause, his voice low, persuading his listeners to silence, and speaking words of which only Sarmin and Govnan understood the full meaning.

'The priest knows war is coming, whether this marke wishes it or no. The church of Mogyrk has decided to test its strength in the desert. That much is plain enough.'

A longer pause and then the babble of outrage as the high and the mighty competed to pour scorn on such defeatist talk. Sarmin settled back into the Petal Throne and let his advisers advise, but the words flowed over him leaving little mark. *War is coming.* Those words stayed. Those words stuck.

16

Sarmin

With the envoy gone, the advisers and slaves banished, the throne room felt empty. The guards, ever-present, were hard not to consider as furniture, so gaudy and without motion. From time to time Sarmin would remind himself of the men behind those impassive faces, of the lives he had pieced together across years from scraps of conversation heard with his ear pressed to his prison door and later from the voices of the Many.

The creak of Govnan's knees as he shifted position brought Sarmin's attention back to matters in hand. 'High Mage, Headman.' He focused on the two men remaining at the base of the dais: Govnan, gnarled and ancient – fire hardened, Sarmin thought him, tempered in the secret flame – and Notheen, tall, ragged, bony; when the desert finally claimed him there would be little to consume. In many ways, in the ways that counted, they looked alike; Sarmin could believe them father and son. They fitted together in some way that could not be seen with the eyes but from a different perspective would be obvious. Lately Sarmin had started to see all those around him as parts of a puzzle, shapes to be manipulated in some high-dimensional and abstract space. It worried him.

'Keep watch on my brother's tomb. If there is alteration, or the Fryth austere comes near it, you let me know.' Sarmin waved them away, his head a sudden single ache as if tidal forces sought to split it along some old fault-line. Austere Adam had come with the peace delegation, but if his church truly meant to test its strength in the desert he might well be its forward scout. The possibility could not be ignored.

He watched them go, Govnan and Notheen, through slitted eyes. In his narrow vision the air around them shimmered and it was almost as if he could see the cracks in each man, as if a little effort would divide them into the constituent parts that meshed so neatly to make them whole.

'I will go to my room now,' he said. 'Ta-Sann, your arm, please.'

Ta-Sann offered him an arm thick with gleaming muscle. With the sword-son's help Sarmin stood. Whispers invaded his mind, ideas and emotions bubbling. 'I am young to feel so old, Ta-Sann. Perhaps I should train as a son of the sword? Would they take me, do you think?'

'Sword-sons are taught from birth, Emperor, sold into the service.' If Ta-Sann felt any discomfort at the questioning no sign of it entered his voice.

'Give me your blade, Ta-Sann. An emperor should know about swords.' Sarmin felt his tongue running away from him, shaping words given to it by someone else. Ta-Sann held out the hilt of his sword as Tuvaini had surrendered his dacarba little more than a year ago. That had been Sarmin's choice, his act and his alone. Maybe this was too.

Fingers met around the thick hilt. Sarmin struggled to lift the hachirah, a gleam chasing the gentle curve of the blade as it turned in his grasp. With effort he held it high. To their

credit not one of the sword-sons flinched when he swung at
the air, almost losing both grip and footing. Sweat stuck his
silks to him. *What am I doing?* He could see the necessary parts
of the sword interlocked, bright lines zigzagging through many
dimensions to separate iron from chrome, sharp from heavy.
It could all come to pieces in his hands, he had only to pull
here . . .

'Take me to my room.' He let the sword fall and the clatter
of it set the plumes bobbing on a score of startled imperials
stood along the walls.

The sword-sons didn't need to be told which room. Sarmin
had a canopied bed of silks and bright tapestries hung around
an oak frame within a galleried chamber that dwarfed it. The
gold in that room, held in statuettes to many gods and in
cunningly wrought birds, jewel-eyed on jade trees, outweighed
him. A dozen emperors had slept there, and Sarmin had slept
there for a time, but it was not his room.

The sword-sons cleared his path, concubines scattering as
their escort returned them to the women's halls. Ta-Sann
helped Sarmin climb the stairs, their footsteps lost beneath
the whispers and cries of the Many. 'I'm sorry for your sword,
Ta-Sann.'

'My Emperor?'

'I should have treated it with more respect.'

Ta-Sann, perhaps wisely, had nothing to say to that.

In the quiet ruin of his old room Sarmin bid the sword-sons
tie him to his bed. The ruined book haunted him. What else
might the Many do with his hands? His guards required no
explanation, no excuses, no swearing to silence. Another in
Sarmin's place might not have trusted to their discretion.

Ta-Sann and his brothers were human after all, subject to all the temptations of men despite their long years of training, when old methods and magics had been used to purge them of such weakness. Sarmin saw each of the six as part of the next, linked in a circle that could not be broken by small things such as offered wealth or power or the bodies of women. Each of the sword-sons depended upon the others in such a manner that Sarmin had more faith in their loyalty to the oath Tuvaini purchased than he did in his own actions.

'Keep two of your number at my door until sunrise,' he told them as they left. He should have put two more at the secret opening to the Ways, but he was afraid of what they might see, should he find his way free. Afraid of what might befall them.

The door closed on a quiet moment and some small part of Sarmin believed that he would be left alone now, that the silence would stretch into blissful infinity. But with the next breath the unguided Many returned to lift him from his flesh, burdened with their memories of times gone, places sketched and shadowed, bodies lost to sword and sickness, flashes of recollection so bright and perfect in their detail that a lifetime's contemplation might not seek out all meaning from them. And a voice, inside him but not of the Many, said:

—*She is coming.*

'But she came!' Sarmin twisted his head towards the unbroken lines beneath his window. 'She brought me the urn.' It remained unopened, a rounded shadow against the wall, threat and promise together.

—*She is coming.*

'Who? Who!' He strained his ears, but the answer, when it

came, rose from within. A vision, a scene remembered through the eyes of one of the Many he bore, one of the dead.

In the mountain dark he stands, shivers by the clan hall. Someone has to take their finds to Her. Someone. And it falls to him. They leave him in the dark with the cloth bag limp in his hand. A dozen white-stars, not much for a day's work on the high ridges, but the tiny blooms are rare as opals. He watches as Costos hauls open the clan-hall door. For a moment firelight colours the two older boys, strains of 'The Peaks of East-March' reach out, scattered notes from Voice Zanar's harp. The door bangs shut behind them.

He shakes himself, this boy of the mountain clans, this boy whose memories flow in an emperor's head, shakes himself and sets off. He starts slow and gets slower. No one hurries to see Her. She'll be pleased with the flowers, the very first in the briefest of seasons. She'll be pleased and she'll let him go without looking into him the way she does, the way that leaves people feeling ill-suited to their skin.

No light shows in the Megra's hut, nothing to lead the boy across the slope of scree-stone. The frost-shattered gravel shifts beneath each step; creet bushes, stunted and long-thorned, try to trip him. The muted sounds of the hall grow fainter and he leaves the village home-stones behind him, coming in time to the walls of Her round-house.

'Megra?' She won't be asleep. She burns no lights, eats cold food, sits wrapped in furs all winter before a cold hearth, but she never sleeps.

'Megra?' Her hut stands away from the village, from the stink of the tanning hall, from the mustiness of goats and the choking rich-ness of composting waste. The wind over the ridges brings the promise of rain and the faint tang of granite.

He sets a hand to the walls of her hut, round like every other save the clan hall and tannery, but built of different stone – older rocks shaped by some lost people and worn beyond corners or edges. The blocks must have been carried at least from Crowspire to build this place, but no one could say why. Pressing his fingers to the smooth stones it seems for a moment that he can hear an echo of those vanished people, chanting, deep-voiced, around the crack and snap of fire. The moment leaves him.

'Boy?' The Megra's voice through the slit window. To hear her speak you might think her young, or at least a mother with young sons.

'It's Gallar. I've brought the white-stars.' He moves around the curve of the wall to the hide flap that hangs as a door.

'Just Gallar?' she said.

'Yes.'

'Well bring my flowers, boy.'

And he ducks in, pushing the hide away.

'Sit, before you break something,' she says. The darkness offers nothing of her. Gallar doesn't mind – she looks too old to be alive. When he'd been small he would hide behind his mother if the Megra came to their hut. The first time she touched him – when he had the red fever – he screamed. He had thought her fingers would mark him for ever, though what with he couldn't say. He'd recovered though and she had let him see the ring of gold she wore always on a thong about her neck. Too big for a finger, too small for a wrist. He'd run his fingertip along the inner surface and she'd read the words there for him. Different for every person. 'Be brave,' she had said. Her face had softened for a moment. 'I was sick and you made me better,' he had told her, being of an age that likes to tell such things. 'We're none of us one thing,' she had replied. Wisdom of her own on offer this time. He'd asked who gave her the ring but she left without answer.

A cough reminds him he is not alone in this darkness.

'The white-stars.' He opens the bag half convinced that some glimmer will escape it, but even the whiteness of the stars can't break the night inside the Megra's hut. He just wants her to take it so he can leave.

'Do you know what's coming, boy? Have you smelled it on the wind?'

'Rain?' She doesn't mean rain.

'Something is coming. Something worse than wickedness.'

Gallar imagines her withered lips twitching as that young voice falls from them. Had she stolen it? Roggon said she had. 'What's coming?' he asks, wanting to be gone, wanting to run from her and the bad thing both.

But the Megra doesn't answer. Instead like any ancient she slips to something new.

'Old Helmar came here once upon a when – did you know that? He was a man grown, with nothing but a century on him, and I ran barefoot no higher than his hip.'

Gallar doesn't ask who Helmar was. The Megra speaks to people as if they know everything and treats them as if they know nothing.

'Bad things are coming, boy. Helmar could have told you. He didn't just catch people in his patterns, he caught the past too, and the future.'

The slither of the cloth bag being taken, the wet noise of chewing. Is she eating the flowers?

'Don't ever eat a white-star, boy. Poisons the body quicker than it opens up the mind. But if you're hardened to it – ain't nothing better for seeing. For really seeing. Helmar would have known what's coming through and through. Me, I have to chew poison just to catch a glimpse of–' She draws in a sharp breath. Another. A low moan. '. . . empty, the desert is empty, a place without time where the djinn howl in silence and the wind moans–' She sounds in pain. 'There's a hole in the world. A hole that devours and the sands are running through it. There's a–' She stops, cut off, and for a moment he thinks she's fainted. The sudden sound of a chair scraping on stone makes him flinch.

'I'm leaving, boy. You should too. Yrkmen are coming up the passes, austeres laying their patterns. Rangers with them. Anyone who stays here will be dead by dawn.'

'What?' His mind can't make sense of it. Yrkmen in the mountains? Fryth was their ally! And they didn't need to take the high passes . . . 'You were talking about the desert! You never said about Yrkmen!'

'The death of all of us is coming from the desert, boy. That's for tomorrow though. The Yrkmen are here today and they'll kill you just as good.'

17

Sarmin

'Do you believe in the gods?'

Sarmin blinked. He had been half in dreams, wondering at his last night's vision. Though tied to his bed he had travelled far, to speak with a wise woman of the mountain clans while Yrkmen swarmed the passes, bound for Fryth. He recalled none of it from *Histories*, the book that had been ruined. Now Mesema's voice pulled him back to her room where sunlight fell in bright spots against their cushions.

'Do you?'

It seemed so odd a question. He answered as he would have answered before he saw the nothingness in Beyon's tomb. 'Ask me if I believe in stone.' He rolled across the rugs to be closer to Mesema, sprawled on her piled cushions, naked and still complaining of the heat.

'Do you believe in stone?' she asked him, lifting her head to watch him in the sunlight that reached them through the perforations overhead.

'I do.'

'And why?' She lifted up, a sway of milk-heavy breasts, and reached for her fan.

'There are slaves—' Sarmin bit off the words. She wouldn't

allow her body-slaves into the chamber when he visited. She would rather sweat in private than be cool beneath the gaze of others. And he liked it also, being truly alone with her, in the sunlight, without even the Many haunting him.

'Why?' she asked again.

'I see it, touch it, it's all around us.' Uncertainty tinged his words. The nothingness in Beyon's tomb made everything he felt, everything he saw, feel temporary, delicate.

'And the gods?' she asked.

'I have only to walk to the temple and I can see them too.'

'You see stone there, cut into the shapes men have imagined, impermanent.' Her hand fluttered and a breath of the fan reached him, an unseen caress.

She was right without knowing why, and irritation washed over him. 'Should the gods be hidden? Nothing but ripples in the grass?' His annoyance was erased an instant later with shame at mocking her.

'The Hidden God watches over the Felt, or so my people say. The Red Hooves believe that the Hidden God revealed himself to them at last and that he is Mogyrk, still faceless but ready to guide those who will hear him. They say that he lives in the houses they build him from stone, as the Cerani say Herzu and Mirra and Ghesh and Meksha and so many others live in the statues that are made for their temples.' She rolled onto her back, spotted with bright points of light. 'The gods of the Felt roam the sky and grass, but only the Hidden God cares if we live or die.'

'I believe in the gods but they don't care if I believe or not.' *Do they care about us at all?* 'Any more than that room cared if I were in it or not.'

'Do they not give you your magic?' Mesema asked.

'They put it there in the world, just like they put arithmetic there, and the wind. I don't need to bother them each time I use it any more than Donato needs their approval to calculate the tax on a caravan or a leatherworker needs it to put his tools to good use.'

'I had a friend, Eldra of the Red Hooves. She followed Mogyrk,' Mesema said.

'The girl who travelled with you?' Sarmin remembered the blue feathers Mesema kept from the arrow that killed the Red Hoof woman.

Mesema nodded. 'They don't believe like you do, at least Eldra didn't. It's a different kind of faith. Just one god, always on her mind. She needed to speak about him all the time, and it's a greedy faith. They hold that all other gods are false, just mistakes and imaginations.'

Greedy, indeed. Mogyrk's end had been selfish, slowly drawing the world into death with him. Sarmin waited for Mesema's next words. It was the Windreader way, to approach new topics along familiar paths. A nation of storytellers . . . he wondered how long it might take to relate even the simplest information in their longhouses when all of them gathered in the besna-smoke and made tales out of the day's events.

'Windreaders live among the gods. We move through them every day, see them work. The Yrkmen have a dead god. They carry his corpse like a burden and demand you see it and know that all other gods are false. They need to stamp this fact on each thing they meet, like a herder marking his beasts with iron.'

'You're worried about this peace envoy?' Sarmin watched the points of light slide over her as she moved. She had once taken a softer view of Mogyrk. Perhaps her father's death at Mogyrk hands had altered her opinion.

'I want you to be worried,' Mesema said. 'I want you to understand how these people think, not just what some scribe has put down about the church of Mogyrk.'

Oh, but I am worried. About this and so many other things. Sarmin sat and drew his knees up to rest his cheek on, bare feet among the cushions. He watched his wife and she watched the ceiling, the only sound the flutter of her fan and the distant wail of a Tower mage threading the sky with spells so old the words lost meaning long ago. He wanted to feel alive, to abandon himself in her flesh again, but her nakedness left him unmoved. Perhaps it was the other women he had seen on his way to her; finer figures and softer skin could be found by walking into the hall and pointing. The greatest beauties of the known world roamed this wing, women from the hot south and the frozen north, from beyond the western mountains and the eastern sea. Forever they drew his eye, invading his imagination.

Mesema rolled towards him, tilting her head in that way of hers. What pleased him most were her imperfections, the faint pink lines on her belly where her child had stretched the skin, the scar on her collarbone, some riding injury from long ago. The things that made her Mesema.

She smiled, knowing where his eyes roamed.

'What are you thinking?' she asked, perhaps the first question the first woman asked the first man when Mirra and Herzu scattered words into the world.

'I—' Sarmin opened his mouth but caught his tongue. In that instant Grada had filled his thoughts, solid, strong, honest with dirt, not shaped like the girls strewn before him, but every inch alive. 'Marke Kavic.' The envoy's name came to his rescue and Sarmin repeated it, laying the emphasis where Azeem had placed his, the word's edges sharp and alien. 'He has brought an austere of Mogyrk with him and demands reparations. And so the courtiers make him wait, to show their displeasure.' He wondered again whether the priest knew of the emptiness that filled Beyon's tomb, whether he could use it to destroy them all.

'Watch the austere,' she said, as if she knew his thoughts. 'If we do not respect his dead god he will move against the peace. And your mother, too. She is asking questions about the war and my people.'

Without answering he stood and pulled on his robe. Mesema watched him with disappointed eyes, but she said nothing. Many unspoken words lay between them now – about the Many, Beyon's tomb, and his vision of the old woman – but tonight was not the time to begin speaking them. It was better she not know how fragile her safety lay, how precarious his mind. But he had brought something for her to see, one thing he could share. He lifted the urn, still sealed, for her inspection. She stood up, wrapping herself in silk sheets. He was reminded of the day she had run into his tower room, hair wild and blood on her arms.

'What is it?' she asked.

'It contains papers, records.' He turned it between his hands. 'I cannot open it.'

Mesema held out her arms. He handed her the urn and she tested the weight of it, frowning. Then in a swoop she smashed it against the floor, scattering shards of clay across the rug. Scrolls and parchment fragments spilled out from between the lid and what had been the base, some tied together with strips of leather, others loose and crumbling. Sarmin smiled. 'I'd forgotten how quickly you get to the heart of a matter.'

She leaned over the smashed pottery and he kissed her, once, twice and more, heat demanding he hold her, run his hands along her skin.

Mesema pulled back and smiled, colour in her cheeks. 'Will you stay a bit longer?'

'I—' In the distance, a baby cried. *Pelar?* The child was Beyon's, given to Mesema hours before his death – a final gift, the promise of another person to love, but the memory cooled Sarmin's passion. The pile at her feet drew his eye. He longed to explore those burnt scraps, dry, rolled-up scrolls and ragged books. Perhaps he would stay and explore Helmar's secrets with her – Sarmin and Mesema, as Sarmin and Grada once had explored the desert.

But Mesema raised her hands, blue eyes knowing, and pushed. 'Go. Read.'

Whenever he left Mesema, Sarmin had a falling sensation. The feeling of an opportunity missed, a chance passed by, just fluttering out of his grasp. He gathered his documents and made his way to the corridor.

Dust hung in the air, motes made golden by the last rays of this day's sun. Sarmin held one of Helmar's scrolls, listening all the while to the rising voices

—he should not – I worked the fields, I always – the horsegirl is filth, she smells of – I'm lost! – I would hit him until he understood – the child is the foremost – he will kill him! – the desert is where hope dies—

Perhaps Helmar had known how to free the Many. Perhaps Sarmin could gain command of his mind through studying the old parchments brought by the priestess. Her predecessor had visited the palace centuries ago, when Helmar was just a boy, held in the lonely room. The Tower had seen his potential, as they had seen Sarmin's. They thought he might swear to earth and fire both, the first to do so in for ever, and called the priests of Meksha to his training. The scrolls contained their story as much as his.

The priests wrote of Helmar's testing, of the fits he had as a child, the way he spoke in other languages and had visions – and the patterns he saw, even before the Yrkmen took him. The scrolls the priestess brought were nearly all fragments, some so brittle from age and fire that they crumbled when he tried to read them. His mind strayed to Grada. He had set her on the path of the concubines; if they were part of a larger scheme then he would know it, and he trusted nobody else with the task. And it was well to send her from Azeem, from the old men, away from their glares and their judgement. As busy as they were forcing Marke Kavic to wait upon their pleasure, as much as they occupied themselves with drawing up demands to go with the peace, they would still have made time to disapprove of Grada.

Ta-Sann, sword-son, entered and fell into his obeisance, muscles rippling as he moved. 'Master Herran requests an audience, Your Majesty.'

—*Kill him.* One of the Many spoke.

Sarmin put down the scroll and eased up from the bed. His joints ached just from the short walks he had taken today. A lifetime in a tower room had not prepared him to journey the breadth and width of the larger palace. 'Send him away, Ta-Sann.'

The empire needs a Knife, the old assassin would say for the seventh time. *Not only because of war: Helmar was not the first heir to surface from the confusion of our history and neither will he be the last. Any man armed with old writings, ambition and time could be a danger to you if he sets to digging among the lost lines and bastard lines. You need a Knife.* The master assassin had brought several candidates before him in recent months, but Sarmin had little interest in such matters; with a Knife comes the pressure to use it.

In any event he would continue with Knives the same way he had begun, on the day Tuvaini had opened a new door for him – he would not be given one, but he would choose his own and take it. Herran's men had been calm and deadly, suited to their duties, but none had fitted; none carried that mix of tragedy and strength that in the end allowed Sarmin to forgive Eyul, even for his brothers. Eyul, like the holy weapon itself, had carried his scars and the insults of time. The hand that held that Knife must have known many tasks, must have touched life and been touched by it. It was not enough that they be a killer and no more.

Sarmin touched the Knife at his hip. It was always at his hip. Without it no one could be the Knife. The power rested with Sarmin, and Sarmin alone.

The Many rose in Sarmin's mind, flooding his ears with their voices. 'Ta-Sann . . .' Ta-Sann would know what to do. He fell back on the bed, his legs no longer doing what he willed, his eyes seeing beyond the constellations on the ceiling.

—it's in the desert – help me – the girl – I had a tortoiseshell brush, where has it gone? – he is going to kill the – all those pretty girls gone to waste—

The voices rose as sand in a storm, burying his sight, and he knew no more.

18

Grada

Grada dreamed many dreams, some of them her own. Nightmare followed nightmare, taking her so far from her flesh she thought she would never wake again, but always the spike of her pain anchored her and drew her back. Once through the slits of eyes glued shut with sleep she saw an old man loom over her, an ancient with a bald and wrinkled pate, two teeth only standing in his gums, huddled together as if for comfort. That was no dream; she smelled his breath and could never have imagined a stench so foul.

She tries to wake. Tries to wake. Tries to wait silent in the dark as the sleeper passes by on bare feet. This is the many-windowed house, the pale moonlit house high on the Rock among the Holies, on the street that joins the shrine of Herzu to that of Mirra. She can't recall the name of the street – perhaps they named it 'life' for what other path do we walk between birth and death?

The sleeper is gone, tugged along his path by dreams of his own. He? He had a man's smell to him. It is enough. She is not here for him in any case. Those she has come for will be guarded; they will be in their beds on the third floor. Grada moves on, trailing fingers along the wall, counting each doorway against the map she carries in her mind. Five she must give to the Knife today. Five. But more than five will die, no matter how careful she is.

She finds the stairs and starts to climb the spiral of them. Moonlight whispers down from tiny windows in a high dome. She treads at the very edge of each step. Marble, they will not creak, but old habits die hard. A frown as she wonders where that old habit came from. A pause as she remembers rickety ladders of bamboo lashed together with hide strips. Creeping up them, desperate not to wake him . . .

Wake who? She shakes off the question and continues up the stair. Her foot hurts, twinges of pain from her big toe, bruised . . . broken? Some accident early in the day. If she has to run, those chasing her will die.

She passes the second floor. More steps. A deeper shadow ahead, one could imagine it a man. She lifts her Knife, not pausing or slowing, nothing so undoes surprise as hesitation. She needs to place hand and blade with precision, to kill quickly and to silence any exclamation. He is already leaning against the wall, so he won't collapse in a clatter.

Even at the last as he turns his head she doesn't quicken her pace. The palm of her hand flat to his mouth, pushing his head back against the wall, wet lips and bristles on her skin. The point of her Knife is planted and pressed home, slicing through flesh, biting through a rib bone, finding the heart.

She pins him to the wall, a faint rattle of keys as he slides to the floor, spluttering beneath her hand, legs twitching as they stretch out before him. He surges up, arching, his breath escaping in a tortured hiss, then slumps. Grada wipes her hand on his cloak. Tugs out the Knife. He sits at the base of the wall, legs out before him, head bowed over his chest.

Murder. Many voices whisper the word within her head. Murder. Some approve.

Grada pauses, listens. Nothing. The Knife weighs heavy in her hand and for a moment she can hardly keep from letting it drop. There's a sour taste in her mouth, hard to swallow – the taste of guilt.

'Good. Spit it out.' An old man's voice, as edged and as sour as the taste she's trying to get rid of. 'Better out than in my old mother used to say.'

'Nobody cares about your mother, Anx, just bring her round.' A nasal voice, not familiar, not Rorrin's.

Grada realised her eyes were screwed shut, and opened them. The daylight surprised her and she squinted against it. Her mouth wanted to ask where she was, but she refused to let it. Sitting on a bed across the room a dark-haired man, dim and blurred in her vision, linen strips about his forehead and across his nose.

'Meere?' she said.

'There she is.' Meere lay back on his pillows. 'I should know better by now than to be surprised by a girl from the Maze. Anx, go get Rorrin. No telling what this one will do when she finds her legs.'

'Bastard.' Grada drew a deep breath, preparing to sit up, and instead found herself gasping as white agony lanced her ribs. The door creaked and Anx left.

'I suppose I am,' he said. 'But I've a broken nose and battered skull to pay me back for it.'

'The caravan? The slave women?' The room grew more distant, Meere's nasal tones more faint.

'Herzu! You don't give up do you, girl? The caravan was followed, until it was unloaded. Its cargo will have been followed too, but it's just a precaution. I know where they're bound.'

'Where?'

'Take it easy, Maze-girl.'

'I said where!' Through the slits of her eyes the room looked a thousand miles away, revolving as it fled from her.

The creak of the door. 'Grada.' Rorrin's voice.

'Where?' She spat again but the taste of guilt wouldn't leave her mouth.

'The Holies. They will have been taken up to the Holies.' So distant she could hardly catch the words. 'I know which house.'

'She will sleep now.' The ancient's voice. 'Natural sleep. The coma is broken. And see, the wound is clean and stitched.'

Grada slept again despite the pain of her wound. Anx's drugs still had a hold on her and pulled her down the moment she gave up the fight. She dreamed of the house on the Holies, of a butterfly broken in her hands, of a hole in the desert where the sands ran out for everyone.

'Herzu!' And she jolted upright, wrapped in sweat, cursing a second time for the sharp agony lancing from her side. Evening had invaded the room. Anx stirred in the corner, resembling a discarded robe more than a man. Grada slipped her legs from the covers and set bare feet to the dusty floor. All of her felt heavy. All of her felt sore. Her nakedness dismayed her. Had the old man undressed her? She snatched her robe from the stool it draped and shrugged it on, brushing at the crusted blood around the slit Meere's knife made.

'You should stay in bed.' The discarded robes stirred again and spoke.

'I have things to do.' Grada patted around for her pack. She winced as she slung it around her shoulder. She slipped her sandals on.

'Mirra helps those who help themselves.' Anx lisped on each 's', two teeth not being enough to put an edge on his words. 'You need to rest.'

Grada suspected the old man was right but she made for the door. 'Are you going to stop me?'

Anx laughed, an old woman's cackle, and settled back. 'I'll rest for you. Tell Rorrin I put up a fight, will you?'

Grada answered with a grunt.

'On the stand by the door.' Anx flapped a thin arm at it. 'Meere left it for you.'

'I want nothing of his.' But she looked anyhow. A long knife lay on the wicker stand, not a street knife intended for honest butchery and set instead to butcher men, but a dacarba fashioned for war, a triple-bladed spike. She set her fingers to the hilt, rough with the skin of river shark, a large jewel set as the pommel. Jade perhaps, it was hard to tell in the half-light. 'An emperor should have this. It will only get me killed.' A scabbard and belt dangled from a nail in the wall.

'Meere said you wouldn't take it.' She could hear the shrug in the old man's voice.

'Meere should be half as clever as he thinks he is.' She closed her hand around the hilt and snatched up the belt.

Grada ducked through a doorway and followed a corridor to the sound of the street, buckling the knife-belt beneath her robes as she went. An arch took her into an alley narrower than the corridor, and at the end she heaved on a door of ancient driftwood until it juddered across the dirt floor. Without a backwards glance she stepped out into the flow of the Maze.

The folk of the Maze can smell weakness, blood too. Grada let neither show, shifting her pack to hide the stain on her robe. Shadow had merged with shadow, stirred by the street traffic into a pervading gloom, broken here and there by a lamp set back from a trade window, yellow flames drinking rock oil through short wicks. She wanted to go to the Holies, to the house Meere spoke of, to follow the charge Sarmin had set upon her. In a deep pocket her hand turned the disc he'd given her, over and over, fingers slick on the obsidian, feeling out his features.

'Mother of—' A pothole made her stumble, fresh pain bringing the curse, the agony on pain's heels taking her breath. She had seen the long stair from river to rock; she would collapse before she made it halfway up. Perhaps even the bridge would defeat her. 'Another day.'

She leaned back against a wall. They say in the Maze a wall can be your best friend. Noorians passed before her, bound in their purpose, each a mystery to the other. A man glanced her way, eyes haunted, a hunger in him. The gloom took him. There had been a time when every One knew the Many, all secrets and sorrows shared until they grew too thin for care. Grada bit her lip, as if more pain might sharpen away the Longing. For her it had been a gentler step away from the Many, taken first into Sarmin's pattern, sharing with him in thought and desire, before being abandoned to herself once more, a second step. For most it had been one quick expulsion, a second birth of sorts, spat from the warmth and safety of the Many into the world again, raw and naked against the night.

She sniffed and set off once more. Not everything that *felt* right *was* right. The smokers in their dens love the poppy as it eats them from within. Even here in the Maze, thick with the stink of smoke and sewage, she caught the sweet tang of poppy-sap. How much more of it must have been borne down the Blessing since the Longing came, hidden in bales of cotton or barrels of grain, how many more meadows sown in the mountain valleys out past empire to satisfy the need?

She passed urchins seeking friends for their sisters, half a penny master, half a penny, clean and young. Hawkers, their tiered sticks swaying with quail, roast starling, rats tied by their tails and smoked over rosewood, old women clutching trays, 'Sesame twists. Dried rose and besna nut. Ants in honey.'

Three men of the Arak spilled from an alley to join the larger way, their skin tarred black in the way of their tribe, the stink of oil in their hair. A snatch of their laughter and the hustle of the Maze swirled them away. Somewhere close by a shriek, sharp and terminal. She moved on.

'. . . dead god . . .'

Grada could have missed it in the muttering river of the Maze, could have misheard, but the phrase snagged her, drew her gaze across the street to a corner where two women met, cowled and veiled. She chose one and followed as they split. She selected the one that carried a small string bag of limes, the other had a heavier load and logic put her on a home-ward course. Grada's woman showed no flesh save her hand where it clutched the bag; the fingers had the gnarled look of a woman turning old, or a twenty-year-old who spends twelve hours a day washing other people's clothes at the river.

Grada followed, pausing now and then to wave off flies and to keep her distance. In the Maze narrow alleys kept the heat of the day; the flies quieted with dusk but rose in buzzing clouds when provoked. Some climes suffered flies of the stinging kind, or that suck the blood. In Nooria the flies stabbed.

The woman stopped once to inspect a stall. She showed no

signs of guilty conscience, no sign that she was engaged in sedition. The finding of a Mogyrk church in Nooria had never been hard nor easy. The church buildings themselves were plentiful but had served new purposes for so long that the people around them no longer remembered what they had been. Two years ago she might have been inside of one and never recognised it for what it was. But since the loss of the Many the Longing had drawn Noorians into all manner of new pursuits, new ways to fill the void inside, and the Mogyrk priests had answered their call. Now statues of their dead god shone behind silk-draped altars, and the people of Nooria drifted in and out of their doors, in secret, out of sight of the royal guard.

Grada's mark grew furtive, quickening her pace, throwing glances left and right, but never behind, never where Grada walked, openly following. The woman veered into the narrow gap between two buildings – gone. Grada passed by, turned at the corner and came back, taking the same path. The gap proved so narrow that she had to draw her shoulders together.

'The second austere . . .' She strained to hear more, but only the buzzing of flies met her ears.

The alley ended in a high wall and a low heap of refuse, so pungent it drew tears to her eyes. A doorway veiled in beaded strings gave to the left just before the heap and she pushed on through. Incense sticks smoked in niches to either side of the entrance, filling the corridor beyond with a haze that gave battle to the reek from outside. The low drone of prayer came from somewhere up ahead. Grada patted through her robes for the dagger at her hip then descended a stair and through a second curtain to enter a low basement, the bead strings streaming from her shoulders, clicking one against the next.

Six or seven people knelt on the dirt floor, lamps in niches affording enough light to avoid tripping over the worshippers. A man stood by the entrance, swaddled in sand-robes, but said nothing. Grada moved to kneel beside the woman and her limes. She bit down hard on the gasp that wanted to escape. Something warm and liquid trickled down her ribs below her wound. She hoped it was only sweat.

'. . . was born of Yi-ith, and she begat Jedah. And Jedah brought the word of Mogyrk to the people of Mythyck in the time of Ansos . . .'

Grada risked a look around at her fellow faithful. Five women, two men, one of those fat with flour on his apron. She wondered how he'd made it between the buildings. Perhaps he was greased specially for the occasion? Her lips twitched at the thought. Once she would have shared it with Sarmin. He would have laughed. The other wore the head cloth of a dock-counter, up from the river quays with his abacus under his tunic no doubt. She wondered if it was a good sign that he had to travel so far to find a church, or a bad sign that his need was so strong he would brave the Maze to worship.

'. . . into the desert that we might follow. Praise be his name.'

'Praise to Mogyrk.' Grada muttered it with the others.

She knelt in the heat, her knees starting to ache, listening to the droning priest and wondering what hold such a dull faith had on her fellow citizens. The basement held no statues, no fearsome warrior god to inspire, no toothed horror to breed a righteous fear. Just words and more words. And after a while one realised that the stink of the alley overmastered the incense to reach in even here.

'Praise to Mogyrk,' she repeated with the others into the pause.

'For Mogyrk went before us, brothers, sisters, to prepare a house of many rooms. And in this house there is a place for all men, for each of us and everything, for each blade of grass and grain of sand. So it is written, and so shall we be unwritten. Death waits for every man; life is but a heartbeat, death eternal, and into this eternity Mogyrk threw Himself, for me, for you, His love for the world boundless. In this house we shall be many, no one of us alone, held within the love Mogyrk died for.'

'Praise to Mogyrk.' The words came unsought. The Many. That's what Mogyrk offered. Faith in togetherness. Grada felt it, the promise, the temptation. The priest walked among them now, between the kneeling faithful, a clay cup in his hand, letting each person drink.

'The dead god's promise.' And he tipped the cup to Grada's lips. She drank deep. The promise tasted only of water, giving no hint as to whether it was poison or cure.

19

Sarmin

Sarmin sat once more on the carpet, gritty with the debris of
ruined walls, and lay back to watch the gods. In the shadow
and soft flicker of his lantern they returned his inspection:
Herzu hooded, just the gleam of his eyes on show; Mirra full
of grace, her compassion wrought in five lines by the skill of
an artist long gone to dust; Meksha with fire in her eyes; Ghesh
wrapped in midnight; Torlos of war, battle dressed; many others.
Beyond the door sword-sons stood guard. The Fryth waited on
his presence while viziers, generals and priests waited on his
word; provincial lords travelled up and down the Blessing; babies
sucked their mother's milk and knew nothing of the emptiness
growing in the heart of the empire. But in here, in this high
tower, this small room, nothing had changed.

Sarmin returned to the undamaged wall below the window,
to the place where the design had spoken and lit visions
within him. Twice the pattern had spoken to him. Not in the
old way, through some devil or demon concealed in plain
sight within the intricate sprawling scroll of the ancient decoration, but in a new voice, a raw and powerful voice that rang
him like a bell and woke echoes among the Many that remained
trapped within him.

Sarmin's fingers had learned to fear the tight-woven lines of the design but he overwrote their reluctance with his will and set them trembling against the patterning. The voice had warned of a woman who approached, and he'd seen her through the eyes of a mountain boy. Seen an ancient woman who spoke of the Pattern Master as an old friend, a mentor, a lover maybe. 'Show her to me,' he said. 'Why is she coming here?'

'She comes!' The voice pulsed through him once again and the boy's life swept over him.

Gallar stands alone, uneasy in the woods – burdened by the exhaustion of his escape through the high passes, the ache of his long descent into Fryth running in each muscle from heel to hip. The mountain-born are used to seeing mile upon empty mile, used to the wind and silence, the surety of rock. In this forest every direction ends in tree, soon or sooner still, everything is malleable, even the trees have give, and each part of it whispers or creaks or rustles.

The outpost announces itself first with the smell of wood-smoke, then with the smoke itself seen rising into an evening sky through breaks in the canopy. Mule dung on the trail, the buzzing of flies, the stink of men lingering among the trunks, and the path breaks without preamble into a wide clearing.

The trading post stands three storeys high, a log-built hall with stone foundations, turf-roofed, surrounded by a score of buildings that are no more than shacks, stables to the rear, trade goods beneath awnings to the fore. Gallar stops in the tree-line. Nothing moves in the lengthening shadows, save a scrawny yellow dog sniffing between the lean-tos. A mule brays from the stables. Silence.

Far back, past the shack, among the trees on the far side of the clearing, something catches his eye. In the gloom beneath the foliage

. . . something moving, things moving, not men though, or if they were, not moving like men. He frowns, takes a step back.

'Hold.' The sharp point of a blade pricks him between his shoulders.

Yrkmen! They beat me here! *Gallar raises his hands. 'I'm just a traveller.'*

'Hold.' Noises from the bushes, rustling. He has walked right past them and now they'll kill him. He had wanted to be brave but fear unmans him, trembling in his raised hands, the tingling of pins and needles across his cheekbones, making him want to piss himself like a child.

Two men walk around him, knives in hand, both hung about with cut vines. Each of them wears an iron helm of strange design, white-enamelled, also wreathed in vines. It is impossible that he could have missed them. The elder of them, tall with a grey-speckled moustache, watches him a moment through narrowed eyes, cocking his head to the side. Gallar tries to return the look but his gaze keeps slipping to the dagger point held between them.

'Yrkman?' The soldier makes it sound wrong.

'I'm a traveller. From the mountains.' *Gallar realises the hands holding the knives are too dark for any Yrkman or Fryth. Even in high summer the men of Fryth never scorched to such an olive tone.*

Behind the boy's eyes Sarmin recognises the men as soldiers of his army of the White Hat, men from Nooria or the cities strung south along the Blessing. Far from home.

'Come.' And the tall soldier leads off, one of his companions moving back up the trail.

A prod from the sword or spear at his back gets Gallar's feet moving. In the stories Voice Zanar told this would be where the hero made his escape. A lunge, a twist, and he'd be off with a stolen weapon and men bleeding in his wake. But Gallar finds himself nailed to *reality by certain knowledge that a spear thrust would outpace any move he might make and that his shaking hands have no chance of stealing a blade.*

They cross the clearing, following the gradient in a series of rough steps, aimed for the far side. Soon enough Gallar understands what had first caught his eye. Men swinging from the boughs of a mountain oak, ropes about their necks. Ten or more, swaying gently, toes pointed to the ground, hands bound behind backs. Closer still and even the twilight can't hide their faces, dark with blood, eyes bulging in unreal almost comic exaggeration of what should be possible. Their heads, cocked to the side at broken angles, recall how the soldier had first looked at him. Is this his fate then, to cross the high pass just to die choking on a rope?

It starts to rain. At first Sarmin only hears it, pattering on the leaves above. He wonders what it is. The first droplets find Gallar, spilling from leaf and twig, cold and shocking. The tempo builds until it's a downpour beating at the canopy. Sarmin has never seen such rain; a season's water will fall in an hour.

The soldiers here are not so well hidden, and more plentiful. Dozens emerge, their armour foreign to Gallar's eye, overlapping scales of iron on linen. Most hold long spears with narrow steel heads, weapons unsuited to the forest. One approaches, this man with bronze chasing on each scale of his armour, his white helm without camouflage, its back extending into lobstered iron plates to guard his neck and running with water. Sarmin knows him for a first-spear captain.

'Yrkmen?' He speaks the word better than his men.

'I'm from the mountain tribes.' Gallar can't keep the terror from quivering in his voice. 'I'm not from Yrkmir or Fryth. From the mountains.' He tries to point towards the peaks but the man behind him slaps his arm down.

The officer shakes his head. 'You are from Yrkmir I think. A spy. There is room for you on the tree.'

Sarmin tries to order the captain to stop. He knows this is memory. It has to be memory. But even so he tries, and fails.

'No, don't!' Gallar falls to his knees in the soft dirt, as if that might stop them. 'I'm from Hollow!' He screams as two men drag him to his feet. 'I hate the Yrkmen.' Someone loops a rope about his neck, a coarse thick rope that makes him retch even before they tighten it. 'No! They killed my mother! All my people! With magic!'

'Hthna.' The officer holds up a hand. Hearing Cerantic through Gallar's ears is strange and for the first time Sarmin realises Gallar is thinking and speaking a language he doesn't understand. The captain steps closer. 'Hanging is easy, boy.' A pause here and there to select his words, his lips struggling with their shapes. 'You die hard if you lie to me.'

'I'm not lying, I'm not, I never lie.' Gallar rushes his words, speaking too fast for the man but unable to stop. 'I saw it. I saw them die. They put a pattern on us. Everyone died—'

The man's hand closes around Gallar's throat, intense dark eyes on his, face close enough to smell the spices on his breath. 'A pattern?'

'I swear it. A pattern. I swear it by the highest rock. By my home-stone.' He remembers the lines curling over everything, everyone, his mother becoming dust even as he told her to run. None of them would listen. He remembers the pain as the pattern-lines wrapped him too, the agony as the scars of the old pattern – the illness that had made him Many, had flared into angry echoes of their old form and burned the new marks from him.

Even in the midst of this remembered suffering Sarmin can wonder – how can this be memory? This boy was cured of the Pattern Master's curse. I saved him.

The soldier barks a command and steps back. He waves to the left and with a tug of the rope Gallar is led deeper into the woods. They pull him choking through a wall of thorny bushes into the beaten-down circle at their midst. Two white-helmed soldiers stand guard over a hunched figure crouching at their knees, a stick figure in wet rags, hands bound at the wrists to a heavy wooden yoke across its shoulders. The prisoner looks up as Gallar stumbles in, bright eyes staring at him through a dirty straggle of hair.

'Megra!' he gasps.

'I know my name, boy.' And her gaze returns to the leaf mould and broken thorns.

'You ran and left us!' Gallar spits the words at old Megra, crouched in the tatters of the woollen shift she had always worn so proudly.

'Stayin' wouldn't have helped,' she mutters, eyes bright behind grey straggles. A dark gap stands where one of her teeth should be, old blood at the corner of her mouth. 'A hundred winters and I still got my teeth,' the Megra had been wont to boast. His Ma used to whisper the Megra was a lot more than a hundred winters and that she stole her teeth from corpses. Whatever the truth, she has one fewer now.

The soldiers thrust Gallar to the ground, broken thorns jabbing through his leggings as he falls. He gathers himself up and crouches opposite the old woman, pausing to pull prickles from his hands then wipe the rain from his face. He tries to take the noose from about his neck but one of the men barks at him, lowering his spear.

'You could have told Hound Marka . . .' Until this moment, until he actually sees her, Gallar has accepted the Megra's treachery, but now she lies within arms' reach he can no longer credit it. The woman had watched Hollow grow, known its children from birth to death, and their children after them.

'Hound Marka paid more attention to birdsong than to me. Woken in the night he would have thrown me from his hall.'

'You could have tried! Someone would have listened.'

'Did they listen to you?' The Megra shakes her head. 'Hollow would have argued until dawn and died all the same. The rock clans won't leave their home-stones on the say-so of an old woman.'

He wants to shake her, to hit her, the need for it itches across his knuckles, he wants to see her spit the rest of her teeth into the gloom. 'They'd listen to you before a boy like me. You could have done something.'

She shakes her head. 'The austeres were already writing their trap around Hollow when you came to my hut.' Overhead the rain beats at the leaves, loud and furious, running down to pour on all below in spurts and dribbles. The Megra hunches, old and frail, a knot of misery in human form. The rope itches at Gallar's neck and the memory of the sensation as it had tightened below the bulge of his throat makes him retch again.

Gallar wipes sourness from his mouth and says nothing. The Megra is right and it angers him. Her fear angers him, a worse betrayal than any other – that the Megra, so old, and tough, has surrendered to her fear. And now she hunches in the rain, utterly defeated, the pivot of old tales, a threat to scare children, just an ancient woman, soaked and waiting to die.

The people of Hollow would not have left. But even so, she should have stayed to try. The Rock Hounds would have waited on their enemy, stood their ground, the common people too. The Hollow had been watered with their blood for too many years to just leave it. None of them had any give in them. The sharp-angled language of the soldiers returns him to the moment as they exchange an observation.

'Who are these people?' Gallar asks, leaning in towards the Megra.

'Cerani.' Her hair hangs before her face, water drops forming and falling from the ragged curtain of it, forming and falling.

Gallar can make no sense of that. Desert men from the ends of the world, here where the mountains keep Mythyck from Fryth? He wants *to ask more but sounds of shouting, louder than the rain, turn his head towards the clearing. He stands, cold water running into the few dry places remaining to him. The Megra stays huddled as if she knows nothing good is coming. Be brave. He remembers the words from the Megra's ring and wonders why they come to him now, demanding to be spoken. 'Be brave,' he says. 'We're none of us just one thing.' It seems important to say those words, to remind her. Perhaps he forgives her too, but those words won't come.*

The shouts grow closer, several men, then a sudden silence filled by the drone of rain on leaves.

'What did the ring say for you?' he asks, wondering if the soldiers have taken if from her or is it hidden, or lost.

'Helmar gave me that ring,' she says, spitting rain. 'Long ago, before time corrupted us both. It said: You are my salvation. It still says it. A lie.' She spat bitterness with the rain this time. 'He's dead. He lived too long and now he's dead. Past any salvation. As if a twisted thing like me could have saved him even when there was a chance.'

And Gallar knows they are lost, he and the Megra both. She wouldn't be spilling secrets with the rain if they weren't about to die. He puts his hand on her shoulder. Rags and bone, soaked through, but there's something in that moment. Be brave.

A few seconds pass, then more rustling and two more dripping soldiers break into the circle of thorns. One points at Gallar, the other man takes hold of the dangling end of the noose and pulls him behind them as they leave again.

They return to the hanging tree, to the swaying corpses, running with water now. There are men beneath the tree, close to the trunk, faces obscured by the legs of the hanged. A score or more soldiers come pressing in from deeper in the forest, a nervous air about them, as if the rain doesn't agree with these men from the dry lands. Lanterns hang on lower branches at wide intervals, the rainclouds having ended the day prematurely. Several of the lights dangle from the hanging tree, one close to the face of a victim, black-faced, eyes bulging, the blood on his chin running again in the rain.

Still more soldiers arrive, these ones hurrying, barking orders or questions to the others. The men by the base of the tree turn and between them Gallar sees a clansman, on his knees, blood covering half his face from a cut high on his forehead. They jerk the man to his feet by the rope about his neck. A man of Rella by the look of him, only ten miles from Hollow if a crow flew above the Ridge of Tears. The officer who'd spoken to Gallar stands beside the clansman and now leads the other soldiers as they bring him out from under the tree, knocking aside the feet of the dead men swaying above them. They have bound his hands tight behind his back and already they're purple with trapped blood. The officer says something and one of his men slings the spare loop of rope from the noose over a tree branch.

'No!' Gallar starts forwards, only to find his own noose tightening as his guard holds fast. 'No!' He chokes it out. The Rella man can see what's happening to him – why isn't he fighting, trying to run?

The soldier reaches high, wraps the rope about both hands and leans back, letting it take his whole weight. A single short cry escapes the clansman. He staggers across the forest floor, drawn onto his toes beneath the branch. A second soldier joins the first and the man's feet leave the ground, his legs scissoring wildly, kicking up fallen leaves and wet rot as he loses contact.

Gallar vomits acid and falls to his knees unable to look.

'Get up.' The officer's boots gleam beside the watery yellow splatters of Gallar's vomit. 'Up,' he says again in his broken accent.

Gallar struggles to his feet, his legs almost too weak to stand. 'I didn't do anything.' His father would not be proud. His father would tell him to stand like a man and not beg.

'You knew this Fryth man.'

'No.'

'And now you lie.' The officer slaps him, an almost casual blow with the back of his hand, but enough to stagger Gallar and have him spitting blood into his hands.

'How many other Fryth are hiding in the trees?'

'None.' Gallar looks wildly for help he knows isn't there. 'I don't know.'

The man sneers at him, a wrinkling of his long nose. Water glistens in his sharp dark beard. 'I can't trust a liar. The old woman knows about the austeres. I don't need you.'

A quick command to Gallar's guards and the officer turns on his heel to walk away. Yet more soldiers have arrived, some setting up more lanterns, others tying a wide canvas to make a shelter from the rain, yet more rolling out rugs beneath it.

Someone important is coming! Sarmin wonders if it is General Arigu. The boy's fear infects him but an anger builds too. These are Cerani. His army. And Arigu has stolen them. Set them to hanging innocents, to killing men and boys in mountains and forests far from home.

'Wait!' Gallar calls at the officer's back. 'What—?'

The sharp tug of the rope cuts him off. One of the soldiers hits him on the back of the neck and shoves him forwards. Gallar falls into the mud beneath the tree. A man laughs, just a short bark of laughter, a little way off. And still the rain keeps falling. The echoes of the Many ring in his head. He tries to speak over them, heart pounding, it's so wrong, so unfair.

'I'm fourteen – I don't want to—'

Sarmin tries to speak to the boy, tries to offer some comfort, but he has none to give, and Gallar cannot hear him.

The rope jerks him to his feet, then off them, the pain excruciating, worse than he has ever known; stars explode in his vision. The scream *that needs to be heard won't come, can't come.* I'm going to die. *Raw terror chases away all thought. Sarmin's terror, Gallar's terror. Neither of them can escape the moment – both suffer the agony. The thrashing of his legs seems distant, the useless hands clutching at the rope around his neck, weak and belonging to someone else, only the pain is his, and even that is being taken away, piece by piece. He sees his Ma, at the hut door, younger, back when her hair was still like wheat and she sometimes smiled. He sees that butterfly, the one he dreamed of, failing to take wing. The sharp scent of white-stars fills his mind, a vision of them, a dozen of the flowers glistening in his palm, then only one white-star, just one, bright and fierce, rushing towards him from dark infinity, growing, filling the world, taking him home.*

Sarmin found himself on the floor, choking. With effort he relaxed the fingers knotted about his throat, sucked in cool air, choked and retched. His neck hurt. His hands ached. Looking down he saw his palms slashed red, as if marked by the rope that had hanged him. Hanged Gallar – he corrected himself. He sat up, spitting dust, rolling his neck, looking back towards the wall he had pulled the vision from.

'Arigu.' The name fell like a curse and summoned a cold anger. Sarmin had fought to stop this war, known it to be both foolish and wrong. But now he had seen it and his convictions ran deeper than bones. 'Arigu.' And he stood, ready to find Azeem, issue orders, demand action.

—I was a soldier.

'No.' Sarmin tried to reject the voice but his strength had gone. The Many would take him as they often did when he slept or lay exhausted.

—I sailed the Blessing ten years and seven.

The Many came whispering from the back of Sarmin's mind, diminished now by the emptiness of Beyon's tomb – but still they were the Many, whole lives, hundreds of personalities left stranded by the Unpatterning, lost and lorn, without form or voice, his to hold, his people. They surfaced from the depths of imagination, insinuating themselves into his thoughts as if they were new ideas or sudden memories. In the cartodome the walls held a painting, a work of the Yrkmen, made in coloured oils on stretched canvas and executed with such skill that a man might think it a window onto some distant place. Beyond clifftops the painter showed the vastness of the sea, as wide and unknown as the empty desert. And on that endless expanse of heaving foam-flecked water, a lone ship, its motion captured in the stillness of oils, tossed by waves.

When the Many came at night, when Sarmin's mind sought sleep, he felt like that ship, alone and without anchor in a place far from any surety of solid ground.

—I hammered pots of copper and plates of silver in the Street of – I knew a girl from Honna Province with hair like dark water falling – Mine was the truest heart that man had ever known – Four times I bore a child and none drew breath – I ran from – I killed – I loved—

The tide rose and lifted Sarmin from all thought or care.

Sarmin regained himself in a cold dark place. He found himself hunched, turning some smooth object in his hands. *The Ways.* Only in the Ways could a man be cold in Nooria. One of the Many had brought him here from his room, taking the secret door and the staircase that spiralled down within the thickness of the walls until it reached the tunnels. He shifted and his shadow moved. He shifted again and turned towards the lantern set behind him on the rock.

Sarmin's hands held a skull, fingers hooked through its dark sockets. He almost dropped it but some instinct made him keep hold. He looked around, trying not to feel the smoothness of the bone between his fingers. The walls stood straight, dressed with blocks of stone. *Not the Ways then, but still some deep place. The dungeons?* Had he come through a hidden door into the oubliettes? He made a slow circle, still crouching. The cell rose high above him but he would not have space enough to stretch his arms wide and still make the turn. The narrow door stood ajar: old wood, inches thick and black with age. Sarmin rotated the skull to face him. *Someone more forgotten than ever I was – with no comfort but cold stone, no bed or books, no window, no freedom but death.* Had one of the Many brought him here to silence his recriminations with shame? To make him face up to his duties? Perhaps one of the sets of memories that seethed within his mind had once been entirely confined behind the dark eye sockets that now regarded him.

Silence wrapped him. No sound from any others unremembered in their tiny cells, nothing of the palace's clatter and stamp reached down this far, no cry of Tower mage or hawks' keening, just time sliding past unheard, by second, minute and year. He had ordered the dungeons emptied. If their crimes were as forgotten as the prisoners then they were freed, or executed if their crimes were remembered and not forgiven – but each man saw the sky, and spoke with an acolyte of Herzu on the wall-tower where the wind comes in from the desert. And so he was alone, the cells abandoned.

Sarmin set the skull before him, wincing at the clack of bone on floor slab. The sea of the Many had stranded him on strange shores before, but none so lonely as this. He sat still and let his eyes explore the stonework with that same inten-

sity which once found every angel and each devil in the detail
of his own prison walls. Time's river flowed. Twice the lamp
guttered but did not die, and at last Sarmin's gaze settled
upon a stone in the wall . . . in the wall, but not of the wall.
It drew him to his feet and he worked it free by fractions of
an inch, breaking nails and skinning a fingertip. At last he
held it, a dark smooth stone, one edge disguised with dirt and
dust to better match the wall. It had a weight to it, more than
such a stone should, and a warmth . . .

When the sound came, Sarmin took it for the return of the
Many, but they held their peace, perhaps kept back by
whichever of them had walked Sarmin to the oubliette in the
first place. *Again!* The scrape of shoe on floor-slab. Sarmin set
the stone dead centre of the cell on the floor beside the skull,
slid the hood across his lantern, and sat behind the door with
his back to the cold wall. Footsteps approached but the Many
came faster, some new person from among the unreturned
now overwriting him like sudden inspiration. *No—*

'Are you well, Magnificence?'

Sarmin shook his head and found focus. His mind had gone
silent and the oubliette, skull and stone had been replaced by
soft silk, feather mattresses and a harem girl, pale as milk
with golden hair, naked and smiling. A pre-dawn light filtered
down from tiny windows high above.

Silk covers slid from Sarmin as he sat, pooling around his
hips. He too was naked.

'Who?' He stared at her, finding her face and knowing it to
be familiar. 'You're a slave?'

'They call me a concubine.' She pouted, rolled to her front,
then grinned. 'But I'm a princess when you are with me, My

Emperor.' Her words came sharp and angled, exotic as her looks.

He knew her then, a slave from the north, one of many such offerings made by some or other lord who curried his favour. Grada had gone to find out more about them. She would find information about these women, these gifts from his courtiers, and then she would return to him. A sharp longing for her twisted his hands in the silk. 'Your name?' he asked the girl who was not Grada.

'Jenni, My Emperor.'

Jenni then. By the blue and white of the walls, shown here and there in the glow of jewelled lamps, Sarmin knew it to be the Ocean Room. Mesema's old room. The unreturned stole his nights and haunted his days, but never had they taken him so far from the life he had chosen. Never had they taken him so far from his wife, from Pelar, from Grada. 'Where are my clothes?'

What had he said to her? Or rather, what had been said with his mouth?

Jenni slipped from the covers and went to gather his robe and slippers. Watching the lamps' glow move across her slim body an echo of want rang through him – just an echo, though. It had been another man's desire, just as she had taken another man's lust. A voice rose from the silence, soft and low.

—You should have her killed.

The advice Beyon would have given. Beyon's body-slaves had died to keep his secrets. It wasn't the story of their coupling that begged the girl's death; that would earn him Mesema's disappointment, but Sarmin had far more damaging tales to tell. Just a handful of words whispered in coitus and passed on could see him dead and his brother Daveed with him; both of them given to the old Knife in new hands, and baby Pelar set upon the Petal Throne.

'Should I dress you, My Emperor?' Jenni smiled and reached towards him.

'No.' *Better run, girl.* 'Just go. And say nothing of this to anyone.'

'My Emperor.' The smile fell away and she went swiftly into her obeisance, the lamplight throwing the knobs of her spine into a relief of light and shade.

Sarmin waited for her to leave and then found his path to the Ways through the hidden door in the corridor. These secret doors were better locked now and new doors of iron sealed key junctions within the Ways, but all of them surrendered to the emperor's own key. Mesema's chambers were so near that he heard Pelar crying out for his milk. The sound cut through him like Grada's knife, and in the darkness, as the hidden door closed behind him, he leaned against the wall and covered his eyes. *Mesema.*

Blind, Sarmin found the way with outstretched fingers and with his first step wondered how a man who could not rule himself might speak for a nation and heal the emptiness that threatened to consume them all.

20

Rushes

Silver trays lined up in the Little Kitchen, gleaming in the lantern light: evening meals for generals and scribes. Rushes hoped that if she grabbed the first one and hurried out as quickly as possible, Gorgen wouldn't notice her. 'Who's this one for?' she whispered urgently to Hagga, but Hagga didn't answer, her mind on other things as she shaped the bread for the next meal.

And then Gorgen was there, pressing against her from behind, drawing his hand over the small of her back, still bruised from the beating she had received. 'That one is for General Lurish,' he said, leaning down, his breath tickling her ear.

She stepped away from him and gathered up the tray, trying to turn towards the door, but Gorgen caught her elbow. She tensed her fingers around the silver and wine sloshed over the edges of the blown glass. Unbidden, Marke Kavic of Fryth came to her mind; the way he had defended her, like a sister or a friend. But the austere – he had been like Gorgen, except smarter. Trickier.

Fingers pinched her skin. 'Has Mina been sneaking around in the root cellar?'

Rushes swallowed. 'No.' She wondered whether he knew about Mylo and the secret meetings, or had simply discovered some missing food.

He accepted the lie, for the moment. 'What about you?'

'No. Please, Gorgen, I'll be late!' She made herself meet his gaze, opened her eyes wide to show him how honest she was.

It was no good. He took the tray from her hands and bowed his head as if he was sorry, but he was not sorry. He was glad. 'You're going to get it.' He pulled her down the corridor, past the steps to the dungeon. The entrance stood empty and cold but the thick wooden door drew her eye. She dragged her feet, but Gorgen only pulled harder. Sahree's stone was still down there. It called to her at night, when she tried to sleep. She imagined holding it in her pocket, the weight of it at her side. Imagined feeling safe.

Gorgen pulled her into a storeroom where the shelves were loaded with dried fruit, flour and nuts. With so few in the Little Kitchen the shelves had fallen into disarray. Rice scattered over the wooden floor drew her eyes up, to where a bulging sack tipped forwards, ready to spill. Gorgen would be in trouble if it fell; Naveen might beat him hard. She was about to say something when he shut the door and cast the room in darkness.

She backed away, bumping her shoulders against a cask. If only she could hear his thoughts, know his mind. 'What did I say, Gorgen?'

'You said you didn't go down to the cellar,' he said, but his voice sounded strange, muffled. 'But a fine lord tells me you were running from there the other night. Crashed right into him, dirtied his silk robes.'

'I don't remember that,' she lied, listening to the sounds

from the hallway. If only Marke Kavic would return for wine and a little bread, as he had before.

'I remember your voice, Rushes. When we were all together, like that. Happy. You remembered things. Butterflies and little flowers. It was so real. And now you lie to me.' He turned towards her; she could tell from his breath on her cheek, and she flinched away. *Happy.* She remembered Beyon in his tomb, his hand empty, no knife. How did he cut his throat with no knife? *Look*, she had sent to the Master, communicating her delight. *It is done.* She cast off the memory.

'Mylo is a bad person. An enemy. You should not have lied about being there. Those Mogyrks will all be hanged once I tell on them. But I won't say anything about you.'

You beat me and you insult me. You hate me. But she knew it wasn't true. She had always feared this, feared learning that he wanted more than just to hurt her. Rushes tried to take a step back and found the cask again, pressing between her shoulder blades. The olive oil within it made a sloshing noise. 'Why?'

'I remember your voice,' he said again, sounding like a little boy. 'Why do we all have to be alone now?'

It was a question they all wanted answered, all the Unpatterned. The loneliness was sometimes unbearable, it was true, but it didn't make Gorgen what he was. Though she had not known him before the Pattern Master came, she judged that he had always been this way. 'We're supposed to be alone.' And he would have to get used to it; nobody would want to be with him.

He grabbed her hand, too tightly. 'Well I don't want it. You're a horsegirl. Do what you horsegirls do.'

'I'm not a horsegirl. I'm a kitchen slave.'

His hands pushed down on her arms now, keeping her still, so she couldn't run away. 'You Felt girls will roll in the grass with any Rider, but you come down here and put on airs.'

'What are you doing?' She struggled to get away. 'Stop it.'

'Do what I say, or I tell the low vizier where you were.'

'Stop it.' Vomit rose in her throat. She remembered Lord Zell's hand on her thigh, and the look on his friend Anut's face, heavy-lidded and intense. It had felt just like this: wrong, shameful. The same fright took hold of her as it had then, and she tried to push him away. It felt as if she were pushing a rock.

Something inside her grew still. When she'd been one with the Many, she heard their voices as a constant chatter in the back of her mind, but when help was needed, always a singular voice came forwards. *I was a cook. I was a fisherman. I was a thief.* She just needed to remember one voice, one history. *I was an acrobat.* Through that One she felt Gorgen's hand on her right arm, the space between herself and the door, the strength in her legs. She brought up her foot and pushed him away, and he fell backwards, making a little gasp of surprise. *I'll get it, now.* Quickly she ran to the door and out into the corridor, hearing the rice behind her, falling in a stream from the high shelf. He would blame her for that too. *They'll catch me, Gorgen and Naveen and Back-door Arvind, and when they do, they'll kill me.*

Rushes ran to the steps that led to the dungeon. Halfway down the hall a patrolling Blue Shield was just turning her way. Her shoes were soft; he hadn't heard her. He picked at his fingernails as he walked, the picture of boredom, but soon enough Gorgen would enlist him in the hunt. *The stone. I need the stone.* She scrambled down to the heavy door. It was not locked.

It was late; the priests had long ago returned to their dark temple and the dungeon stairs stretched down into a black emptiness. She could not be trapped here. She knew every entrance to the Ways, even from the bottom of the world – or at least, she thought she did. Sometimes the palace spread out in her mind like the face of an old friend, hidden paths, forgotten rooms and all; at other times, she had only a sense of where to go.

She entered and pushed the door closed behind her, shutting out all light. She wondered why she didn't hear Gorgen chasing her. Perhaps he was sneaking right behind her. She felt in the darkness for a bar or a lock, but then she remembered: that was not how a dungeon worked. A person could be locked in, but not locked out. She descended the stairs, shaking, listening for his angry breathing, the air moving around his fists.

These stairs were more uneven, and steep, than she expected. Rushes had to press flat hands against the smooth stone at the sides to keep from tumbling. She moved through the dark, but it lay blacker still below her; sunlight never touched these walls. She slowed her steps, taking more care. Far beneath, someone moaned. She suppressed a whimper.

In time it grew so dark that she was forced to sit on the cold, gritty stairs and scoot her way down. A scent of mould and wet stone rose around her. She moved in the blackness for so long she had time to think about how she had run. Maybe she shouldn't have. Maybe if she had stayed, Old Hagga would have spoken up for her. Or maybe not. She wondered what Gorgen would do to her this time, or whether he might feel sorry. Perhaps he would act as Mylo preached and forgive her. If only Emperor Beyon were still alive, she would feel safe.

She scooted one more step, and found herself on the floor with her legs splayed out in front of her. She began to crawl, feeling her way across the room. This wouldn't work; she would never find the stone this way. She gasped when her hand found a pool of icy water and decided to stand, using the wall as a guide. Where were the guards? Had all the prisoners truly been taken by Herzu?

No. *Someone* had moaned.

She felt her way through a doorway, and then her hands were trailing against iron bars. These were the cells. She listened for prisoners, but heard none. Perhaps they kept still and listened to her breathing, the brushing of her skirts against the iron . . .

The bars ended. Once again her fingers ran against stone, and then the stone took her around a corner. At last, in the distance, she saw flickering light. Her steps slowed and she watched with caution. Anyone could carry that lantern. A guard, a prisoner, another person running away like herself. Stealth was key. *I was a thief. Keep to the shadows, keep quiet.*

Rushes crept forwards. Whoever held the lantern was not moving. He, or she, was sitting in an open cell, waiting. Fear overtook her. What would she see there? Images from the Many filled her mind. Bodies, cut apart, naked and cold. Couples writhing together, or pleasing themselves in less conventional ways. Sick, starving or injured people, desperation making them quiet. As she drew close, her shoe scraped against an irregular stone. She stopped, but someone had heard her; the lantern went dark and a scuffling whispered against the walls.

Did someone approach? She listened with all her mind, but no sound reached her except for the distant drip of water.

'I know you came for it,' said a man, somewhere ahead of her in the dark, 'but it's mine.'

The voice sounded familiar. Rushes stood where she was, saying nothing.

'It's mine!' he said again.

She opened her mouth to speak three times before she found her voice. 'You mean the stone.'

'He's taken everything from me, except the stone. I'm keeping it.'

A madman. She backed away. 'I won't take it from you,' she said. 'I was only scared, and I thought that stone would help me.'

'The stone can't help you,' he snarled. The light reappeared and swept across the walls and iron bars, as if the speaker waved the lantern like a flag. Rushes backed away.

'It won't work for you,' he said. 'For him it will, but I won't let him have it.'

'I said I wouldn't take it from you. Please, I promise.'

The light moved again and a slender man emerged from the cell. He held the lantern low and to his left, so that his face was in shadow but his blue robes and the elegant belt around his waist were brightly lit. He stopped and cocked his head, studying her, before crouching down upon the stones and putting the light in front of him. She saw his chin and the lines of his cheekbones, and drew in her breath. The emperor.

'Red-Rose,' he said, leaning forwards, showing his eyes, wild and gleaming. 'Why didn't you tell me it was you?'

She let out a breath. Emperor Beyon had called her Red-Rose. Had he told his brother? Surely he meant to be kind if he called her by that name, though her body believed otherwise, shaking so badly that she had trouble getting down on her knees. 'I did not recognise Your Majesty.'

He said nothing to that, only turning to look at the grey walls. 'Are you a prisoner?' he asked. 'Did I send you here?'

'No, Your Majesty. I came here myself.' She prostrated herself on the cold granite, praying to Mirra he would leave her there, that he would pick up his lantern and go on with his strange business, whatever it was.

'Why?' His voice carried a command within it, clear as any whip. 'For my stone?'

A cold sweat ran along her skin; her stomach roiled. 'No. I ran from the Little Kitchen, Your Majesty.'

'Why?' he asked again.

She opened her mouth, but found her tongue too heavy to speak. Her shaking grew worse, as if the rock below her shuddered and heaved.

And then the metal of the lantern clanged beside her and she felt his hands, warm and soft, pulling her upright to face him. He put a finger against her cheek and she froze, the terror digging deeper now, bringing bile to her throat. 'Red-Rose,' he said, 'what have they done to you?' The way he spoke reminded her of another man, another time, as if someone else watched her from the emperor's eyes.

She said nothing – could say nothing – but his eyes were like the Many, bringing forth all the pieces she'd hidden away. Her brother; Demah; Emperor Beyon, dead, with the pattern around him; Lord Zell and his friend; Gorgen. They each fitted into the design of her sorrow, and as he held her gaze it made itself whole. A wail escaped her, a rough, naked sound that trailed away beyond the iron bars. Shame and regret made Rushes heavy, so heavy she feared she would fall away from his strong arms, through the stone floor and far into the rock, all the way down to where Meksha burned her secret fires.

But the emperor released Rushes and the floor held cold and steady beneath her knees. He stood and she recognised his fierceness, the set of his shoulders, ready to fight. His brother Beyon had always looked so before dealing his justice. But it was not Rushes he meant to punish; he walked away from her without another word, into the darkness from which she had come, moving quietly.

The emperor had taken the stone. Sahree's stone. Her luck stone. What could protect her now? When she had wiped away the last tear, she lifted the lantern and moved towards the entrance to the Ways.

21

Nessaket

Nessaket made her way between gryphons and gargoyles and past chairs and benches to the great statue of Herzu, gleaming in the light of high wall-sconces. His face looked down at her from a height of twenty feet, fangs gleaming, eyes fierce. The dead baby in his left hand looked downwards too, eyes blank. She had achieved little; Herzu was impatient. All Nessaket could offer in recompense was a sacrifice. She reached into the pouch where Dreshka had placed a dove for her, trained by the palace birdman to trust her hands. She took it from the velvet and it fluttered its wings, adjusting to its new freedom. She wrapped one hand around its body and twisted its neck with the other before climbing up on the altar to place it in Herzu's right hand. All was silent.

Tuvaini had once told her that he dreamed of Herzu as a handsome, tall man, not unlike himself. Perhaps gods revealed themselves within their worshippers, showing themselves both kin and stranger, human and deity, at once. Nessaket had never dreamed of Herzu; He did not favour her. She knelt on the rough mat that surrounded the altar. The stiff fibres below her knees were meant to cause discomfort and, over time, a unique pain. Nessaket prayed until her knees were on fire.

Once finished, she examined the dim corners of the nave. She did not see Dinar among the seats and statues, but this was not unusual; he often retreated beyond sight of the worshippers, his priestly tasks shrouded in power and mystery. This did not concern her. As Empire Mother, she had her own power; he would come. 'Dinar?' she called, moving to the side of the altar where a door led to the private chambers. It stood open but only blackness moved beyond it. 'Dinar!' He would hear her. He would come.

And he did, appearing as a darker form cut from shadow, a dream of Herzu himself, finally granted to her. 'You are here,' he said, as if he had been waiting. 'Come.' He moved back into the swell of night, beyond her vision, and she had no choice but to follow, blindly, feeling her way along the wall. For the first time she wondered what occupied his time beyond the altar, here in the dark, but she would show no fear. After a minute an open door shed light onto her path, and she could see Dinar ahead of her, his muscled arms hanging to his sides, his shoulders straight and square, a bloody knife in his hand.

No fear. She continued to move towards him and stepped into a bright, dirty room that stank of vinegar. Lit candles were scattered over every surface; the light flickered a sickly yellow and gleamed against his bald scalp. Besides the table she had seen, a desk and a chair stood against the wall, and a set of tall, disorganised shelves marked the far edge of the room. Every surface lay covered with books, melted wax and spatters of what looked like blood.

'I need deadseeds.' Deadseeds would take care of any unborn heir inside of a concubine.

Dinar moved to the shelves and tossed a book aside, then

two. Finally he lifted a ceramic canister tied to a rope and shook it. Nodding to himself he cut the rope with the knife and returned to her. 'Deadseeds.' He put the canister in her hands and regarded her with flat, cold eyes as he produced a small pouch and held it up for her inspection. 'And pika seeds.'

Nessaket turned the cold clay in her hands, heard the plinking of the deadseeds within. She had used pika to kill Tuvaini's lover Lapella and it had not been a kind death.

Dinar spoke into the silence. 'The empress sent a slave to fetch pika seeds of her own. But you hesitate.'

Nessaket thought of Mesema, her honest face, the way she spoke without thinking. 'The empress is not capable—'

But Dinar grabbed her hands and slammed them against the wall, holding them there as he spoke, his breath against her face smelling of garlic and bitter root. 'You think I will protect your son when you do not protect him yourself?'

The pressure against her hands grew intense; tears came to her eyes. 'I am the Empire Mother! I—'

'Empire Mother twice over,' he agreed, twisting the skin around her wrists, 'and what have you accomplished? Beyon satisfied his bloodlust here in the palace, but we could have done more. So much more. The whole world under Herzu's great gaze.'

Nessaket jerked her hands from his grasp. The pouch full of pika seeds dropped from his palm and made a soft landing on the floor. 'Arigu and I would have succeeded but for the Pattern Master.' All those plans, so carefully laid upon the pillows. Her betrayal of Beyon. For a moment she saw his dark eyes, the way they had been before his brothers died, when he still loved her. 'But that future has not been lost. When Pelar is on the throne, and Daveed his trusted adviser, a man of Herzu—'

'Why speak of the future, when today a Mogyrk austere wanders the palace freely?' Dinar stepped away. 'And when the emperor is ready to declare peace with him?'

'I have slowed the negotiations. But they will go on if steps are not taken. His wife—'

'His wife is more powerful than you? A tiny child from a land where the god hides away?' Dinar smirked. 'Perhaps so; after all she asked for pika seeds. Perhaps she will use them and your suffering will please Herzu.'

She thought of Arigu, gone beyond the mountains; Tuvaini, dead; Beyon, dead. 'How dare you? I am the Empire Mother.' It could not all be about suffering. There had to be something at the end, some reward, some reason for all the pain and betrayal and blood.

Dinar turned and walked out into the dark corridor. She lifted the pouch of pika seeds and followed him. He would not get the best of her. He came to another door, opened it and stepped in, and now she saw how he had occupied himself while she prayed. A massive golden hand lay upon the floor, large enough for two people to lie end to end in either direction, cupped for sacrifice. A man lay upon it, motionless and covered with blood; his eyes were closed. Dinar had peeled back the skin of his chest and secured it with hooks. What he had done with the reddish murk below she could not tell. It looked like the red, pulpy centre of a blood-orange. Dinar had sewn shut the man's mouth; behind the black threads that held closed his lips she could see cotton stained with blood. A chamber-pot scent mixed in the air with another, something of rotting leaves and dead things.

'You want to give your son to Herzu. You should see what it is you do not understand.'

Vomit rose in her throat, but she could not look away from the tortured man. He held a fascination.

'Look.' He held her shoulders and pushed her towards the prisoner. 'Look at the bone beneath his flesh.'

She followed the line of a colossal finger, eyes on the white solidity of breastbone. As she drew close the man screamed inside his throat, moving for the first time, his legs thrashing against her shin. 'He's alive.'

'What is pain to a dead man? Of course he is alive.'

She drew back and watched Dinar use his knife to clean dried blood from under his fingernails. 'Only by stripping away the flesh do we find the spirit of a man.'

She wondered if it was possible for Mesema to go behind her back, to obtain pika seeds in secret. As she herself had gone behind Beyon's back. 'No,' she said, 'love can be stripped away. Trust. That, too.'

'Yes.' Something in his face told her that he preferred to do it with a knife. 'When all is stripped away, one shines with the dark of Herzu.' He turned to her, smiling like a cat, his knife gleaming where the blood did not cling to it. 'Now you understand.'

Nessaket held the canister to her chest. 'I do.' Herzu demanded all or nothing – war or peace – with Daveed making up the balance. She backed away, out into the dark corridor. Dinar had forgotten her, absorbed in his sacrifice. Images flashed in her mind as she walked to where her guards waited: black thread through a bloody lip, bloody rib bones, Dinar's smile. The god grew impatient. The pouch filled with pika seeds felt heavy in the palm of her hand. Something terrible would have to happen.

22

Rushes

Hagga came into the Ways, calling across the blackness, her voice accompanied by the tempting smells of bread and apple. 'Come along, child,' she said. 'You can't hide in here for ever.'

Rushes pressed herself against the wall, though she knew Hagga couldn't see her. She'd found this little platform in the Ways when she was still with the Many. Stairs rose from the commonly used paths and led to a narrow ledge just big enough for her to sit with her legs drawn up. Perhaps a door had once graced this landing, but no longer.

'I'll leave this food here,' Hagga said at last, turning away. Her door to the Ways opened and shut, a bright flash of yellow lantern-light, and then darkness.

A trap. Rushes didn't move, though the flesh of that apple filled her mind. She listened for Gorgen first. He would be waiting nearby, still and quiet like herself, angrier than ever. At long last she let her feet down to dangle over the edge. Far below in the chasm lay bones upon bones, the new fallen among the ancient. Some of the Many had walked across that floor, picking their way between rib cages. Gold gathered there too, some coins so old that the faces stamped upon them were no more than legends. The Many had not been interested in coins. They had always let them fall, turning away, seeking something more useful.

She rolled to her feet, one hand on the wall. The stairs were just five paces away, and her shoes were soft. If Gorgen was out there, he might not hear. His silence frightened. He was one to shout and bluster, not wait in the darkness. Whatever punishment he had planned must be worth some patience. In all the whole day and night she had been hiding she had not heard him, not seen him, once.

A scuttling sounded below her. A rat, maybe, running between bones and over gold. Or a person. She remembered the emperor in the dungeons; remembered his wild, bright eyes. That too had been a dark, lonely place. She scooted down the stairs, peering into the darkness. The apple was closer now, just over the bridge. She could smell it, a smell of freedom, of trees and open air, but the bridge scared her, so narrow, and with a drop to either side. She fell to her hands and knees and began to crawl.

And heard a rustle, fabric against fabric. *Gorgen!* Rushes froze, but whoever shared the Ways with her moved off, up another set of stairs, on his own business. A coincidence. Not Gorgen. The rustle sounded again, this time joined by heavy breathing, and then a voice.

'You have the seeds?' A man, or so she thought. His tone was high, but commanding.

A woman answered. 'Yes.'

They carried no lights and spoke so quietly that Rushes had to creep forwards, straining to hear.

'What did you tell the priest?'

The woman spoke with an accent, hard on the consonants, akin to Marke Kavic's way of speaking. 'That the empress sent me. As you told me.'

'Good.' He spoke with relish, as if a tray of delicacies lay before him. 'All eyes will fall upon her when we use them. But first our slithering friend. The brother dies before anyone.'

'It won't be easy. I can't get near—'

'He will be bitten. A charm has been set. The snake will find him.'

'And then Sarmin the Mad.' She spoke as if she looked forward to it, as if the emperor had done her some harm.

'What did you say?' Rushes heard the cold reproof in his voice. The woman had overstepped, but she continued unawares, her voice firm with stolen authority.

'He told me himself he is not the emperor. That Beyon's son—'

Rushes flinched when she heard the slap. 'I told you that if you spoke of that again I would hurt you. See to the boy. Now go back before they notice you're gone.'

Rushes held her breath. If this man noticed her, found her hiding and listening to his words, he would kick her into the abyss without a second thought. Zell or Gorgen would beat her, anger guiding their words and their fists. But this man had neither anger nor kindness. She could feel it in him, an emptiness.

The woman was not afraid of him, though. She did not see what he was. 'And then you'll send me to Gehinni Province, as you said?'

'With a bagful of gold, just as I promised.' Rushes did not believe him. It came out of his mouth with too much ease, practised and smooth. 'Just remember your training in the desert. Stick to the ways you've been taught.'

The door Hagga had used swung wide and in the light of the corridor Rushes saw the silhouette of a large man, more wide than tall, and a flash of his scarlet robes. Then he was gone, and their corner of the Ways fell dark once more. As for the woman, she was moving up the steps, signalled by a soft shuffling and the whisper of silk.

Rushes reached Hagga's plate and stuffed the fruit into her pocket before following in the wake of her unknown companion. They moved upwards, the other person lithe in the dark, hopping easily over the missing stairs and the cracks in the narrow walkways. At the entrance to the women's wing Rushes ducked into a shadow, but there was no need. The iron door that should have required a key swung open in her direction, blocking her from the other person's sight.

She thought on their words. The important thing right now was the slithering friend. Someone had brought a snake into the women's wing, and they meant to kill the emperor's brother.

The Many were gone; the eyes that might have followed the mysterious woman through those gleaming halls did not exist. Rushes had to brave it herself, though they would surely send her to Gorgen after she found Empire Mother Nessaket. But Prince Daveed might be hurt if she didn't warn them. She tried to grab the edge of the door before it closed. Heavy, it slipped from her grasp, but something else stopped it – a piece of stone tile, placed near the bottom. Rushes waited, exploring the width of the crack with her fingers, testing the strength of her hands as she waited for the corridor to clear.

She took a bite of the round, firm apple Hagga had left for her. The sweet and sour taste brought a tear to her eye. With the Many one did not taste, feel or smell, not with one's own body. Perhaps if Demah had taken an apple with her that morning, she would have remembered that. Perhaps she would have felt that sweetness on her tongue, the juice tickling her gums, and thought that it was worth being alone.

The corridor in the women's wing had fallen silent. It took all of Rushes' strength to pull open the door and step through, and by that time the hall was not empty. Three concubines saw her and began to shout.

'Filthy slave! What are you doing, spreading dirt in our halls?'

She looked at her dress and her shoes. Dirt and moist stone had turned them grey.

'You need a whipping!' But they passed by, and did not call the guards. Things were not as they were downstairs. Rushes moved down the corridor, her dirty shoes sinking into the rich carpet, until she saw Nessaket leaving her room, escorted by six guards. Rushes slipped into a niche that held a seat with cushions, keeping her shoulder to the near wall, watching the men. There were ten guards in all and four lingered by the door, their attention on the Empire Mother as she walked down the hall, her black hair swinging against her shoulders.

They would never let her wait here. By the time Nessaket returned, they would have discovered her and dragged her down to Gorgen. She darted forwards and slipped behind their backs into the Empire Mother's room. Once there she took her place in the shadows between two wardrobes, far from the single lantern that cast a soft light around the mirror.

Madness. She would be killed for this.

No sooner had she pressed her shoulders against the wall than a guard entered the room, walked to a gilded cradle that had been set beneath the window and looked down. 'Sleepy tonight,' he said aloud.

'He loves to sleep.' Rushes jumped at the sound of a woman's voice. She had not seen her when she ran in. She leaned out and looked: small, with short dark hair, probably a nursemaid. When the guard turned she snapped back into the darkness, hoping he would not see her bright hair. He passed by without looking.

The woman sang a song to the babe, about ships fighting on the ocean and a child who floated away. Rushes listened, caught by the fate of the child on the waves, but also by the spray of salt water, the snap of the sails, and the clash of swords on a rocking boat. When the song was finished she remained with her eyes closed for a time, relishing the images, forgetting that she had sneaked into the Empire Mother's room. But soon she remembered how foolish she had been.

Perhaps the nursemaid would take pity on her, help her get back to the Ways. She in turn could warn the nursemaid about the snake. No one need know she was here, dirtying the silk rugs. She reached a quick decision. It was the best plan. The tiny woman, a servant herself, might understand.

She crept out, skirting the lantern, keeping to the shadow. As she neared she realised the nursemaid was sleeping, chin against her chest, one arm extended over the prince. Rushes paused, wondering whether to wake her. She might cry out, and then the guards would come.

Movement drew her eye to the window-screen, a shimmer of brown on brown, a curve where there should not have been one. A snake slithered in through the latticework; it must have come through from the balcony. Its head extended over the cradle where Prince Daveed lay sleeping, his chubby arms extended to either side.

She knew snakes; she knew them from the long grass and the summer heat of childhood days. She remembered her father sticking a long branch beneath a boulder and lifting a snake from its middle. 'Keep your distance,' he'd told her, his indigo eyes intent on the danger. 'Use as long a stick as you can find.' Then he took it away from their little hut, where it could not cause them any harm.

Rushes looked around the room. The only thing that resembled a long stick was the fireplace poker. The silk-clad all had fireplaces, though she had never seen one used. She lifted it and tested the heavy iron. She could not hold it extended for very long, so she would wait for the right moment. She crept back to the cradle and watched the snake's slow movements. It was only one third of the way through. It had not seen her, or did not think her a danger; she remembered one threatening her father, the way its scales seemed to shiver, the angry position of its mouth. This one was relaxed. She waited. Prince Daveed moved his head, just a little, and she tensed her fingers around the iron. She tried not to think what would happen if the nursemaid should wake up and scream, or if Nessaket returned and began to shout. *If only I had that luck-stone.*

At last the snake bobbed its head and slithered down to the edge of the gilded cradle, but half of it remained wound through the window-screen. She prayed to Mirra it would come all the way through before anyone moved and frightened it. She extended the poker, slowly, beneath the snake's middle, feeling the ache in her arm muscles, afraid of dropping it and waking the baby.

With a quick movement the snake dropped and just as quickly Rushes lifted the poker under its belly. *I'll be bitten. It will slide off and escape.* She ran to the balcony, threw the poker and shut the door. A dull thud came as it hit the wooden screen and then a clatter as it fell upon the tiles. Without pausing to judge whether anyone had heard she hurried to the screen and fastened the shutters. She backed away and leaned against the fireplace, counting her breaths until they slowed.

'Very good, Red-Rose.' The emperor stood behind her, his white robes glowing in the light from the single lantern. She stifled a yelp of surprise and forced her feet to stillness; she would not run, though every part of her wanted to do so. She shivered, recalling his touch. He knew everything – about her brother, Beyon, Gorgen – all of it. He had gleaned it all from her eyes that night. It made her feel sick, butterflies crawling along her skin.

In her fright she forgot her obeisance, but he did not notice, jerking his head towards the balcony. 'I will kill it,' he said, drawing a dagger from his belt, a twisted one, and ugly. He opened the doors, stepped out and disappeared into the night. She heard a scrape of metal on stone and he returned, grinning in a cold way, like the Fryth priest. 'It is dead.'

At last the nursemaid woke, looking around the room in confusion as she blinked the sleep from her eyes. The emperor leaned over her and gave her a kiss, but even in that affectionate motion Rushes detected an air of scorn. 'Little Mother. You may leave.' She gave Rushes a curious look before bustling from the room.

'I think we can do without her guarding skills,' he said, to nobody in particular, looking down at his brother Daveed. 'Look at this one. He is not so strong. Pelar will be the strongest.' He lowered his voice. 'Pelar is my son.'

'Yes, Majesty.' Rushes wondered why he shared it so intimately, like a secret. Everyone knew Pelar was Sarmin's son and heir. She wondered how he had killed the snake so easily – Emperor Sarmin, who had lived most of his life in one small room with neither snakes nor any other animal.

'I killed that filthy kitchen boy,' he continued, the grin returning to his face, 'I found him in the pantry and I snapped his neck.'

Cold claws held Rushes' heart. 'Gorgen is dead?' She thought of Gorgen, standing by the fire, talking, taking off his belt to give her a whipping. He had been terrible and fearsome, but always alive, with thoughts and fears and wishes of his own.

Rushes remembered the overfull rice sack, the kick she'd given. She went over it in her mind: the acrobat's memories, the feeling in her legs, the run for the dungeon, and then the emperor's fierce look in the lantern light, the set of his shoulders when he left her. 'Your Magnificence!' Her knees failed her, and once kneeling, she fell into her obeisance at last. Turning her face to the floor allowed her to hide the horror that must be written there.

'I said that I would protect you. I kept my word. Not like my brother.'

'Yes, Your Majesty.' But it had been Emperor Beyon who promised to protect her. She swallowed. She had imagined something, built on the ghost of a memory, but it was preposterous. Impossible.

He took her right arm and lifted her out of her obeisance. Emperor Sarmin was thin and wasted, but he loomed over her with shoulders as wide as his brother Beyon's. Rushes clenched her teeth against a scream as he reached into her robes, but it was a smooth-edged stone, the luck-stone, he pressed into her hand. 'He wants this,' said the emperor, 'and I can't let him have it. Throw it into the deepest part of the Ways where he will never find it.'

Who? Again she thought of the Mogyrk priest and his cold smile. 'Yes, Your Magnificence.' Her shaking hands wanted to keep it, to keep holding it. She put it into her pocket and it felt heavy, a reassuring weight at her side.

'I have kept my promise to you. Will you keep your promise to me, Red-Rose?' His dark eyes threatened. She remembered that look.

'Yes, Magnificence. I promise.' But in truth she was not sure; oddly, with Gorgen dead and the emperor as he was, the palace felt more dangerous, not less. She curled her fingers around the stone. It made her feel safe.

He touched a hand to his forehead as if it hurt. 'One moment – I will return.' At the door he said something to the guards, who looked in and saw her at last. Their expressions changed from dismay to surprise when the emperor commanded they allow her to stay.

Rushes watched Prince Daveed sleep and turned the stone in her pocket. It grew warm against her skin. The emperor did not return, nor did the Empire Mother. Eventually someone would send her back to the Little Kitchen. Would they ask her about Gorgen? She could not tell anyone who had killed him, nor would anyone believe that Emperor Beyon lived on in his brother's body. She had not believed it herself until he reminded her of his promise, though she had recognised him in the dungeon. Emperor Sarmin did not know her real name – Red-Rose – nor had he ever promised to protect her.

But he had changed. When he spoke with her she saw his anger and his determination, even to keep his promises. But he used to carry sadness in his eyes, and speak with kindness. That was gone. She wiped a tear away. Perhaps those parts of him were already in heaven. She remembered his grey skin, the blood pooling in his lap, the pattern around him shining like light through a window that pierced the world. Perhaps those parts would forgive her for her role in his death.

She waited so long for the emperor to return that she began to doze herself, and forgot to be frightened. When Nessaket finally entered, her face twisted in anger, Rushes remembered enough to cringe. She had seen that look so many times and knew what came after, the crack of flesh on flesh, the feel of fists against soft places, but the Empire Mother stopped an arm's length away and allowed Rushes time to fall into her obeisance.

After a minute in a tight voice Nessaket said, 'Rise.' Rushes stood and the Empire Mother paced the small floor, hands clasped tight behind her back. 'My son the emperor boasted of his kill,' she said. 'And he said you found the snake and rescued my son. Some would say that if you found it, then you are the one who put it there.'

'I would never do it, Your Majesty!'

'Do what, Rushes? You must say it.'

'Bring the snake, or hurt anyone, Your Majesty! Please, I am just a slave!'

Nessaket stopped pacing and stared into her eyes for a long moment. Rushes was reminded of the emperor in the dungeon, but this time her secrets were not laid bare. It was just the two of them, face to face, and finally Nessaket turned away and hit the high wooden screen. 'You are telling the truth – I can tell.'

'Thank you, Your Majesty.' Rushes did not allow herself to feel relief just yet, not when the Empire Mother looked so angry.

'If it wasn't you, then the snake-bearer has not been caught,' said Nessaket. 'There are so many who want Daveed dead, it is difficult to sort who might have done this.' Nessaket paced back and forth, muttering to herself, a frown marring her forehead. Eventually she stopped before the mirror. 'First pika seeds, and now a snake.' She spoke more to her reflection than to Rushes, and so Rushes kept her silence. As important as her information might be, she could not speak unbidden. Nessaket took in Rushes' filthy clothes, her soiled shoes. 'I know who you are. You're the girl I sent to listen. Now they say your master was killed, and you were seen running away. Should I send you back?'

'I did run from the Little Kitchen, Your Majesty, and I know it was wrong, but please don't send me back there. It's beatings, and worse. I'd rather go to the dungeon, as dark and cold as it is.' Then she sucked in her breath, trying in vain to bring all those words back to her mouth.

Nessaket frowned. 'I don't care what you'd rather! But if you can show that you listened, as I have asked you, I will keep you here – for now.'

Rushes cleared her throat and curled her fingers around the luck-stone in her pocket, wondering where to begin. 'Your Majesty,' she said. 'I heard them talking about the snake in the Ways. A man, and a woman.' She didn't know their names, or what it all meant, but she could remember their words, and their voices.

'Tell me,' said Nessaket, 'and you will become mine.'

Rushes began.

23

Nessaket

Someone had tried to kill Daveed, and it would happen again. They had not waited long after Pelar's birth to make their move, and they would not stop until he was dead.

Nessaket sat with the pouch of pika seeds. *One for sleep. Two to make sure there's no waking. Five to kill.* She had killed Lapella with five and she had not relished it. Yes, she had hidden in the shadows of a wall-niche and watched Demah deliver the candied dates, but not out of pleasure. It had been her plan and her responsibility. Eyul had said something to her once, long ago, when Beyon was just a boy. *Killing becomes too easy if you don't look.* And so she had looked, all the while until it was over, letting herself into the woman's room and standing over her as she died. Eyul had been right – killing had not grown easy.

Dinar had stated the price of Daveed's safety. Kavic's death. Could she do it again?

The mirror showed Rushes hovering over Daveed. Could she ask Rushes to deliver the poison? Perhaps Marke Kavic would trust her, see her as a fellow Fryth, and eat whatever she brought him. They could make desert candies. Pika seeds were bitter, best hidden in honey.

Or perhaps she should save them for the concubine from the Ways, the one who had brought the snake to her balcony. The one who had obtained pika seeds, and meant to use them. She did not doubt the specifics of Rushes' account. The girl had a good memory. Nessaket had tested her.

But which concubine, and who was her master? Rushes had described him only as cold. But just as the concubine was that man's instrument, he might in turn be obeying the orders of someone more powerful. If she chose to protect Daveed in that way Nessaket might never be finished killing.

But she could stop the concubine using other methods. Exposure. Blackmail. Threats.

'Let Dreshka tend to the boy,' she said to the girl. 'You should be in the Great Room, listening to the women. Find the one you heard talking in the Ways.'

'Yes, Your Majesty.' Rushes did a quick curtsey and left her alone with Daveed. Nessaket looked at the cradle, so very small, the child within it even smaller. So vulnerable. If she should die . . .

Could I do it again? She imagined the palace in thirty years' time, with her grandson Pelar on the throne and Daveed at his side, wearing priests' robes. She tried to imagine her son in other ways – as a trusted adviser, or perhaps a general – but she could not see him alive in those positions. Not in thirty years, and not in twenty. A priest was the best role for him, the safest role. She poured the seeds out into her hand. Five shiny red crescents. Just enough for one death, with no room for error. If she killed Marke Kavic, it would secure Daveed's place with Herzu.

Nessaket wished she had given birth to girls instead of boys. Her life would have followed a different path, and all her children would still be alive. She would not be counting pika seeds. She would be combing hair, giving advice, living in a softer world.

Had she never counted Mesema as a daughter? Over time she had come to find the horsegirl tolerable, but Mesema was too hard around the edges, too clever and wilful. On her first day in Nooria she had walked into the temple of Herzu, bold as a lion, and laid a hand upon the god-statue. She'd enraptured Beyon before Nessaket had even had a chance to speak with her or guide her; she remembered he came into the women's wing, nearly frantic that he couldn't find her.

She'd enraptured Beyon. Why had Nessaket never considered that before? Mesema had been with Beyon in the desert. Had they made love there, out on the sands?

It was possible – more than possible. And if Pelar was Beyon's son, then he, not Sarmin, was the emperor.

The shock of it put Nessaket on her feet. If it were true, then Mesema needed only to tell someone – Govnan, Azeem, Dinar – and Emperor Sarmin and his young brother would both be dead. Mesema would become the Empire Mother, and in controlling Pelar control the world.

And yet she took no advantage. Was she biding her time, waiting for some signal from her people or their Hidden God? It was difficult to know what to make of Mesema; she played by inscrutable rules, born in high grass, drawn from the wind with sky-washed eyes.

Nessaket replaced the seeds in the pouch. Whatever Mesema's intentions, she had honoured their alliance thus far. She deserved a warning about this concubine.

Nessaket checked Daveed's blankets. Lately she had become afraid that scorpions or fire-dust hid in the folds. There were many ways to kill a child and Nessaket could imagine all of them. She checked the balcony where the dead snake had earlier been laid out and where a guard remained to ward against further attacks, and gazed towards the roof, where Siri's garden lay dead. The concubine traitor would have dropped the snake from there, a violation to her old friend's memory, but also a mistake. If the woman had stood there, looking down at this balcony, there might be witnesses, or a clue. Nessaket ordered the guards to set watch over Daveed and headed into the corridor.

She felt exhausted. It was not the kind of tiredness that led to deep and restful sleep, but the kind that tore at her, pulled her down. The last time Nessaket had felt happy was with Arigu, and before that, when Siri was alive, when they spent long days on that roof garden, Sarmin running, little Amile laughing, every one of them trying to keep up with their beloved brother Beyon.

Half of Nessaket's men rushed to make a circle around her as she walked to Mesema's Tree Room. The rest stayed with Daveed. Once there she pushed past Pelar's dozen guards to where Mesema sat with her books at a new, shining table. Sarmin had taught her to read after they were married; Nessaket thought it a mistake. 'You should not read, My Empress,' she said. 'You'll ruin your eyes and get ugly creases on your forehead.' Was it because her son was the true emperor that she did not care how she looked?

The empress shut her book and put it aside with a smile. 'There are worlds in books, whole nations beyond our reach, with new gods and songs and stories. The only way to know them is to read of them, for we can never get there if it takes us our entire lives. I always wondered why Banreh loved his scratchings so. Now I understand.' Banreh was the new Windreader Chief. She spoke as if she was fond of him, and yet she pushed for peace – surely against his wishes. The girl was made of contradictions.

Nessaket motioned to the door. 'Come.' They made a tour through the women's wing, Nessaket and her half-dozen well-armed men, followed by Mesema, Pelar and their own guards. They passed slaves and concubines, a confusion of faces to which she could give no names. *Which one? Which one of you?*

The only way to the garden was through the room of Old Wife Farra, a corner room, large and well appointed, if in an older style. The door stood ajar, ready for visitors, though it was akin to putting bowls of bitter nut on the dinner table; nobody was interested. Most of those who had known and loved Farra were dead or gone. Her sons had fought Tahal for the throne, and lost; her daughters had married away. Most days she sat in her gilded rocking chair, lost in memories, rising only for meals. Dread turned Nessaket's stomach. Here was a woman whose life had shrunk to almost nothing. *How long before my life is the same? Ten years? Twenty?*

Farra sat up in her chair and squinted about the room when all of them entered, a confusion of men inside the soft room and then Nessaket and Mesema, in the middle. 'Who is there?' she called out in a quavering voice. Her body-slave, nearly as old as Farra herself, had been dozing on a long couch, but soon fell to the floor and made a clumsy obeisance.

'It is I, Nessaket, with your empress.' She walked forwards to where the woman could at least see the outline of her form. Looking down she saw withered scalp, wisps of white hair.

'Nessaket, Majesty.' Farra lifted her eyebrows. 'What brings you?' The Old Wife did not so much as look at Mesema.

'Blessings of the day,' Nessaket said. 'Farra, has anyone been up to the garden recently?'

'I don't know. I can't see . . . can't see much these days.' Farra sighed again, her thin shoulders drawing up like the wings of a bird.

'Where is the key?'

'Yes,' said Farra, folding one shaking hand over the other, 'you need the key.'

Nessaket sighed in frustration and looked to the slave. 'Where is the key?'

The slave stood, and with slow, shuffling steps she moved to a mahogany dresser with brass pulls. Mesema cast a questioning look at Nessaket. Of course she had not known about the roof. At last the old woman opened a drawer and pulled out a long and rusted key. 'It is here, Your Majesty.'

'Has anyone else asked you for it?'

'No, Your Majesty.'

'Bring it,' said Nessaket, feeling a buzzing along her skin that overwhelmed even her annoyance. She was about to climb those stairs again, see the old garden. The last time she stood there, it was to look down upon Siri's broken body in the courtyard. The day before that, Siri had wrapped Kashim in his burial linens, and Beyon was given his crown. They had loved one another, she and Siri, but not after that. And then Siri had jumped. Nessaket allowed herself to feel the emotion, just for a moment, and realised it was no longer anger.

The woman handed her the key and she turned it in her hand, feeling the old weight of it. Already she was lost in memories, like Farra. She opened the door for herself, the first time she had done so in years. The key made a grinding sound in the lock. She heard the mechanism tumble and turned the knob.

The stairs rose up, into the night. Nessaket climbed them, breathing in the open air, Mesema and Pelar close behind. Pelar made a sound of joy when he saw the starry sky above him. The stone lay cool beneath Nessaket's sandals. Statues of Mirra and Pomegra bracketed long flat flowerbeds set in a square around benches and a dried-up pool. The beds no longer contained flowers, not even dead ones. Nessaket poked at the cracked dirt. Siri used to carry up the water by the basinful, never asking the slaves to do it for her. She had always said that watering the flowers made her feel at peace. That peace had been broken long ago, but the attack on Daveed was nevertheless an attack on its memory.

A guard lifted his lantern and as the light ran across the roof-stone Nessaket caught a gleam of metal along the low wall. She pushed aside stacked clay pots and lifted a long-handled snake hook. It had been put out of sight, but not hidden. She would give it to Govnan, see if the spirits of stone and fire could tell who had held it. It was something, but she had hoped for more. She called for more light and searched for a lost earring, a scrap of silk, a hair-tie – but she found nothing. In sudden anger she threw a pot against the bench. It shattered, making a sudden sharp noise in the gloom.

Nessaket said what she had come to say. 'There is a concubine working against us. She has pika seeds and means to use them, to kill one of us and blame the other.' She did not say who was to die and who was to be blamed.

Mesema frowned. 'And the snake?'

'Her work.'

'Hm,' Mesema said, looking more thoughtful than frightened, 'Which one?' Perhaps fighting the Pattern Master had left her so brave that the threat of assassination did not alarm her. Or perhaps she had already known.

'If I knew who they were, I would have told you.' Nessaket turned back to the pots, turning them upside down and shaking them.

But Mesema moaned and stumbled forwards, her free hand extended over the low wall as she sought for balance. Nessaket jumped up and grabbed Pelar just in time to keep him from going over the edge. Perhaps the news had been too much for her, after all. Putting a hand on Mesema's elbow she said, 'It's too soon since the birth. You should not have climbed—'

The empress waved a hand. 'The Hidden God has shown me something . . . no. Nothing. He has shown me nothing. And such nothing . . .' She straightened, but she remained shaken. 'I am well. But what I saw . . . such a thing that is impossible to see. I do not understand it.'

Nessaket frowned. If the girl had seen nothing, how did it count as a vision? 'A deception,' she offered. 'Prophecy is unreliable.'

'Yes, that must be it,' Mesema agreed, putting a comforting hand on Nessaket's arm. The kindness of the gesture made Nessaket uncomfortable, as if Mesema knew some truth, and pitied her for it. She looked to the statue of Mirra, where the moon reflected off the marble with a soft glow, and felt there was something she had missed. She sat on the wall of a flowerbed and her guards took their places around her, silent, faithful.

Pelar lay quiet in her arms, another child for another garden. She should have honoured Siri by keeping it alive. She had been away from it too long, forgotten its purpose. Mirra honoured the children, the flowers and everything soft and dying in the palace. Siri had known it. It had not saved her, but she had found comfort here. Priest Dinar had always said a person must save herself, and it was true; but maybe Mirra could give one the strength to do it. She thought once more of Marke Kavic.

Could I kill again?

A cloud slid past the moon, casting shadows across the face of the goddess, and looking at those carved features for a moment Nessaket felt that Mirra's eyes moved in the darkness to settle upon her. She had never put much faith in Her, had seen her prayers go unanswered time and time again, but this once she felt she had received an answer.

No.

Dinar would not forgive her. Nor would Arigu, she suspected, should he ever return. She could not trust her son the emperor, nor his snake of a vizier, Azeem, who must naturally put Pelar first. The courtiers – those satraps, merchant princes, governors and generals – would sooner kill Daveed than speak his name. That left her with just one ally: the empress, Mesema.

24

Sarmin

Sarmin walked the corridors of the women's wing, treading a carpet of whispers. Dark-eyed girls from desert tribes watched him from alcoves, the olive of their skin inked black by nomad needles in patterns that were old before Helmar ever worked his magics. Pale women like Jenni from across the Jagged Sea, grey-eyed beauties, reed girls from the Blessing's delta, and more, more than he could know or name or want, some intent, staring, some languid, gazes sliding from him to the sleek-muscled sword-sons tight about him as he went. Past the empty rooms where Beyon's wives had lived, still vacant, all save one, though concubines lay elbow to elbow in the nooks and chambers of the harem. Such richness of colour and flesh could only feed the emptiness of his brother's tomb; it could not survive it.

Ta-Sann rapped lightly upon the door to the Forest Room with the hilt of his hachirah. In time a servant girl opened it, just a hand span, not looking out but glancing over her shoulder, brow furrowed with impatience. 'I've told you—' She registered Ta-Sann's towering, muscled presence, the glimmer of his yard-long scimitar. 'Oh.' And seeing past him to the royal purple of Sarmin's silks, she fell into her obeisance so fast he feared she might injure herself.

'I would see my wife and son.' Sarmin waved the girl up, though she could see only floor. 'Rise. Rise.'

'My Emperor! The empress is visiting the royal stables with Old Wife Lana to see her . . . The empress is absent, My Emperor!'

'I'll see my son, then, and perhaps Mesema will return whilst he and I are talking.' He hoped so; he could count on one hand the number of times he had seen her since the presentation of Pelar. A few short weeks ago he and Mesema had spent their days together, but now he allowed the Fryth negotiations to explain his absence. In truth forcing peace upon the lords and generals no longer seemed so great a challenge. They had used the last few days to launch a flurry of demands, but it would be a simple task compared with countering the threat from Beyon's tomb and laying claim to his own skin.

The servant stepped aside and Sarmin followed Ta-Sann into the muted greens of the Forest Room. Tree trunks rose in greys and browns along each wall, picked out in startling detail. By some artifice of the artist's craft the painted ceiling carried those rising trunks to dizzying heights before exploding into branches and more branches, each one thick with emerald leaves through which a painted sun threw dappled light.

Sarmin walked past Ta-Sann to the gold-leafed cradle where his son lay blinking. 'You know, Ta-Sann, I have never seen a tree. Nor has the empress. Sand and grass we know between us.' For a moment though he saw a forest, with rain falling in curtains in the gloom between the trees and dark shapes hanging from branches. Sarmin shivered, shaking off the memory. He reached into the cot and lifted Pelar beneath the arms, marvelling at the softness and warmth of the child. 'So tiny . . .' He shook his head. 'Are trees truly so tall, Ta-Sann?'

'On the islands trees grow taller than these, My Emperor,

wider too, and more wild.' Ta-Sann's low voice held a wistful note.

'Taller?' Sarmin addressed the comment to his baby and smiled, jiggling the child to find his smile's echo. 'Will you climb such trees, Pelar? You have a good start with a room like this.' He carried his son to one of the couches nearby and sat, cradling him on his lap. Little Pelar cooed to himself, looking about, wide-eyed, dribbling onto Sarmin's purple silks. With index finger and thumb Sarmin unclenched one of Pelar's fists and let it close again upon his smallest finger.

'What a grip!' He watched the baby's face. 'Do you see, Ta-Sann? An iron grip! Will he be a warrior, do you think?' *May I give him the chance to live that long.*

'I cannot say, My Emperor.'

Sarmin let Pelar's questing mouth fasten upon his knuckle. The baby gummed it wetly, the strength of his bite surprising. The emperor sat watching his brother's son, swirling a finger across his forehead to make dark curls of his hair. 'There's a magic here.' He said it to no one in particular and no one answered.

The child shifted slightly in Sarmin's lap and, in that moment, Pelar's face turned towards him. His gaze was unfocused, the dark and liquid eyes of innocence – Beyon's eyes, Mesema's eyes – and something quivered in the air between them, the ancient magic of blood and bone, father and son, so deep that beside it all of patterning seemed crude scratching on the surface of things.

Long moments and no words, only Pelar's sucking and occasional growl of complaint at not being rewarded with milk. Sarmin sat in the dim coolness of the Forest Room and understood a new thing, a thing not written in his books.

'Would you die to protect me, Ta-Sann?'

'I would, My Emperor.' Ta-Sann laid a long-fingered hand on the hilt of his hachirah.

'Why?'

'I was raised to protect the emperor. If you were to die and I still lived then my life would have had no meaning, my purpose would be spent.'

'You've told me this before, Ta-Sann,' Sarmin said. 'Today I understand it.'

Afternoon found him shuffling through the parchments brought by the priestess. Helmar had written something about a stone, precious to Meksha, in the foundation of the palace. Sarmin frowned, knowing he had read something about the stone before, or been told it, but the memory eluded him, fluttering away. He looked at his hand, cupped, as if it remembered the weight of such a stone. It might be a clue, a path to follow, to stop the palace from falling through the world like water through a torn skin. The bottom of his lantern held ashes. Was there something the Many did not want him to know? Had they used his fingers, held parchments over the flame? He laid a hand on the Knife, the one that had killed the Pattern Master, and looked down at Helmar's parchments. *You are gone, Helmar, but you left too much behind.*

But one of these parchments had not been left by Helmar. Lightly coloured and supple against his fingers, it matched his own supply from inside the drawer. Sarmin turned it towards the light from the window, the writing on its surface making no sense to him at first, an unpractised scrawl where he was accustomed to seeing a scribe's smooth lettering or Helmar's careful, looping cursive. When he recognised the words he dropped the parchment with a hiss of fear.

YOU are not the emperor.

It was written by the same man who had destroyed his *Histories* – but in truth Sarmin's own hands had done both, driven by another man's rage and another man's will, just as another man's lust had been spent in Jenni. Who was this man, and what did he want? A darkness welled in his mind. The Pattern Master had made Grada kill his guards and drive a knife between his ribs. How much harm might his own body do before he could wake to himself? He had woken Grada but there was no one to wake him. He ran his fingers across the scar she had left. *Grada. Where are you?* He longed to hear her mind's voice, but he had broken that bond, the last bond he'd had with any of the Many still alive. At times it felt as if he had cut off his own right hand.

Govnan shuffled into the room without announcement or fanfare, as if he were bringing a meal or cleaning the slop bucket. But looking into his eyes one could not mistake him. He was High Mage of the Tower, the third pillar of Cerana, and adviser to the Son of Heaven.

Sarmin tucked the note into his robe. 'Govnan.'

Govnan sighed, eased into his seat and laid his walking stick across his knees. 'There is little to say. The tomb dissolves.'

'And the austere?''

'I cannot know for certain. I see no pattern. He has not approached.'

Sarmin waited. Normally the high mage had much to say, and more elegantly. After a silence he asked, 'Can your rocksworn not replace what has been lost? Replace the stone as it fades away?'

'They can.' Govnan paused, and the space between his words told the rest. 'It only slows the nothing. Gives us a few more hours. My rock-sworn have not the strength. Had we more mages . . .' But there was no time to recruit and train mages, and nobody to do it.

And so it fell to Sarmin. There was nobody else.

But he did not know what to do, or if the Many would allow him to do it.

After a moment he noticed Azeem in obeisance at the door. Sarmin was not certain how long the vizier had been waiting, but now he stood and said, 'Rise, Azeem. How goes the empire?'

Azeem rose and smoothed his silks for a moment before speaking. 'The empire is strong, Magnificence,' he said, though his voice sounded wary. 'Only one small blemish on its proud face disturbs our peace today.' As he spoke Govnan shuffled out, leaning heavily on his walking stick. Sarmin thought to stop him, to ask more questions, but he knew the old man was at the limit of his power and beyond. He could not solve this. Instead he turned to Azeem.

'What is that blemish, Azeem?'

'Nooria has received refugees from a town upriver, Migido. Also from the desert. These people say—'

'Migido?' Sarmin recalled the bodies in the marketplace, the blood making a sickening pattern beneath the sun. Helmar's work. He looked down at the parchments on his desk and felt the world spinning. 'Nobody lives there.'

'The town was abandoned during Helmar's rule, it is true, but it is located along the river, where barges load pomegranates and olives for shipment to Nooria. Such a place attracts settlers. It was soon half-full with new residents.'

'And now?'

Azeem looked at the carpet, picking between unfamiliar words. 'Some kind of natural disaster, Magnificence. I cannot tell whether it is a sandstorm or a blight. The way they talk about it is . . . odd.'

With dread Sarmin remembered his dream, the grey spot that grew in the desert, devouring the tent and the boy. *Hollow.* Beyon's tomb. *An emptiness that devours.* Migido had been another anchor point for Helmar's pattern. How many had there been, in the sands and in the cities? How many wounds had been opened to the world? They could not move from the palace if nowhere was safe. He thought of Pelar and his brother Daveed, both so small and helpless, both so loved. 'Allow the refugees into the city, Azeem,' he said, his mouth feeling strange with fear, 'It is my order they be given bread, salt and water. Here they will be . . .' – *safe* teetered on the edge of his lips – 'welcomed.'

Azeem nodded, his eyes still on the carpet, his mouth twitching with the need to say something more, something uncomfortable.

'What else have you come for, Vizier?'

'Not I, Your Majesty,' he said, motioning towards the door. 'It is the Marke Kavic. He wishes to speak with you.'

25

Sarmin

Sarmin paced. Memories crowded his old room, and the story of his life ran across each wall. The Many clamoured at him with each step and in time he feared one would seize him, speak new words to the world with his mouth, have him act out their desires and their rage, take him once more to the dungeons or into a stranger's bed. Ta-Sann should tie him down. Now.

No. He would not allow himself to be taken. He would speak with Marke Kavic, begin to put a shape to the peace.

Azeem cautioned against an informal meeting, especially here, in this ruined room, but Sarmin had always longed for visitors before the Pattern Master came, and he found he could not refuse one now.

The young marke entered, flanked by three of his tall, blue-clad guards. They were flanked in turn by Sarmin's own sword-sons, hands on their hachirahs. In Sarmin's memory the room had never been so full. Sweat dripped down his back as he watched the marke make his obeisance. Soon the small chamber would become intolerably hot.

'Rise,' he said, too quickly; he imagined Azeem, somewhere behind him, pursing his lips in disapproval, and even more so when he said, 'Ta-Sann, your men can wait outside.'

'Magnificence—!' Ta-Sann looked with horror upon the Fryth and their swords. But the marke motioned to his men, and when they filed out to the landing Ta-Sann could not ignore the gesture. He allowed the sword-sons to leave, and at last only four men remained in the room – Kavic, Azeem, Ta-Sann and the emperor.

Sarmin eased into his chair with a sigh of relief.

'A fine evening to you,' said Marke Kavic, subtly rubbing the plaster dust from his cloak.

Sarmin was pleased by the man's informal tone, but he must be careful; an emperor did not make friends.

He remained silent until Kavic remembered himself. '. . . Magnificence.'

Thankfully he had not taken so long that Ta-Sann had drawn his weapon. 'A fine evening indeed,' Sarmin said. He looked at Kavic more closely than he had in the throne room. He had a strong but narrow face, and his eyes were a colour of blue Sarmin had seen once before – but where? He had thought the man young, but he was not so very young. Thirty, or thirty-five. The marke examined the broken walls and window with an air of appreciation, as if he found this room just as fine as any other in the palace, and Sarmin once again was charmed.

'Your Majesty, may I express my sympathy for the loss of your father-in-law. He was a great warrior. When he was hit with one of our arrows he was ahorse, urging on his fellows. I saw him fight and I was impressed with his bravery.'

Sarmin imagined the scene. His visions of the Megra allowed him to conjure the scents and colours of the Fryth mountains, the feel of the sun and the rain, the voices of the soldiers, the fear of death and the grief of loss. Only the sensation of riding a horse eluded him. 'Thank you,' he said, wondering whether

Kavic was moved to speak by affection for his own father-in-law. Did he have a wife? A child? Was he afraid for them – did he keep secrets from them? He could not ask, with Azeem hovering behind.

When Sarmin said nothing more, Marke Kavic continued, eyes focused in concentration as if he had memorised the words, practised them. 'Your Majesty, since our negotiations begin in the morning, I thought we might speak outside the hearing of our advisers.' The marke himself had only one, the Mogyrk austere. That he had come here without the priest meant something – perhaps more than Sarmin realised. Sarmin watched the man with interest, delighting in his strange accent and exaggerated politeness. 'Advisers have agendas of their own, Majesty. My grandfather is the duke, not I, but I am familiar with the back and forth that comes with rule.' He paused before finishing with blunt words. 'I want you to know that I am committed to the peace.'

Sarmin smiled. 'As am I.' He saw the other man's relief in the relaxed set of his shoulders. He wished he could ask him things, about Fryth, and about his life there. He wondered if Kavic had brothers, if he rode horses, if he knew how to climb a tree. Once Beyon had come to this room and Sarmin had thought of him like a new book that he could not keep. He felt the same of Kavic.

'Do you know the story of how we became a colony of Yrkmir . . . Your Majesty?'

Sarmin had read all he could about Fryth, once he realised he was at war. 'Fifty years ago your grandfather, the Iron Duke, held off the Yrkmen for over a year.'

'He did,' said Kavic, with a sad smile, 'and that is how he earned his name. Iron for his will, and duke where he once had been king. Our city is against the mountains, and a river rushes through it. My grandfather had everything he needed and would not come out from behind his great wall. It came down to fighting, and numbers. They had five times our men with more coming every day. Once they had my grandfather on his knees they made his people take down their wall, stone by stone. In its place they built one of wood, thin and useless. One that reminds my grandfather, every day, that we depend upon Yrkmir to protect us.'

But it had not protected Fryth from Arigu. Had the Yrkmen, too, been held up by snows, or had their First Austere decided to let the colony fall? Kavic had told him that story for a reason.

The marke said no more about Yrkmir, instead nodding towards Helmar's writings, scattered across the desk. 'Old papers,' he said, 'Majesty.'

'Parchments – yes. I am studying a . . . different historical matter.'

'That is a Mogyrk symbol, Magnificence,' said Kavic, the honorific rolling from him now with no hesitation. He tilted his head towards a particular fragment and Sarmin looked at the symbol drawn there, a half-moon suspended over a concave triangle. Sarmin had put this and many others aside as a mystery, but now excitement built inside of him. 'Do you know this kind of magic?' he asked, leaning forwards, watching the marke's eyes flicker over Helmar's work. 'Do you know what it means?'

—Put it away. Put it away now.

'It's my cousin who follows the path of Mogyrk, Majesty,' Kavic said. 'While my own meagre familiarity comes from attending rituals and feast days. These symbols of devotion are important at certain times of the year.'

'Devotion?' Sarmin remembered how the pattern had wrapped itself around his brother Beyon and stolen him, shape by shape, and yet this was Kavic's religion. He must be more cautious; Austere Adam could be using Mogyrk's signs to exploit the hole in Beyon's tomb, hollowing out the great city of Nooria, even as the emperor was being charmed by the marke.

Kavic waved a hand, as if pushing aside Sarmin's concerns. 'I have heard that only one pattern came here, Your Majesty. That is the same as one grain of sand finding its way to Fryth, for there are many patterns, and few of them do harm. Mogyrk Named everything and these are the Names.' Kavic motioned towards the symbol Sarmin still held in one hand. 'With those Names we can call upon the essence of things to aid us.'

To replace that which was lost. To rebuild. If Mogyrk's own death had made this wound then His own magic could heal it. If Sarmin could learn all of Helmar's pattern-marks, gain mastery over them, he could fix Beyon's tomb. Fix Migido. Fix himself. 'Better than our Tower calling upon fire and stone,' he breathed, leafing through the parchments, excitement in his fingers.

Kavic frowned and backed off. 'We do not subjugate anything to our will, Your Majesty, even the elements.'

He will speak to me of subjugation? Frustration and outrage together guided Sarmin's tongue. 'The Pattern Master enslaved his people, stole their memories—'

'The Pattern Master was Cerani, Majesty!' The marke blinked, as if surprised by his own words. Behind Sarmin Ta-Sann shifted; Azeem cleared his throat. Sarmin let the silence last. The conversation he had begun with such hope was now ruined. No matter how much he liked a man, he would never make a friend. He put down the parchment and waited two breaths before speaking.

'My wife is like you,' he said. 'She speaks the truth without thinking. I find it a valuable trait, even if those close to me do not.'

'Thank you, Magnificence. Apologies.' Kavic's eyes flicked to the vizier and away.

Sarmin imagined Azeem's sour face.

'No need . . .'

—the mountains, so cold – never wanted to hurt her, oh please, I just had the knife – there he was, grinning like a rat on feast-day – kill him – please, where am I? – home, see my little girl – kill him!—

Sarmin stood, so suddenly that the desk rocked beneath his fingers. 'You should go. We will continue this in the morning.'

—Kill him!

'You should go,' he said again, fingers digging into the wood. The Many nearly had him now.

Kavic made to kneel, but Sarmin waved a hand. 'Go. All of you!'

It took too many seconds for all three of them to leave the room and Sarmin came close to pushing them. Once they had gone he bolted the door and made swiftly for the decoration that spoke to him in memories, that had shown him the horrors of the war in Kavic's land. Gallar's death, throttled on a rope beneath a tree, still haunted Sarmin's quiet moments. He'd no desire to share more pain. But perhaps the voice would drown out the Many and keep them from turning his hands to other tasks.

With his fingers above the patterned wall he hesitated. Was the design the same? Had those dark lines made some subtle shift? There was a time when he would have known without a moment's consideration. The Many howled at him, a shrill chorus of wants and fears. His hand wavered, pulled by divergent needs, few of them his own. 'No.' And he set his palm to the wall.

The rain soaked through her shift quick enough, the goatskins underneath, thick with mutton grease, held out longer, but now she can get no wetter. The rain has reached her bones. There's precious little over them but papery skin these days. The Megra crouches in her misery.

Behind these memories Sarmin sits wrapped in confusion. The Megra was never patterned, surely? She knew Helmar, knew enough of his tricks to escape? And yet her memories are served before him. And are they even memories or is this now? White Hats in the Fryth valleys, nervous of a Yrkman advance across the borders . . . all of it fits with the likely chaos of Arigu's war.

The rain drips from her hair, tears for the boy. He hadn't known he wasn't coming back. There's some bliss in ignorance, but not much. All that effort following her through the high pass only to end his journey fifteen miles from where it began a similar number of years ago in Getrin Hallartson's round-hut, Getrin standing over his new wife as she struggled to push out a child she'd been too old to have. Gallar they'd called the baby. The Megra had been there, exchanging her herb-craft and common sense for two chickens and a sapphire smaller than the nail on her little toe. She'd slapped his pink arse and made him say hello to the world, told his parents some empty nothing concerning the favourable alignment of stars. She hadn't seen this end though, not seen it clear, but she knew it would be soon enough and not good, worse than the father's end, and the father's death was going to be a slow and lonely one.

'I don't care. I don't care. I don't care.' She whispers it to herself, beneath the fall of the rain. Even her voice doesn't sound her own, the

missing tooth changing it, putting a sharp edge on each 's'. Her mouth hurts too, a constant sick-making throb. There haven't been many hurts this bad in her two hundred years, nor a pit of despair so deep. 'I don't care. I don't care.' Two hundred years, few of those lived well, most of them spent as a wrinkled crone, and still she isn't ready to let go. There's a little bliss in ignorance. The Megra would trade in another fifty years to be ignorant of what she is.

'Knowing what you are doesn't mean you can change what you are.' That had been the first of the curses Helmar gave her, each wrapped like a gift, and she, being young and foolish and in love, had taken them all.

The Megra hunches in the wet, touching the pain of her missing tooth with her tongue, quick investigations, wincing returns. She supposes the boy hanged with the others. It fits the pattern. Helmar would have known, he would have been able to tell her before the child was born. It seemed he knew everything in those days. He saw the great design clearer then than when he came into his strength and they called him Pattern Master. He had been old when he first came to Hollow, a traveller bound for the pass, but a hundred years hadn't touched him. The pattern stands outside time, and through it, penetrating days and minutes as completely as centuries.

'A man can't truly see the pattern without being seen by it, without becoming it, and when a man truly sees what is written under each second, beneath each beat of a heart, then the days slide around him and no longer dare to take their toll.' That was how he put it. That was how he saw it back then. But even Helmar didn't see all the design, maybe no man ever could, and so time touched him, albeit with the lightest kiss, and with time he changed, soured, saw less and less of what once had filled his vision, until the pattern shrank to little more than a means to power.

The Megra looks up at the two soldiers inside the ring of thorns with her boys – both of them, nervous beneath their white helms and the scales of their armour, far from home, maybe a decade or two more than Gallar had to toughen them up. She finds it hard to tell these days. They all look like children, vicious stupid children dressing up in their fathers' armour, holding their fathers' swords.

'The day he left me Helmar held my face between his hands and said he would never see a woman more beautiful. He said I was his mountain flower.' She laughs, a harsh sound in her ancient throat. 'Told me he loved me and I would never wilt or wither. Told me he would set a gift on me.'

The two men watch her with distaste. One raises the butt of his spear. The Megra looks away. The Pattern Master's gift had soured, keeping her beauty only long enough for it to become a curse, for it to brand her a witch, a thing apart from her kind. She had wilted and withered both. Dying though, that proved to be another matter. But perhaps that too would come soon enough. Her own knowledge of the pattern was ever a crude thing, a knowing more felt than seen, as if discovered through blind fingertips, one corner at a time, but it was clear enough that whatever end had stalked her through the years was now catching up fast.

When the guards look away the Megra touches the wrap hidden beneath her shift. 'Be brave,' the boy had said, had dared to instruct her, barely dry from the womb and . . . and now dead. She slips the ring out, hidden in her hand within the veil of her hair. Helmar taught her to see past darkness lifetimes ago. That trick she had not forgotten. The gold gleams, ageless and without stain. Helmar told her once that gold, all of it, was made in a single heartbeat in the dying scream of a star. She had watched him pour the metal from crucible to mould, brighter with heat than it would ever be again. They had passed the ring between them before it cooled enough, giggling and gasping, tossing it one to the other before the metal burned their hands. She had clung to him, pestered, laughed, as he set the words there, stamping each line with a steel tool.

'What does it say? What does it say?' she wanted to know.

'What you need to know,' he said. 'What you need to hear.' Ending his sentence as every other with a quirk of the lips, setting on his words, seemingly so clear, a seal to render them inscrutable, as ambiguous as every part of the man, and past that quarter smile the briefest glimpse of darkness, so fleeting that it might only be imagination.

She snatched it from him then and read, devoured the words. 'You are my salvation.'

'What does that mean?' She laughed but the words set a chill in her. 'Salvation? That's silly. I should write that for you.'

He had taken the ring from her, folding it in his palm, too wide for a finger, or even thumb, too narrow for a wrist. He took it and left her with a kiss. 'My sweet Meg.'

In the dark of the forest, in the shadow of her hair, with the cold rain running and more than two centuries aching in her bones, she reads: 'You are my salvation.'

A guardsman's kick shakes the Megra from her thoughts. More rustling, lanterns swinging, shields against the thorns, and the officer who pulled her tooth strides in flanked by several men, all dripping.

'Up, woman. My captain has come. He will want to question this . . . expert. General Arigu is keen to meet the Yrkmen so let us hope your tale pleases us.'

Sarmin wants to stay, to watch this woman who once loved Helmar, to understand this war in his name, to know why Gallar died, but the scene is fading. The forest, the rain, all growing faint, reduced to patterns of sound and light. He tries to hold on but it's fingers catching sand and the moments slip from him.

Sarmin came to himself upon the floor of his room, on his side, one cheek buried in the dusty rug. A moment and he scrambled to his feet, urgency guiding his movements. The Many must not take him this night. Negotiations would begin in the morning and he could not wake in another strange place, his feet having moved along the path of another, his lips having spoken another man's words, his Knife . . . He remembered his *Histories*, stabbed a dozen dozen times, and felt a coldness in his stomach.

At the door he called for Ta-Sann and his fellows to bind him to his bed. They used elaborate knots of twisting silk, making patterns that belonged to great boats and the men who sailed them. Once secure he began to drift, the memories of those who were lost rising before him in the same bright clarity as if he had lived them. And in those images he saw one, something so recent that its smells and sounds came to him unbidden. His own hand held a parchment fragment, dark with age and covered with the script of the man who had once lived alone in this same tower room, a man who had also loved patterns. And what was written on that fragment was his own name.

26

Sarmin

'My Emperor!' The words came again, reaching past dreams.

'What?' Sarmin kept his eyes closed against the glare of a lamp close by.

'My Emperor, the vizier has urgent news.'

'Azeem?' It would have to be him, disturbing the first peaceful night in for ever.

Sarmin sat and shielded his eyes. One of the sword-sons loomed above him, lamp in hand.

'Is he here, then?' The shadows offered no hint of the vizier.

'Waiting with the council in the throne room, My Emperor.'

'The council?' *Some disaster must have happened.* The last traces of sleep fell away as Sarmin stood. 'Mesema! My son?' It was as if Grada stabbed him once again, the metal scraping against his bone.

'I have only been told to wake you, My Emperor.'

Sarmin reached up to catch the unyielding ridge of muscle along the man's shoulder. 'Tell me! I am your emperor!'

'I know nothing – forgive me.' The man bowed his head and Sarmin walked past him, the other five sword-sons closing around him, bracketing him three before, three behind as they descended the stair. The palace halls glowed with the light of hundreds of lamps as if to leave a shadow no hiding place. Not since the night that Sarmin wedded Mesema had so many lamps been lit. Squads of palace guard hastened by without falling into obeisance as Sarmin passed – only in war might such insolence be tolerated. Had Yrkmir's armies crossed the desert? Had the emptiness reached the palace, reached Mesema and Pelar?

The throne-room door stood open. A crowd of men had gathered within and was still growing while curious women were being swept out, a river of colour and silk. He caught a glimpse of Jenni's face, then others, just as pretty, all gone in a moment. Among those who stayed Sarmin picked out the faces of Lord Jomla, General Merkel and Herzu's priest among his acolytes, before they fell into obeisance like river-corn before the scythe.

'Tell me of my wife and child – tell me now!' Sarmin shouted.

Azeem rose from the sea of backs. 'They are well, My Emperor.'

'And my brother?' *Daveed. He has fallen into nothing!*

'Prince Daveed is well and with the Empire Mother, My Emperor.'

'What then! Why am I here and all these before me?' He swept his arm at the prostrate nobles. 'Rise! Get up!'

Azeem walked to the dais, opening a path among the priests and nobles so that Sarmin could ascend to take his place above them. Sarmin lowered himself onto the cushions. 'Speak!' He sounded like Beyon, infected with that same impatience now.

Azeem cleared his throat. 'The envoy from Fryth has been killed.'

'Killed.' Sarmin tried the word out for size.

'His throat was cut.' Azeem nodded as if it were a question.

'And his guards?' Sarmin pictured the two huge warriors.

'The one set to watch over the envoy is dead. The other and the priest were in a separate chamber. Both live.'

'And *my* guards? The men I set to honour my guest?' There had only been honour in it – the thought that the men of Fryth were in danger within the palace had not crossed Sarmin's mind.

'Nobody else was hurt. The attacker did not enter the room by the corridor.' Azeem studied the ripples in the silk runner that led from doors to throne.

The Ways! Was there a man of Nooria who didn't know the Ways since the Many ran loose there?

'Captain Shalla believes the killer may have gained access from the roof through a ventilation dome.' General Lurish spoke up beside the vizier.

Lord Jomla broke in with his high, sweet voice. 'Your Majesty—'

Sarmin cut across him and spoke to Azeem. 'And what of Herran? What does he say?' He sought the master assassin among the crowd. If any should know how death was brought into the palace it would be that one, Eyul's old master.

'Master Herran left the palace several days ago, My Emperor. We are uncertain when to expect his return.'

'Gone questing to find me a Knife, I imagine.' Sarmin tapped his fingers on the marble of his armrest. Master Herran had brought several candidates before him in recent months, trying to convince him to take one or other of them as the next emperor's Knife, but Sarmin would have none. *As many candidates as it takes*, Herran had said. 'Are none of the Grey Service here to answer me?' Sarmin didn't expect anyone to step out of the crowd but they would come to him in time.

Only silence for an answer, broken by the shuffling of expensive footwear.

'Govnan! Have the mages brought from the Tower, every one of them.' As few as they were. 'Read the stone, the water, air and fire. Tell me what has happened here.' He saw it in his mind's eye. Envoy Kavic amid the shallow lake of his blood, his throat opened in a long red slit. Where was their talk of peace and reparation now? What red words would that new mouth speak to Fryth and Yrkmir? He saw the sprawl of Kavic's white hands, the twist of his legs on a patterned rug. How wide would the lake of blood grow before this was finished?

In his mind's eye he saw Helmar's pattern-mark, the one that Kavic had recognised. How many others might he have known? Mastery of the pattern would allow Sarmin to heal the wound in Beyon's tomb, stop the emptiness from flowing into Nooria, but that would be much more difficult now with Kavic dead.

Sarmin rubbed his wrists. His bonds had left the faintest chafing. *The rope?* And in that moment a cold thought ran through him and left him hollow. 'Ta-Sann.' Sarmin beckoned the sword-son closer. 'Ta-Sann.' Repeated in a low voice. 'Did you untie me before waking me?'

'No, My Emperor.'

'How then am I free? Was the rope cut?'

Ta-Sann blinked, but only once. 'There was no rope, My Emperor, only grey dust.'

27

Grada

She's kneeling in the greenest grass she has ever known. The only grass she has ever known, though for a moment she remembers a dark garden, grass in short black blades, springy beneath her feet. The shadow passes over and the sun returns to press upon her shoulders. She's kneeling in the long grass with the squeals and shouts of other children all about her, unseen as they play. Her knees are green-stained, her hands clasped together before her, cupping something, trapping it. She feels it skittering against her palms, some thin dry frenzy of motion. When she parts her hands something escapes, bright with colour, patterned with dots and diamonds.

Grada falls back as the thing flaps a wild and stuttering path through the air, crashing into the ground, rising, crashing again. At last it pauses. A butterfly. She knows moths but this is the first butterfly she has seen, braving the sun, iridescent, beautiful . . . broken. She sees the wound, the ragged hole in its wings, and knows it to be her work. Acid bile floods her mouth and she spits and spits, but the taste won't go.

'Grada?' A hand shook her.

'Where—' She bit back on the word. The room lay in darkness, the only light from a lantern set on a stone shelf in the opposite wall.

'Time to go.' Rorrin said, moving into vision.

She swung at him and he caught her fist. The pain in her side stopped her struggling.

'Enough. It's time to go.'

'Your man stabbed me!' she said. He released her and she put her fingers to the wound.

'And Anx made it better.'

'I did my best. My mother always told me—'

'Your mother died before Uthman sowed Nooria's seed, old man.' Meere, from the shadows, cutting across Anx's meanderings.

Grada levered herself up, cursing, 'Torlos' pointy cock!' Meere and Rorrin must have come in while she slept. Only Anx had been there on her return from the Mogyrk service.

Meere sat on his bed, ready for travel, old Anx beside him, bones and skin in a faded black robe sewn with Mirra's hand. An acolyte then, at least once upon a time.

'Why did you stab me?' she asked.

'He said to test your mettle.' Meere looked at Rorrin. 'You caught me by surprise, things got out of hand.' He shrugged, lifting his hand towards his nose then letting it fall. 'You can't get the measure of a man without risking a little blood. It's the nature of the business. And besides, you got lucky.'

Rorrin snorted at that. 'It's your job to make sure people don't get lucky, Meere.'

Grada tried to stand, fell back, gritted her teeth, and stood. 'Don't,' she said, as Rorrin stepped to help her. 'Why would you do something so stupid?' She put her hand to her wound.

Rorrin shook his head. 'We should go to the palace and report.'

'I will see these slaves and where they are for myself before

I go to Emperor Sarmin, heaven bless him and keep him,' Grada said. She looked down at the stain on her robe. The lamplight made the dry blood almost black. 'His Magnificence will ask about this. Even without the robe he will know.'

'And I will tell him,' Rorrin said. 'I will tell His Majesty that if he will not accept Meere as his Knife, if he will not trust my judgement in these matters and accept someone he doesn't know to do his red work for him – then I must make a Knife of someone he does know and trust.'

'You overstep yourself, Rorrin.' Grada shook her head, confused. Sarmin might have the man killed if he came to court ... unlikely, but whatever the emperor did in her defence would tarnish him. The vizier, Azeem, had the right of it: she had no place in the palace. Grada took her hand from her stained robe, stiff with her blood. 'This could be the death of you.'

Rorrin watched her. A moth found its way into the lantern and beat its wings. Shadows danced across them as the creature spun and thrashed. For a moment she saw the glimmer of a broken butterfly. She opened her mouth to speak, but he forestalled her. 'It won't be the death of Rorrin. He is invention, nothing more. The death of me? Perhaps. But I am sworn to the empire and this is the path.' He looked to the others.

Meere stood, his head still wrapped in linens. 'I'm ready, Master Herran.'

'You'll stay here with Anx. Grada, with me.'

And Herran, master of the Grey Service and of the emperor's Knife both, led the way out.

As they moved through the plaza behind the palace, scattered with laundry tubs and waggons, Rorrin said, 'The envoy has been killed.'

'The peace envoy?' Grada looked at him, but his face betrayed neither concern nor fear.

'We need a Knife,' he said, 'tonight.'

They passed through the door and entered the back hall-ways. She could remember walking this way with a bucket of slops, back when Sarmin rode within her. For a moment she missed the emperor so intensely that she did not hear what Rorrin was saying.

'. . . someone small, through the roof vent. One of the girls' hands might show rope burns.'

'Yes,' she said, nodding as if she understood, and put Sarmin from her mind.

Their path through the palace led up, winding through corridors that ran with servant and slave, all wrapped in their purpose, part of the great industry that let the upper eche-lons lead such idle lives within an illusion of tranquillity. In time Rorrin led the way into areas reserved for Sarmin's guests and family. Many halls stood empty, used perhaps once in a year, visited more frequently by slaves hunting dust than by the silk-clad in pursuit of diversion. They passed the Red Room, a place scored into the memories of the Many. In the Red Room where the fountain plays, Carriers first sought to test the Knife. Eyul had fought the Many there and found patterned skin cuts as easily as any other.

They had passed the doors to the Red Room when a woman's cry echoed after them. A single wail mixing fear and resig-nation.

'We should keep moving,' said Rorrin, his voice cold, but Grada had already returned to the doorway and pushed it open. Against the far wall she saw the source of the cries: a woman huddled in the corner, arms shielding her face, while a man beat her with his hands and fists. He was silk-clad; she could see that much, though his robes and hair were dishevelled, and as she approached he turned to look at her. She could not determine whether his lips formed a smile or a sneer, or had found some way to convey both.

'This slave talked back to me,' he said, gaze flickering from Grada to Rorrin. The woman lowered her arms enough to look. Her eyes had gone blank and dull and her hair was stiff with blood.

'You should stop now,' said Grada, and the calm she heard in her own voice surprised her. A man like him could take more from a person than the Pattern Master. She had seen it when her father was alive, and in the dark alleys of the Maze, and in every other place too. The Many had carried their hurts into the design and she had lived enough of it.

'I am Lord Zell,' the man said, 'and I do not take commands from you.' The tinkling of water into the fountain's pool filled the silence. The room felt cool despite its hot colours, the fountain elegant and simple, a beautiful setting for such an ugly scene.

Another man stepped from the crimson folds of the hangings that covered each wall. A bodyguard, to protect Zell as he beat the slaves. She wondered what resistance Zell had met in the past that caused him to seek a guard. This one had not armed himself for the palace except for a dacarba, gleaming in his hand. Its sharp, three-sided blade was designed for assassins, but he was too heavy and thick for that profession.

'I suggest you take a command from the Grey Service.' Rorrin stepped forwards, a hand on his dagger. 'Let her go.'

Lord Zell looked from Grada to Rorrin and grinned. 'Grey Service? Grey hair – now that I believe.' He gave the woman a kick and she crumpled to the floor, curled around her pain. 'I like my odds against an old man and a woman.'

Grada tensed her muscles, testing the pain of her wound. 'You won't.' The blade that Meere had left for her hung over her ribs, over the spot where his knife had punctured her. The beaten slave drew in a shuddering breath and crept closer to the wall.

'We have no time for this.' Rorrin sounded impatient. Grada thought perhaps he should sound worried. What did it take to stand before a naked blade and not feel terror, she wondered. Rorrin must know the butchery a knife slash will do, open flesh gaping down through muscle and fat to the bone, blood splattering out in a hot, spurting rush. And yet it was the delay that bothered the master of assassins, not the threat, not the gleam of steel. Her gaze flickered to the woman, head bowed, crimson fingers staunching a bleeding nose; flickered back to Zell and the tight cruelty of the smile twitching below his neat moustache.

Without words Grada marched towards the bodyguard. As she entered his range he delayed, confused, then lunged, dacarba angled towards her heart. She lunged too, her right hand closing over his wrist, pushing the trajectory of his blade wide as she twisted from its path, turning, presenting her back to him as she controlled his knife hand. She pulled her own blade clear with her left while she twisted into him, arched her neck, crunching the back of her skull into his face. With precision she stabbed beneath her own armpit into the guard's chest. The steel sank home and he cried out, letting his blade clatter to the floor. She stepped away and let him fall.

The man lay clutching his chest, the hilt of Meere's dagger

jutting from it. Scarlet bubbles sprang up around it as the guard fought for breath. Zell's amazement wiped all other expression from his face. He stared for one moment then took to his heels, running for the exit. Rorrin let him pass.

'This was not well done, Grada.' The old assassin looked from slave to guard. 'Our lives are the emperor's and we're not free to spend them on such . . . domestic matters. He could have got lucky and then you'd be the one dying on the floor. How would that help the emperor?'

'Dying?' The heat of the fight ran from Grada quicker than it came. 'He's not going to die?' She looked down at the man. 'I'll get help.' His face had gone deathly pale and his blood spread around him on the tiles.

'And that lord will make trouble. Whispers against the throne. Change is the last thing any one of the peacocks wants.'

'Help him!' Grada pointed at the man. She didn't want his death on her hands, didn't want to see his face when she closed her eyes to sleep.

'I will send word for Mirra's temple to send someone,' said Rorrin. 'Come. We have not the time.' He turned without another glance and left.

Grada followed him from the room. 'You *will* send someone from the temple.'

'I will.'

As they walked Grada collected herself. 'It is dangerous for the silk-clad to abuse the slaves. Nobody notices the slaves, but they are there. They surround you.' She spoke also of herself, of the Untouchables.

'They surround *us*,' corrected Herran. 'You are one of us, now. And if the Knife finds one such as Zell a threat, the Knife can eliminate him. I would advise against it though. Change must be a slow process. Cerana can only be turned by degrees. Some problems are like the hydra. Slice off a head and two grow in its place.'

To that she did not reply. Herran could not give her the Knife; only Sarmin could lay that burden upon her. But would he? The envoy had been murdered, and she knew how much he had wanted the peace. What she did not know was how much such a failure might change a man. As they continued towards the centre of the palace Herran began to speak of schemes, snakes, concubines, war and children. This time Grada listened.

28

Rushes

Rushes returned to Nessaket's room, ears tired from listening. As she pretended to tidy the Great Room the concubines had paid her no mind, sharing their opinions on the emperor's looks, the quality of the food, and the stifling heat of Cerana. Two women had whispered that the emperor made love with one of them, the pale girl named Jenni, and speculated on their own chances. Surely the Empire Mother would wish to know about that, but even more she would want to identify the woman from the Ways. Rushes had not heard that voice. It filled her with dread to think that concubine could make another move, even harm one of the princes, before anyone could put a name to her.

And that was not the only thing. Rushes had thought the stone would be a comfort, but instead it frightened her. Sometimes she thought it twisted in her pocket, trying to find its way out. Many times during the day she caught it with one hand, as one catches a falling sash or pendant. She imagined the stone was angry she had disobeyed the emperor. She should have thrown it in the Ways as he asked, and now perhaps it would start giving bad luck instead of good.

Rushes put the stone from her mind and prepared for the

morning. She checked that Daveed had a tall stack of clean blankets, the brush and comb were side-by-side to the left of the mirror, and the Empire Mother's sandals were just where a person would not trip on them but that, when getting out of bed, they were easy to slip onto the feet. That done, she walked to the Great Room to make sure the shelves had been lowered to the kitchen, so that Hagga and the others could place the breakfast inside them.

When Rushes was passing a mosaic of Pomegra, done in jade and amber, the lantern light flickered up and down the long corridor as if buffeted by a strong wind she could not feel. The guards outside Nessaket's room murmured to one another, hands on their weapons, eyes sharp. Rushes didn't like to be near the guards when they were tense – it was then that they reminded her of Gorgen – so instead of trying to move past them she turned in a slow circle, looking up and down the corridor lined with bright paintings and sparkling tiles. She thought she saw someone fair and slim stepping back into a shadowed niche, so she called out, 'Hello?' No answer came; one of the guards, a grey-haired, burly man, leaned that way and said, 'Hey, there!'

Still there was no answer. Rushes took one step, then another, towards the niche, cautious of the guards, cautious of whoever was hiding there. But the niche lay empty. She looked from the pointed arch to the carpeted floor. Nobody was there.

A scream rang out from the other end of the hall, causing the guards to curse under their breath and draw their weapons at last, but they would not leave Nessaket's door. Their job was to guard little Daveed, not protect the other women. There were others stationed outside the heavy gilded entrance for that. Just as they took defensive stances the concubine named Banafrit came running down the long red carpet. 'It's Irisa!' she cried. 'Her colour . . .'

In moments the corridor filled with a dozen or more women, all of them perfumed, bangled, their lips every shade from pink to blood-red, all moving towards where Irisa lay near a gurgling fountain, and Rushes was pulled along with them, stumbling, her shoulders jarred by their elbows. Irisa appeared to her in parts, through the bend of an arm or the narrow space between two concubines – an arm, a hint of a cheek, the end of her flowing hair. And all of her was white, faded, the colour of a pretty dress left out in the sun too long.

Sickness. Rushes backed away, the stone turning in her pocket. The pattern had begun with just one person and spread, until they all became the tools of its Master. She would not fall victim to another plague. She put in her hand to keep the stone from falling and it was so hot that it burned her fingers; it had turned against her, just as she feared. She backed away, into the soft silks of one of the concubines.

'Watch where you're going!' the woman snapped, pushing her away by the shoulder, speaking with the tones of the north, like Marke Kavic or his priest.

'I . . .' Rushes turned and looked at her, at her pale skin and hair, at the turquoise silk draped from her shoulder. Three other women stood by her, each one just as beautiful, and indignant on her behalf, but Rushes' eyes were drawn back to the woman who had pushed her, for she was the woman from the Ways, and Rushes knew her name. She was the one who everyone whispered about, who had made love with Emperor Sarmin. Jenni.

Turn away. Turn away. The Many would have told her how to protect herself, to pretend. But instead she stood and stared, and understanding dawned in Jenni's eyes. She had not heard Rushes behind her in the Ways – that was impossible. She would have given some sign. And yet she *knew*.

Rushes ran, dodging between the fine ladies and past the paintings and fountains to Nessaket's room. But there the guards stopped her.

'If there's disease, we can't let you in,' said the older one, holding his hachirah across the entryway, the wide steel of his blade catching the light of a thousand gems and gleaming tiles. Brighter than all of them blazed the outline of a person, but it was not Jenni who stood behind her. White and indistinct, the reflection showed no eyes or mouth. It was not part of any painting or tapestry, and not a man but a thing – formed from imagination more than flesh, with arms, legs and a head shaped to trick the eye. As she watched it opened its arms and moved towards her.

She dodged behind the guard.

'Hey, now!' he said, pulling her up by the shoulder of her livery. He had not seen. The ghost had been visible only in the reflection.

'Tell Nessaket,' she said, letting him push her away, 'tell Nessaket it was Jenni.' She felt something cold against her legs, something like the feel of snow or cold water, and she readied her feet, obeying that ancient edict, the primary rule of survival. *Run.* 'Tell her!' she repeated, and then she ran.

'Wait,' the old guard called after her, understanding something of her urgency at last, but she only ran faster.

29

Rushes

Rushes had thought herself safe, but now she remembered: the palace was never safe. The snake should have told her that those happy days in the throne room with Beyon had been an illusion, as was everything else that felt soft and comforting. Only his protection was real. She should throw the stone into the abyss as he had asked; she did not want to betray him again.

Getting into the Ways had grown harder. Since the snake incident most of the exits had been sealed, but she knew of another, forgotten, in an unused corridor. Once inside she hurried along the familiar dark paths, making her way to the secret platform where she liked to hide. It was a long way from that platform to the bottom, where rats ran among bones and coins. The stone could go missing there for centuries. She climbed the final stairs and pressed her back against the damp wall, her fingers clenched around it. She should throw it. Now. Maybe if she did as the emperor asked, Irisa wouldn't be sick and the ghost she had seen would disappear. But it pricked along her fingers like needles, telling her it didn't want to be lost in the Ways.

She sat on the cold rock, brought her knees up to her chin

and held the stone to her forehead. She needed to throw it; she had to throw it. Emperor Beyon had commanded it. And yet her arm would not move and her fingers wrapped protectively around the smooth edges. Only the emperor's stone could save itself thus. She remembered the way Beyon had looked from Sarmin's eyes into hers that night in the dungeon. It was not for her to ask how he could return from the dead, or how he could know so much just from looking. The emperors were near to gods; if nothing else proved it, this did. Surely heaven's light fell upon them and granted powers a mere slave could not understand.

She held the stone, Beyon's stone, a thing of power and intelligence. A longing to return to the oubliettes, where she had first seen it, filled her mind. Those night-filled corridors called to her the same way as her memories of the plains, heart to heart. They called her home.

A trick; it was not safe there. It could not be safe. *But no place is safe.* She stood, tucked the stone into her pocket and moved down, tracking a path to the halls behind the Little Kitchen. Nobody moved through the Ways this night. Ever since Helmar these passages had become a shortcut for those who lived in the palace, even with many exits blocked. No matter where Rushes stood, she could always hear someone else moving, even if it was far in the distance. Guards patrolled, servants carried messages and nobles sneaked to one another's rooms. But on this night the dark stairs and bridges lay forgotten. She quickened her pace.

She took a breath of relief once she exited into the bright corridor and began the short walk to the dungeon stairs, slowing her steps. If the guards heard running they might come to see what was the matter, and then there would be questions. The stone felt warm in her pocket, pleased that she had chosen the dungeon. But it would not be easy. Nothing was ever easy. A man approached from the other end of the corridor, moving fast. He would meet her before she could dash down the steps, and so she slowed, hiding her destination. As he drew closer she recognised Mylo. She felt no pleasure in seeing his handsome face, his easy smile. She did not want to be alone with any man, in a pantry, a hallway or anywhere else.

'Our little Rushes,' he said. 'Where have you been?'

'I work for the Empire Mother now,' she said, looking around. Mylo had a gentle manner, but she was frightened nevertheless.

'Really? And the little prince?'

Not wanting to talk about Daveed she asked a question. 'When is your next meeting?'

'It's—' A noble wrapped in a dark cloak approached, and they bowed until he had passed. '—tomorrow night, if you can make it. After lanterns' turning.'

Lanterns' turning was no longer a time of day that Rushes understood; the women's halls were always lit, even in the middle of the night. Bright and safe. She moved her shaking hand from her mouth and nodded, nevertheless, her feet already moving.

Mylo gave another smile. She wondered if anything could put a frown in its place. 'Will you be there?' Behind him she saw a flash of red; the Fryth priest was skulking along the corridor, keeping to the shadow of doorways, as if he needed to hide, as she did. Were he and Mylo together?

She backed away. 'Maybe,' she said. 'I have to go.' She turned, anxious to leave the priest behind her, but Mylo called, 'Wait!' and she stopped.

'Did you hear they killed the envoy?'

She stared at him. 'No. Who did?' She remembered the Fryth man and his kindness. She thought he was one man she would have liked to know.

'The silk-clad,' he said, as if it were obvious, and all silk-clad were the same. 'Remember the secret signal.' He drew his finger across his chin. 'Mogyrk will claim the palace soon.'

Rushes did not understand him. She hurried on towards the dungeon, reaching the stairs and passing through the doors with no further incident. The dungeons were better lit this time, and filled with the combined scents of night-pots and rotten meat. Rushes descended the stairs, keeping an eye to the room at the base. It was a shorter climb than she remembered. The luck stone vibrated against her leg; it could sense that it was almost home. Men were talking, and women too, and the lower she came the louder it was, a babble of voices, like the market, or the slaves' hall on a festival day. Two steps from the bottom she stopped and peered around the edge. There were no guards in this room, though she could see a man in the room beyond, his back to her. She lifted her skirts and scurried across to the cells.

They were full. Each contained three or more people – dirty, hungry, stinking, they clutched at the bars and begged her in their own language. She did not know whether they needed food, water, or just a glance, a touch, to let them know they still existed, and could still be heard. Tears came to her eyes as she stopped before a little girl, just a few years her junior, red-haired and blue-eyed, her hands clutching the bars. 'Where are you from, little girl?'

The girl stared at her without understanding. Of course. She had been speaking Cerantic. She asked the same question in Fryth, or tried, but the girl still did not answer.

Rushes moved on, hesitating at the turn, facing the long, empty hallway that led to the oubliettes. She could not remember which one it was. The stone twisted and warmed in her pocket. As she walked, the prisoners called to her, still begging from where they stood packed together in the corridors behind. She counted to fifteen. The Many always had been divided into five, and three was her favourite number, the number of times to hit a stone for good luck or walk in circles for a blessing. *Three fives is fifteen. Fifteen is the number of the first priests of Mogyrk. Fifteen is how many days it took Mogyrk to die.* The Many had known this, but she had not remembered. Not until now. She stopped before the fifteenth cell.

The door was made of wood, but a little window had been cut through and fitted with a grille. Rushes couldn't reach the opening, even standing on tiptoe, but she found an old pail, turned it upside down and climbed up. Inside sat a woman, all alone, shoulders drawn up against the cold. She was old, older than Sahree even, skin sagging over her eyes, wrinkles hiding the flesh of her lips. Her spine curved and her knees stuck out, bony and swollen at once. She turned to Rushes and pointed towards her with a hand that had become a claw.

'The stone,' she said, 'you have the stone.'

Rushes felt the trembling at the core of herself. 'You know about the stone?'

The old woman shuffled to the door. 'Put two hundred years behind you and you'll realise we none of us know anything. But I feel the stone. I see it. More clearly than I see you, child. *He* made it. Helmar. And once upon a time he was mine.'

Rushes drew it from her pocket and hissed at the heat of it. She nearly threw it at the old woman, so much did she long to get rid of it. How a stone could know things, make itself warm, she did not understand. The mages of the Tower used elementals for their magic, borrowing power from another place and time. This stone thought for itself, behaved for itself. She pushed it through the grille; it was nearly too large to fit.

The woman cradled it between her palms, cupping it as a child might hold a mouse or a chick. The stone, searing in Rushes' grip, did not bother the woman at all. 'Oh, yes,' she said, nodding to herself, 'yes. Meg has you. Meg has you.'

Rushes backed away. The need to leave the stone behind, to leave the old woman and the Fryth prisoners, overcame her.

'Girl!' shouted Meg, pointing at her again, and she froze. 'You must take it back.' Her stare held Rushes, a communion of a kind as if the two of them were Many, rich with emotion, each conflicting with the next.

'I can't. I brought it here as I was supposed to, and now . . .'

'Take it. It is in the design that you will. His design. Be brave. Take what comes.' She held the stone to the grille, her arm thin as a stalk of cat-grass. Rushes stepped forwards and accepted it, tears running down her face. 'It's all right to cry,' said the old woman, 'I know you're scared. But it's the emperor's stone, now. He needs it.'

'I can't . . .' She remembered what Beyon had said to her on the balcony, using Sarmin's lips: *He wants this, and I can't let him have it.* He had meant his brother. The emperor.

The stone had turned cold and lay inert in Rushes' hand. 'Take it,' said Meg. 'Be strong. You can be strong. We're none of us one thing.'

Rushes wiped her tears and put the stone in her pocket. 'You're from Fryth?'

'I'm from Mythyck, girl, but as far as they're concerned I'm from Fryth.'

'Is there fighting there? War?'

'There was blood and fire and hangings and all of it. But there is much worse to come. All this horror these children think is so important . . . and it's all just a dance on a knife edge none of them can see. Now go on, girl, before I drop dead and can't do anything more for anyone. Tell the emperor I know who put it here in the oubliette. Remember to say *oubliette*. It rhymes with forget. Now go on. Go!'

Rushes hurried to the Ways, past the prisoners, past the dark corners, past a thousand other stones that looked like stones but could be anything else, could trick a person and change into something with a will. She would need to get past a great many soldiers to speak with the emperor, and she would not know whether it was Sarmin or Beyon until they spoke. If it were Beyon she found, he would be angry; he did not take disobedience and betrayal lightly. He had kept his promise to her, though violently; but she would fail him.

And yet that was not really Beyon, the Beyon who was sad and kind as well as angry. The Beyon who hid inside his brother had left parts of himself in heaven, she thought; perhaps the best of him stood with Mirra even now, urging her to help his brother. She thought maybe that was so.

30

Sarmin

'Who could have done this thing?' Only Sarmin and his vizier stood upon the steps of the dais, and the throne room lay empty save for the ever-present guards. Lit in haste, only one in three of the many lamps sconced along the walls held a flame and the room ran with shadows. Sarmin paced, unable to sit, and Azeem followed, careful always to be a step lower. 'Who?' Sarmin could think of a list a yard long, the person who brought the snake to Daveed at the head of it and himself close behind.

'"Why?" is the question that may answer "Who?", My Emperor, and more importantly will give us the hand behind whatever knife was used.'

Sarmin found himself looking at his own hand, sore from tearing at the ropes that bound him in his sleep. The image of Kavic lying twisted in his blood on a patterned rug returned to him. How could he see it if he was not there? But then he had been an absent witness to so much of late.

'There is a question still more pressing than that of guilt, My Emperor.' The jewels on Azeem's robe of office caught the lamplight, returning it in deep reds. Had Tuvaini worn that robe? One like it but not that one – Tuvaini had been a much taller man.

'My Emperor?' Azeem waited at his elbow.

'What question, Vizier?'

'The question of how to proceed. Can the peace be kept despite what has happened? What should be done with this Fryth austere? Can he speak in the envoy's place? What line might he take? Austere Adam is said to be a zealot. He may prefer to see Fryth burn for the chance it might set Yrkmir against Cerana, and count every death a new martyr for his faith.'

Sarmin returned to the Petal Throne. 'They will see that a peace can't stand or fall on the death of one man.' He nodded, finding comfort in agreeing with himself. 'This Iron Duke of theirs . . . Mala . . . Malast?'

'Malast Anteydies Griffon, My Emperor.'

'This duke must be able to see that two cut throats don't require ten thousand more to die in his streets, Fryth and Cerani both.'

'It's not the death of one man, though I understand the duke favoured his grandson Kavic. The envoy carried Fryth's pride with him. To have him murdered abed in the imperial palace is to wound the pride of every man of Fryth. Wars have been fought for far smaller injuries to men's pride.'

Sarmin remembered Kavic speaking of the man, of his humiliation at the hands of Yrkmir. He watched the shadows flicker and play. He wanted Mesema at his side. The throne was a lonely place. Even his mother would have had good council. 'So we need to heal this wound.' And how can pride be repaired? Sarmin had no idea; his room had not armed him with such talents. 'Shall I call Priest Assar to work one of Mirra's cures?'

'Master Herran seeks audience, My Emperor!' The herald called out from the great doors, eased apart to admit his bulk.

'Let him come.' Sarmin raised a weary hand above his head and beckoned.

'Herran brings only Herzu's cures,' Azeem said. He stepped aside and studied his patterned slippers.

'Master Herran.' Sarmin acknowledged the assassin as he walked the long path to the dais, his feet silent on the silk runner laying out his route.

Herran said nothing until he reached his allotted place, two yards before the lowest step. 'My Emperor.' And he slipped into the obeisance as if age had no finger on him. Indeed he looked more hale than he had at any point in the last year, his hair and eyebrows shaded away from their usual white to a new grey, though Sarmin would not have thought the man vain.

'Master Herran.' Sarmin scowled at the back of the old man's head. 'Your profession has done great harm this night.'

Herran said nothing.

'Rise.' Sarmin's fingertips drummed his irritation out on the armrest. 'Speak.'

Master Herran got to his knees, then showing at the last some sign of age, to his feet. 'My Emperor, it remains to be seen whether the envoy's death is the work of skilled men or of amateurs with fortune on their side – I can assure you that the Grey Service were no part of this. The solution however may lie with the grey men in your service.'

'You will cut the throats of each and every Fryth in their bed and leave us none to war against? Is that your solution?' Some of that bitterness brewed in the long years of Sarmin's imprisonment leaked into his voice.

'Only two more.' Herran inclined his head.

'Two? I don't understand you. I won't send you after the duke and his last remaining heir if that's what you're asking.

I won't have it.' Behind his eyes the pool of Kavic's blood widened until it joined that which had spread around Sarmin's brothers in the long ago.

Herran waited a moment, studying Sarmin as no servant should study his master. The assassin had pale eyes that together with the lines of his face spoke of a mixed ancestry, of blood from beyond Cerana's borders. 'If the envoy had never reached the palace, if ill luck had befallen him in the wild mountains where lawless tribes hold sway, then we would never have had this problem.'

'But ill luck didn't befall them until they spent the night beneath my roofs!' Sarmin studied his fingers, looking for traces of blood.

Azeem coughed into his hand. 'If we say they never reached us. If we send for word of their arrival . . . who will call us liars? Who will call the emperor of Cerana a liar?'

'Austere Adam, for one,' said Sarmin. 'Besides, I am not a liar.'

Herran bowed his head. Azeem licked his lips and continued. 'Would you lie to preserve the peace you seek, My Emperor, to save the ten thousand lives you spoke of?'

Sarmin frowned. Mesema would know what to say to that. His mother would lie without pause for blinking, except that her pride would not incline her towards peace. 'Austere Adam is not—'

'Austere Adam has not yet survived the night,' Herran said.

'Ah.' Finally Sarmin understood. He did not count himself stupid, but his mind did not run so easily down the bloodier of paths. 'No. I won't order a priest slain.'

'We have places he might be held, along with that guardsman,' Azeem said. 'Cells in the dungeon where men might be forgotten.'

The oubliettes. Sarmin remembered the smoothness of that skull beneath his hands, the dry papery feel when he hooked his fingers through its eye sockets. 'No! Not there. I commanded that every prisoner be brought out and the dungeons emptied.'

Azeem and Herran exchanged a look. The older man spoke. 'Your royal father appointed Eyul son of Klemet to be the Fifty-Third Knife-Sworn. He found he needed such a man and that the Grey Service would not fill the need.'

'This I know. I watched the man slit my brothers' throats. Your assassins are forbidden such blood. If he had been a true emperor my father would have killed his sons by his own hand, or let them live.'

'Emperor Tahal was dead by the time the deed was required.' A gentle reminder from Azeem.

'You need a Knife in your service, My Emperor.' Herran's pale eyes sought Sarmin's.

'No.' Appointing a Knife was the penultimate step towards sacrificing his last brother. He might as well snatch Daveed from his mother's arms and throttle him himself as put the emperor's Knife into the hand of a new Knife-Sworn.

'It is not just for the spilling of royal blood that the Knife serves, My Emperor. The Knife serves the empire. The Knife dares what must be done, what needs be done, what honest men and good men cannot bring themselves to say or to command. The hand that wields the Knife is stained; the emperor's remain clean.

'Your father appointed Eyul because he trusted him, with his own life, with the black judgements that taint a man and yet must be made. Your father sacrificed Eyul to the Knife that the empire might survive, that the people within her borders might live and thrive.'

The Many began their whispering, the hush and flow of their words reaching from the darkest corners of Sarmin's mind, rippling like the shadows across the throne-room floor. 'Your search is over before it starts then, assassin,' he said. 'I've grown between four walls, alone, forgotten. Who would I trust as my father trusted Eyul? Who would I trust to kill in my name and not to ask my permission or tell me the result?' *And if I had such a person how could I sacrifice them?*

Herran turned away, towards the doors, and clapped twice. A figure stepped through with no announcement. Hooded, the visitor walked towards the throne, avoiding the silk runner, taking careful steps as if favouring an injury.

'Who—' The herald would announce every visitor without exception; only the guards entered without remark. The guards and servants.

Halfway to the throne the figure stopped. Further back than noble supplicants, further back than merchants or low-ranked officers would halt, further back than the lowest of servants.

'Grada!' And as he spoke she threw her hood back and watched him with dark eyes. The Many whispered; they lifted their voices so Sarmin could hear neither assassin nor vizier. He saw both men though their words didn't reach him – saw them in their many parts, their bright fault-lines, the way they fitted the pattern all around them. Grada however stood unmoving and did not speak. No lines crossed her; she stood dark and whole, her purpose clear, fitting only a single pattern, a puzzle of two parts: his and hers.

31

Sarmin

Did I kill Kavic? Did the Many kill him with these hands? Sarmin held his palms before him for inspection. No stain, no trace of blood. But someone inside him had made dust of the ropes that bound him to his bed. Someone had been free to do it. And envoy Kavic lay dead, the image of his spreading blood seared on Sarmin's mind like memory although only the killer would have seen it flow.

'Not memory,' he told the gods. 'Imagination.' He had not killed Austere Adam. He had ordered him into the oubliettes instead: not what Sarmin wanted to do, but better than cutting the man's throat.

Sarmin stood in the tower room where he had counted out his youth. Too many steps ached in his legs and they told him to sit, but he remained standing, eyes on the painted ceiling from where the gods looked down upon him.

A knock and Ta-Sann's voice through the door. 'My Emperor?'
'Yes.'

'High Mage Govnan is here with . . . a servant.' Even Ta-Sann, who could cut through the niceties of court like a blade, had not the words for Grada.

'Let them come.' Sarmin stood, anticipation flowing through

him. At last he and Grada would speak without the eyes of the court upon them.

Govnan walked in, hobbled with age but carrying no extra burden from the climb, Grada behind him, frowning, not even the hint of a smile when his eyes caught hers.

'Well?' Before Govnan had even begun his slow descent into the obeisance.

The old man put his hands together, knuckles overlarge, skin patterned by age. 'There was no magic in it.'

'But what did you discover?'

'The elements have little to say in the matter.' Govnan bowed his head. 'The spirits in the stone, the air, within the flame of lamp and lantern, they see much but it means nothing to them. They don't care about what we care about. No stone was broken, no fire set, just flesh cut, blood spilled.'

'And what does Herran say?' Sarmin looked to Grada.

'That the killer came in through the roof vents by removing a screen. That they must have had a slight build to fit. That they sifted poppy-dust into the room first, to drug the envoy and his guard.' She shrugged, a hint of anger in the motion.

'You don't agree?' Sarmin asked.

'Herran isn't wrong. His men don't miss much.'

'What then?' For a moment Sarmin missed the days when the edges of their thoughts had met within a pattern of two, and questions need not be spoken.

'The *how* is less than *who*, and both are less than *why*,' she said.

'And you know why?'

'I know who.'

'Well?' When did it change to this? From sharing minds to pulling answers from her like nails from wood . . . The Many granted him that memory, the feel of the grain beneath one hand, a hammer the other. Honest work.

Govnan coughed. 'Perhaps this news is for the emperor's ears only?' The look Grada shot the old mage held enough heat to suggest she too might be flame-sworn, but he simply glanced away to the ruined wall, coughing into his hand, or perhaps chuckling. 'To leave the Light of Heaven alone with an Untouchable might set tongues wagging. But nobody would think it unseemly for an emperor and his Knife to meet in solitude and discuss their secrets.'

'I am the emperor! I decide what is seemly!' Sarmin hadn't meant to raise his voice, but it rang loud enough to bring Ta-Sann through the door.

Govnan nodded. 'You would think an emperor would decide who his armies wage war on, too.'

Sarmin bit back the reply to that one. Once it had been books that schooled him. Never answering back, their lessons learned by repetition, day upon day. Govnan offered a sharper wisdom. Sarmin drew open his robe. The Knife hung at his hip, where it always rested. A thing like that should drag at a man, should carry more weight than mere steel, and yet it never had. Perhaps because it was never his to wield. Perhaps only once he gave it into another's hands would he feel the burden of it.

'Herran wants me to give you this.' Sarmin drew the Knife from its scabbard and held it up for Grada to see. Ta-Sann's eyes followed the blade's glimmer, the first time Sarmin had ever seen him distracted. Grada though, looked past it, into Sarmin's eyes. A bold stare no subject should ever give their emperor. He looked away, down at the pommel of the Knife, a dark stone, swallowing the light.

'I'm not a killer. I have never killed—' She broke off. She would be remembering the guards on the bridge, their blood on her hands.

'I know.' Sarmin met her gaze again and for a moment a resonance of their old bond shivered in the space between them. He felt her strength, sorrows, fears. 'Who else should I give the Knife to?'

'I'm not—'

'I don't want you to kill, Grada.' He held the hilt towards her. 'What better Knife-Sworn for a new empire, for a new peace, than one who will not cut?'

'No, I don't—'

'Please,' he said.

And she took the Knife, surprise in her eyes as she found her fingers tight around it. Sarmin stepped back and sat upon his bed frame, burdened with new guilt.

'Witnessed.' Govnan bowed, turned away, this once not waiting to be dismissed. He set a hand to Ta-Sann's shoulder at the door, and both men left.

Alone at last. Sarmin looked up from the bed frame, a weak smile twisting his lips. 'Grada of Nooria, Fifty-Fourth Knife-Sworn, Daughter of Mella.'

She returned his smile at that. 'The emperor speaking my mother's name. A thousand fortune tellers could have told her that and she would have believed none of them.'

'Who killed the envoy, Grada?' He needed to know.

'A harem girl. Jenni of Yrkmir.'

'What? Jenni?' A glance at Grada told him she knew, knew that he had shared Jenni's bed. It should be nothing. The harem was there for that. There should be no sting in the accusation. No accusation. But Grada judged him even so, and it stung.

'To fit through that gap in the ceiling it had to be someone slim, a woman or a child most likely. I went to the women's wing. There your mother told me of the concubine Jenni, identified as the one who threatened your brother with the snake. Now she has disappeared.'

'Jenni? She's not a killer.' Sarmin barely knew the girl. No, not a girl, a young woman – but surely she couldn't have murdered two grown men? Wouldn't have. He saw Jenni's smile again and how it had fallen away, broken, when he dismissed her. It was one of the Many who had shared her passion, not him, never him, but his fingers remembered her curves, remembered counting a path down along the ridges of her spine.

'You were right to have me watch the concubines. More than a fifth of your harem have been trained to kill,' Grada said. She pursed her lips. 'Give them a dagger and they're more dangerous than I am with this.' She held up the Knife.

'No—' Sarmin watched the blade. 'Which ones?' It didn't really matter; he knew few of their faces, and fewer of their names. 'Who gave them? Whose gifts are they?' Surely no single lord had given so many of his harem. How many traitors were there?

'Many men gave them, and none were given by the man who had them trained. They were sold on, gifted, placed and traded in such a manner that each stood a decent chance of ending up in the palace. Many did not. A lot of gold has been spent.'

'Herran told you all this?' They sounded like Herran's words, like his cleverness, not the rough speech of the Untouchable who had stabbed him long ago . . . or at least it felt long ago, though the scar was still red.

'Some of it. Some I have learned this evening.' She spoke with her own voice, changed but hers. They had both changed since they left this room. He wouldn't recognise himself if he could look back, nor if he could have looked forwards from then to now.

'And Herran has let this stand? Left me surrounded by enemies? Left my son—'

'We only understood the truth of it yesterday. Herran would have come to you immediately but you had the envoy to tend to, and you have little time for your Grey Service at the best of times.' She shrugged. Herran made that shrug. 'The arrests will soon begin, slowly, one girl then the next, so there won't be panic, rash acts. Jenni will be found. Your son will be kept safe.'

'But I was—' He remembered waking with Jenni beside him, her sweet smile in the morning light.

'If Jenni had wanted you dead wouldn't she have stabbed you while you slept?' She left 'together' unspoken. Beyon's Knife would never have cut across him; Eyul kept his temper sheathed.

'That wasn't—' He broke off. The emperor didn't explain himself. *That wasn't me.* Sarmin could explain to Grada, but the emperor didn't explain, not even to his Knife. The empire rested on his authority and any crack in it would spread, fork and fork again, reaching out until the whole edifice of his power came crashing down.

'Ta-Sann, Azeem, all those that watch you said you kept your distance from the harem. You told me to watch the slaves from the north. I thought you were suspicious of these women, these gifts.'

'I was.' Again he did not explain why he had ignored that warning when his body found its pleasure in Jenni. 'But my brother – the snake—'

'You killed that snake yourself,' said Grada, 'fortunately.'

Sarmin had been told of this, though the memory was not his. It was a comfort, at least, to know that some of the Many he Carried would commit good deeds as well as bad.

Grada held the Knife by her hip, turning it this way and that to watch the light slide across the blade. 'Why me?'

He reached for the memory of reading Helmar's records with his own hands, his own eyes, but another man's will. 'I have been reading Helmar's history. One parchment fragment held the last words he spoke to his tutor. He talked of patterns and of symmetry. Said that any pattern reaches out to for ever, and that just as a grand pattern can hold memory and reaches back to capture and contain the past, such a pattern also reaches forwards and does the same to the future.'

'And what are a sick boy's ramblings to you?' Only Beyon had ever spoken to him like that. Beyon and Mesema. As if he were just a person, without title or any right to wisdom. Sarmin sensed more value in that honesty than in all the counsel of the wise, slanted as it was towards hidden goals. 'Helmar hated you, hated all of us.' Grada held up the Knife. 'You killed him with this!'

'There was more on that fragment, Grada. My name was there. He called me his brother in captivity. Little of that boy who wrote to me remained by the time he returned here. Maybe just enough to let me stab him. I killed the Pattern Master. But three hundred years ago Helmar, son of an emperor, my ancestor and blood, reached out to me, knowing I would save him from what he became, and offering me peace in thanks.' Sarmin hoped that it was true, that he could heal the damage Helmar had done.

'And he put the Knife into my hand,' Grada said.

Sarmin said nothing but held her gaze. He had sent Grada away to spare her the old men's judgement. He had never wanted her to take the Knife. And yet here she was, Eyul's ugly blade in hand, perhaps as damned as any before her.

'Jenni may know a secret.' The words left him slowly, unwilling. 'Something more dangerous to me, to the empire, than any dead envoy.' Sarmin thought of Daveed, saw the baby's soft arms and balled fists reaching from the basket their mother put him in. If Jenni knew – if he had told her – if one of the Many had spoken of Beyon and Mesema to Jenni, even as he spent himself in her . . . How long had she waited to tell whoever placed her in the palace? Had knowledge of Pelar's true heritage brought a snake to the women's halls?

Sarmin looked away from Grada, from the Knife she held, and watched the gods instead, Herzu grim as ever but somehow vindicated. 'That secret cannot spread.'

...

32

Grada

Herran stood waiting in the cartodome, hands on the circular
edge of the great central table. He waited without motion,
leaning out towards the blankness where nothing but
unadorned marble described the inner desert.

'Tell me about the house.' Grada still thought of him as
Rorrin, any other name would feel wrong on her tongue, so
she afforded him neither name nor title. Perhaps Rorrin was
his true name in any case, and Master Herran the invention.
She wondered if that was something the Many had taught
her, or just imagination.

'You look different,' Herran said after long inspection.

Grada looked at him, from the toes of his soft boots to the
grey of his hair. Some would call it an insolence, not at all
how she was raised to look at men of power, but she had
stabbed an emperor and this was just Rorrin, who crawled in
the sand with her that first day. He was older than she had
first guessed, closer to seventy than to fifty. Age had its claws
sunk deep. In the desert, in the unforgiving light of day, she
hadn't seen it, but here in the kindness of lamps and shadows,
he showed his years. Here he allowed her to see.

'You knew from that first day, didn't you?' She pushed back her robe to reveal the Knife at her hip.

'I knew from the moment we met.' Herran permitted himself a smile. 'I caught you by surprise, alone, vulnerable, and your first words to me were interrogation. Without hesitation you wanted explanation. Focused on your goal. Straight to the point.'

'I'm a labourer. I wash, fetch, carry, clean. I'm not a warrior, not an assassin.' Grada remembered the men by the river. How did she do that?

'You're a natural, Grada. The still point in the storm, action in chaos. That's in the blood, and as like to be borne out in a peasant as a prince. But I had more to go on. We soon learned that any skill worked through a person by the Many left its mark. The Pattern Master housed archers in the bodies of men who had never touched a bow. When the emperor freed those men they found they could still shoot a sand hare from a river barge. And your hands, Grada, were given to the best assassins in the Many to work the Pattern Master's will.'

Grada held her hands before her, palm up for inspection. Too broad, too thick of finger, sun-stained, coarsened by hard work. She flexed her fingers, recalling the weight and grip of the Knife.

'They still have that cleverness, don't they, Knife-Sworn?' Herran didn't require her answer.

'I would rather have had a potter's skill, a weaver, something honest.' A mother's touch that remembered softness and babies.

'Feh, and who would buy a pot from an Untouchable? Who would walk on the rugs you wove? Now you are the Knife, Chosen of the emperor. It is given to you to keep this empire safe. As the blood fights infection while the mind leads us through our lives, Sarmin will plot our path, while you will keep the body politic healthy. By cutting out the rot.'

'I'd rather empty chamber pots.'

'But that luxury is not yours, Grada.' Again the narrow smile, twisted with regret. 'Fifty-three good souls have carried that blade before you. None of them would have chosen to. If they had then they would have been the wrong candidate.'

'Whatever you think, assassin, I am not a killer.'

'Why then did you take the Knife?'

'Sarmin needed me to. He wants a Knife who will serve in a new way. Sarmin is a different kind of emperor. Things will change.'

Herran said nothing, only watched her.

'A Knife that doesn't slit throats is still useful. A sharp edge can be turned to many purposes.' Had Herran told her that? They weren't her words. 'I'll find a new way.'

'You will find there is no other way.' Herran shook his head. 'The greater good stands upon many small evils. Better to accept that lesson than be forced to learn it.'

Grada turned away, walked the perimeter of the cartodome where endless map scrolls lay stacked in their marble pigeon-holes, ordered, capped with turned rosewood, the whole world picked out in inks, captured and stored. They stood among the greatest collection of maps ever assembled and Herran told her there was no other path to find?

'So, tell me about the house,' she said, returning her attention to the assassin.

Herran glanced quickly around the cartodome as if suspicious even of the walls, though the Ways did not reach into these levels. 'Lord Jomla owns it. He lives there when he visits the capital, though he entertains at the Yellow Manse on the west side and would have his guests believe it is his home.'

'And who is this Lord Jomla?'

'A man grown rich off trade. His estates sit at a point where the river Xeres ceases to be navigable and caravans out of Hedrin may ford it. Barges from the West Ports unload there. War suits his purpose. Imports will multiply, his coffers grow fatter still with the taxes and duties.'

'The empire has many rich men. Why is this one seeding his agents through the emperor's harem?' She thought of Jenni, slim and exotic, leading Sarmin to her chamber. The chatter among the servants for month after month had been of the emperor's lack of interest in the women's wing. Was he sick? Too weak? Was Cerana's emperor not a true man eager to exercise his rights? One of the royal cooks had said a real man held prisoner for so many years would lock himself in the harem and do nothing but rut for months. Grada had wanted to slap the crone's last teeth out, but the serving girl chatting with them owned that Sarmin was too in love with the empress to look at his concubines, and that had stung deeper than the old woman's slander.

'Meere has been following the servants of the house when they leave on errands. One went to the artisans' district across the Blessing. To the tall house of Mechar Anlantar.'

Grada shook her head.

'A famed maker of toys. Jewelled birds that sing, silver acrobats that tumble on a flat table, driven by coiled springs.'

'Meere might have followed, but I'm not understanding. If this lord wanted himself a gold song-thrush, what of it? How does it explain him?'

Herran spared a quick glance towards the blank heart of

the desert, as if it worried him. 'Meere robbed the servant on his return. He had toys for a child, not toys for a grown lord. Jomla has many wives but no children. And his tastes do not run to them. If he is keeping a child in his secret town house then the reason should concern us.'

'Everything about that man should concern us,' Grada said.

'The child could be an heir to the Petal Throne, some lost shoot like the Pattern Master was, a branch that should have been pruned by a Knife of yesteryear. Why else would Jomla hide a child so well? None of the lesser servants know the boy is there. It must be a boy. I've had agents follow every member of that household, try all their tricks to get a placement, to befriend even the lowest scullion . . . nothing. It took crude robbery to get even a hint.'

'If he has an heir then why set his spies to murdering envoys? Kill Sarmin, kill Daveed, kill Pelar, and the throne can be claimed for any petitioner whose blood will satisfy the Tower. One snake is all they have sent against them.'

Herran shook his head. 'The royal babies are very well guarded; the emperor's brother has as many or more guards than even his own son! And harem girls have no contact with them. As for the emperor himself, well, he doesn't visit his harem.'

Grada knew better, but perhaps Sarmin's visits to Jenni had been few, or even singular. Perhaps he had visited only her, only once. Perhaps. She found her hand on the hilt of the Knife, wanting the edge to sharpen away such foolishness.

'So what then?' she asked.

'Spying. Secrets are more valuable than diamonds. Jomla must have thought that one of his beauties would catch Sarmin's eye in time. And if none of them did . . . well, that in itself would be a secret worth having. And to stir up trouble between Daveed's mother and Pelar's . . .

'In any event, before this business of the envoy a clever man might have thought to play Settu with these pretty pieces, to turn one of them perhaps, or if a piece could not be turned, feed it lies, the kind that might choke Jomla and teach a subtle lesson to those who watch him.'

'Jomla knows a secret.' Grada set her fingers to the dark stone in the Knife's pommel, its surface cold with whispers.

Herran tilted his head. 'What kind?'

'The worst.' The killing kind. 'Meere should take the Grey Service and see that it never spreads.' She had known when she took the Knife that throats would have to be cut, all the voices between Jenni and her unknown master silenced. Now though a hollow nausea grew in her stomach.

For a long time Herran said nothing. He stared at the map of empire, tracing a fingertip along the course of the Blessing.

'Meere believes Jomla keeps an heir to the throne in that house. Someone in the line of succession who could be placed on the throne should a sickly young man die, a couple of babies cease to breathe.' He tapped a nail on the legend, Nooria, set in stone. 'Jomla is no fool. If he has a candidate for the Petal Throne he will have evidence, genealogy. He will have strong reason to expect this person's blood to prove royal under the Tower's inspection.'

'Meere could—'

'Only the Knife-Sworn may take a royal life, Grada. If he has an heir then only the Knife can cut a path to peace.'

'Bring Jomla and whoever is with him to the palace. Put them in the dungeons. Have the high mage test these claims and theories.' *Don't send me. Don't let me find that this house in* the Holies lies on a street of palms between the shrines of Herzu and Mirra.

'Would Sarmin have you cut the child's throat if you asked him?'

Grada didn't answer. To put words around that question would be dangerous. Whether it came to her as a stain left by the assassins who used her body to kill, or was simply a lesson from the streets of the Maze, Grada knew better than to seal away options before she absolutely had to. Choices were the key to survival, even if all of them were bad.

'Would he have the child taken to the dungeons and thrown into an oubliette?' Herran asked.

Grada said nothing. Sarmin had all but emptied the dungeons, and set free any man whose crime could no longer be recalled.

'Perhaps our emperor is kinder and would set the child in more salubrious surroundings: secure, secret but dressed in silk, maybe with some books for company?' Herran proved relentless. Sarmin would never subject a child to the fate he had suffered alone in his tower.

'He would have the child as an honoured guest, free to roam, guarded for his own security.' Grada nodded as she said it. 'He would defy his council and each day some new plot would grow from the mere fact of the child's existence, some plan to steal him away, raise a rebellion around him.'

'Ta-Sann would never ask Sarmin's permission to block a sword swinging at the royal neck. He wouldn't canvas Sarmin's permission before he stepped in front of a spear thrust to save him. As the emperor's Knife you may act in his defence without seeking permission. And you may do so in the long game. Ta-Sann acts in the split second. The years are given to you. That privilege is given to no other. If the emperor orders against a course of action, however, you will of course obey.'

'You're sending me to Jomla's manse.' Grada bit her lip, tasting the blood.

'You are not mine to send or to tell, Knife.' And Herran bowed to her. Nothing this day had scared her more, except perhaps the pity in his eyes before the bow took them from view.

33

Sarmin

Sarmin sat back upon the frame of his old bed. Grada's foot-steps on the stairs had passed beyond hearing, and Ta-Sann and the sword-sons kept their silence behind the door. Only the distant wail of a Tower-wizard could be heard beneath the muted hubbub of Nooria rising over palace walls. Even the Many within him held their peace. He had taken them in, refugees from the Master's pattern, hundreds without bodies to return to, and it had cost him, but dozens had flowed into the nothingness in Beyon's tomb like water through a crack in the world. After that a voice left him each day, fading into whatever the future held. Soon the Many would be the Few, and perhaps in a year Sarmin would be alone in his thoughts once more. Trapped in the bony prison of his skull, but at the same time, free at last.

He thought of the oubliettes deep in the dungeon, of the skull he'd found there, picked clean by rats, and the stone hidden in a crevice between the great blocks of the wall. Would he taste the loneliness of that cell when the Many left him? He would miss them, even though they plagued him, used his body, spread his secrets. In the streets of Nooria those who had been patterned and then set free fought the Longing, and Sarmin would join them in that battle. Set adrift without the sickness of the Many they felt lost, like men from whom a hand has been taken, reaching out to touch with absent fingers. Azeem told him many such sought new comfort in the secret churches where men praised Mogyrk, perhaps believing that the faith of the Yrkmen, the code preached by their austeres with stories of the one dead god, would return to them something that had been taken.

'My Emperor?'

Ta-Sann's voice at the door jerked Sarmin from his thoughts so suddenly that he nearly fell into the bed ropes.

'Yes?' More harsh than he had intended.

'A slave-girl has come with a tray of food.'

'Send her away.' His stomach contracted around the thought of eating.

A moment's silence then voices from behind the door, Ta-Sann's rumble and a girl's high tones, raised but struggling against suppression as if truly she wanted to shout.

'She has brought you a stone, Excellency.' A rare note of surprise entered Ta-Sann's voice.

'To eat?' Sarmin asked.

Silence.

'She wants you to see it, Excellency. She is just a serving girl. She is . . . dishevelled. Perhaps she is mad. I will send her away.'

Again the girl's voice reached Sarmin. He caught the word 'Rushes.' A name? It held a touch of the familiar.

—*Send her away.*

A whisper at the back of his mind, not his own voice, but not a stranger's. 'Bring her in,' he said.

The door opened and Ta-Sann led the servant through, a

second sword-son following behind her. When Ta-Sann stepped aside to reveal the girl she was comically small and frail bracketed between the bulk of the two guards. A pretty girl, maybe seven years his junior, gripped by a nervous energy, more bony than slim, her eyes blue and darting, hair the colour of amber. She held a silver tray as if it were her child, wrapped in her arms, its edge tight under her chest, gleaming covers hiding each dish.

'Show me this . . .' Whispers rose in him, one stronger than the rest.

—*Send her away.*

The image came to him of a jagged stone, clutched in a man's hand, both coated with blood, hair, fragments of bone, flecks of brain.

—*You don't want to see.*

'No, take her away, Ta-Sann. Tell the kitchens to keep her.'

The girl made no move in her dismay and Ta-Sann set a hand to her shoulder to aim her at the door. As he turned her somehow the dish closest to the edge of the tray slipped and fell. The second sword-son had his blade at her throat before the item hit the floor. Cover and plate flew apart and something dark shot forth, coming to rest a yard from Sarmin's feet. A stone, dull black, smooth-edged, a comfortable fit for a man's hand. A shock of recognition ran through him.

The sword-sons took the girl to the doorway, her toes brushing the carpet, body rigid against the threat of the knife by her neck.

'Wait,' Sarmin said.

Ta-Sann stopped and set the servant down.

'I—' Sarmin looked up from the stone to the girl. 'Where did you get this?'

She opened her mouth but no words came out. Sarmin stood, waving away the sword-sons' blades. 'What's your name?'

'Rushes, My Emperor. Also Red-Rose.' With the knife gone she found her voice more easily. Instinct drew her towards the obeisance, but Ta-Sann's grip kept her upright.

'And where did you get this stone, Rushes-called-Red-Rose?'

'It was yours, Emperor.' She wouldn't look at him. Sarmin wondered at which point he'd become something that terrified young women. He turned the stone over in his hand. It held a warmth. He would have said from Rushes' grip, but she had not been holding it. The stone was as he remembered it. It had seemed important then, back when he dug it from the wall of that cell, and it seemed so now.

'I don't remember giving it to you.'

'I—you didn't, Magnificence. Not exactly.' A tear fell from behind the veil of her hair and glistened on her cheek.

'I would trust your memory in these matters more than mine, Rushes. I'm not calling you a liar. Why did I give it to you? What were you to do with it?'

'You told me to take it away. To throw it in the deepest part of the Ways.'

'Then how is it here?'

Rushes shook with sobs now, her words hard to understand. 'I kept it. I know I shouldn't have. But I needed help. I needed— It felt wrong to throw it away. I kept saying I would. I—'

'Did you know, Rushes, that the greatest crime in Cerana is treason? Not theft, not murder, not the slaughter of innocents. A man may go to the Maze and hunt children like rats, use them for pleasure, throw their corpses in the midden, and yet it is a lesser crime than for him to not do what I say. If I were to tell that man to pass the salt at table and he were to tell me no . . . that would be a greater crime.' Rushes tried to answer but he spoke over her. 'I was not myself that day. You've done no wrong.'

Rushes lifted her head, enough for Sarmin to see her eyes past the fall of her hair. Sarmin turned the stone over in his hand, turned it again, squeezed it. It felt heavier than it should. 'I am pleased to have this back. I have . . . read . . . about it. But why have you brought it to me after all these weeks?'

For a moment Sarmin thought he would get no answer. He opened his mouth but the girl shuddered and spoke. 'My Emperor, there's an old woman in the dungeons—'

'No! The dungeons are empty.'

'I—I spoke with an old woman, My Emperor.'

'I ordered the dungeons cleared!' Sarmin turned to Ta-Sann. 'Summon my vizier.'

As Ta-Sann relayed the order to one of his men Sarmin motioned for the girl to continue.

'I wanted to put the stone back in that little cell. I needed to. The stone insisted.' She paused and looked at her hands, turned up as if for inspection, or to catch her tears, though she had stopped crying. Her voice took on a sing-song tone, as if she were too deep in memory to remember where she was. 'But the cell was locked. An old woman put her face to the window. I wanted to give her the stone, asked her to put it back, but she wouldn't take it. She said I must take the stone to the emperor and tell him that she knew the man who hid it there in that . . . she called it an oubliette. Rhymes with forget, that's how she told me to remember it.'

Rushes' head snapped up, sudden as if startling from sleep, her hair swinging to either side, leaving her face to face with Sarmin, eyes wide and staring into his. 'I didn't want to come to you. I didn't. I was scared. But it's important. I know it is.'

'Ta-Sann, have this prisoner brought to me. This old woman.'

'Here, My Emperor?'

Sarmin thought of having her taken to the throne room, of sitting above his captive in the Petal Throne, lord of all Cerana. 'Here,' he said. 'This is where it began.'

Azeem entered the room, robes swishing, with Ta-Sann behind him, returning from sending for the old woman. The vizier took in the scene with a quick glance: Rushes, red-eyed, still clutching her tray, held in turn by a sword-son, and Sarmin standing in the wreckage of his former prison. The vizier's eyes caught for a moment on the stone in Sarmin's hands, then moved on.

'My emperor has need of me?' He went into the obeisance, and Sarmin let him, counting out his temper while the man kept his face to the dusty carpet.

'Rise.' Sarmin waited while Azeem got to his feet, traces of plaster on his cheekbones making sharp contrast with the darkness of his skin. Sarmin remembered when they had spoken together of the Islands. *We are both strangers here.* His anger softened. 'I ordered the dungeons emptied, but I'm told we keep old women locked there now?'

Azeem bowed his head. 'The dungeons were emptied, My Emperor, in obedience to your command. Each prisoner was released or executed according to their crime, and each man to die was first taken to the wall where they spoke with priest Dinar of Herzu's order and saw the sky.'

'The dungeons *were* emptied . . . but now they are being filled again?' Sarmin saw the gap he had left in his order.

'Even so, My Emperor. Prisoners from the Fryth campaign arrived during the night in waggons from the front.'

'Vizier, the man I want in your slippers is a man who obeys the intent of my commands, not one who contorts around the letter of them. That island of yours . . . ?'

'Konomagh, My Emperor.'

'It may be that you should consider a return to it.'

'As my emperor commands.' Azeem bowed lower. 'But before I empty the dungeons again may I offer the reasons for placing the Fryth there?' Sarmin sealed his lips, and taking the pause for assent Azeem continued. 'The prisoners arrived after Envoy Kavic and Austere Adam, having taken the longer route. They were still being processed when news of the envoy's death reached me. Many of these prisoners are soldiers, violent men with grievances. To loose such men outside the palace on a night when their envoy had been murdered would have been unwise. Moreover discussions in the throne room touched on the possibility that the envoy never arrived in Nooria but was attacked by bandits and slain along the borderland trails on his way to your palace.'

'Herran did suggest that,' Sarmin agreed.

'Such a fiction would be hard to maintain if freed prisoners from Fryth were allowed to wander, perhaps picking up news of the envoy's arrival in the city, or even rumours of his fate.'

'An emperor is not allowed to apologise.' Sarmin set a hand to Azeem's shoulder, then turned away to look at the wall where his councillors had once lived in the scroll and detail of the decoration. Had he been mad? Had he projected parts of his own personality onto imagined faces? Or had he summoned the wisdom of spirits living behind what men took for real? He touched his hand to the broken plaster, rubbed the powder between his fingers. Aherim had spoken to him from the pattern written here, the sternest of the angels, cautious in his council. Zanasta too, oldest of the devils, and given to secrets. They had bound him to this room more securely than locks and guards. Mesema had given him his freedom when she destroyed them. *I miss them.*

Sarmin wiped his hand across his robe. 'Sometimes I sound like my brother. A man with the lives of five hundred thousand and more in his hands should not be quick to anger, nor quick to take offence, nor slow to forgive.'

'Emperor Beyon was a great man.' A girl's voice.

Sarmin turned in surprise and found Rushes covering her mouth as if scared of what words might escape next. 'I loved him too, Rushes.' He smiled. 'And I can see where you got your name. Perhaps that's why he liked you. Both of you led by the heart. Rushing in.' Sarmin met Azeem's eyes, pleased that the vizier didn't look away but watched him closely. 'Good men, great men, men of the heart, all of them can make bad emperors.' Sarmin's gaze returned to the stone, so ordinary in all respects and yet somehow fascinating. 'So tell me, Azeem, how many prisoners do we have in the cells?'

'Two hundred and six, My Emperor. General Arigu's report indicates over three hundred departed his camp in Fryth. I understand there were many casualties along the route. Privation and disease led to high rates of attrition.'

'And how many old women are among them?'

'I believe there are twenty women, My Emperor, I was not informed of their ages.' From the expression that passed across Azeem's face Sarmin judged it physically pained the man to be found wanting in information.

A knock, and one of the sword-sons entered at Sarmin's

permission. 'The prisoner is being helped up the stairs, My Emperor.'

'Would this be the old woman you alluded to, My Emperor?' Azeem tilted his head in question.

Sarmin held up the stone, not quite a perfect circle, not quite smooth, not quite black. 'What can you tell me about this?'

'I—' Azeem blinked. 'Nothing, Your Excellency.' Again that look of acute unhappiness.

'Well our guest claims to have more knowledge, so I have extended her my invitation.'

It took less time than Sarmin anticipated for the knock announcing the prisoner. Fryth bred its old women tough it seemed. Perhaps the mountains there made the two hundred steps of his tower feel like nothing. Govnan had once told him that mountains, like the sea, must be seen to be believed, and lived in to be understood.

She walked in behind the largest of the sword-sons, at first obscured by his frame, then revealed. He knew her in that moment and the sight of her took the strength from his limbs. For a moment he stood once more in the gloom beneath innumerable trees with the deluge shedding cold across his shoulders. Stick-thin, ragged, gristle and wrinkles over old bones, somehow she radiated a strength that made the island warriors look frail in comparison. The Megra looked first to the stone, then to Sarmin, her eyes hard, the colour of flint. Sarmin had seen her through Gallar's eyes and now she stood before him in the place where he had watched her from without and from within.

'I never thought to see another.' Her words, dry with age, wrapped in the harsh accents of the east.

Ta-Sann motioned to his brothers that they should put the woman into the obeisance. She must have been instructed, but like all these northerners she would rather break than bend.

'Leave her.' Sarmin waved his guard back. Beyon would have had her legs broken. That or swept her into his arms, calling her Grandmother and laughing at her audacity. Either one a possibility depending on his mood. 'I am the emperor Sarmin. What is your name, madam?' Sarmin had no desire to admit his knowledge of her, a stolen glimpse tarnished by the act of theft, though he had not been the one to steal it. He wondered what the Megra thought of his own stiff formality. She looked to have seen a hundred summers, but two hundred would be closer to the mark. Did a hundred summers bring wisdom, and if so, what did the wise think of Sarmin?

'They called me the Megra.' She shook her head. 'A Yrkman pattern killed all the people who knew my name. All save one. A boy escaped, and your soldiers strung him from a tree.' She extended a finger towards the stone. 'It wasn't chance that put me in that cell. I knew a man who spent a year in it, lifetimes ago. I could taste him still, on the air, in the darkness. I helped the guards select that one for me. That man called me Meg. His Meg.' She made to spit, as if a moment of sweetness had turned sour on the instant.

In Sarmin's hands the stone grew suddenly warmer, more heavy.

'Tell them to leave.' The voice came from behind him, not from within, not from the Many. A stern voice remembered from a thousand nights alone in this room. 'All of them but Meg.'

'Aherim?' Sarmin wanted to laugh.

'My Emperor?' Azeem looked surprised. None of them had

reacted to Aherim's voice, only to Sarmin speaking the angel's name.

Aherim! Always so stern! 'Leave me. All of you. Only the Megra is to stay.' Sarmin clapped his hands to startle them into action.

Ta-Sann led his brothers from the room, ushering Rushes with them. Azeem followed, looking worried, but saying nothing. As the door closed Sarmin whirled to face the wall beside his bed. He'd half expected to see Aherim's face written back across the broken plaster, half expected that the scrolling decoration that concealed and revealed him would be spreading out across the wall once more like vine tendrils growing as he watched.

'Aherim?' he asked.

'I heard a voice too.' The Megra spoke behind him.

'You heard Aherim?' Sarmin glanced back at her.

'I heard a voice.' She nodded. The Megra took six steps and set her bony hands to the wall beside the door where the decoration remained.

'There used to be many voices here. Angels and devils. But you had to hunt for them. It took years to find some of them,' Sarmin told her.

'They kept you here?' She didn't wait for his agreement. 'They kept him here too. Year after year. He grew up here, until the Yrkmen brought their war into the desert. His brother hid him in the dungeon then. For safe-keeping. In an oubliette. To forget.'

'Who?' But Sarmin knew the answer.

'Helmar.'

'The Pattern Master.' Sarmin's hand remembered how it had felt to thrust the Knife into Helmar's chest.

The Megra traced a single line through the complexity of the scrollwork. 'He told me they brought him to a bare room. He was too young to understand, but he grew into it. They let him paint the walls. He would spend months at it, then rub it all away and start again.' Her nail ended its path where one of Mesema's blows had cratered the wall. 'This is all his work. He wrote himself here.'

'My angels . . .' Sarmin hunted for his next breath.

'Echoes of Helmar, reflections of him, aspects and fragments.' The Megra turned her flint eyes towards him. 'We're none of us one thing. Someone told me that once.'

Sarmin held the stone up, his arm trembling with the effort. 'Then this is his? The Pattern Master's stone?'

'Helmar's.' She nodded. 'He made one for me, back when I was young, and he was . . . less old.'

'She loved me.' Aherim's voice, from the walls, pulsing at the edge of hearing.

'You *loved* him?'

A long pause and the Megra nodded, a smile of remembrance softening the hard angles of her face for a moment. Her teeth perfect, just one gone, leaving a black slot. *We're none of us one thing.* A hint perhaps of the mountain girl Helmar once met. Then a shrug. He could almost hear the creak of her shoulders. 'A passing thing. Love is like that. The Voice in my village, Voice Zanar, used to sing that love came like a cloud's shadow on the mountain slopes. When you're in it you don't see that it's always moving. Just a boy of fifty that Zanar, but he had it right.

'I kept that stone. Kept it as my home-stone. Close on two hundred years sitting in the middle of my hut, watching me get old. It's still there now I expect. Filthy rangers wouldn't have a use for it. They'd be too busy stealing my copper pans.' She shook her head and made to spit again, before thinking better of it. Her hair hung in grey rat-tails, mottled scalp showing beneath. Dirt crusted on the ragged wool of her dress; she smelled of decay, but still Sarmin felt a resonance between them. Something shared. Perhaps just the knowing that develops in those who have been too much alone.

'Tell me about Helmar's stone. You asked to see me, put a charm on that girl to get your way. What is it you have to say?' He swapped the stone from one hand to the other as he spoke, and her eyes followed.

'It holds a power and a secret,' she said.

'I know. It drew me to his cell, kept me there until I found it. But what power? What secret?' Perhaps it was a key to the pattern, to reversing Helmar's work, to healing Mogyrk's wound.

'Ha! If I knew that I wouldn't have let the austeres destroy my home, or your soldiers lay hands on me.' She paused and looked away from the stone. 'I wouldn't have let them hang that fool boy.'

'What was his name?' Sarmin saw Gallar had meant more to her than she wanted to let show. But sometimes what a person wants is not what they need.

'Gallar. Almost grown but still a boy. We're none of us one thing – he said that to me. Be brave, he said. Always spouting nonsense. Look inside, he said, as if an old woman needs a child to teach her to see past surfaces. A foolish child, wasted, hung from a tree. Did you know your soldiers hang men in foreign lands, Emperor? Shopkeepers, woodcutters, charcoal men, foolish boys, all throttled on ropes under a tree. That's the lesson age teaches us. The one about waste.'

'I've tried to stop this war. It's nothing of mine.' But the ache in his throat, the memory of the rope tightening about Gallar's neck for the last time – that told a different story. Sarmin owned the war as he owned the empire. Responsibility had to lie somewhere, had to be claimed. Sarmin turned the stone over and found no insight. 'So all you have to tell me is that it's powerful?'

'The truth?' The Megra reached out again to the wall. 'I wanted to see you. To see what there was of him in you. To see where he had been kept so long. To see you in Helmar's room.'

'You took quite a risk. The Reclaimer's line are not famed for their patience.'

Again the shrug of ancient shoulders. 'I'm an old woman with no roots left, waiting to die. They brought me a long way to reach Nooria. It didn't seem so big a thing to travel the last few hundred yards and see Helmar's heir.'

That sent a shiver down his spine. *Helmar's heir.* Sarmin went back to where Aherim and Zanasta had hidden in the detail. He knelt before the wall, careless of the Megra. Had the faces still been there they would have been positioned level with his shoulders, an angel for one shoulder and a devil for the other, to whisper in his ears.

'All this time I spoke to the Pattern Master?'

'To echoes Helmar left behind, yes. Echoes of a young man, much like you, sharing a similar fate.'

'I never killed. I—'

'And yet people died, and you became emperor. As did Helmar. And every day more people die, more throats are cut, more boys hung from branches with a rope about their neck. It's the way of things, what we do. People hurt each other.

Sometimes good men shed more innocent blood than the bad ones do.'

Sarmin set the stone before the wall. For an instant he saw himself setting the stone down on desert sands, stepping back, stepping away, watching that one dark point dwindle among the white and blinding expanse of the dunes.

'What do you know of the desert, Megra?' The question bubbled up within him and he claimed it as his own, though his thoughts had been very much on what lay before him.

'The desert?' A shrill note entered the old woman's voice. 'You ask a woman of the mountains about the desert?'

'Yes. What do you know of it?'

'You won't make me go there?'

'No.'

A long pause and then: 'Only what Helmar knew. Only that the story of men is being unwritten in the desert. Only that nothing lives there . . . and that the nothing is growing.'

She looked old. As old as her years and weary with them. Sarmin turned towards the scrollwork by the window, the place where he had found the voice and seen the first steps of the Megra's journey towards him. 'Here,' he said, and pointed. 'He still lives here.'

The Megra stepped in closer, tilting her head. 'It's his name.'

And Sarmin tilting his head in the same way saw what had eluded his eyes for so many years, lettering reduced to pattern and slanted through a confusion of calligraphic swirls. Helmar.

The Megra reached the wall, knelt, as swift as if she were a child, and set her withered hand to the writing. It seemed that the room released a long-held breath and in that moment each part of the wall stole into motion, the lines the Pattern Master wrote there so long ago flowing and unfolding, drawn like water to a spout. Lines writhed in black and blue across the Megra's hand, wrapping her fingers, curling up around her wrist, sinking in. In the space of five heartbeats all trace of Helmar's work had vanished, sunk into the Megra, deep as bones.

Sarmin turned, taking in the blank walls. Only the ceiling retained its panorama of the gods. Without their decoration the walls became alien, a close friend suddenly without a face. 'He's with you, now? In you?'

The Megra stood. She smiled. He wondered if she had smiled in his lifetime. 'Memories, fragments of who he was, hopes . . .' She set a hand to her face as if touching it for the first time. 'Dreams.'

Sarmin stared at the walls once more and their blankness recalled him to his need, to the nothing growing close at hand, ready to erase more than painted lines. 'And the stone, can you tell me its secret now?'

'Nothing's ever that simple.' The Megra shook her head, a dazed look to her where before all had been bitterness and calculation. 'Let me think, boy, let me think. I'm full of dreams.'

'Ta-Sann!' Sarmin rose to instruct the sword-son as he entered. 'Escort the Megra to High Mage Govnan. Please ask him to consider her an honoured guest who must, for now, be watched over until we can establish why she was sent here with the other prisoners from the Fryth incursion. Tell him there may be much to learn from her.'

34

Nessaket

It was mad to plant a garden while the women's wing was dying. Five more women had gone pale, the latest named Gala, a merry girl from all reports. Priest Assar only shook his head and gave out phials of poppy-milk: Mirra could be no help in this. And yet Nessaket had ordered plants moved from her temple to be planted here, on the roof. If she waited until Jenni had been caught, or there was no more plague, or for the end of the war, then Siri's garden would be dead for ever. Let it live one last time. Even if Nessaket had to flee, back to the forested home of her parents or the oceanside manse of Tuvaini's, she would first see blossoms on this roof.

A few days ago the pika seeds in her pocket had meant everything. Though she had chosen not to use them, Kavic had died anyway. Events had their own way of coming about, as if they had already been written into place and needed only time to arrive there. It made the fluttering of the courtiers appear futile, senseless, the struggles of a butterfly caught in water. The garden gave better results.

Dreshka finished planting the last of the roses and wiped the sweat from her brow with a dirty arm, smearing her face with soil. 'Stupid girl,' said Nessaket, wishing Rushes were here instead – but she had disappeared after giving her warning about Jenni. She hoped the girl had not met an ill fate – she was the best spy Nessaket had found thus far. She rocked Daveed in her arms and looked out over the edge, ignoring the guards who hovered, hands reaching out towards the baby lest she lose her grip.

'Apologies, Your Majesty,' said Dreshka. 'I am a stupid girl.'

Nessaket sighed and looked towards Beyon's tomb. Odd stories had been told about that place. A curse on her son, they said, for bearing the pattern while he sat the Petal Throne. Now ghosts haunted his grave. And that was not the only place. Some of the women insisted the women's wing was haunted. 'Foolishness,' she said aloud, though the sight of the tomb disturbed her. It was more than the fact her son was buried there – she had grown accustomed to dead sons. No, something about the shadows there made her uneasy.

Shadows. That would be where Jenni was hiding. The Grey Service hunted the palace for her, the better she did not give warning to her master. But Nessaket was certain she had not left, that she lurked somewhere in these soft halls, waiting to strike. For Jenni's master could offer her nothing but death now, unless she completed her mission.

Six more guards climbed the stairs, three and three, with Mesema between them, Pelar in her arms. She smiled and gave Nessaket a kiss on each cheek before pushing between another set of guards to settle on the bench. Nessaket sat beside her and together they looked at the new rose bed.

'She has not been found,' said Nessaket, before the empress could ask.

Mesema sighed. 'At least we have not been poisoned.'

Nessaket silently agreed. She did not know if she would ever eat normally again, without picking apart her food to check for the crescent-shaped seeds. 'I am glad to see you well. This sickness . . . We may need to leave this place.'

'We will survive it,' said Mesema. 'Disease has tried to defeat us once before, and failed.' *Us.* Mesema had named herself Cerani. 'We will stay.'

But this pale-sickness was not the pattern, and killing its master would not cure. She had lived through other plagues before the blue marks had come, plagues that had killed nearly all the children. She did not feel the empress's confidence. Her throat felt dry. 'Dreshka . . .' she began, thinking to ask for a cup of fresh water, but a high, keening noise made her turn.

Dreshka fell to one side, her arm jerking among the thorns of a rose bush, blood appearing in streaks where the thorns tore her skin. Her head rested on the stone wall, and she held her eyes open with a confused, lost look. At first her legs kicked lazily away from the garden bed, as if she were cooling herself in a pool, but then with more power, her back arching, head finally falling backwards to hit the floor on the other side. Her body twitched between soil and roses, legs spread scandalously apart, urine running down to pool upon the tiles.

Mesema screamed. Nessaket put out a hand to stay her. She had seen this before.

The guards lifted Dreshka from the bushes and held her down on the tiles, whether from propriety or to try and save her, Nessaket could not guess. She could not be saved. Spittle flew from Dreshka's mouth as she tried to speak. 'Ah—Ah—Ah—'

Lapella had died silently. 'Shhh,' said Nessaket. 'Don't be afraid.'

The convulsions had Dreshka now, pulling her up into the air as if hauled by ropes and dropping her again. Her skull made a rapping noise against the roof, *rap rap rap*. 'Can't you stop her head from doing that?' asked Mesema, tears streaming down her cheeks, hiding Pelar's face so that he could not see.

It would go on like this for several minutes. Nessaket had seen it before and did not wish to witness it again. 'Kill her,' she said to the guard at Dreshka's shoulder. 'Stab her heart.' To her credit Mesema made no protest.

The guard drew a dagger and hesitated. 'She'll die anyway,' Nessaket insisted. Dreshka's chest was heaving so much that the guard struggled. Five of them held her down, two of them sitting on her hips and legs, so that he could do it. The slave-girl jerked once more, then went still.

Nessaket crouched by the girl, careful not to touch the blood with her silks. She examined Dreshka's dirty hands, checked her pockets and reached inside her robes. There she found it. Linen folded into a square, containing a bit of bread, some half-eaten cheese and the stem of a candied fig. 'The servants' meals,' she said. 'Of course. She wanted to kill the slave who could identify her.'

'But this wasn't her—'

And Lapella had been barren. 'Yes,' said Nessaket, 'sometimes things don't work out fairly.' She turned to the guards. 'Take her away.'

Besides her anger and pity Nessaket felt victorious. Jenni had wasted her only weapon. She might still be in the women's wing, hiding in niches or under beds, but she posed no threat. By doing nothing but planting flowers Nessaket had defeated her. It would not be long, now. She would be found.

35

Sarmin

Sarmin held his gaze on the Pattern Master's stone. A year spent in darkness within that oubliette and Helmar had kept this simple river stone, made a hiding place for it, treasured it. He must have turned it in his hands ten times a thousand times. In the blindness of that place he set his brilliant mind upon this stone and worked wonders. *And I can find no single hint of any piece of magic.* He had hoped it would free him from the Many, stop the emptiness from spreading out from Beyon's tomb. That was what Helmar had promised, when he had reached out to him from the past. The stone was the key to the pattern.

He sat alone in his room. Azeem pestered him with messages and with visits, pleading for him to hold court, to be seen in the Petal Throne, to be emperor. Even the priests visited him, clambering up the many stairs to stand before him sweating in their robes and symbols. Dinar of Herzu's temple, his shoulders as broad as Ta-Sann's, almost scraping the sides of the doorway as he entered, had talked of duty.

'In time of war the emperor must lead, Excellency.' He held his staff of office tight, skin pale around the black tears tattooed along the arcs of index fingers and thumbs.

'We are still at truce, High Priest,' Sarmin had told him. 'Herzu is patient – do they not say that of him? He has no need of wars to hurry us through his gates.' Sarmin kept the Pattern Master's stone in his hands, smoothing it between them as if it were his own creation and he was finishing off the final touches.

Assar of Mirra came too, his grim face given colour by the climb, a man ill-suited to sharing out Mirra's love.

'The empire has been sick with this plague of patterns for generations, My Emperor. Even with the agent of the disease removed our recovery is not complete. Such conditions leave scars and the road back to health can be slow. The Longing grips our people and a new sickness emerges. We need our emperor among us, showing our strength and unity. The loneliness of this tower is an illness too, and surely your wife—'

'The empress needs your attentions more than I do, Assar.' Sarmin cut across him, his tone sharp. 'And if I am alone here then you are years too late with your company.'

Others came, last of them a pale young woman, a native of Kreshta, south beyond even Konomagh, and newly appointed priestess of Ghesh – Sarmin had been introduced briefly at Pelar's birth feast but couldn't recall her name. She strode in past the sword-sons with such purpose that Sarmin imagined they would have stood nose to nose but for Ta-Sann's intervening arm. Her passage blocked, the priestess came to a halt, diaphanous robes in blackest silk swirling about her like smoke.

'I bring you the blessings of Ghesh, My Emperor.' She made the bow that the holiest may offer in place of obeisance.

'Ghesh, clothed in darkness, eater of stars.' Sarmin smiled at her seriousness. 'Zanasta used to speak of him often.'

'I—'

'Remind me of your name,' Sarmin interrupted her. Better to put her on a new course than explain Zanasta. Perhaps though Ghesh would approve of his having been raised by demons.

'Maniloot, My Emperor.' She had no accent. Perhaps she had been raised in Nooria despite her looks and the strangeness of her name.

He held the stone to his ear, tapped his fingers to it. 'And have you come to urge me to my throne room, Maniloot? To have me scold and chide my collection of wise men, to line up my lords and satraps, generals and governors, and keep the game in order?' He returned Helmar's stone to his lap, looking for the thousandth time to find any hint of pattern in the vague mottling across its surface.

'No, My Emperor. All Settu strategies are the same when the board is burning.'

Sarmin glanced up at the woman. She was even younger than he had first thought. Perhaps as young as he. A child for the priesthood. Her life spent directing prayers to Ghesh, begging he ignore mankind and continue his long voyaging between the stars. 'You're worried about the war? The truce—'

'The Fryth are not the threat.' A sharp intake of breath from Ta-Sann. A priestess does not cut across the emperor.

She knew, then. Sarmin felt a hollowness inside, remembering the Megra's words: *The story of man is being unwritten in the desert.* He remembered standing in the tomb, feeling the Many flow away from him like water into a crack. 'Wouldn't Ghesh approve of nothing? He's famed for extinguishing the heavens one star at a time, after all.' The worship of Ghesh had always niggled at Sarmin. He couldn't find it in him to pray to a god only in the hope of being ignored.

'The void that grows among us, beginning in the deepest desert, is not the emptiness of dark heavens. The darkness is being unwound together with the light, both robbed of meaning. This is not the desert spreading, My Emperor. The sand may drift against our walls, the dunes march out and choke the Blessing, but in the heart of the desert sand itself is unravelling, grain by grain, into nothing.'

'And what then do you ask of me, priestess?'

She looked at him, her boldness gone. 'Save us.'

And Sarmin, finding he had no more words, no questions or encouragement, let her go.

Azeem returned to press his forehead against the carpet with no mind to the plaster dust that ground itself against his dark robes. He gave off a sharp odour of sweat and worry, unusual for such a fastidious man, and he spoke first in a breach of protocol that had Ta-Sann stepping forwards. 'I bear urgent news, Majesty.'

Sarmin waved off the sword-son, sweat trickling down his back as he considered what new disaster might have befallen them. He needed more time – time to invent a story about Marke Kavic, to deal with Jomla's conspirators, to heal the wound that bled from his brother's tomb. Time to unlock the secrets of Helmar's stone. *And yet the world does not wait for me.* 'How stands my empire, High Vizier?'

Azeem stood and brushed white powder from his long face. 'The empire stands strong, but the White Hat army less so this day. Messengers have arrived in Nooria, sent through the mountain passes from Arigu's second in command.'

'No word preceded them on the wind?'

'Silence from Mage Mura.' Azeem let that hang in the air

a moment. The wind-mage Mura was one of four remaining to the Tower, that cornerstone of empire, the might of Cerana manifest in runes and elemental skill. They had sent her to Fryth to help secure the peace. 'We have been betrayed by our horsemen allies. Their new chief—'

'Banreh.' Sarmin had seen him once, through Grada's eyes, sun on yellow curls.

'Yes. Banreh the Lame, they call him. He and the heir to Fryth—'

'But the heir is dead.' Throat slit. Sarmin remembered the blood, or thought he did, and yet Grada had told him it was Jenni who killed the marke.

Azeem cleared his throat. 'Marke Kavic had a cousin, Majesty, who conspired with the Windreader chief. Treacherous savages!' The last he spat out with uncharacteristic emotion. 'They must have learned, somehow, that Marke Kavic is dead.'

In the time of the Many such information could be shared with a thought. Now, though, it would take weeks. Word to be passed from mouth to mouth, along trade routes, over mugs of beer at the roadside. How could it have happened so quickly?

'And the army?' Sarmin turned the stone in his palm. Even now he wanted to turn away from Azeem, to focus on Helmar's work.

'The army approaches through the desert, Your Majesty, but without Arigu.'

'Nor the mage?'

'Nor the mage.'

Sarmin passed the stone from one hand to the other, feeling its smooth warmth and the promise of magic shiver against his skin. Cerana's great general and one of its last mages, missing. Perhaps dead. Whatever the Pattern Master had fore-seen of this war, the stone kept hidden. 'Keep this quiet for the moment,' he said at last. 'I do not wish the empress to hear of this from anyone but me.'

'Yes, Magnificence. But if you would just come down, meet with council, be seen by the lords . . .'

'No.' Sarmin held the stone to his lips. He would eat it if he could, crush it between his teeth and taste its secrets like salt against his tongue. 'I am not finished.'

Azeem knew when he was defeated; Sarmin liked that about him, at least. His gaze lingered on the stone in Sarmin's hands for just a moment, and then he was gone.

'My Emperor?'

Sarmin looked up from the Pattern Master's stone. His eyes ached with looking. His mind trembled with half-felt touches of hidden magic.

'My Emperor?' Ta-Sann behind the door where once the guards had served to keep him in.

'Yes?'

'The empress requests an audience.'

Sarmin rose quickly to his feet, crossed to the door and threw it wide. 'The empress is always to be admitted!' Beyond Ta-Sann Mesema waited in silks of pale green, jade about her throat in strings, her hair piled and golden, tamed by ivory combs. Two slaves waited with her, Tarub and Willa, and looming behind them an imperial guardsman, their escort from the women's wing. 'A crowd!' Sarmin made an apolo-getic smile seeing them all huddled together on the small landing.

Mesema bowed her head and walked on in, alone. She held

her shoulders straight and her chin high as she waited for Sarmin to close the door. Once his men and her ladies were shut from the room she said, 'You keep too much to this room, Sarmin. Your subjects talk of it. Mad Sarmin in his tower. You haven't even let them repair the walls.' She kicked dust from the carpet as if to prove her point, and glanced about frowning at the blankness, as if aware of a change but unable to say what it was.

Sarmin let himself grin. 'Azeem would have taken a week to say all that! He would have circled around what he wanted to say dropping endless subtle hints in the hope I wouldn't force him to speak plainly.'

'Azeem is not your wife.'

'Maybe he needs one of his own, to teach him new ways?'

Mesema shrugged, glancing about for somewhere to sit. 'If he wants a woman he will find one. The Old Wives say he has no taste for girls.' She shrugged again. 'When he speaks to you, listen for the message – he is a good man.'

Sarmin watched as Mesema sat in the chair where his mother had sat on her visits as she watched him grow, an hour a month, checking on him as a gardener might. Mesema had seldom looked more lovely. She was recovering from her pregnancy, less pale, less thin, her silks pressing against her form. Even so his gaze fell to the stone in his hand.

'Marke Kavic is dead,' she said, 'but we may still try for peace if you would only leave this room. Now that Banreh is chief, I know you'll have the Windreaders on your side. I can help you to convince him.'

Azeem's news tickled against Sarmin's lips. He should tell her what Banreh the Lame had done. Soon the dusty, defeated army would trickle into Nooria, cursing the name of her countryman, aiming threats at her people like arrows. And yet he remained silent, turning the stone against his palm. Marke Kavic's death and the loss of the peace was his failure, one of weakness or madness he did not know; but it was one more thing that would come between them. He did not want her to see him that way, to worry with him about his lost time, the things he did when another governed his body – not before he found what Helmar had left for him. Once he had solved the mystery of the stone and saved Nooria, healed the wound, then he could tell her how badly he had failed in Fryth.

'And the people would whisper louder of madness if they knew that you spent your time up here staring at a stone.' Mesema pursed her lips, the compassion in her motherly. In that moment more than any other he wanted her to want him, needed her to need him. And yet he had left her in the women's wing to live a life separate from the threats that consumed his time. Had he meant to protect her, or protect himself from the clear insight of her gaze? He watched her as she spoke, waited for her to reach out, to show that she wanted to touch him. But instead she folded her hands in her lap. 'They tell me it came from the dungeons. Some old woman brought it to you out of a cell?'

Sarmin sat before her, cross-legged on the carpet. He leaned forwards and placed the stone on her lap like an offering. 'Helmar made it.'

'The Pattern Master?' Mesema flinched as if he had placed a rat-spider on her legs. 'It can be nothing good!' She raised her hands to her shoulders, palms outwards.

'Perhaps.' Sarmin sighed and retrieved the stone. 'But he wasn't always the creature we saw. He grew here.' He set his fingers to the floor. 'Walked my paths, shared my blood. He was a young man full of passions, hopes, ambition, all locked away here year upon year. I can't hate him, Mesema.'

Mesema said nothing, only looked away to the narrow slot of sky through the Sayakarva window. They sat in silence for a time.

'Gala fell sick last night,' Mesema said.

'Who?'

'Gala! She's one of your harem. I thought I mentioned her . . .'

It pulled them apart. How many times had his lips spoken to Mesema with another man's voice? 'Has Assar sent a healer?' he asked.

'Assar came himself.'

Sarmin blinked at that. 'Mirra's own priest attending a concubine? Was her illness that interesting?'

'Her hair turned white and she won't speak.' Mesema drew her knees up, hunching in, all of a sudden a nervous girl lost within an empress's dress. 'And, Sarmin, her eyes . . .' A shudder ran through her. 'She's not the first. Irisa fell ill before her.'

Sarmin stood and went to the window, rising to his toes so he could look down upon Beyon's mausoleum, a squat, wide building out beyond the palace walls.

'I'm scared, Sarmin.'

'Yes.' The mausoleum's ceiling had fallen in two days before. He had heard it as distant thunder. Now the outer walls shed their plaster in white clouds, teased away by the wind like funeral smoke, bare and pale brick exposed beneath.

'And the guards speak of ghosts, here and in the city also. Tarub saw one, in the Red Room, a reflection in the fountain.

She won't speak of it. If you ask her what she saw she tells you: "Nothing", but it haunts her. She won't walk anywhere alone. Willa sleeps with her now.'

The djinn. Notheen had warned of them. Sarmin pressed the stone to his forehead. 'The trouble spreads from the tomb.' He turned to face her.

'Beyon's tomb?' She coloured at that.

'Yes.' At last she knew. He had kept it from her so long. 'It isn't pattern work. Something new, or rather something old, from the desert, bleeding in through the hole Helmar made when you—' He lifted a hand to stop her objection. 'When Beyon died.'

'I have Seen it,' she said, to his surprise, 'but I didn't know it had come to pass.' She leaned closer, eyes intent. 'Can it be stopped? How can I help?'

'I don't know.' Sarmin brought his shoulders forwards, trying to shrug off the helplessness. 'The mages might . . .' He let out his exasperation in a long breath. 'I don't know.'

'Will your gods help us?'

Sarmin looked at her and for a moment saw once again the young girl on her horse, trekking the grasslands. The tribes spoke to their Hidden God, and he spoke back. 'Our gods in Cerana are not so . . .' He groped for the word. Real? 'They don't help, only watch.' He gestured to the ceiling where the pantheon crowded amid painted heavens. 'If I were to set the priests to healing this wound, and were they to fail, it would erode Cerana's faith at a time when our people are already flocking to the Yrkman church.'

'What then?' She showed no mercy, and why should she? He was emperor, Sarmin the Saviour, the light of heaven, pattern mage. He was her husband. What mother wouldn't demand the same when her baby lay in the path of destruction? 'What will you do, Sarmin?'

'I . . . I don't know.' His hand rose, the black stone filling it. 'Perhaps this . . .'

'But you said pattern-magic wouldn't work, you—'

'I don't know!' His answer came out louder and more angry than he had intended. He knelt beside her chair, before the shock on her face had time to harden into something else. 'I'm sorry. I don't know. And I'm scared too.'

A dull rumbling rolled across the silence that followed. The wall of Beyon's tomb falling. There would be no hiding it now. Somewhere away towards the kitchen wing a high wail went up, perhaps another person emptied, perhaps another djinn staring hungry from the shadows. Mesema took his hand, squeezed it, hard. 'We'll find a way. We are Cerani. We carry on.'

36

Sarmin

Sarmin went to the Megra. In the *Book of Etiquette* an emperor is instructed never to visit but always to summon. The world flows to the feet of the mighty. From the Petal Throne the emperor may see all that concerns him, for he is the light of heaven. Sarmin had spent days upon each page of that fat tome, but a year into his freedom it occurred to him that a man who can have his brothers killed, who can send an Untouchable to kill an heir and find none to stop him, should hardly be instructed by a book, however many pages it may possess.

Ta-Marn knocked upon the door then pushed it open. An emperor at least does not wait on permission.

In the bright room beyond, the Megra sat with an old servant woman, one of his mother's perhaps; she seemed familiar. They sat amid white cushions scattered in abandon, a Settu board between them.

'Who is winning?' Sarmin walked past Ta-Marn. The serving woman sent the board spinning as she fell into her obeisance.

'No one, now.' The Megra gave him half a gap-toothed smile. They had traded her crawling rags for a grey shift from the kitchen staff.

Sarmin riffled through the pages of the *Book of Etiquette*. Were commoners even permitted to play Settu? Were women? It occurred to him that he didn't care. 'Perhaps we could speak alone. Ta-Marn will escort . . .'

'Her name is Sahree. You should let her up. She's an old woman and not well.'

'Ta-Marn will escort Sahree to a seat in some other chamber.'

The sword-son followed his instructions and the Megra scooped up Settu tiles, standing some on the board. At last they sat facing each other, the light streaming in through high windows.

'Has the high mage found you useful, Megra?' Sarmin asked. He had wondered what Govnan would make of her, that rare individual at once older, more shrewd and more sour than himself.

The Megra licked the corner of her mouth as if tasting the memory. 'I remembered a thing or two that his Tower had forgotten. His kind have spent too long looking into the fire, watching the skies, contemplating the deep places. The secrets most worth having are to be found close at hand. Always.'

'Helmar told you that?'

'I told me that.'

'And did these secrets please Govnan?'

'They puzzled him. Good secrets are always a puzzle.' She took the last grape from a copper bowl and set it in her mouth. 'His mages seek new accords with their cousins in flame and air. The void has opened on man and elemental alike, and fear breeds compromise.'

'You know about the problem in my brother's tomb, then?'

'You have so many brothers in tombs, Emperor.'

'In Beyon's tomb.'

'Helmar's work is coming undone. Your man from the desert thinks you should move.'

'A city cannot be moved. If the people are taken from it the city remains. If these stones crumble, Cerana is done. What people would serve an emperor who cannot hold his capital?'

The Megra squashed the grape beneath her tongue and sucked the juice. 'I am too old to care.'

'I have a wife, a baby son, Helmar's blood. Is there no secret you have that might save us?' Beyon would have threatened a stake and fire.

'Your Notheen has the right of it. Leave. Take your wife, your child, some gold. Live free in some other place. You will be happier.'

Sarmin smiled at the thought. A small house of seven floors, in some city compound, Mesema and he and Pelar, a few servants, no duties but to spend gold and grow fat. 'I would be happier – but I am Sarmin the Saviour. It is not my part to be happy. And besides, the nothing would spread, would follow us. Sooner or later we would run out of places to flee.'

The Megra pursed her lips and nodded. 'It picks up pace, like a fire. An ember has smouldered for a thousand years but now the flame is woken.'

'And so I must stay. Be brave though I have never been before, look inside myself for the person I need to be. And all the hope I have is this stone.' He pulled it from his robe. 'Helmar's stone. And I think that if there is a key to it then you must be the key.'

The Megra looked suddenly as if her years had fallen from a great height and landed upon her all at once. She shook her head. 'I've been too long alone. Helmar taught me to see through darkness and I chose instead to live in it. The years ruined us both in the end. Carried us away from ourselves in a river of days until the past became lost to us and the current left us stranded on new shores, me to be alone with my cowardice and selfishness, Helmar to madness and cruelty. I hold new memories of him now, new understanding. It is better this way, but some hurts cannot be undone, only . . . stepped away from. You understand?'

'How was he before – when you loved him?' It seemed important to know the man who made that stone, who pressed his secrets into it.

'Bold.' She smiled. 'Exciting. Curious. Full of life in all its colours.' She looked at Sarmin without seeing. 'I don't know where the pattern came to him. The Yrkmen had such magics, and they taught him as a child after they had taken him from Nooria, but theirs was magic of a cruder kind, old and learned by rote, a blunt power that could be put in the hands of any fool with half a mind and ten years to study it. The Yrkmen austeres could only destroy, only take a thing apart. But Helmar found new pieces to the pattern, new symbols. He spent fifty years finding ways to build, searching all that time for a pattern that could repair, that could remake broken things. And not just dead things that men had made then fractured, but life, living creatures, men, flesh, blood and bone.'

'I have heard of such magics in Yrkmir. Pathfinders who lead a body back to health.'

Megra spat into the copper bowl, careless of her royal audience. 'He taught his captors the rudiments, all that they could follow. But since he left they have lost more of what he taught them than they have discovered with all their schools and academies.'

'But did he succeed?' It felt odd to speak of Helmar, who set the foulest disease on his own people, as a healer, a man who dedicated his youth to enchantment that would do Mirra's work on earth.

'Close.' The Megra pinched the air with finger and thumb to show how close. 'But in the end the puzzle broke him, and he left it all behind.' She shook her head. 'It haunted him, that failure. Leaving things behind became a habit. I was just another broken thing left in his wake.'

'But—' Sarmin held the stone between them.

'Don't think him infallible. He was no Mogyrk walking out of humanity into godhood. He made mistakes. Time and again, even at the start. He called me his salvation, you know? Me? And here I am old enough to be grandmother to the most ancient hag in Nooria, a bitter thing, and him gone mad and stabbed to death with his family Knife. Where's his salvation now?' She spat again and set her fingers to her chest as if feeling some old pain there beneath the tunic. She drew a deep breath, as if remembering. 'Still. He believed in me. I know that now. I took that from your room. His honesty. He believed in me. That's something.'

'There's something here – I *feel* it.' Sarmin set the stone on the Settu board between them. Pieces rocked and toppled. 'I need the key. He called you his Meg and he loved you in his way, loved you before he fell. You know . . . something.'

'Why? Why must I? Because you need me to? You are young indeed if you still think the world works like that. I had a young . . . a young friend who thought that way . . .'

'And?'

'The world rose up and choked him.'

'There's more here, Megra. I know patterns. In my way I know Helmar. I know his pattern, his grand work. A pattern reaches. In a way that's all it does. It spreads itself, it reaches, it covers and contains. A true pattern reaches back, roots itself in our histories, and it reaches forwards, buries its branches in our future. You are here for a reason. Find the courage to hold to that reason.'

The Megra closed her eyes, shook her head, denial written through her. 'I can't.'

'Your friend, Gallar. What would he say?'

And against all expectation a single tear escaped the Megra's wrinkled eyelid, tracing a gleaming path down her cheek. 'Be brave. He told me, be brave. Helmar's message to him.' She clasped her hand to her thin chest, heaving in a breath.

'How? How did Helmar speak to your friend?'

The Megra drew the thong from around her neck, slowly, and at its end a golden band emerged from the top of her tunic, making slow rotations. 'Helmar made it for me.'

'What is it?'

'A message.' She sealed the band between her hands. 'A message for each person who reads it.'

'And what does it say?'

'For me, "You are my salvation". Something new for you. It's worthless. I am hardly his salvation. Don't ask me for it.'

'I must. For a moment at least.'

Without protest, as if she had always known she would part with it, the Megra offered up her prize, and Sarmin took it, drawing a sharp breath at the thrill coursing from the gold through his fingers, swirling in his chest like undirected excitement. He held the ring to his eye, and turned it, reading.

'A lie can still be true.' He looked again, turning the ring, studying the inside and the outside, hunting the edges of its magic. 'A lie can still be true? What does it mean?'

The Megra shrugged. 'All good secrets are a puzzle.'

37

Grada

Those who cross the desert, even its fringes where the dunes are ripples and the hardpan shows like scalp on a balding man, should not expect to arrive at their destination other than worn and weary, hollowed by their privations. Even the Arak who trade with nomads in the outer wastes work metal for salt and return hunched against the wind, burned through every crack in their paint, sand-coated, the humps of their camels hanging flaccid.

When the first of the White Hats emerged hatless from the desert, the Cerani in countless villages along the Blessing thought them deserters. More than one was stoned to death before his dry tongue could shape an explanation. They came: first a handful, then in tens, then hundreds, scattered for thirty miles both up and downstream of Nooria, like a handful of pebbles carelessly launched from Fryth that had showered down around their intended target.

Many, when claiming to be soldiers, were laughed at, so few scraps of their uniform remained to them. Rag-tails, the villagers jeered, flotsam blown by the desert wind – escaped prisoners perhaps, or survivors of ill-fated caravans doomed by their own ignorance and greed. The goodfolk had little patience for beggars, especially those pretending some right to their support and at the same time mocking Cerana's great army of the White.

As the numbers built, as the same tale spilled time and again from cracked lips, and waggons started to roll in – the horses half dead, the cargo of corpses almost too dry to interest the flies – a whisper of disaster started to spread along the Blessing's banks.

Grada saw the first of the great retreat from the west wall. She had taken to jogging from Tewel tower to Maseem's tower in the early dawn, to stretch the scar where Meere's knife had driven in and to exorcise the tenderness below. Perhaps three hundred yards of dusty red brick walkway lay crumbling between those two watchtowers, and she would jog, then stride, then finally stagger the distance, five times. Today though she stopped, leaned out, her hands upon the dusty parapet, and heaved one breath after the next, no longer feeling the echo of Meere's blow with each inhalation. She watched the first units of the Army of the White emerge from their own dust clouds, advancing along the river road towards the Gate of Storms.

'Herzu's Teeth!' An old wall guard ambled from his guard box, as bandy-legged and toothless as all the men set to such duty. He came alongside Grada, clutching his antique spear for support as much as for show. 'Are they bandits? Should I sound the alarm?'

Grada shot him a dark glance. She wondered at what point she had turned from a woman such men would barely trust to wash their linens to a confidante, a commander almost. Did he even know she bore the emperor's Knife, or had her station somehow informed her stance and communicated itself to the world by nothing more than surety?

The old man stumped away towards the iron bell, rusting in its great hoop, waiting for the day's sun to fill it full of heat.

'Don't,' she told him, and he stopped. 'They're Cerani. White Hat.'

'No?' The old man returned to the wall, trying to blink the rheum from his eyes. 'Arigu's men?'

'What's left of them.' A messenger had come in days before. Sunstroke took him before he recovered enough for coherence, but it was clear some great reversal had occurred in the green valleys of Fryth.

Grada nodded. 'Arigu's men.' Would the general be with them, she wondered.

'The gods have deserted us.' A foamy trail of spit made its slow path down the guard's chin. 'The palace haunted, the emperor mad, and now our gods run before Mogyrk!'

'Shut up.' Grada suppressed the strong urge to push the old man from the wall. 'Remember yourself!'

The man looked down, jaw working. Grada snorted, glanced once more towards the river road, and hastened towards the nearest stair.

At the Gate of Storms a crowd of hundreds had gathered. Labourers and foremen, slaves and masters, traders and their customers. Grada pushed her way through, breathing in the stale sweat, cardamom, the tang of lotus sap, the stink of sewers sloping to the river. Shouts went up as soldiers set the gates wide, the squeal of ancient hinges rising over the hubbub.

'Look at them! Look at them!' A child in tatters, wild with excitement.

The first of the White Hats came through in ragged order. These had their helms in the main, the cloth covers, the 'hats', as torn as the urchin's clothes. They kept their gaze to the road, and marched with a remnant of pride, burned black, dusted pale. Those that followed came in a loose rabble, limping, leaning on staffs, hobbling like the old man on the walls.

'Not a wound on them!' A baker hollered it from the crowd. A fat man red from the oven heat.

'What cowards run without a wound?' Some woman lost under cowl and veil, a hysterical edge to her calling.

Grada lifted her gaze above the limp banners of the White Hats to the sky beyond where vultures circled in their wake. 'No wounded man would survive the journey.' She spoke to no one in particular.

'Mogyrk has cursed us!'

'Will the Yrkmen come?'

'The emperor is mad. Everyone says it.'

Grada turned away, forged a path through the crowd with sharp elbows. A hundred yards back she paused in the shadows of an awning, the stallholder presumably at the gates, his melons abandoned. She watched more children tear along the street towards the excitement, widows and old men following on with less speed but scarcely less interest. Perhaps all the shouters were right – the Yrkmen coming, the gods were fleeing before Mogyrk's curse and Sarmin was mad. Perhaps they were all right. She set her hand to the Knife. It didn't matter. She would serve. She felt strong, whole, the ache in her chest more habit and imagination than truth. Across the street, above the rooftops, beyond the river, the rock of the Holies rose, hazing in the distance, drawing her gaze. She would serve. As if one act of sacrifice, one act of loyalty, would stand against the desert and the Yrkmen both.

It was time.

Flies buzzed around Grada even as she crossed the Blessing, even as she walked the high arches of Asham Asherak's great bridge where the breeze normally kept them at bay. The meat drew them. Raw and bloody in her pack, cloth-wrapped, the flies could smell it and gave Grada no peace. At least they couldn't smell the poison that Meere had soaked into the joints. Dogs won't eat what flies won't touch. Everything else, they'll at least try.

'You're sure Jomla keeps dogs?' she had asked Meere. Not out of disbelief but of a desperate hope he might be speaking from expectation rather than observation. The assassin had only narrowed his eyes and continued to poison the mutton.

Already it felt too close to the dream that had echoed through her these past months, laced through with the recollections of the Many. Perhaps some god was steering her there, to the house where the Many remembered some sin greater than the rest. Or maybe simple chance aimed her at a place where she herself had once been put to work killing for the Pattern Master. Chance and the crumbled remnants of his prophecy. Chance or the gods. Did Herzu point her at this house to close some cycle of death, or Mirra to heal some wrong? Grada prayed to both that her fears were without grounds and that a different house awaited her with different results.

'Every noble of consequence has a place on the Holies.' Grada set her hand to the Knife. 'You've cut more throats on that rock than everywhere else put together. You—' She caught herself muttering and sealed her lips tight. She was already talking to the blade.

The robe Herran had given Grada was older than her, black and flowing. 'Six Knife-Sworn have worn this before you,' he said. Her fingers had found a repair as she slipped into it.

Tight little stitches invisibly sealing an inch-long tear on the back. 'All of them were skilled. Not all were lucky.' Herran did the fastener about her throat, the clasp made of dull black bone, with nothing to gleam or catch the eye.

Out on the bridge the robe fluttered behind her with the breeze. Few remarked her passing, though she no longer passed unseen beneath the good citizens' contempt. Perhaps a close inspection would convince them of her heritage; they might see the broad cheekbones, the brown of her eyes, and recoil – 'Untouchable!' – but for now she walked among them as an equal, with only the flies paying real attention.

The sun dipped behind the great rock of the Holies, still white and fierce as it threw shadow over the Blessing. Grada left the bridge and began the long climb to the mansions and shrines far above. A narrow track for carts wound a still steep but more leisurely path back and forth across the granite slopes of the west side, but Grada chose the steps: nine hundred of them, hand-cut into the stone. Bearers passed her, bowed under crated luxuries bound for the nobility above, their legs hardened to the climb by a lifetime of up and down. She reached the top with a little of the day's light still glowing in the sky, her muscles warm, sweat beneath her robes. The rock plateau stretched out for acres, once bare and wind-smoothed, now encrusted with the houses of Cerana's great and good. Some even had gardens, the soil shipped up the Blessing from greener lands and carted in sacks up the winding track on the west side.

The taller towers and highest domes caught the reflected crimson of the sun, sinking into the desert out past her sight. She looked once at the directions in her hand, inked onto a scrap of papyrus. Street of Gods, turn left past the Red Manse.

The Knife bumped at her hip as she paced. She could walk the length of the Street of Gods, descend the west side and find passage south with one of the nomad caravans that came to trade, make a new life in some distant city. Sarmin would allow no pursuit and her hands would be clean of murder. Or if not her hands then at least her soul. It had been others that used her to kill before. This time it would be her own will behind the blade, her own crime.

Crime or not, Grada turned left past the dull red walls of Satrap Honnecka's manse. Herran had shown her the *Book of the Knife* before she left, a huge tome kept in its own room in a high tower at the rear of the palace. On the line that joined the towers of the Knife and that of the mages lay the room where she had once stabbed Sarmin. The room where Sarmin had made a pattern of two and bound their lives tight together. Sarmin's single window had pointed only at the mages' Tower, though, and he never had a view of where the Grey Service lived.

'The only crime the Knife-Sworn may be guilty of is failing to obey the command of the rightful emperor.' Herran had found the page unerringly and read for her, his fingers tracing the script without touching it. He closed the book with two hands, the cover as heavy and final as a coffin lid.

Grada walked by Mirra's shrine, the black dome darker than the surrounding gloom. Life comes out of the darkness of 'before', the midnight nothingness that waits behind memory and beyond imagining. Ten more paces and the healing shrine, Mirra's cradle of birth, lay behind her. A row of ancient palms, dust-grey in the twilight, led her on. At the far end of the street Herzu's shrine waited – a point of light, the alabaster still brilliant, finding and returning whatever radiance the sun left in its wake. Grada kept her eyes on that bright point, taking slow steps along the street. The leaning palms and the high garden walls of great houses gave the feeling of a tunnel. The day's heat radiated from the flagstones but the air grew colder by the moment. The wind rose and the palms whispered together, sharing old confidences.

In the time it took Grada to reach the gates of Lord Jomla's manse the day had gone. She slung her muslin bag of meat over the wall where it dipped lowest, following some artist's notion of ocean waves. She heard the bag break branches, rustle leaves, then hit ground with a wet thump. Slow steps took her on to Herzu's shrine. In the east the moon rose and the shrine glowed with the new light, pale as bone. Grada considered entering, but what words had she for gods? Instead she sank against the base of the nearest palm, letting the moon shadows swallow her. She took the Knife from her hip, still scabbarded. The street lay quiet, but the glimmer of a blade might catch a hidden eye. Each of these houses would have guards, each a fortress of wealth, though the times when families fought openly here and factions claimed and reclaimed territory were long gone, remembered only in the shape and style of the older homes.

In the darkness at the base of the tree Grada counted out the path that had led her to this place. A path not of choices but of being chosen. What had the Pattern Master seen in her to send her as his weapon into the palace? Helmar had been a royal, emperor by right, when he chose her as his Knife and sent her to kill Sarmin – the first royal blood she spilled. Helmar had been emperor enthroned when she had stabbed him amid his blood-pattern in the desert past Migido, he had been attested ruler of all Cerana. And still she killed him there. It had been her right. She was Helmar's Knife. Now she was Sarmin's. But why had Helmar chosen her? The Pattern Master had so many choices, and if he had wanted an Untouchable he had a thousand and more among the Many, among the dirt and squalor of the Maze. But he took her. Without allowing her a choice. Perhaps he sensed he was not the first to do so.

When Sarmin made a pattern of two parts from himself and her, Grada had no say in it. He had invaded every part of her life without invitation, without permission. Only that he lay dying and that her hand had delivered the wound made it forgivable, this and the way they had fitted together, each weakness countered by a strength, each strength by a weakness. Herran had chosen too. Meere offered no choices. And Govnan left her in that room, left her with Sarmin in the room where she shed his blood, and while the emperor said please, and while she knew he would accept her refusal, there was, from the moment he held the Knife's hilt towards her, no choice.

With the moon full risen Grada rose too, retracing her steps along the street of palms. She might have nothing to say to the gods, but it seemed they spoke to her, laughed behind their hands even as they laid out for her the same night she remembered from her dreaming with the Many, the same street, the same house.

'That is all that will be the same though.' She spoke the words silently to the Knife, the cold pommel stone against her lips as she walked. 'That was memory. This will be choice.'

38

Rushes

Rushes saw them everywhere: Mylo's followers, identified by their secret signal, a finger across the chin. They gathered over simple meals and work-tables in every place where marble changed to plain tile, where silk tapestries gave way to white-washed walls, and where the silk-clad did not venture. They whispered and planned, though their Fryth austere had disappeared, likely into the dark oubliettes where Rushes had first found the Megra.

Rushes was hiding from Beyon, from his wrath at her betrayal. She kept herself hidden in plain sight, among other female slaves, far from the women's wing or the Little Kitchen. She found that if she walked back and forth in Nessaket's livery nobody questioned her. Nevertheless her eyes scanned for threats, and she walked on the balls of her feet, always ready to run towards the Ways.

The whispers eddied along the corridors; Irisa was dead. The physician had left the women's wing, his satchel clutched at his side, all the herbs and potions within it useless when it came to a girl who had lost all colour and will. At the end of her life the concubine had at last been given a room of her own, the bed high, the walls painted with birds. But it was said she did not notice, that her eyes stared straight ahead, at nothing. And now more fell ill, not just concubines but slaves too, and some of the silk-clad. When people spoke of the sickness they used the word 'catch', as if a person reached for it like a ball. Instead Rushes believed that the sickness was trying to catch *her*, and so by always moving, she tricked it.

Lanterns were lit day and night, reflected in gleaming door-knobs and bright mosaics, but the brightness did nothing to keep the ghosts away; they drifted through the halls, form-less, but threatening all the same. They watched and waited – for what, Rushes could not tell. When frightened she thought it best to proceed normally, completing tasks as if she noticed nothing amiss, but sometimes she felt a coldness sliding along her skin and she knew that a ghost had passed too closely.

So when Kya, who carried the silk runners to and from the administrator's hall, grabbed her arm and whispered, Rushes screamed – but it was only one of Mylo's secret messages. Every few days she received a new one, usually instructions to appreciate Mogyrk's blessings or to pray for strength, but this one was different. 'Fire is the signal. You must bring some-thing precious to the courtyard.'

'What?' But Kya was gone, her arms wrapped around her purple bundle.

Rushes did not see how fire could be a signal. Fire burned everywhere, in the lanterns and the ovens, all day and all night. And what was meant by something precious? She spied a group of slaves standing around a table polishing silver candlesticks, their voices low, so she came closer, pulling a bit of silk that she used to polish Nessaket's comb from her pocket.

'They say Lord Zell beat her so hard she could barely move.'

'They'll kill all of us by the end of it, with their patterns, their beatings, or their ghosts. I tell you . . .'

'. . . waiting in a grave for another . . .'

'Excuse me,' said Rushes, and all turned to look at her, eyes narrowed in suspicion. She drew her finger across her chin and they relaxed, nodding and returning to their work. 'Who died?'

'Mina from the Little Kitchen,' said a young woman, hair the colour of the oak door behind her. 'She got beaten.'

'W—What?' Rushes stumbled and turned, her mouth moving with no words.

'Some silk-clad caught her,' she said, expression going dark with what was left unspoken. 'After that they took her to Mirra's temple but there was nothing to be done.'

Mina. Dead. Rushes had seen Lord Zell in those passageways, cloaked in black like Herzu himself, hunting girls in the Little Kitchen. Nobody would stop him. Nobody could. Rushes got away, but Mina had been caught. Her chest felt tight, so tight she could not breathe. She wandered, crookedly, her shoulder bumping against the wall, drained of hope, the Longing filling her at last.

Her mind fell deep into memory – Gorgen, her brother, Emperor Beyon, Mina, Demah, Zell – and her feet went their own way, turning and stepping, following a well-worn path into the Ways. She huddled against the damp stone, smooth from the touch of a thousand hands, some shining and clean, others filthy, bloody.

She could jump. It was what Demah had chosen, what many others had chosen. It was the easiest way. To just stop. Stop worrying, stop trying. She moved forwards, feeling with her feet for the edge of the stone. She would not be alone. There were bones down there, thousands of them. It would be like being part of the Many, only all would be quiet. Peaceful.

But she remembered the apple Hagga had given her, here in the Ways. How it had tasted. How a butterfly looked, fluttering in the sunshine. The Empire Mother's perfume and how Daveed felt in her arms, squirming and reaching for her hair. The things that coloured a life.

Daveed. She remembered him, the curl at his temple, his smile. He did not have the choice to go on or to stop. He was helpless in a hall where ghosts moved and illness picked one girl, then another, without regard, and where slaves planned their secret rebellion. She had betrayed Beyon but she did not have to abandon Daveed. *Fire is the signal.* Mylo's followers were everywhere, perhaps even in the women's wing. *Something precious.* She backed away from the edge. Daveed did not have a choice to stop. She had to protect him.

39

Sarmin

Out beyond the city where the sky fell to earth, curving on its suicidal plunge, the blue brilliance of heaven shaded through bars of crimson dawn into a dun haze, and out there, where distant dunes rolled in an endless sea, sky met sand without a join.

From Qalamin's Deck the whole of Nooria may be seen, spread out in a dirty, sparkling, glorious and shameful carpet of many hues, washing up against the desert walls, twisting in the confusion of the Maze, crowding down to the banks of the Blessing, leaping Asham Asherak's great bridge and huddling in splendour atop the rock of the Holies. Sarmin stood in the morning sun, the breeze still sharp with night's chill as it toyed with his silks. Somewhere a child howled. Smoke lifted from innumerable homes, workshops, cook fires, kilns, furnaces, the red heat of industry, thin columns resolute until the wind made mock of their intention and scattered them into haze. Somewhere a child bawled. A baby. Long shadows everywhere: the city reaching beyond its walls, the Towers of Knife and Mage throwing dark fingers out across Nooria.

'This is my city.'

White sails on the swiftness of the river, camels clustered in dun clots within the stockyards west, goats beside them in smaller pens, caravans circled within their lots, safe from the desert behind ancient walls. The morning sun found gleams on the swollen turrets of prayer tower and town house, starlings lifted in dark clouds from roofs along the streets of Copper and Brass.

'My Emperor.'

The voice came from behind him.

'Ta-Sann? Is that you?'

'Yes My Emperor.'

The flat roof of Qalamin's Deck stood less high than the Towers of the Knife and of the Mage, less high than the room where Sarmin grew, but in all of Nooria there was no other place a man might stand and be closer to the open sky. Azeem had asked that the sides be walled. So many of the palace household had jumped to their deaths in the past year, servant and noble. Gravity held no prejudice; it would take them all. Sarmin had told the vizier that a man seeking death would find it easily enough. Emperor Qalamin had watched the stars from this place, mapped the heavens and their progress in minute detail, spent his life at such work when his attention might better have been directed towards the surface across which his rule was spread. Even so, a wall, even a rail, would steal the aesthetic of the place, and save no lives.

The child's sobbing kept breaking Sarmin's line of thought. He looked down. The embroidered toes of his slippers inched out over the Deck's edge. A fall of over a hundred feet yawned below and it reached up for him. He took a quick step back, dizzy, suddenly nauseous.

'What am I doing here?' Another step from the precipice. 'Ta-Sann?'

'My Emperor.'

Sarmin turned, feeling for the first time the weight in his hand, and in the crook of his arm. Daveed hung screaming from Sarmin's right hand, dangling from the breechcloth wrapped about him and knotted in Sarmin's grip. Nestled in the fold of his other arm, Pelar, sleeping despite the older boy's howls.

'What?' Sarmin sat heavily, cross-legged, almost a collapse. 'Daveed?'

Ta-Sann stood five yards back, hachirah in hand, aflame with the morning sun. Ta-Sann alone.

'Where are my guard?'

'Securing the stair, My Emperor, by your command.'

Sarmin's arm ached, a throb at once sharp and dull, deep in the muscle. An image came to him. He had been holding Daveed out above that drop. Sarmin drew his brother to him, the child quiet now, trying to crawl away on some or other investigation.

'I was going to drop him.'

'So you said, My Emperor.'

With the image and the realisation came a new insight, a taste of the person that had brought him to the roof, that had held the child over that empty drop, trembling with cold rage. One of the Many, not a stranger, but someone within, and so close, so familiar, that Sarmin's mind shied away from framing their name. The image came again. Of his fingers knotted in that cloth, starting to loosen.

'Why didn't you stop—?' Sarmin closed his mouth on the question. *Because I am the emperor and I may do as I choose.*

He pulled both boys closer to his chest, Daveed squirming for release. Anger rose from some deep place, a hot tide, tightening every muscle until Daveed squealed, half-crushed in Sarmin's grip. 'Take my brother.' He relaxed his hold and offered Daveed to Ta-Sann. 'Return him to my mother. Safely.'

Ta-Sann took the baby and bowed. If he felt relief that the infant had not been cast over, none of it showed in his face. 'I will send Ta-Marn to attend you.'

Sarmin only held Pelar closer and looked away across the city. When Ta-Sann's footsteps had passed beyond hearing Sarmin spoke to the quiet.

'Beyon?' Again with more command. 'Beyon!'

Somewhere behind his thoughts the Many stirred. Their ranks had thinned when Sarmin stared into the nothing within Beyon's tomb. Hiding in the ranks of the Many had become more difficult as they became fewer.

'Beyon! He is our brother! Would you truly have dropped him?'

He is a threat. Beyon's voice, but spoken from a great distance, robbed of its old richness. *A threat to the emperor.*

'He is our *brother*! He's no threat to me. I command you – leave him be.'

You are not emperor. An anger like ice underwrote the words even as his lips moved to copy them. *My son is emperor and you have stolen his throne.*

'It was you.' Sarmin exhaled the realisation. 'You with Jenni. Did you tell her? . . . You did! You would have delivered Daveed and me to the Knife!'

My son is emperor and you have stolen his throne.

'What else did you tell her? Did you set her against the envoy?'

A smile twisted Sarmin's lips, a smile he didn't own. *My son will have an empire vaster than mine. What right do you have to deny him with . . . peace?* Sarmin's tongue twitched against the word in Beyon's disgust.

'You're not Beyon! Beyon would never kill his brothers. Beyon saved me!'

That Beyon was a child. He saved you and now you steal the throne from his son, the true emperor. It was a mistake to keep you in that tower, a mistake to go against tradition. And within a year of my death that mistake stands revealed. You stole my wife and my son's throne before I grew cold.

'Mesema was never your wife—'

Traitor!

A numbness stole through Sarmin's arms and against his will he set Pelar down on the paved roof.

Still we can give my son his throne back . . .

Sarmin stood, his legs no longer his to command, an emperor not even ruling his own body. On the cold stone Pelar stirred but made no cry. Sarmin turned towards the edge. Two steps brought him to the precipice.

'No!' And some effort of will prevented the next and final step. He held there, trapped between two intentions, trembling at the mercy of the wind. 'You're not my brother. Beyon was . . .' And what was Beyon? Brave, cruel, generous, unforgiving, as twisted in his way as Sarmin by the heritage they shared, deformed by the weight of expectation.

I was what, traitor?

'More than this!' It came to Sarmin clear and whole, an understanding surfacing from unseen depths. 'Beyon was more than this.' He had believed the Pattern Master's work of symbols, of intricate and infinite complexity, captured all that a man was or could be. But he was wrong. The pattern stole part of a man, and Sarmin had returned that part to the afflicted, but it couldn't take all a man was, couldn't hold all a man is. The pattern could record ambition, sketch memories, but the depths of a man couldn't be spelled out in symbols, no matter how many or how layered. Love could not be held in a code of circles in circles, in the blue and the red. What controlled him now was a crude caricature of Beyon: ambition, pride, duty, but not the essence of the man – not the love.

The pattern was a lie.

Fall, damn you!

Sarmin's foot shuddered, aching to obey. He wondered if Beyon's pattern would have any hold over him at all if at least some small part of him didn't also want to take one more step.

A single sharp cry rang out behind him from Pelar, a sound that had no place in any child's throat. Sarmin turned, pushed by two wills. Pelar lay naked save for his cloth, having kicked off his wrapping. Sarmin dropped to his knee beside the boy. His skin held the white of plaster dust, his thin limbs lay limp.

'No!' Sarmin reached for his son, and as he did Pelar's eyes flicked open. Sarmin's hand stopped, inches from the boy. He had seen those eyes before: in his dream of the desert, where a child had stood from the crumbling remains of a trader's tent, white dust bleeding from him. He had the same eyes, the colour of forever, empty, holding only nothingness.

Pelar's wrappings held a worn and faded look, the colours faint, cloth paper-thin. He watched Sarmin without expression, without blinking. A shadow fell across them both: Ta-Marn come to guard his emperor.

'Oh, my son.' Sarmin smiled for the boy, his eyes blurring. He knew now that the man in his memory would never have run from that child in the tent if it had been his own boy standing there. He reached for Pelar and in his head the pattern that was not Beyon screamed for him to run. Pain ate into Sarmin's hands as he gathered Pelar from the flagstones. He held Pelar to his chest and his purple silks went pale where the boy touched them, fragile, tearing as he moved. Each touch ached, and inside Sarmin the Many faded, unwritten by what flowed from Pelar. He stood, finding his son at once both frighteningly light and almost too heavy to be borne.

'Go ahead, Ta-Marn. Fetch High Mage Govnan, fetch all the mages of the Tower, every priest, tell the empress. My son will not be taken.'

'My Emperor.' Ta-Marn bowed, and straightened, frowning. 'I should carry the prince. He is harming you.'

'Go!' Sarmin shouted. Then more softly, returning his gaze to the empty child. 'Love is hard to capture, harder to unwrite. I will manage.'

40

Nessaket

Sarmin had come at night, cold-faced, surrounded by his sword-sons.

'What do you want?' she had asked, edging in front of the cradle, looking at the pointed swords and blank faces of the emperor's guard. Saying nothing he pushed her aside and took her son, took his softness and his curling hair and the way he laughed when he saw something new.

'Where are you taking him?' she asked, her mouth numb with fear, clutching at Sarmin's arm. Later she would remember that, not being able to let go of his arm, as if she were sinking into sand and Sarmin her only rope. At last his sword-sons pulled her away.

Nessaket had felt such fear only once before, on the night Tahal died – and it hollowed her again. She fell to the floor, pleading with Mirra – but this was Herzu's work. And then, a miracle: Ta-Sann returned her boy. The sword-son simply laid him in her arms and left the room without a word. She remained on the floor, holding her son, wondering what intervention from god or man had saved him.

And then she heard a scream. At first she did not move. Screams were not uncommon these days. The women's hall was filled with ghosts, spies, and the strange illness that crept along the halls, paling one girl and then another. But the scream came again and Nessaket recognised Mesema's voice. She stood, feeling the ache in her legs from hours on the floor, and made a sling from a piece of silk. Slipping Daveed inside she went to her door and cracked it open, peeking out. A slave-girl stood there, a new one, peering down the hall. She looked frightened.

'What is it, girl?' *What more could happen?*

'Something happened in the empress's room, Your Majesty. The emperor is there, and . . .' The slave scrambled aside as Nessaket moved forwards, her feet sure and quick on the path to the Tree Room, her thankfulness for Daveed's health transformed into anger. So her older son's night was not finished. She would know the cause of his strange behaviour, learn why he had taken her boy. In her fury she imagined even the ghosts slipping out of her way like fog.

A single lantern lit Mesema's room giving the tree-paintings a sinister look, tall giants waiting to crush everyone below. The empress stood by a pillowed bench, tearing at her hair, dark kohl running in long streaks down her face. 'This was you!' she screamed at her husband the emperor. 'This was you!'

Both of them circled the bed, or what was on it: Pelar, pale, withered, hair gone white. Like Gala, Irisa and all the others. But where Pelar lay the covers began to fade and crumble, as if they were a hundred years old instead of newly made. 'Mirra save him!' Nessaket brought a hand to her mouth. She had never wanted him born, had wished he was a girl, but to see him like this . . .

We should have fled, after Dreshka died. Too late, too late.

Sarmin had done this to him. He had taken both the boys this night, and Pelar . . . She looked at her emperor son, who spoke in an even voice, his eyes distant. 'This is the nothingness, the illness that devours,' said Sarmin.

'Don't tell me what it is!' cried Mesema. 'You fix it!' She rushed forwards, meaning to pick up the boy. 'You fix it!'

Sarmin held out a hand. 'Carefully.' Mesema's hands slowed, and she gathered Pelar as if he were made of the most delicate glass, hissing as if it hurt her hands. 'My sweet boy,' she said. 'My darling boy.'

'I will make him well,' Sarmin said. 'I will fix it.' The last he said more quietly: a promise to himself, or an edict.

Mesema said nothing. Nessaket wondered if he truly had the power to cure the boy. She watched Mesema's arms and the child within them, fearing he would break if held too tightly.

Sarmin left the room, his sword-sons trailing him, gone without another word. He would leave the room bereft, no Pelar cooing in his cradle, no sweet smell from his skin. Only a colourless shell remained of the child. Nessaket chased after Sarmin, treasuring the feel of her own healthy baby, the weight of him in his sling. 'I would have a word with my son the emperor,' she said.

Sarmin stopped and turned, his gaze far away, his mind on patterns and magic.

'Why did you take the boys? Where did you take them? Why would you do such a thing to Pelar?' As she spoke his copper eyes cleared, focusing on her own, so that she knew he listened.

He laid a hand on her shoulder, an intimate gesture from a man she had not touched in years. 'It was Beyon.'

'What?' She took a step backwards. Had he learned that Beyon was Pelar's father? Would that make him kill the boy?

'It was Beyon,' he said again, his eyes growing distant once again. 'Rising up from the Many.' He turned towards the Great Room, his sword-sons behind him.

Or had Sarmin gone mad – was it the Cotora family curse come upon them? With no real answer from her son, Nessaket returned to Mesema. 'Come,' she said, nudging the girl. 'Let us go and honour Mirra in Siri's garden. Mirra might help us.' *She helped me earlier. It is possible.* Awkwardly she put an arm around the horsegirl and guided her into the hall.

Women crowded around, trying to catch sight of the stricken prince. Spies might be among them, but Nessaket found it difficult to care. Pelar drew her gaze; she could not discern where his skin ended and his white silks began. Mesema stumbled along, her face nearly as pale as her son's now, allowing herself to be led. Guards followed, six, a dozen, and once they reached Farra's room Nessaket bid them guard the door. Grief was a private affair and they would keep anyone from entering. Farra was absent. They climbed the stairs. Each of them held a bundle, Nessaket's olive-skinned and kicking, Mesema's drained and still.

They sat on the bench in Siri's garden, surrounded by bare flowerbeds. The sun began to set, casting an orange light over the city below them. Their view beyond the palace walls looked out over the river and the long barges that carried fruit and nuts from the groves into Nooria.

Mesema lurched forwards and knelt before the statue of Mirra, hunched over Pelar in prayer. Nessaket understood. She had knelt for hours, pleading with Mirra, before Ta-Sann returned Daveed. They sat in that way for some time, Nessaket watching the night fall along the edges of the city, Daveed asleep in his sling. It was then that she noticed a seedling poking its head from the cracked soil. She leaned over it, brushed her finger against the green leaves. A sign from Mirra, surely.

Footsteps sounded on the stairs, light and quick. *Rushes?* Nessaket did not know why the girl came so quickly to her mind. But it was not Rushes; white-blond hair appeared above the stairwell, followed by smooth shoulders tied with blue silk. Jenni. Nessaket pulled Daveed closer, crushing him against her chest, and glanced at Mesema, who remained unaware, lost in her prayers. How had the concubine got past the guards downstairs? Then she realised – Jenni had been in the Old Wife's room already, waiting. Was Farra dead, then?

Jenni reached the top of the stairs and turned in a slow circle. 'I have not seen this roof before, Majesty.'

A lie. 'Leave us,' said Nessaket.

'May I see Prince Daveed, at least?'

'No,' said Nessaket. 'Leave us.' But the girl moved her hand, and steel gleamed there, catching the sun's last rays. Where had she kept that knife? Now she moved forwards, holding the blade in a way that showed she knew how to use it.

Jenni slashed. Nessaket barely had time to raise her arm up to protect Daveed. The knife sliced her arm, bouncing off bone, leaving a bloody trail between wrist and elbow. A sharp hot pain, no more than that.

Nessaket held her son close, his face crushed against her chest, blood pulsing over fingers clamped across her wound. Mesema looked around from her position at the statue. 'What . . .'

Jenni danced backwards, keeping them both within their sights, as Mesema pushed to her knees, a flowerpot in each hand. She threw the first; Jenni ducked easily out of the way. Quickly Nessaket picked up another flowerpot and threw it, but the woman was trained, a fighter and an athlete. Two unarmed mothers with flowerpots were no match for her. If these were her last moments, Nessaket felt foolish more than angry or frightented. Unprepared, like a girl at her books who had studied the wrong lesson.

'When the emperor lay with me, he told me the truth.' Jenni held the knife held low, Nessaket's blood dripping from its edge. 'That he is mad, and the empress is a whore.' She moved forwards, twisting, light on her feet, a dance almost.

Something dark broke from the stairwell. *Rushes!* Arms extended, she shoved Jenni, palms to shoulder blades, pushing, steering her to the garden's edge. Three quick and stumbling steps and Jenni hung in that moment of unbalance, arms flailing. The knife fell, and she followed it, her scream not sounding until her tumble took her from their sight. An instant later and a dull thud cut the cry short.

Nessaket said to Rushes, 'Don't look down!' She remembered seeing Siri from the same angle; she did not want the girl to see it too. Rushes stood, stunned, not looking at anything in particular, then she finally focused on Nessaket and fell into her obeisance. Mesema looked, though. She went to the edge and looked down, nodding to herself with satisfaction.

'Rise, Rushes.' Nessaket looked to Mesema, her arm beginning to hurt now, a long ache in skin and muscle. 'How is Pelar?'

The child lay before the statue where Mesema left him. 'The same.' Mesema pressed her lips together in fear.

The same was better than worse. Daveed stirred and began to fuss when Nessaket put him on the bench and unwound the silk from her neck for a bandage. She quieted the boy, feeling guilty. She remembered when illness had swept through the women's wing, leaving Beyon as the eldest. She had felt guilty then too, even as she offered thanks to Herzu.

'She brought the snake, and killed the envoy, too,' said Rushes, motioning towards the edge.

'Yes, child; you have done well,' said Nessaket. She hissed as she pulled the silk tight around her wound. Assar would need to look at this.

The girl shook herself, as if waking. 'Your Majesty! The Mogyrk slaves are going to do something. They said fire was the signal. When they see it, they're supposed to go to the courtyard behind the Little Kitchen.' She kept talking, faster now, as if time itself would run out on her. 'They are looking for precious things to take with them. I—'

'Mogyrk slaves?' Nessaket blinked with confusion. How long had Mogyrks been fixing her food, carrying her silks? The world shifted under her feet. At least the ghosts and spies she could see. The concubines had surrounded her, but the slaves surrounded everyone.

'The Mogyrks,' growled Mesema, stalking forwards. 'This is all their fault! Show me this courtyard!'

Nessaket held out a hand to stay her. 'I know you have the will for it, but not the strength. Stay here with Pelar.' She motioned towards Rushes. 'I am going to send the guards up now. You watch Daveed.'

Rushes held the baby tight, her blue eyes round over his dark curls. 'Where are you going?'

Nessaket looked again at Pelar, Beyon's son. Tahal's death had changed her, and Beyon too. Neither of them had ever been what they could have been, not while the grief and anger held them. *I will be a better mother this time.* It was too late for

Beyon, but she could protect his child. 'I am going to talk to that austere,' said Nessaket. 'I am going to stop this.'

Nessaket found two guards in the dungeon's anteroom, two of the four who watched over three hundred Fryth prisoners. It was Sarmin, she knew; Sarmin had emptied the dungeons completely, assigning the soldiers to other tasks. Now that the dungeons were full, there were not enough men to manage them. Both men fell into obeisance at the sight of her and her four guards. 'Rise,' she said, 'and tell me where to find the second austere.'

A grizzled guard stood, his jacket too small for his fat belly, his eyes both curious and kind. 'I will take you, Majesty.'

Nessaket followed him between the crowded cells, looking at the faces of the Fryth behind the bars. They called to her in their language, begging for water, perhaps, or for their freedom. Mogyrk worshippers as they were, she should not feel sorry for them; and yet she felt drawn by their hungry eyes, the desperate tone of their calls. She quickened her step, as one hurries past a bad odour or a cloud of smoke.

The guard indicated the austere's cell and she dismissed him. Adam stood inside in his red robes, straight, shoulders square, as if he had been expecting her.

'Austere Adam,' she said, 'I am sorry to meet you again under such conditions.' She looked past him at the bare cell.

'Treachery is as treachery does,' he said, with a lift of his right shoulder.

She made to argue, then put it aside. To admit they had not actually meant to kill Kavic might be worse than to let him think they planned it. 'I come about the disease that spreads nothing into a person,' she said. 'I understand Mogyrk has done this to us.'

'The Pattern Master Helmar is responsible,' he said, 'not Mogyrk. Mogyrk is nothing but love, safe harbour, protection.'

'I am a woman of the world,' she said, 'and you do not need to speak such platitudes to me. Tell me how to cure the illness.'

He laughed. 'There is no cure. You will be eaten slowly, your colours, your memories, your feelings, and then your body, piece by piece. It is foretold. There is no way that it can be prevented.'

'Lies!' she said, grabbing the bars. 'I will have you tortured until you tell me!' Shouting rang out at the guards' station. She heard metal on metal, quick movement. Fighting. Who attacked? Slaves? Yrkmir? Her guards stepped away to investigate, hands on their sword-hilts. She had brought only four, and left the rest to watch over Rushes and Daveed. She turned back to Adam, and he smiled.

'You should find somewhere to hide, Your Majesty,' he said, 'for my people have come to free me.'

Her guards rushed around the corner, meeting some threat she could not see; she let go the bars and walked to the edge of the corridor, peeking around the bend. Six slaves were fighting the guards with kitchen knives, lanterns, clubs. *Slaves.* She had not heeded Rushes' warning. This was the Longing. This was Mogyrk. Nobody understood how things should work any more. For a slave to fight a guard . . . The five who had attacked were quickly defeated, but more slaves came, running down the stairs with whoops and jeers. The room became a jumble of movement to her eyes, but it seemed there were five slaves for every guard, holding fire pokers, wooden bats and kitchen knives, their faces lit with a determination she had never known was there.

A young man stepped out from the fighting, calm, as if taking a morning stroll along the banks of the Blessing. He held a key in his hand and with it he opened the cell doors. He had a lovely face, the colour of tea, and his hair curled round his forehead with a soft gleam. The freed prisoners ran, towards the fighting, the stairs and the palace, but the young man looked down the long row of empty cells and saw her. He smiled, moving close, and when he spoke, his voice was like honey. 'Empire Mother,' he said, 'this is the will of Mogyrk.'

So entranced was she that it took her a moment to process his words. 'Mogyrk?' she asked, as he raised a club in his hands. 'What—?' The wood came down, and all went dark.

41

Rushes

When the guards came Empress Mesema stood, walked to the stairs, and left the garden without a word. She was pale, trembling, not the clever lady Rushes had heard about from Demah. It was Pelar's sickness. Rushes wanted to tell Mesema that the emperor might have been someone else when he took Pelar, that she shouldn't be angry at Sarmin; but she was gone, disappearing down the stairs, and she missed her chance.

I killed Jenni. I should feel sad, she thought, the loss of a life, but mostly her heart beat fast and her skin felt cold. She had been so frightened when she saw Jenni holding the knife against Nessaket and the baby, and the moment when she ran had been filled with such determination, such will, as if the Pattern Master still lived inside her.

She stood, and all the guards clustered around her like flies on old meat. She froze in fear, but then she remembered that they were protecting Daveed and they meant no harm. She let them lead her down the stairs and through Farra's room into the hall, towards the crib that waited under Nessaket's window.

Her pace was slow. She felt tired. She could not remember the last time she had slept. When she got to the room she sat down as the guards searched the room and Daveed's bedding. They searched for mundane threats; they were no proof against ghosts and the pale-sickness. Finally they took position in the corridor and in every corner.

She put Daveed to bed, and waited. Nessaket had gone to speak with the second austere. She wondered if Mylo would be with him, speaking of Mogyrk's arrival and all of his other plans. She dozed. A scent tickled her nose, bringing her back to her mother's smallhouse on the plains. They used to gather around the cooking fire during the winter, warming their hands over the stew. But it was wrong; this was not a palace scent. She stirred herself alert, stood up and checked Daveed. He was asleep in his silks, his cheeks red and round. But half the guards had left the room – unthinkable – this was all wrong. She ventured towards the corridor and looked out. People were shouting, running. Smoke spilled into the corridor from one of the Old Wives' bedrooms. *Fire is the signal.*

She gathered Daveed and hurried towards Mesema's room, a trail of guards behind her, but a sudden plume of flame, like water rising from a fountain, blocked their way. She smelled lantern-oil; this fire was no accident. She felt the heat against her skin and backed away into the guards behind her. 'Fire,' she said, stupidly. They took off their jackets and beat at the flames, but the burning carpet created a terrible smoke and Daveed woke up and began to cough.

'Shush, shush, little one,' she whispered, coughing herself, turning towards the Great Room. She would head for the big doors; surely they would be safe if she could get to the other side. But what of the empress, and little Pelar? No time to think of them. *Must get out.* She ran, a dozen concubines running with her. But the doors were blocked. The guards struggled to pull them open, panic in their voices. 'Open at once!' they shouted. 'The royal princes are trapped inside!'

Someone on the other side shouted, 'Mogyrk's will!'

The guards kicked and clawed. Smoke billowed into the room, hot in Rushes' lungs, burning her eyes. Barely able to see, she stumbled against the wall. The baby coughed again and she clutched him to her chest, heart beating fast. *We must get out!* Screams echoed around her. A hot wind blew against her cheek, attended by a rush of flame. She jumped back as fire burst from the jewel-coloured cushions. It was then she saw Gala, pale as winter snow, run through the room, mouth open in a skeleton's grin, laughing like a demon from Herzu's hell. Not just Gala; something rode on her back, drove her through the crowd of screaming concubines like a warhorse. A ghost. This was what they had been waiting for – for Gala, and others, to be empty enough for them to ride. The horror filled her lungs as much as the smoke, stopping her breath.

The guards drew their swords and moved in on Gala, coughing and wiping at their eyes. Only one remained with Rushes and Daveed now, one faithful protector, but against fire he could do nothing. She had to save Daveed. *The moving shelves!* She hurried to them. 'I can take the prince this way, down to the Little Kitchen,' she told him, taking out the shelves as she spoke. He helped her climb in, knees up, Daveed cradled against her chest. 'Release the brake and lower me,' she said.

'I can't protect the baby in the Little Kitchen,' he said, suddenly doubtful of the plan. He was an older man, fatherly, and she wondered if he had children or grandchildren, if he protected them as he protected Daveed.

'Quickly! He will burn!'

He frowned, but assented at last and closed the door, leaving her in darkness. It reminded her of Gorgen, in the pantry, and she clamped her lips together to keep from screaming. Just a minute or so. It would take only a minute to get down to the Little Kitchen. She prayed that Empress Mesema had found a way out, away from the flames.

The guard lowered her in jerks and bounces, every time feeling as if she would fall and break her bones and the baby too. But then she was there, pulling up on the door that Old Hagga always stood by, where Mina used to put the trays, and she slid out onto the floor of the Little Kitchen. She gave a sigh of relief and gathered Daveed against her breast. His coughing began to subside, and he looked around the room with interest. That was a good sign he was feeling better. Her eyes on the baby, Rushes took a step forwards and nearly crashed into Mylo.

Mylo smiled at her, but not with the beatific smile she had come to know. This smile was the smile of a wolf or a grass-cat. 'Good! I knew you'd figure it out,' he said. 'and you brought me something precious. Is that Prince Pelar?'

Rushes backed away, holding Daveed to her chest. Mylo was supposed to be in the courtyard, or locked in the dungeon along with his priest. 'No. It's Daveed.'

'Where's Pelar?'

'With his mother.' She looked around. 'I thought you would be in the courtyard.' *I thought I would be safe in the Little Kitchen. But no place is safe.*

'Soon,' he said. 'Give me the baby.'

'I'll carry him,' she said.

He lifted a club, sticky with blood. *Whose?* 'Give him to me.'

'No!' Others wandered into the kitchen now, some curious,

others angry, kitchen knives and fire pokers in their hands. Hagga was not here. Had they hurt her? She turned back to Mylo. 'Why—'

The blow came sharp and quick, a cracking against her skull. *Daveed!* But she did not drop him. The last thing she felt as her knees buckled and her sight grew dim was gentle hands, lifting the silk bundle from her arms, and Daveed kicking, wailing, beginning to realise he was not safe any longer. The lesson came too early for him. *Not fair . . . Daveed!*

42

Sarmin

'A lie can also be true?' Sarmin scratched more of his pattern into the wall, scoring the plaster in white lines. 'What help is that?' The truth of his own pattern ached around him, each stroke cutting something more substantial than the surfaces about him, a flat light leaking through them to bathe the room in that glow which settles before the worst of storms. 'A lie can also be true?' He saw the pattern everywhere now; each exposed brick a mesh of earth symbols, fire symbols, the coded geometry of its construction, the ancient waters where silt settled, the imprints of the men who shaped it. His bed no longer held form but shaped itself from patterns enumerating trees, branching, folded, self-referencing, remembering days when twigs and leaves had danced to please the wind.

For the year since Helmar died on the Knife Sarmin had drawn no pattern, made no study of the magics.

'These enchantments are your heritage, My Emperor,' Govnan had told him. 'The skill for such seeing is found so rarely – a gift of your blood.'

'What good ever came from Helmar's work?' Sarmin had asked, and the high mage had no answer.

Sarmin had never craved the power of the Petal Throne, let

alone desired to claim still deeper control with patterns new or old. Helmar's need to rule a nation of puppets, a world enslaved to his will . . . it had always been the miserable ember of lost ambitions, of a hope turned sour.

Sarmin closed his eyes, unsteady with exhaustion. He pressed the heel of his hand hard against his forehead. For the thousandth time the image of Pelar swam before him, lying white and unmoving on the flagstones. He shook it away, shook away the pain, opened his eyes to focus on the symbols before him. He'd been wrong; patterns could speak of more than men, but whatever they spoke of they told only a story, not the truth. The pattern of fire held heat and light but the vital essence of fire, the wildness, vitality, endless variety – all that lay too deep for the pattern to catch.

Sarmin found he could write the stories of many things within his patterns, but he could craft no symbol for the nothing. The end of all things lay in the heart of the desert, and now because of Helmar it devoured the palace and threatened everything Sarmin loved. And though the pattern had brought this curse to their doorstep, not in all of its language were there words to speak of what attacked them.

'Gods help me.' He saw Pelar again, still as pale, still as small.

Ta-Sann knocked and entered, a silver tray in hand. Sarmin would admit no servants now. 'You must eat, My Emperor.'

'Eat?' The tray spilled patterns, fire signs chasing water signs coiling up where steam should rise, the life of a fish written limp across a plate, corrupted with other stories, stories of salt and spice, even the tray itself a dense mesh of symbology speaking of the deep places where ore is mined, the furnace in which the silver sweated from the rock.

'For your strength, My Emperor.' Ta-Sann himself glowed with the essay of his life written through him, making a ghost of his flesh; his loyalty, memories and wants all coded there in threaded lines woven into bones.

'I have no strength.' Only the stone held no pattern. It was simply a stone, black and uninspired, scooped no doubt from some turn of the Blessing where the river piles up its discarded toys. The stone and the nothing held no pattern, the unwriting from the desert.

'Nothing I do here matters.' Sarmin spat the words and rolled back against the wall, shoulders pressed flat against it. 'Helmar's patterns are false. Their language is too crude, too blunt. Men cannot be written into it. Not all of a man. Not the core. Not what matters most. That was not my brother.' He stared at Ta-Sann as if the man had contradicted him. 'That was not my brother. Beyon loved me.'

Sarmin had last looked from the Sayakarva window on the previous evening. The nothing appeared as a stain against the eye, a blot on the imagination, seated in a sinkhole of sand and dust, whiter than bone, where once Sarmin's fathers had lain in their splendour. Soon the outer wall would fall and the courtyard where Eyul killed Sarmin's brothers would erode into rotten pieces. The nothing would touch his tower and it too would topple. Panic ran in the corridors, djinn haunted each shadow and stole the unwary, empty men and empty women wandered without purpose or will, corrupting all they touched, and slaves ran through it all, blood on their hands, fire in their wake.

'The empress—'

'I cannot go! I will not watch my son drain away. Do you understand that?' He found himself shouting.

'My Emperor.'

'I didn't ask you to say "My Emperor". I asked if you understood what I said.' Sarmin advanced on Ta-Sann, his body alight, rage flaring through him, throwing the shadows of fire signs across the walls. Something in the sword-son's patience exasperated him – as obdurate in its way as Helmar's damned stone.

'Does Govnan do anything for Pelar? Are all my mages useless? Every single one?'

He slapped a hand to Ta-Sann's chest, solid like the timbers of the throne-room doors. The sword-son flinched despite himself. Sarmin saw only patterns, this thing, that thing, written out, twisted, coiled, interwritten, interwoven. He could hook his fingers about any piece of it and pull the symbols forth, rob Ta-Sann of some vital part of who he was.

Sarmin spun away with an animal cry, rage, frustration, Helmar's stone raised high like a weapon, ready to open skulls.

'The food—' Ta-Sann pursued his path with dogged determination.

'Damn your food!' Sarmin spun again, roaring the words, the stone leaving his fingertips before regret could close them. It flew straight and true, with deadly speed, a single black dot, a single point of simplicity in a room of swirling pattern-stuff.

Ta-Sann moved so fast it didn't seem human – as if his entire life had been spent tensed for this moment, waiting to spring. And even so the stone grazed his ear before hammering into the doorjamb. Plaster and brick dust plumed. The stone fell.

'I'm sorry.' An emperor never apologises. Page six of the *Book of Etiquette*. 'So sorry.'

The two halves of Helmar's stone slid apart, the split running along the length of it, a finger's width of the inner surface exposed. All patterns fled: the ancient ones still showing in the painted ceiling and the patterns overlaying Sarmin's vision – all of them erased. And the room filled with light. Ta-Sann stepped away as Sarmin advanced, a hand raised to shield his eyes from the glare.

Look inside, Gallar had said to the Megra.

Sarmin reached for the stone. His hand felt the ghosts of jagged edges and emotions bled into him, all of them, from melancholy to madness, joy to rage. He slid the two sides together again, sealing away all but a thread of the light within, and stood, trembling. Then, like a book, like the only book that ever mattered, he opened the two halves before his face.

'A butterfly?' Written there in crystals of many hues, every pattern of its wings, every scale captured, formed with exquisite care from without, melted and reset, melted and reset in the long night of that oubliette so many years ago. Helmar was ever Meksha's child, a son of rock and fire. 'A butterfly.' And Sarmin fell, stricken so suddenly that he never felt the ground.

In a bright summer meadow he's running with the slope, out of breath but laughing. It's hot and the heat folds round him, flows through him. The air is full of seeds, floating on their white fluff, swirling in his wake, like the memory of the first snow that falls fat-flaked and lazy into the early days of autumn. Sarmin understands he is caught in someone else's memory. He has only read of snow.

He's a child, chubby-armed, almost chest-deep in the longest greenest grass he has ever known, running without direction, chasing butterflies, swinging a thin stick with no hope of hitting. There's no tiredness in this memory, he runs and runs some more, always laughing.

And Sarmin laughs too, he has found Helmar before the austeres of Yrkmir, before the dungeon, before even the tower. Sarmin has days like this walled within the record of his past – someday he will open those too.

Butterflies rise before him in hues too vivid for the world. And then he stumbles. Just a little trip, a snagged foot, a headlong plunge into the lushness of the grass, his stick snapping beneath him. The sky is so blue, as if the heat and brightness of the day has woken its true colours, given them meaning. Motion draws his gaze from the sky, something fluttering but wrong. There in the canyon that his fall scored into the grass is a butterfly, lunging skyward, failing, veering in crazy spirals, battering against the green stems. Is it sick?

This is why he's here, Sarmin knows it. This is the anchor point, the fractured moment that has defined a life, defined many lives. A child's stumble, an instant's thoughtlessness and something beautiful lies broken. A lesson every child learns. Perhaps the first and sharpest truth of all those that slice us through the years, that carve away innocence, make bitter men of joyous boys.

The thing is a frenzy of beating wings, iridescent green slashed with crimson. For a heartbeat it pauses on the ground. A jagged hole spoils the symmetry of its wings, breaks the interwoven pattern of their markings. Some swing of his stick has taken a chunk from the back of both wings. The butterfly rises again in its broken dance. And falls.

Helmar's hands close around the insect, cupping, holding. The crazed fluttering continues, the beat of broken wings within the darkness he encloses. The feel of it against his palms turns his stomach.

This is the first lesson. What's done is done. Beauty is too easy to destroy.

'No.' Helmar refuses the lesson.

'Let it go.' A whisper from Sarmin's lips. Madness lies in such refusal.

Deny but one truth, however small, and your world must twist and twist again at each turn through your days to accommodate that lie, until at last there is no hint of truth in any corner of your existence.

'No,' Helmar says again, and opens his hands, just a crack, to study his captive, now resting on the lower palm.

There is a pattern here, boldly stamped in brilliant green, metallic blue, a symmetry of circles within circles, curves and divides. Where the wing is gone the eye fills in what is missing, symmetry demands it; completeness requires that this circle is finished, this line carried to the end.

The child closes his hands again, closes his eyes, tight until the reds and greens a summer day leaves behind the eyelids flare bright as fire. He sees the pattern, the necessary pattern of the butterfly, whole, intact, brilliant in memory. He sees it, he lives it, he prints it into his hands, stamping it with every breath, every beat of his heart.

The pattern is not the butterfly, Sarmin tells him. *The butterfly is so much more. The butterfly is whatever mystery of insect blood and insect bone serves such creatures, it is egg and chrysalis, it is dew sucked from grass and nectar from flowers. It is this morning there, that morning here, a close escape, five miles in the grip of a sudden gale. The pattern is not the butterfly.*

The child sees the pattern, whole, complete. He believes it. He opens his hands and the butterfly flutters away, gone amongst the floating seeds.

The pattern was no more than a story, a tale of the butterfly, but it showed it the way to be whole once more. It showed the butterfly how to heal itself.

The pattern was a lie. The pattern was also true.

43

Grada

In darkness, betrayed only by the moon, Grada climbed the wall. Her fingers found easy holds, a wall built for show rather than security. Below her bushes seethed in the wind, dogs lay hissing and choking on their last breaths, and the grounds stretched out to a moon-pale mansion. Everything as she had dreamed it so many times, even the grass.

She crossed neither fast enough to draw attention nor slow enough to present a lingering target. At the windows she checked first the ones closest to the great stair, then moved along the front of the house trying each in turn. She pulled hard, hoping to force an entrance before she reached the shutter that the dream told her would come free. Nothing gave. She reached the shutter she knew would yield.

'I could leave it, try the next instead. I could walk away, find a caravan, head south for a new life.' The words twitched behind her lips. Duty bound her to the task. 'Knife-Sworn are a rare breed,' Herran had told her. 'It's a combination of loyalty that once given goes bone-deep, and independent thought that remains unclouded by that loyalty. Either quality is rare and each seems to preclude the other, but still time and again the emperors of Cerana find such servants. The priests tell us it is the gods who send the Knife-Sworn to the emperor in time of need, and I cannot argue.'

Grada pulled at the next shutter and it gave as she had known it would. She clambered through into the blind dark beyond. In the corridor she passed the sleepwalker from the dream, guided only by sound. Grada moved on, trailing fingers along the wall, counting each doorway against the map she remembered from Meere's papyrus. Meere wrote a number there too, five. Jomla, both his wives and his counsellor, who like the emperor's vizier would be privy to all schemes and secrets. That made four. Fifth would be the boy, the heir. Grada wondered if he would have toys now, if Lord Jomla had sent again to the tall houses of the artisans, to Mechar Anlantar, and if his servant returned this time with model soldiers, mechanical acrobats in silver and jet, a drum perhaps. Would she find the child clutching his gift in the depth of his sleep? Herran had said five given to the Knife would be enough to cut out the rot, rebottle the genie, kill the secret. But once the cutting started more than five would die, no matter how careful she was. Grada remembered the Pattern Master centred in his pattern of death, corpses laid in dismembered intricacy all around him, thick with flies. And now she was supposed to fill this house with more bodies, bleeding out in the dark, and all because of pillow talk, of secrets whispered into blond hair in the aftermath of Sarmin's lust. It made no sense. Sarmin was not that man, and she had known him to the core. And yet here she was, chasing secrets.

She found the stairs and began to climb the spiral of them. Whispers of moonlight from tiny windows in a high dome let her find the very edge of each step, a habit from the Maze where any stairs are most likely salvaged from old river barges, creaky with rot. Jomla's stairs were marble and silent, but old habits die hard.

She passed the second floor. More steps. A deeper shadow ahead, one could imagine it a man. It will be a man. In the dream she killed him. And what else can she do now? Whatever plan might come to her, whatever gambit that might avoid slicing the life from Jomla, it couldn't start with being captured as an intruder. Waking with the emperor's Knife at your throat carries a certain degree of terror with it. Having a woman of the Untouchables captured like a thief in your house, coming down to the servants' quarters with your guards to view her and congratulate the man who took her . . . that's hardly a position of strength. In the dream she stabbed him, took his keys, and the voices of the Many whispered 'murderer'. In the dream she was bound to her course.

I have a choice now. The Knife is in my hand. I have a choice, many choices. All of them bad.

This is memory, the darkness holds Grada and this could be memory, the remembering of crimes already committed by another's hands. It could be remembered . . . should be . . .

It was never memory. This house on the Holies had waited for her, held in the fearful symmetry of Helmar's pattern, the Pattern Master's great work reaching both forward and back to capture histories and futures. In the darkness Grada at last allowed herself to understand what she had always known, allowed herself to let hope slip away, a warm tear to slide down across one cheek.

Ahead, at the top of the stairs, the guardsman would be waiting, unseen and unseeing, dozing or patient, he waited. Grada's hand tightened around the Knife. She climbed the last few steps, each of them feeling like a step down, like a descent into some black deed. Her dreams gave the man to her, they wrapped the darkness where he stood into the shape of a man, and she moved towards him without pause. An indrawn breath hissed from him and her hand lashed out, the pommel of the Knife striking his forehead. He jerked back and his head struck the wall behind him with equal force. She pinned him to the painted plaster, a faint rattle of keys as he slid to the floor.

'Choice!' She wanted to shout it. In the dream she stabbed his heart. For the moment it seemed the world around her seethed with pattern, the outrage of the Many echoing around her defiance. But at the end of it the guard lay at her feet and the Knife bore no blood. She savoured the victory.

I am the emperor's Knife. I cut, and no pattern can bind me. The future is mine to make.

Still the sour taste came to her mouth, hard to swallow. Jomla and the others, the child, none of those problems could be fixed by knocking them insensible. She moved on. Meere had told her the place wouldn't be a fortress, but even so it seemed too easy. 'The rich politic against each other these days, they don't murder one another in their beds,' Meere had said. 'Better to dominate and rob your rivals than to kill them and see them be replaced by some unknown who knows his chance to survive lies in murdering you first. This is what civilisation gave the Cerani.'

Grada set the pommel of the Knife to her chin, thinking. Jomla first. Jomla would be easy. The house reeked of his guilt. Without his ambition, without his dreams of treachery and power, the child would not be here, would not be at risk.

A light burned in the corridor that led to Jomla's room. Grada eased herself to the corner. In a niche opposite the door to Jomla's bedchamber an oil lantern sat, its flame dancing.

Standing before the door a single guard: tall, tending to fat, but powerfully built and wearing a ring-mail shirt. A slim sword curving at his hip, a knife in his belt, the red glass of the pommel capturing the lamplight.

Grada stepped back and scraped the Knife along the wall, old steel grating on plaster. Properly the guard should wake his master and warn of trouble if he suspected any – if he suspected nothing then he should do nothing. If everyone did what was proper the world would have fewer problems. Maybe none at all. As Grada had anticipated the man came to the end of the corridor, carrying the lamp with him. He turned the corner and Grada stabbed him in the neck. This man though not wary was not unaware and stood too tall to risk a non-lethal stratagem against. The Knife sliced off his protest and bit through his neck bones, halting the progress of fingers towards sword hilt. Grada bore him to the ground, the clatter seeming loud enough to wake the whole household. And yet none stirred.

Grada suppressed a grunt of effort as she rolled him across the spilled and burning oil from the lamp, extinguishing the flame. She waited by his twitching corpse, listening hard. No sounds of alarm, no boots on marble stairs. She counted twenty beats of her heart then pulled the Knife from his throat and let the blood flow. In death the man soiled himself and smelled rank. Grada had twisted the heads from a hundred chickens in her time – men had no more dignity in death. Emperors may lie in golden caskets within tombs of worked stone, but even they died like any other man, like any other animal.

She rolled the man twice more until he lay along the wall where he might be passed by in the dark rather than tripped over. He really had been a big man. Perhaps in his prime he might have stood among the imperial guard. She mouthed a prayer to Mirra for his soul. The words felt empty without sound to give them voice. She filled and lit her own lamp, a small one of fired clay. She would need to see Jomla die.

Ten paces brought her to Jomla's door. It would be locked from within. Meere had given her a vial of acid to destroy the mechanism but she had smelled the stuff at work. It ate metal slowly and released sharp odours that might wake a sleeper. The emperor's Knife was always on the grand scale a simple solution to a complex problem, or seemingly so. Grada opted for the same direct simplicity on the small scale. She knocked on the door with the hilt of the Knife, three loud raps. A pause then three more. When the muffled query came from inside she simply called in: 'Fire.'

A man awake and suspicious would have a dozen questions, not least being where had his night guard gone, but Lord Jomla thick with sleep and focused on the threat of fire came to his own door and unlocked it for her.

With the door ajar between them Jomla blinked at Grada, lifting a hand to rub the sleep from his eyes. Meere had told her she need only kill the fattest man in the house to be sure of Jomla. She could believe the house held no one more corpulent. Jomla's chins continued down into the embroidered silks of his nightshirt. She kicked the door wider and lifted the Knife.

Jomla's eyes widened, 'I have gold—' The rest spluttered through a sliced throat, the Knife biting deep to find his windpipe. He fell with a heavy thud, thrashing, refusing to die, rising up spraying blood. Anyone who has seen a pig slaughtered knows how long these things take. The Emperor Sarmin would have been appalled. In the stories of valour told to princes, death comes in an instant, or slow enough that sad farewells might be recorded for posterity.

Grada stepped over and around Jomla, careful of his flailing legs. Oddly they were almost thin, as if he were a great jelly on stork's legs.

One wife, young and slim, sat in the wide expanse of Jomla's bed, the silks drawn up around her. The other, an older fatter woman, lay in a separate bed, asleep even now. Grada had thought to find them in separate chambers but Meere had warned that Jomla liked to keep his possessions close.

'I—' The young woman clutched her sheets tighter still, as if they might protect her, eyes flitting between Jomla and the Knife. 'Don't hurt me.'

'I won't,' Grada said, stepping close. The secret doomed the wives, not the Knife. She came to kill the secret, not to kill people. But secrets spread, especially between the sheets. And hadn't this all sprung from pillow talk?

'Please!' the girl begged, her black hair framing a pale face in curls.

'It's all right,' Grada said and stabbed through silk into the wife's heart. 'It will be quick.'

For the sleeping wife the end came quicker still.

Jomla's vizier, Nashan, slept unguarded one floor down, though a guardsman died between the lord's bedroom and that of Nashan. Like the fat wife, the vizier died without waking. 'It's a kindness to die in one's sleep. All men should sleep first, then sleep deeper.' She found the words on her lips, perhaps the credo of the assassins who used her back in the days when the Many flowed through her veins and the Pattern Master chose her victims. Did Helmar select her as his Knife for a joke, she wondered, an insult, to set an Untouchable against the light of heaven and kill him in his sleep? And now Sarmin followed in his relative's footsteps, putting the Knife in her hands, the lives of the highest and most mighty into her keeping.

Grada found herself outside the heir's bedroom, the light and shadows dancing across his door. 'I never wanted this.'

Her dreams had painted this door for her many times, a butterfly carved into the satinwood. She put her lamp in the niche opposite and set her fingers to the lines of the butterfly's wings. She glanced to the Knife, a dark drop of blood forming at its point as she looked, dark and gleaming, swelling, pregnant with possibility. She watched it fall. An age passed and it hit the carpet without sound. The pattern it made she had seen each time in her dreaming.

I'm not bound to this. I make the future – not you, Helmar. I am the Knife.

The pattern pulsed around her, echoing in her skin, tracing the invisible scars where once the Pattern Master's design had wrapped her.

I could do anything. Scream, shout, set a fire, walk away. I am not bound to this dream.

But in the end her hand closed around the handle of the door. This one locked from the outside and yielded to the fourth of the many keys she had gathered on her bloody rounds. The door opened on oiled hinges and a blackness yawned before her. She stepped through on damned feet.

The child lay atop his covers – a boy of seven years, maybe eight, sweat-tousled, naked but for a loincloth, thin-limbed, pale. Grada sank to her knees beside the bed, setting down her lamp. Tears blinded her. It didn't matter that Jomla was dead, for he would never have acted alone. Petty satraps and governors, their lords and generals, would have been lined up behind him, and as long as the boy lived, as long as he might be set upon the throne to pardon the treason of those who put him there . . . they would seek him, seek to own him.

'He's innocent.' She held the Knife's blade flat to her lips, whispering the words.

Had Eyul wept as he killed Sarmin's brothers? He killed a Tower mage too, an Island woman, Amalya. Sarmin had said the assassin had loved her, but gave her to the Knife when the pattern took hold upon her.

'Gods help me. I cannot do this.' And yet each alternative led to blood. Oceans of it, innocent and guilty, men, women, children as young and as pure as the boy before her. In the game of Settu the push sets the tiles falling, each one toppling the next in branching chains until the work is done and an accounting of the fallen must be made. Grada knew now that the push had been made further back than she had ever known, and that all her life the tiles had been toppling around her, each crashing against the next, a tide that had lifted her and swept her to this point. The old steel trembled on her lips.

A gleam caught her eye. On the table beside the bed, clock-work animals in copper and silver, Mechar Anlantar's work, two lions, two bears . . . a cow on its side. Grada swallowed a cry that would become a scream if she let it escape. She set the point of the Knife to the hollow at the base of her throat. 'Gods help me.'

44

Sarmin

'—be kept a secret. It's imperative—'

'—been left hollow like so many other—'

'—panic in the streets, Azeem—'

'—something you can do?'

'—dangerous to touch him.'

Sarmin rose through a sea of disjointed conversations, fragments, snatches. Familiar voices: Ta-Sann anxious, Govnan resigned, Azeem insistent. Voices came and went, minutes chased hours, and still he rose, still blind with the depths of his journey.

'It's better that he stay here. We can put it about that he's in seclusion seeking a cure for this plague.' Azeem's voice.

'Already there are rumours he's been hollowed.' Govnan, sounding old. 'And the outer wall will fall within hours. Moreth gives it strength but it can't last. The people will see.'

Sarmin sat up. He had been lying on the carpet of his tower room. Only Govnan and Azeem were present and the two men had their backs to him, the door closed. His tongue had stuck to the roof of his mouth and a great thirst consumed him.

'Water.' His mouth too dry for more words.

High mage and vizier both jumped, then turned too fast

for any dignity, and stared, Govnan with his mouth open, Azeem with the broadest smile. Sarmin couldn't remember ever seeing the man smile. He tried to grin back.

They came quickly to his side, Azeem taking jug and glass from a silver tray set on the floor by the wall. It looked like Ta-Sann's tray, the food taken from it. Sarmin coughed on the water, struggling not to choke.

'The stone!' Sarmin cast about him. 'Where is it?'

Govnan drew the two halves of Helmar's stone from his robes, the butterfly caught there in crystal and colour, held perfect on both the inner faces. The work that Helmar had wrought with the magics of fire and rock, a picture written within the rock, unseen until the day Sarmin split the stone open. He took the pieces, closing his hands about them.

'How are you—' Govnan shook his head. 'We thought the nothing had you, like the rest.'

'How is my son?' Sarmin grabbed Azeem's wrist, pushing the water glass from his mouth.

The vizier's smile vanished. Govnan paused, just a moment, before speaking. 'I fear little time remains to Prince Pelar . . .'

Sarmin got to his feet, pulling on Azeem's arm, almost pulling him down. He staggered once, found his strength, then hauled open the door. 'How long?'

'My Emperor?' Azeem bowed his head. Ta-Sann stood outside the door. He turned, and for an instant Sarmin caught a flicker of relief on its swift passage across his face.

'How long have I lain there?'

'A day, My Emperor. We feared to move you . . .'

'I understand. Lead on, Ta-Sann. Take me to my son.'

Ta-Sann inclined his head and set off down the spiral staircase. Sarmin followed, taking the steps two at a time, Azeem at his shoulders, Govnan struggling to keep pace.

'Wait!' Ta-Sann stopped so suddenly that Sarmin crashed into his back, managing to turn at the last instant to keep from breaking his nose. The warrior had anticipated the impact and there was no give in him. Sarmin bounced off, nearly taking his vizier down, his shoulder feeling as though he'd charged a door.

'What—' Sarmin checked himself. Ta-Sann would only command him if his life were in danger.

The sword-son took a step back up the stairs, Sarmin scrambled back to keep from being stepped on, Azeem still supporting him, hands under his arms. Another step back, facing down the stairs, the occasional glimpse past Ta-Sann to the gleam of his hachirah held out before him. Govnan descended around the curve of the stair behind them, and stopped.

'It is one of the hollow ones. A palace guard,' Ta-Sann said, backing another step.

'Show me.' Sarmin shook Azeem off and moved to Ta-Sann's shoulder, lifting up on his toes to see over.

The guard had been a young man; Sarmin half-recognised him, even robbed of colour. He had been young, now he seemed ageless, his flesh marble, hair translucent, and eyes like the nothing itself, promising destruction. His armour had fallen away and what remnants of his uniform remained had been bleached as pale as his skin, hanging in crumbling tatters. He climbed another stair, swaying, hypnotic as any cobra's dance, and where his fingers trailed the stonework, dust fell.

'How can he be walking?' It made no sense; the nothing emptied, it didn't add.

The man's eyes found Sarmin, a sick smile twitching on his

face as if the corner of his mouth were tugged by hook and string. He climbed another step and Sarmin retreated as Ta-Sann stepped back.

'I will have to kill him,' Ta-Sann said. 'My blade will be ruined though. Best we meet no more such—'

'Don't kill him.' Sarmin hurried back a few more steps to gain height for a better look. He turned back at Govnan's side.

'Notheen speaks of the djinn in the empty quarter. The nothing draws such spirits to it, like flies to a corpse, a great gyre about which they swirl.' Both men retreated two more steps. Soon they would be back at Sarmin's room. 'The nomads fear them, for djinn will possess a man and misuse him.'

'The desert's a bad place to hunt if you're after men!'

Govnan grunted, steadying himself with his staff. 'Loneliness makes a man easier to take hold of, and being alone breeds loneliness. The desert has ever been their domain.'

'And what man is more easily possessed than one who has been emptied?' Sarmin clapped his hands. 'They're vultures to the nothing's death.'

'You can't evict this spirit? It worked with Ashanagur.' A touch of old man's peevishness in Govnan's voice as he remembered Sarmin parting him from his elemental. Even with the djinn advancing, some small part of Sarmin noted that neither Govnan nor Ta-Sann was giving him the honorifics demanded by his station. He rather liked it.

'Patterns are just symbols; their power lies in the minds of men. They're a key.' Sarmin reached the landing. 'The real world, beyond our imagination, is deeper than any pattern that can be drawn. Patterns are lies.' He thought of Beyon and the lie of Beyon that had hidden patterned in his head, an imperfect representation, without love. 'Into the room. We'll lock the door and go by the Ways.'

'But—' Govnan allowed himself to be pulled through the doorway. 'But parting the djinn and the man on the stairs. Is that so different from what you did with Ashanagur?'

Ta-Sann followed them into the room, slamming the heavy door behind him. He drew the bolt across, a new addition since Sarmin's captivity.

'I only have symbols for what I know. No part of the pattern revealed to me has power over the djinn. I know patterns about men, but only men believe the lies men tell. A pattern can divide a man's flesh, split his bone, but only because first it tricks the mind. And the man on the stairs has been emptied. There is nothing of him for the pattern to deceive. If there were then I might give that part strength to throw off the possession.'

Ta-Sann moved to the secret door to the Ways, less secret now that a small metal knob had been affixed so the door could be opened from inside the room. He pulled it wide and waited for Sarmin to follow. Behind them a light blow sounded against the door.

'Time to go,' Govnan said, glancing back. It wouldn't be strength that brought down the door, but weakness.

Descending the hidden stair took them through the thickness of the wall, spiralling down, turn by turn. Ta-Sann did not speak of his fellow sword-sons, no speculation as to how the empty man passed their guard at the base of the stair. Govnan made a light, a white flame dancing across the back of his hand, like a street magician walking a coin back and forth across his knuckles. Even without Ashanagur imprisoned within him the old mage held an affinity with the realm of fire.

A turn, another turn. Tuvaini had walked these paths with Eyul, a lifetime ago. Last year. Tuvaini had been on that first visit. Bound to open that door for the first time in an age, to open that door and change Sarmin's life for ever. The nothing – that was a door opening too. A door that led nowhere but through which everyone was going to be drawn.

'What did you see?'

Sarmin flinched as Govnan spoke behind him. 'See?'

'We thought you hollowed. But you went somewhere, in your mind? Somewhere deep?'

Sarmin stumbled and steadied himself with a hand to the rough stone of the wall. 'I saw . . .' A butterfly. Made whole. A lie made true. They came to one of the iron doors that now sealed important junctions. Without secrecy to secure the Ways other methods had been found. Sarmin unlocked it and they continued down. The steps gave out and the Ways took them into the natural rock into which and around which the palace had been built. He paused at the first fork.

'To the left,' Govnan said. The passage would twist, divide, rise, fall and come at last to the door in the women's quarters. 'The prince is with Empress Mesema in the Forest Room.'

Sarmin took a step that way. Paused. 'Wait.' He lifted his hand. His skin ran with the pattern: deep, intricate, circle in circle, triangle over triangle, the red and the blue, layered. 'A lie.'

'My Emperor?' Govnan peered at Sarmin's fingers, seeing only flesh.

'Man is more than that. Beyon was more than that.' He shook his head and the pattern-sight left him. 'Azeem, go to my wife and son. Make sure they are defended. We will go to the right. Ta-Sann, take me to the tomb.'

'There is no tomb, My Emperor.' Ta-Sann watched him. 'There are no tombs. Just the nothing. It has taken them all.'

'Even so. We will go there.'

And Ta-Sann set off to the right without further reply. Sarmin envied him his loyalty. Loyalty can remain when even faith has gone, a view so narrow it makes every choice seem simple. Azeem they left, finding his way in the dark.

They crossed the chasm where Grada had fought and killed imperial guards on her way to murder him. Sarmin felt the pull of that drop to either side of the narrow span of stone. Djinn lurked in those depths now, willing him to fall.

From chasm to rough-hewn corridor, a flight of steps, then a long sideways shuffle following some natural fissure in the rock. Behind them, at the edge of Govnan's illumination, the shadows seethed. Djinn filled the darkness, following, as if sensing some threat to their feasting.

At last, dry and dirty, they reached the long stair that would take them up to a storeroom near the door to Satreth's Plaza where the tombs of the emperors had stood. The Ways would take them directly to several of the tombs, but Govnan had reports of collapse in those tunnels.

The storeroom held a musty scent of disuse and rat droppings. Ta-Sann had to force open the door from the Ways, toppling several sacks of millet flour, sliding others across the floor. He moved into the room with hachirah held across his body in a two-handed grip, his shadow swinging before him in the steady glade of Govnan's white flame.

'Come.'

And Sarmin moved out, Govnan at his back. Ta-Sann opened the door to the corridor beyond, a broad servants' avenue leading past storerooms left and right on its way to the main kitchens. Shafts of sunlight struck down through skylights along the length of the passage and dust motes caught the light in the shaft closest. Sarmin paused in the doorway to watch. 'A pattern.' Some inner engine sought to attach meaning to the motes' slow swirl, to the brief brilliance given to each, and the obscurity that followed. He drew a deep breath and smelled smoke.

'My Emperor?' Govnan trapped behind him. 'Sarmin?'

'Sor—' Sarmin caught himself. *An emperor does not apologise.* He stepped into the corridor and the high mage followed. The sound of distant screaming reached them along the passageway: terror, but more than that, shouting too, anger and pain. 'I hear fighting?'

'More trouble with the slaves,' Govnan said. 'The hollow ones have everyone terrified. It wouldn't surprise me if half the servants are gone by morning, fled downriver.'

Sarmin shook his head. 'None of that will matter unless we can end this. Not the war, not what happens here.' *Not even if the palace is burning.*

'If you would give me an hour I could assemble the Tower mages . . .'

Sarmin turned towards the door that opened onto the plaza. The wood had a fragile look, pale like driftwood abandoned by the river and bleached in the sun. 'Would they help? These . . . how many mages is it now? Four? They can't save my son and he hasn't touched the nothing, just been lapped by its outer waves.' He pointed to the door. 'What's out there is so much worse.'

Govnan shook his head, such a small motion it almost wasn't there. 'What can any of us do? The nothing unwrites the elements, unpatterns, undoes.'

'We can try.' Sarmin managed a smile. 'That's all we can do. Running won't save Pelar. And, whatever the books might say, an emperor should sometimes apologise. But what he should never do is run – certainly not from his capital. Notheen and his people are an idea set in motion; the nomads carry their world with them. Cerana though, it is an idea fixed around a centre. And if the centre gives, the rest will not hold.

'Open the door, Ta-Sann.'

The sword-son reached out for the black iron ring of the handle. It tore free in his grip, the wood crumbling around the fixing plate as if devoured from within by dry mite. He made a tentative jab at the middle of the door with his hachirah and the whole structure collapsed, falling in sections, pieces exploding into dust as they hit the floor.

Through the doorway Sarmin could see nothing – not darkness or light, no hint of the sky, just a space that refused to register on his eye, as if the corridor neither ended nor continued but simply denied inquiry. Along with the sense of an endless fall just waiting to seize him, Sarmin felt the nothing's touch, feather-light, searching for any loose end by which he might be unravelled. Ahead of him Ta-Sann's huge form looked diminished, his darkness shaded to grey.

Sarmin advanced on the doorway. He reached up for Ta-Sann's shoulder and pulled him away. The warrior slumped back, easily turned, no protest in him.

'No!' Govnan's cry behind him, too late, as if he too had been spellbound by the nothing, a moth bound to its flame. 'No.' Weaker this second time. And Sarmin turned to face his undoing.

Through the Many Sarmin knew what it was to be blind. Staring into the midst of nothing made less of his eyes than those of a man who has never seen, and yet it seemed vision was all that remained to him. The nothing filled and hollowed him, he fell into it, or felt he did, with the unwriting all around him, seeking out stray threads of his life and starting to unwind them.

This is a power that can undo stone, dismantle wind and water, break fire into pieces and devour each part. There is nothing I can do.

The Many had been wiped from Sarmin, and yet somehow he knew the voice that echoed in him was not his own. 'Out!' and he drove the djinn from him. Impossible or not his task might be, but the spirits would try to stop him, for the nothing sustained them. They would ride its destruction until the last moment of time was devoured and they too found oblivion. They would allow no threat to it, however small.

Sarmin tore his vision from the nothing and looked back along the corridor. Ta-Sann stood with Govnan, neither of them able to watch him. In the distance figures moved, not with the broken gait of hollow men but with speed and purpose, drawing closer. Closer still and Sarmin saw that some had the pale flesh of the hollowed: temple guards, imperial guards, and a concubine, silks tattered and streaming, her white hair wild, while others were slaves bearing crude weapons and no sign of the nothing's touch. All of them ran without cries or threat, eyes fixed on their emperor.

'They're possessed!' Govnan raised his staff, though it could be small defence against so many.

Sarmin saw it in the same moment as Govnan – the djinn riding on each man's back, invisible yet somehow made known through the sheer malice radiating from them.

'Stay clear.' Ta-Sann drew his hachirah and stepped forwards to block the corridor. He took the heavy blade two-handed and rolled his head as if getting the cricks out of his thick neck. The walls to either side allowed for an uninterrupted swing but with no room to spare.

The swiftest of the attackers died first, the hachirah decapitating him as he came within its arc. He fell in two pieces showering pale blood. Behind him another man, then two more, then a multitude. Ta-Sann turned with the scimitar's momentum, his foot lashing out to strike the second man beneath the chin with force enough to separate vertebrae in his neck. That man fell boneless and the two that followed tripped over the corpses before them.

Even for Sarmin, echoing with the threat of the nothing, the scene held a fascination that pinned him. Ta-Sann jerked the hilt of his scimitar into the face of the next man, the iron pommel making a ruin of the slave's forehead. The cutting edge followed on a descending arc to sever a reaching arm. The sword-son mixed brutality with grace, each blow underwritten by rippling muscle, driven not only by corded arms but the thick power of his torso, the strength of his legs.

A storeroom slave, blooded from some other combat, slid along the wall to flank Ta-Sann and found the end of Govnan's staff rammed hard into the side of his head. The djinn-born cunning left his eyes and he toppled in confusion.

With a roar of effort Ta-Sann divided a hollow man, his hachirah given no pause by the decaying armour. Dulled by the corrupting nothingness lacing the hollow men's blood, the scimitar's work became harder from each moment to the next – and such a battle is counted in moments.

Twenty men, more, thirty, ranked back along the corridor, slowed only by those before them. 'Sarmin!' Govnan risked a glance back at him. 'He can't last!' Even as the high mage spoke a slave woman threw herself onto Ta-Sann's shoulder in the moment his scimitar bedded itself in the body of a Herzu temple-guard. The sword-son launched himself into a wall, crushing the woman between his body and the stone. The abandoned hachirah fell with his last victim, tripping another man. Two glittering knives appeared in Ta-Sann's hands and he bellowed at his foe with such a voice that even the hollowed paused for half a beat. 'Sarmin!' Govnan cried again.

Turning his back on Ta-Sann's last extravagant stand felt like all kinds of betrayal, but still Sarmin turned. He held the two halves of Helmar's stone before his face, let his eyes wander the brilliance and intricacy of the pattern, then lowered both and looked once more upon the nothing.

The stonework about the empty doorframe crumbled now, falling into dust, swirling into memory. Sarmin felt the skin of his cheeks, his forehead, lips, start to respond, to unwind and flow towards the nothing.

This is the death of god. The one god of whom all others are shadows. The end of all things. Let it take you.

'No.' And Sarmin looked again. Looked for the edges rather than the centre. The nothing was a wound, a rip in the fabric of being. Helmar had broken the butterfly then made it whole. And centuries later that same boy in his wrath had broken the world, pierced the stuff of eternity to anchor his grand pattern. The last of his anchor points he sank through Beyon's tomb, through his death, through that moment, that day. Before that there had been Migido, before that three others. Five was ever the number of the pattern. But before five comes one, and long before Helmar's puncturing work Mogyrk died in the desert, a wound in creation that had made Helmar's attacks seem pinpricks. And now Mogyrk's death infected the wounds Helmar made, spreading the terror of the deep desert into the heart of Nooria. As a pebble can start an avalanche, Helmar's self-destruction had brought the dead god's suicide crashing down upon them all.

Sarmin saw it, he looked with new eyes, even as those eyes were unwound from the business of seeing, and he beheld the nothing as a jagged hole punched through existence, a blankness in the complex, breathtaking, beautiful, dirty world. A world deeper and more real than any pattern, as far beyond description by mere language as the wings of a butterfly.

Surrender to it. Lay down the burden of your days, Sarmin Tahalson. This is the end. Your life has been only lies, nothing but rumour that Mogyrk now unspeaks.

Sarmin walked in the dream, in the green of the grass, the blue of the sky, he held the butterfly broken in his hands. This was not his memory. A lie. And yet he could taste it.

'A lie can also be true.'

The memory of Helmar opened his hands and the butterfly stood remade. The pattern of the world might yet show creation how to be whole again. Show the nothing how to be something.

'You are my salvation.'

The Megra brought Helmar's past with her, seasoned with the bitterness of experience. Sarmin reached for the edges of the nothing with unwritten fingers, with the memory of them, intention. To draw those edges together would tear him apart. Helmar gave him the magic, wrote it in stone, and with it he could heal this wound, and the act would be Helmar's salvation. The boy who had shared his room, shared his fate, twisted by circumstance and years, twisted beyond recognition into the thing that was the Pattern Master. Was he born to craft the magic that might save the world? Yet Sarmin was afraid. He wished Beyon were at his side. 'I don't want to die.' Vanishing hands remembered the softness of his son, Pelar so warm and heavy in the cradle of his arms.

'Be brave.' The face of a boy, mountains behind him rising higher than Sarmin's imagination would ever have painted them. Was this Pelar? The boy Pelar would become? White flowers in his hands glistening like stars, dark hair wind-swept across his brow, his grin so wide, no trace of fear in him. 'Be brave.'

Sarmin took hold of the wound. Everywhere the pattern ran through the world, the story of things, the tale of each grain of sand, each breath of wind, the threads of being. 'The pattern is not the thing, it is the story of the thing. Neither lie nor truth.' And as Helmar had once let the pattern of a wing guide the stuff of the world – the unseen vitality of shape and form that burns in each grain of that which is – as Helmar had let the necessary pattern of the butterfly lead the world back to the place where a butterfly sat perfect on his palm, the injury he did it now a lie, Sarmin let the deeper pattern of his city rewrite all that had been lost, filling in each stolen brick, each lost moment, even down to his brother's bones and the hidden decay of his dead flesh. With all the strength that ran in him he strove to draw the edges of the wound together. And it hurt.

Crimson dots. Lines of crimson dots on white. Some large, some small, arcs of them, as if spattered on a canvas by the careless lash of an artist's overladen brush. Crimson and white.

He tried to make sense of it. A pattern here, but what pattern, what meaning?

Crimson dots. He had a name once. Crimson and white. The 'S' hissed on his tongue, begging the remainder of his name. Arc crisscrossing arc. 'Sarmin.'

He woke beneath bodies, an arm across his face, and pain – an ocean on which he floated beyond sight of land. Above him on the plastered ceiling of a corridor, arcs of crimson spatter made abstract testimony to the violence wrought below.

Sarmin sat, the arm that was not his own slid away, other arms, a man's leg lacking a body. The effort and agony of that movement ground his teeth together but he could give it no voice, it lay beyond words. Bodies lay everywhere, slaves, guards, an Old Mother, her face turned away. Four yards of the fallen lay before the doors to the courtyard, closed and solid. The gore and ruin pooled and ran – it stank, of burning and a hot abattoir stink catching at Sarmin's throat – but though the dead might lie broken, not one of them lay pale, not one of them hollowed.

And with a groan Sarmin lay back among the dead and let dreams take him.

45

Sarmin

The guards closed the doors behind Sarmin as he entered the women's wing. Soot coated the walls that had once been painted with images of Mirra and Pomegra. The carpet consisted of ashes mixed with long, bright threads. Doors twisted from their frames, scorched and broken. The stink of fire reminded him of the smell of his room after Govnan raised the elemental and burned the stairs. Bitter and heavy. Women and guards had been found along this floor, red with the death that smoke bestows and black with the kind offered by fire. Traitor guards had barred the doors, trapping them all inside.

He had declared the empty wing, the wing where Beyon had once hidden with Mesema and his Knife, the new house for the women. Nessaket was there now, unconscious, struck down by a blow to the head from a delivery boy purchased one year ago from a satrap's estate. Murmurs and confessions allowed the story to be pieced together. The boy had been a follower of Mogyrk, and colluded with Austere Adam through a network of priests and worshippers. Neither of them had been found, nor had Sarmin's brother Daveed. He had been spirited away as had Helmar so many years ago, taken by followers of Mogyrk.

Daveed. Flesh called to flesh and he ached for his brother, his round face, his curls. *I will find you.*

Azeem told him Mesema had gone to the ladies' garden to find relief from the flames and then had never left it. Sarmin had forgotten the garden, where he had once played as a boy, Kashim's mother Siri watering the blooms as the children pushed around her. How bright those days had been. He passed through Old Wife Farra's room, charred and stinking, and climbed the stairs to the roof.

The garden had changed. Once, a riot of colour burst from roses, honeysuckle and clematis and green things grew in every bed. He remembered Mother Siri, holding her jug of water – but today it was Mesema he saw, and only a few weak seedlings pushed forth from the soil. His wife knelt beneath the statue of Mirra, Pelar's silks laid out on the ground before her. As he approached she moved to pick up the boy, to protect the child from him, her sky-coloured eyes angry and cold. He stopped a man's length from where she sat and held out a hand, his eyes drawn to Pelar, pink and squirming in his makeshift bed. Cured. Tears stung his eyes. 'Azeem says you will not come downstairs.'

'There is nothing but death and lies downstairs,' she said. 'Give me a tent and let me live outside in the air.'

'You are Cerani now. Remember? You took my hand. You said, "We are Cerani. We carry on." Did you not mean it?'

'How could I mean it when I didn't know what it meant? When my own husband keeps the truth from me . . . if you had told me that you Carried Beyon I would not have let Pelar go.'

He knew that more than Beyon stood between them. There was Jenni, too. Sarmin looked again at the boy. He longed to hold him, to smell his skin. Daveed and Pelar both had a stubborn curl at their temples, just like Beyon's, inherited from some ancestor they no longer remembered. *Daveed!* His heart split into two like Helmar's stone. 'You are the empress,' he reminded her. 'There are duties, especially with my mother fallen. Your clan—'

'My clan has betrayed you. Have you not heard of it? I heard it from the concubines as we huddled up here, waiting out the fire. Concubines, Sarmin, told me that Banreh slit our soldiers' throats in the night. What could drive Banreh to such treachery other than Cerani madness, the same madness that drove you to infect Pelar?'

'It is gone,' he said, risking a step closer. 'And even so, you have duties.' A flash of blue caught his eye. Behind her, a butterfly searched for a blossom.

'You instruct me like a servant,' she said, pushing yellow curls from her eyes, 'because you do not need me. Leave me to the garden and to my mothering. Once, we defeated the Pattern Master together, but now you pursue your own fascinations, make your own assaults against the dark without me. This victory was yours, and I was there only to witness the destruction that came with it. I could have been at your side . . .'

'You could not have helped. I needed . . . protect . . .' The words left him. He remembered when Mesema had smashed the urn, just as he had smashed the stone, and when she smiled at him from across the room on the first day he saw Pelar. Those were the last happy days he could remember. Before Jenni, before the envoy. He had wanted to need her, to feel that closeness he felt with Grada, bone to bone, the intimacy he had pushed away when he handed Grada the Knife. But Mesema offered something else.

'Please,' he said, kneeling, looking into her eyes, 'we are friends, are we not? From the first moment when you came to me in my room, you were my friend. My only friend, now.'

She met his gaze, lips trembling, with tears or a smile he could not tell. 'I would like a friend too.'

It was a start.

46

Sarmin

Sarmin had thought that sealing the pattern wound would kill him. He had thought the effort would sunder him and the dead god's doom would consume them all. In the end all that had broken was his magic. The world no longer presented him with patterns – perhaps it never would again. The loss troubled him only when he thought of the other wounds where Mogyrk's loss echoed out, consuming all around, and of the great wound centred in the desert, dwarfing the five made by Helmar's work. But those threats lay far away, and Nooria would carry on.

Sarmin had also thought that somehow saving the city, saving the empire, would leave it a better place, a world with new priorities where petty concerns no longer drew men down into childish squabbles. And yet here he sat once more, lofted above his subjects in the Petal Throne, whilst lords squabbled on the dais steps, entreating for advantages so slight or obscure as to be ridiculous were in not for the fact that lives depended from such matters.

Now, though, talk turned to Mogyrk's faith riddling Nooria like a disease, and to the rebellion that had seen slave turn against master in the very halls of the palace. Sarmin's own mother had been struck down by a mere delivery boy – they spoke of it with alarm – and yet they did not know her son had been taken, hidden among Mogyrk traitors passing through the Ways, lost in the sea of people that was Nooria. His heart called out to his brother. *I will find you.*

'These slaves must be taught their place.' Lord Zell raised his voice and his hands, each to the barest fraction below the level at which the guards might strike him. With Ta-Sann gone that level lay lower than before, the surviving sword-sons on edge, haunted by their failure to be at his side that day.

'And how should such lessons be taught?' Satrap Honnecka from his seat on the third step.

'In blood!' Lord Zell jerked his hands down, and Ta-Marn flinched a hand towards his knife. 'In blood. Hang them from their guts in the streets, boil them in the squares. Would we not break a knife that was turned against us? Strangle a dog that bit its master? Can any Cerani tolerate defiance among his properties?' Spittle flew from Zell's thin lips. Sarmin wondered how it felt to be such a man's property.

Away across the crowds – of lesser nobles, Old Mothers come to court, concubines and entertainers, lined and ready for their turn – the great doors of the throne room opened a crack to admit a single figure, clad in black. Sarmin let Zell's ranting flow around him, robbed of meaning, as he watched his Knife draw closer. For the longest moment he thought Eyul approached, so grim and lined was the face above that black collar. Dark circles surrounded Grada's eyes, the whites red with broken veins. She walked with that brittle step that speaks of warrior's tension, held herself taut, her whole body a simple threat to cut away any hand that might be set upon her. Where she walked people fell silent, stepped back. On the dais

Zell held forth, facing Sarmin, head raised to stare at his emperor, his mouth wide and red and full of complaint.

'A slave is property, no more. I can use my property as I will, and do so. If I blind a girl for missing a discarded garment on the floor, if I cut out a man's tongue when I find it too sharp ... what then remains for punishment of crimes like treason? I say horror. We must show them true horror and—'

Grada came up behind Zell and slit his throat, pushing him aside to sprawl down the dais steps. She held the Knife dripping before her and all held silent.

'I was wrong, Sarmin. You were wrong.'

Ta-Marn and his three brothers drew their blades. The lords leaped to their feet, clamouring, the spell of silence broken.

Grada barked a harsh laugh at them. 'I stand Knife-Sworn, it is not given to you to interfere with my purpose.'

Sarmin stood from his throne. 'Let her approach.' He waved the sword-sons away.

Grada climbed the last two steps. 'We were wrong. This Knife cuts just as all the others. I am just as damned.'

Sarmin blinked back tears. He took a step towards her. Reached out and set his hand to her shoulder. 'I had hoped we could remake it, forge a new path ...'

Grada lowered her head. 'This Knife cuts.' She glanced back towards Zell in the spreading pool of his blood. 'But it cuts both ways.' She pointed at the dying lord with the Knife, its ugly blade hung with his lifeblood.

Sarmin looked out at the sea of still faces, outrage on the high and the mighty, curiosity here, surprise there, each turned his way. He had laid the burden of the Knife on Grada, misused her as badly as Helmar before him, damned her. He sat lord of an empire so wide a year might turn before a man could walk from border to border, heir to an unbroken chain of emperors, blood of the Reclaimer . . . and even so, she stood before him, untouchable, blooded, and showed him truth, showed him the path.

'The Knife-Sworn protect the emperor from whatever threats may come,' he told his court, lifting a voice unused to speech and finding in it the same power of command that had run through Beyon's. 'The emperor is the empire. And as ever, even with the threats of Yrkmir and the desert, our greatest enemies lie within.' He let that settle with them and swept his gaze across the dais steps. 'I wanted peace and Arigu gave me war. I wanted reconciliation, and a traitor within murdered Envoy Kavic. I wanted security and yet my own lords lead such poisonous lives that our people turn to a foreign god and our slaves turn traitor.

'I have tried to be Sarmin the Saviour, tried to be Sarmin the Kind, the Peacemaker, but Cerana doesn't need such emperors. The weakness of this empire is born of the strength of my convictions, its cruelty of my kindness, its war of my peace.

'From this day I will be a new emperor, the emperor Cerana does not deserve but needs. I will gather my power to me. My Knife will cut, cut and cut again until my word is law, my will imposed, my desire your only concern. Cerana *shall* be united under one will, focused to one goal, obedient to one man.'

Mesema entered through a side door, her hair piled into a complex arrangement of curls and butterfly pins. He held out a hand to her and she walked towards him, high shoes slowing her path up the dais steps. Only one glance for Zell and his blood. He thought of Pelar, stronger with each passing hour since the sealing of the first wound. Their son, Sarmin's and

Mesema's. Together they would find Daveed. Together they would . . .

We will make a better world.

Mesema arrived at his side and gripped his hand for the briefest moment before stepping back, taking her place at his side. Sarmin let his gaze return to the steps below him, the old men in their jewels and silks, wrapped in their plans and ambitions. None of it mattered. He had lived a lifetime with this cancer and if Cerana were to stand against the future the sickness must be cut out. Let them gaze upon his fierce empress and his blunt, honest Knife. He leaned forwards and set a kiss upon Grada's forehead.

'Go to it, Knife-Sworn.'

ACKNOWLEDGEMENTS

Thanks to Ian Drury, Jo Fletcher, and everyone at Jo Fletcher Books who helped this book to completion. Thanks also to Sarah Swart, without whom *The Emperor's Knife* would not have been finished, and to Teresa Frohock and Michelle Goldsmith for their emergency consultations. Finally thanks to all the readers of *The Emperor's Knife*, because your enjoyment is what it's all about.

ALSO AVAILABLE

THE EMPEROR'S KNIFE
Mazarkis Williams

A plague is attacking the Cerani Empire: as the geometric patterns cover the skin, so the victims fall under the power of the Pattern Master.

Only three people stand in his way: a lost prince, a world-weary killer, and a young girl who once saw a path through the waving grass.

'This novel puts great writing to the service of vivid characters, a compelling plot and a wholly convincing fantasy world'
Ben Aaronovitch, author of *Rivers of London*

'Rich and entertaining [with] believably ambitious individuals who struggle to survive in a maze of tradition and intrigue . . . this is strongly recommended' **SFX**

Jo Fletcher
BOOKS

www.jofletcherbooks.com

COMING SOON

THE TOWER BROKEN
Mazarkis Williams

Nooria is at breaking point. The nothing bleeds out the very essence of all, of stone, silk — and souls. Sarmin thought he had stopped it, but it is spreading towards Cerana — and he is powerless to halt the destruction. Even as Cerana fills with refugees, the Yrkmen armies arrive, offering to spare Sarmin's people if they will convert to the Mogyrk faith.

Time is running out for Sarmin and Mesema: the Mage's Tower is cracked; the last mage, sent to find a mysterious pattern-worker in the desert, has vanished; and Sarmin believes his kidnapped brother Daveed still has a part to play.

The walls are crumbling around them . . .

PUBLISHED NOVEMBER 2013

Jo Fletcher
BOOKS

www.jofletcherbooks.com